Go Scorch Yourself

by

Marilyn Barr

Strawberry Shifters, Book 3

This is a work of fiction. Names, characters, places, and incidents are either the product of the author's imagination or are used fictitiously, and any resemblance to actual persons living or dead, business establishments, events, or locales, is entirely coincidental.

Go Scorch Yourself

COPYRIGHT © 2022 by Patricia AS Reuther

All rights reserved. No part of this book may be used or reproduced in any manner whatsoever without written permission of the author or The Wild Rose Press, Inc. except in the case of brief quotations embodied in critical articles or reviews.
Contact Information: info@thewildrosepress.com

Cover Art by *Tina Lynn Stout*

The Wild Rose Press, Inc.
PO Box 708
Adams Basin, NY 14410-0708
Visit us at www.thewildrosepress.com

Publishing History
First Edition, 2022
Trade Paperback ISBN 978-1-5092-4162-0
Digital ISBN 978-1-5092-4163-7

Strawberry Shifters, Book 3
Published in the United States of America

"Look if you came out here to lord over me. Don't waste your breath. I'm at my lowest…so…leave me alone."

"I followed you because I am afraid Sluagh are going to attack. They are attracted to sadness. Your mournful call is bringing the cavalcade to our doorstep."

"Oh well, heaven forbid I ruin your party," she puffs between billowing breathes. She claws at her back as if she truly wishes to open the dress. She spins again and I am faced with the back of the dress. It hasn't a zipper or row of buttons to loosen it.

I take a deep breath and stand behind her. "Tell me not to rip it," I say with such trepidation that it comes out as a whisper. The wisps of hair on the back of her neck dance to my voice as the waves travel along her flesh. I tuck my fingers into the neckline of her dress, careful to only allow the backs of my fingers to touch her. Her skin is on fire and so silky I fear my callused fingertips will snag it.

"Release me," she sobs.

A strength buried inside me surges forward and my claws extend from my nailbeds. I dip the black tips into the collar of her dress and yank. The material gives way, revealing smooth creamy skin to her waist. I have a heartbeat to catch my breath before she whirls around and slaps me.

Praise for Marilyn Barr

"Marilyn Barr is a gifted weaver of stories"
~ *N. N. Light's Book Heaven*

"Marilyn Barr has outdone herself with what is so far my favorite book in the Strawberry Shifters series. Lucien and Betty make the perfect couple, and I loved their dynamic as well as how much they make sense. Go Scorch Yourself is a beautiful mix of serious issues, romantic tension, and humor."
~ *Sydney Winward, Author of the Bloodborn Vampire Romance Series.*

Dedication

To all the siblings who stand up to bullies—and to my siblings, I know I'm difficult but thanks for loving me anyway.

Chapter 1

Why is it socially inappropriate for adults to live in blanket forts? First chased by angry drug dealers and cops and then chased by Sluagh and giant feral cats, I deserve some time in quilted solitude. I have been running scared for over a year. Moving to Strawberry was supposed to be a safe bet but the first friend I make turns out to be Aurora the Cat Whisperer—not housecats but the giant leopard which chased me upstairs.

My next career should be hide-and-seek champion. I'm tired. I just want the security of a nest made of quilts and dining room chairs to nurse my broken heart. Locked in my sister's house, hiding under her expensive duvet, I am one step away from my dream home of a blanket fort.

I will gladly trade the outside world for the life of a hermit, like my big sister, Alison. She was lucky enough to inherit our family's witchy genes while I was skipped over. Not that I'm jealous, it came with sensory processing disorder which has controlled her since birth. "Help me understand, Ally," I say with fear pounding in my chest. "Help me understand your secrets. I have always been on your side, right?"

"Oh Betty, I wasn't keeping all this from you because I kicked you out of my confidence. I was hoping to resolve most of it before you arrived. I hoped the Sluagh invasion wouldn't get out of control and they would never haunt you. I wanted to protect you for once." Just because she has become accustomed to the Kentucky fried monsters roaming this hick town doesn't mean she can't give me a heads up before convincing Mom and Dad to let me move in with her.

I pull my head from her shoulder to look into her eerie golden eyes. Wait...*Protect me*? I have beaten up everyone who made fun of her from schoolboys to mean girls. I have given her husband, Grant, hell more times than I can count for making her cry. Now she wants to protect me from an invasion of soul-sucking phantoms. How? She's a Green Witch. Was she planning on suffocating them with pollen?

"No more secrets, no more bullshit." I extend my pinky finger between us. She reluctantly adds her digit to the oath and nods in compliance. "We can fix it together, but I can't go to battle without knowing the enemies. When you feel you can open up, I will be right here."

She gasps when my words throw her out of the luxurious bedroom in her own house. She slowly withdraws her embrace and stands beside the bed. I glare through the distorted vision of newly formed tears. Since moving to Strawberry, Kentucky, I have noticed a new strength in my sister that always starts with a deep centering breath. I know I'm in for it when her exhale flutters the red lacy ruffles on my bedspread.

Instead of yelling, she surprises me by whipping her dress over her head and dropping it to the floor. As she bends to step out of her panties, her limbs thicken to three times their girth. Her midsection thickens while the pop and crackle of her bones fill the room. Despite knowing my sister's gentle demeanor, I fight the urge to hide in my covers. When she sprouts white fur, I lose my nerve and rush under the bed.

A chuffing sound precedes the clawing at the floor just beyond the lace dust ruffle. I thought I was too dehydrated to cry more tears, but I quickly create a puddle on the floor. What has happened to my sister? Will she eat me? If she is one of those butterfly vampires—a Sluagh?

"Betty, look at me," a growling voice comes from the other side of the ruffle.

"Can you shoot lasers from your eyes?"

"Polar bears don't have lasers," her voice filled with annoyance. A snout rummages beneath the ruffle and I scoot to the opposite side. "Betty please, I need to show you why you shouldn't fear Aurora's leopard. Nate's an animal shifter. Grant and I are now bear shifters, too. If anyone tries to bother you, I will eat them. I promise. Please don't shut me out when I finally have the means to protect you. I can have your back."

"My sister would never hurt me. My sister would never hurt me," I chant to myself. I force myself to stand on the opposite side of the bed, face to face with a polar bear the size of my newly acquired Toyota.

The bear's snout recedes revealing my sister's face on the giant bear's body. I shriek and cower in the corner of the room. "You must recognize me, but I'm having trouble recognizing you. The Betty I know doesn't shrink into corners when faced with danger. Grant and I were infected with the local parasite giving us the ability to shift into our inner animals. Nothing more."

"Did the Sluagh do this to you?"

"No, the strength of a mama bear has been inside of me all along. It took a parasite to bring it out."

The more coherent words come from the bear, the

more comfortable I feel sharing a room with it. I stand tall and face her. "What about Henrik?"

"The pack decided to wait to turn him until after he reaches puberty since it is not until then shifters meet their inner animals. However, Henrik doesn't want to be a shifter like us. He has just discovered he has our family's gift. Betty, he's a much more powerful witch at twelve-years-old than Aunt Sarah and myself combined. Henrik sang the spell to close the portal to stop the invasion of Sluagh."

"Will the pack want to turn me too, to keep me quiet? Can you convince them I am trustworthy? I have always kept our family's secret."

"I am the Pack Leader. I have the final say in who gets turned. If you don't want it, they will have to do it over my dead body," she growls through her fangs. *What? Does my meek sister lead a pack?* Electricity crackles through the room as she begins to shrink. Her limbs narrow and her paws redefine themselves into tiny delicate hands. Left in the place of the snarling beast is a broken doll resembling my sister. She lies in a heap on the floor as I sit beside her.

"When did this happen? I mean I'm happy you found a place to fit in, but how can I avoid going furry," I ask her shivering form. She holds a quaking finger up to me and takes billowing breaths. Pulling the bedspread onto the floor to tuck it in around her, I rock her quietly until she recovers.

"Changing is always worse when you try to rush it," she says with a sheepish smile. I smile in return because this feels so much more familiar. Ally's strangeness has got her into a mess and I'm here to help her through it. "Bergan Pharma, the company Grant works for, belongs to the pack. The board decided to change him with a blood transfusion from a pack member who was born a shifter. I got it because I am a witch and I…I…"

"You couldn't keep your paws off him." She turns pink at my reference to her infatuation with her husband.

"Yes, that's always the base of my troubles isn't it," she says, pulling her dress over her head. "If we have more children, they will be shifters genetically. They will also have the power to change others via blood transfusion and it only takes a couple of drops."

Having her mention more children is jarring. After being abandoned by Grant for over half of Henrik's life, Alison swore she would never consider going through it again. Things must have really changed for them after becoming shifters. The shock is plainly displayed on my face because she continues.

"We mate like bears. We mark like bears and with each marking, our souls connect. Betty, I'm in a happy marriage. Really, I am." To prove her point, she points to the bite mark on the tender space between her neck and shoulder. *Gross.* Freaky bear sex with Grant must be an acquired taste.

"If you are happy then I am happy too," I say hugging her tightly. "So, avoid blood transfers and random animal sex, I think I can do that. Anything else I can do to keep safe? How do I avoid the Sluagh?"

"The Sluagh must avoid sunlight and are most active on the night of the New Moon. They cannot break inside buildings so just stay indoors or with shifters who can defeat them after dark. However, Sluagh can travel in the shadows on foggy or extremely cloudy days…"

"I got the job with Dr. V, though," I say throwing my hands in the air. "Why did you suggest working for him when his office hours are during the night?" I was looking forward to working in the small medical office in Strawberry. It is the perfect solution to my professional and legal problems. I have missed my clinical rotations since graduating and I need to keep sharp for the nursing exam at the end of the month.

"I thought the witches could close the portal before any Sluagh got through," Alison says, twisting my bedspread between her fingers. "Twelve made it into this realm. However, Nate and Aurora already took care of one of them. Ten are in their fortress just west of here but one is missing."

"Missing," I squeak.

"That's why we lock up tight at night, so be sure to be inside Dr. V's office before sundown. We can have a member of the wolfpack—you know Rosie's boys—next door at Paulino's walk you to your car or Dr. V's last patient in the morning."

"Oh, hell no," I groan. "I will not be chaperoned by a kid or an injured patient."

"Because of our witch genes, our souls are worth our weight in gold to the Sluagh. It has something to do with getting back to the Fae realm. I'm not risking you. Frank Junior and Ray aren't kids. They are full-grown werewolves."

My eyes grow to saucers as what she has stated sinks in. The tender-hearted, quiet Ray is a full-grown horror movie monster. I'm grateful Ally showed me her polar side first, so I keep perspective. If my goodie-two-shoes, tiny sister turns into the abominable snow monster, then the eighteen-year-old could be a kind-hearted werewolf. "Who else is a shifter?"

"Everyone is a shifter or vampire except for Dr. V,

Aurora, and you. Grant was converted to a grizzly bear shifter after we moved in. Henrik and Gran are witches, but Gran was a shifter until her mate died. Rosie said she looked as young as us until Vinnie died, now she can't walk without a cane. She was turned the same way I was, so she's my Ghost of Christmas Future."

My jaw drops. "You tied your physical well-being to Grant's mortality. Are you crazy?"

"Not every human couple turns out to be fated mates, so you can imagine my relief. Oh, don't glare at me. When have I made a sane decision regarding him?"

"If I'm ever that in love, I need you to smack me back to reality."

"No way, I want you to have what I have with Grant. It's difficult right now," she says with a brutal twist to the fabric, "but weren't you in love with Evan?"

"No Alison, our relationship was completely one-sided," I snap. "Stupid Junky proved repeatedly he loved drugs more than me. He even said he couldn't love me until he got clean. Why do you think he stole using my hospital credentials? If he hadn't OD'd, then we would have split eventually. There are no wedding bells or soul-merging bites for me." I glare at the ceiling as if I can curse Evan in the afterlife. I know everyone supposedly turns to dust, returning to Mother Earth, but I hope he is reincarnated as a worm.

"Betty," Alison pauses to take my hand in hers. "Your mate is out there." We lightly embrace while she fights back the tears for my lost love. Ally was always a romantic which made her easy prey for Grant's hollow promises. I would say look where it got her but she's a happy, career mom who lives in a palace with a doting husband. The turn-around of her life has left me incredulous.

"I don't care if he is out there. Ally, it has been almost a year since Evan died and I'm just now getting through the day without crying. I'm not doing it again. I will love you, Henrik, and possibly Grant. My goal in life is happiness, not love. Let's start there."

Chapter 2

T'was the night before Christmas and all through the lab, not a creature was working except for this unlucky cad...or at least I hope so. Everyone had left for the Yuletide party at Paulino's pizzeria so I should be able to work in solitude. Nate, the leopard shifter, and my microbiology cohort, was kind enough to find the agar recipe for the fruit plates I needed. It took all day to pour and set the stacks that fill my class II cabinet.

Like candy cane soldiers, the pink-striped stacks of plates stand sentinel behind the plexiglass sash. It will take a few hours to dilute the yeast I need and streak the plates; however, my reward will be a few days at home while the colonies grow. *Aaaah, time off.* Just the thought of my empty house with only my guitar and pet cats for company spreads a smile across my face.

The image is enough to rush my body through donning my protective gear; nitrile gloves tucked into a specially-designed latex apron with pouches for my wings, the second pair of gloves to cover the apron, and finally Tyvek sleeves to act as splash guards. With the sash down, I should be able to get away without using the face shield. Being a vampire, I thought I could skip the protective gear until a wicked skin infection proved otherwise.

I take one last inventory of the contents of the cabinet because once inside, I can't get out. I would not physically be stuck but discarding gloves and sleeves over and over gets expensive after a while. I do not want to incur the wrath of Ryan the Vampire King over something as stupid as wasting gloves.

With a touch of my double-gloved finger punk music echoes through the empty lab and I settle into the cabinet to work. The top three plates get one milliliter of concentrated yeast apiece which I streak across half the plate before rotating each plate ninety degrees to draw the lines of yeast into thinner crosshatches. One final ninety-degree rotation allows me to draw from the second set of yeast lines. This final quadrant will yield colony isolates for genetic verification. Repeat this about thirty times and I will be one-third finished.

"Dear mother,

Can you hear me whining?

It has been three whole days since I have been stuck at work,

This lab has drained the life from me,

For some strange reason, it's now feeling like my home,

And I just want to be alone!"

I belt out my parody with jaded timbre. It is private moments like this when I enjoy being a microbiologist. A decade of muscle memory lead my hands in a dance with the pipets and inoculation loops creating a treasure trove of genetic data. The untrained eye only sees liquid smeared onto gelatin-like molds but a genius like Nate turns it into life-saving medication. The stacks of plates march across the cabinet as I load them with data.

"Lucien, why aren't you dressed?" The bellow of the Vampire King across the lab causes me to jump to attention with my arms still in the cabinet. My forearms bang against the sash with a crash while the pipet flies out of my hands and into my bleach bucket. Twenty percent bleach splashes onto my blotter, instantly burning a network of holes into the plastic with a hiss of yellow vapor.

"I am wearing all my P-P-PPE," I stutter, referring to my personal protective equipment. I guiltily swing my gaze to the face shield hanging next to the cabinet. Bracing for impact, I wait for Ryan's tirade on following the rules of the lab to keep Grant happy. I have his diatribe memorized. Keep Grant happy to keep Alison happy because keeping Alison happy keeps our unfettered access to the Bergan Pharma blood bank. Blah, blah, blah.

"It is time to go to the Yule party," Ryan says, throwing his arms in the air. Oh no, I didn't think I was required to go. I cast a forlorn look at my plate stacks.

"You were going to skip it, weren't you? You were going to play scientist until I left and then go home, weren't you? Lucien, you are testing my patience. Nate has requested a new head of microbiology from another pack. If you are replaced, it weakens our alliance with the shifters. As heir to our colony that alliance is your only function, don't you get it? Since you seem to fail at using Bergan Pharma for that alliance, it must be social." Ryan lectures with glowing red eyes and partially descended fangs.

"I have this project all together now. I'm going to set up the colony isolation for James in the mol-tox department, set up the dilution plates to get vial concentrations for chemistry, and set up long term viability plates to keep Grant's timelines going. When Nate gets back from England—"

"When he what? He can't leave! He's the brains behind everything you do," Ryan yells. If his eyes bulge out any further, I fear they will fall out. He flicks my phone screen to silence the music, leaving only the whir of the air handler to drown out his lecture.

"He solves the puzzles much faster than I do but I get the answers eventually. I can see this project though if I get it set up tonight." I would rather Ryan drain me dry than go to the party. I loathe the vintage vampire routine that Ryan insists we put on to maintain the Hollywood image of us. I will never understand why it is so important Alison thinks we are hundreds of years old.

I slowly ease back into my chair to wrap the completed plates in incubator bags. If they get into the incubator, I can get James his plates on time. The rest will be delayed one day until I come back tomorrow night to finish the work. The separate plate times mean I will have to come in every night during the holiday break while wasting PPE. I hate that Ryan is not making an efficient decision but the one most politically savvy. Hell, I hate politics. I'm even starting to hate Ryan.

"You will look like a rag next to me. Do you have a suit in your office?" He straightens the cufflinks on his red velvet ensemble for the hundredth time since entering. He looks like a 1970s leisure suit edition of Santa and I crack a small grin at the image of him disco dancing in my mind. I finish wrapping everything in the cabinet and prepare to decontaminate the supplies out of it. Ryan snaps his fingers at me when I don't answer fast enough.

"No extra suit, just my jacket. I have been here for three nights and I arrived in scrubs because I only stopped home to feed my cats and drop my laundry." I load the unused plates back into their refrigerator, so I don't have to look at Ryan's disappointed face. Next, I place labels on James's loaded plates and place them in the incubator. With each armful, I must pass by toe-tapping Ryan. He doesn't offer to help, get a door, or even step out of the way as he displays his dominance.

"I will grab your jacket since you are so determined to drag this out. We are late already," he sneers. His heels clap their way down the hall to my office before I release the breath I didn't know I was holding.

I clean out the cabinet but abandon the bleach bucket inside. *I will be back tomorrow.* Hanging my head, I finish the paperwork with the times the plates were finished so they can be part of Grant's official project. I learned from Grant if it is not in the paperwork then it didn't happen.

Ryan returns to throw my jacket over my head and haul me out of the lab by my wing like a child. We turn the corner to head out and run smack into Brad and Molina. Could this get any more embarrassing?

Brad is the lion-shifter acting as CEO of Bergan Pharma but more importantly, he is mated to my aunt with too many greats, Molina. Molina is the oldest in our colony, enjoying the increased lifespan of frequent shifter blood infusions from her mate. Ryan is a typical disgruntled younger child. My father was Ryan's elder sibling until his myelodysplastic anemia took his life.

Myelodysplastic anemia is the syndrome that makes us vampires. Our bone marrow is hollow instead of the spongy red blood cell factory it should be. For generations, our relatives have taken blood from humans to use their red blood cells, but this behavior covers the problems instead of solves it. The result is a race which dies young. I am already older than my father was at the time of his death because I am fortunate enough to get monthly stem cell infusions from Dr. V. Ryan is proof stem cell therapy can prolong a vampire's life expectancy by at least twenty years but even his time is running out.

"All work and no play, Ryan," Molina teases. Her green eyes twinkle in merriment while Ryan's brown eyes seethe with annoyance at the delay. Vampire's eyes are reversed when compared to shifter's and human eyes to allow more light to enter them. Our irises look like crystals balanced in the center of a black void. The enlarged surrounding pupil ring allows more light to enter the shrunken iris.

"Just retrieving our workaholic nephew, Molina. A task I should have left to you since you are also delayed at getting to the party," Ryan replies with an eye roll.

Molina turns pink and sends a secretive smile to Brad. *Oh Brother*. Molina was the first of our colony to come to the States in the mid-1700s and she met Brad before stepping off the boat. Together with Vinnie Paulino and his wife Rafaella (now called Gran), they created the Strawberry shifters pack and the town of Strawberry, Kentucky. Too bad Ryan is not convinced this is enough to secure the alliance between the shifters and the vampires, mostly because female vampires cannot have children.

Stepping into the cold December night, the crisp breeze feels like heaven after several days of stale laboratory air. I am going to suck every drop of enjoyment from this walk across the snow-covered field. The annual Strawberry Yule party is my personal hell.

Ryan pushes me to dance with every unmated female shifter using moves from the Baroque period to maintain our Old World image. Do you know how hard it is to *danses à deux* to "All I Want for Christmas Is You"?

He hopes to secure a match, but every female moons over Nate the entire time. This year will be worse because Nate is getting serious with Aurora, Strawberry's newest human resident. Tonight, Ryan and I will be Strawberry's most eligible bachelors. A fact that makes me want to hide in a hole in the ground.

"Perfect," Ryan whispers, pulling me to slow down. He wants Brad and Molina to get a comfortable distance ahead so he can scheme…again. "The bears are playing in the snow with the Paulino kids, so the party hasn't officially started. I can forgive your dallying if you keep Grant busy with science junk. Give him an update on what you were doing late in the lab. I need a few moments alone with Alison."

Ryan has a twinkle in his eye when he's about to be evil. Trying to break up the marriage between Grant and Alison is as mean as it gets. I hate being a part of this. *Sigh, I guess it could be worse, he could task me to do it.* Ryan's physical attraction to Alison is the heart of the problem. Rosie Paulino is the widow of our former leader, a perfect candidate for the alliance, but not nearly as pretty as Alison.

"Hey Grant," I yell while jogging to where he stands in his grizzly form. "I just l-left the l-lab. M-Micro should have all the colonies ready for further testing by the end of the holiday break, so the Sacc B project is ahead of schedule. Isn't that great?" Do I sound as stupid out loud as I do in my head?

"Sure, Lucien. However, it doesn't matter because

Nate is taking James with him to England. We will be dependent on the bench chemists and George's daytime mol-tox team to analyze the data. You know they move as slow as molasses." Damn it, my colonies will overgrow or die before James gets back. Looks like I will be analyzing my own data too, only to have Nate come home to tell me I did everything wrong.

"I'm sure I can get someone on David's Quality Control team to do it and we can circumvent George. Perhaps his l-lead chemist, P-Paul," I suggest. David is the vampire equivalent of George with duplicate teams to keep the company running twenty-four hours per day. This is Bergan Pharma's secret to success. Having a permanent scientific night staff makes for twice the research and productivity than the average pharmaceutical company. Unfortunately, David has a horrible work ethic after being a nobleman in the Old Country for too long. He acts like Americans live to serve him.

"Fang-tastic," says Grant with a grin that doesn't reach his eyes. His gaze hasn't left Alison during our exchange. Ryan has kissed her hand twice when she partially shifted to greet him. Now he has his hand resting on her polar bear back. I can feel the waves of hostility radiating from Grant, the formidable Grizzly bear.

Ryan is an idiot. A brilliant idea on how I can get retribution for going to this party pops into my head. I stoop to gather a boulder of snow and struggle to roll it toward Grant. A smile spreads across Grant's muzzle as he stands on his back legs and easily lobs it at Ryan.

Splat! A three-foot snow print decorates the back of Ryan's suit completing his Santa persona. I school my face into one of shock while a victory cheer roars in my head. The wet snow will mar the velvet fabric for the rest of the evening, a constant irritant for stepping on the other man's territory. Ryan is just lucky Grant hasn't mauled him yet. The two got into a fistfight over Alison when they first met but Grant was a newly transitioned shifter who hadn't tested his strength. Now it would not be an even match.

"Hey, I could use some help over here," calls Nate in his yowling snow leopard voice. Tommy, the youngest Paulino werewolf, is buried to his neck in the snow while the other kids are rolling with laughter. The eight-year-old has no idea of the danger of hypothermia. His purple-tinged lips surround a smile, but it is fading fast as he notices the panic of the adults. As the bears rush to his aid, Ryan grabs my jacket and pulls me toward the party.

"We've got it, Luc. Tell James and Rosie we will be bringing Tommy shortly," Nate calls when I struggle against Ryan's super grip. I wave in response and turn toward the party. It is no use fighting Ryan's hold on me anyway. His claws go deeper than what people see on the outside.

Chapter 3

"You are here to mate one of those shifters. We need an alliance. Every year it gets harder after you blew it," Ryan sneers when we reach the doors. I'm not sure which wounds my pride more, the way he shoves me over the threshold or the reminder of the worst social experience of my life.

Every time Yule lights are strung in Paulino's pizzeria, I have the same edict from Ryan. Since Patty, the Hawk shifter, is the highest-ranking female in Bergan Pharma, he thinks she would be a partner worthy of our cause. Under his tutelage, I have been groomed to be the sensitive, non-threatening vampire with supposedly irresistible Old-World charm. Too bad his plan was ruined eight years ago.

She was obsessed with Nate and medicating her nervousness with mudslides. I was no match for Nate's modern approach to courting with his lazy smiles and feminist views. We took turns whirling her around the dancefloor until she confessed her affections for the leopard shifter. When he rejected her in front of everyone, she grabbed me in a last-ditch attempt to sling mud at him. Instead, her mudslides landed on me. The Yule party that shall not be mentioned was born and Patty was too upset to ever talk to me again.

Perhaps Nate elected to play in the snow instead of coming to the party to avoid the past drama. Rumor has it he is getting serious with Aurora, but the rumor mill also spins a tale of James getting serious with Aurora. *Sigh*. It is difficult to keep up with the small-town gossip since I spend every waking moment working.

I would be completely in the dark if I didn't have a habit of working into the daylight hours and cannot go home without sun-scorching myself, so I sleep in the bunks at Bergan. Aurora is perched on James's lap confirming Strawberry's most sought-after bachelor is still single. My stomach acid boils at the prospect of another dance competition against Nate.

Aurora's table erupts with laughter calling more attention from the local gossips. *Oh wow...* Who is the beauty seated beside them? Her laughter soars toward the ceiling like a bird taking flight, graceful wings sending melodious waves to my ears. Her black hair catches the light, pale skin so perfect it glistens and ruby lips, add up to a classic vampire princess, but she can't be. All the vampire princesses are related to me.

Head tilted back with her glee; the narrow column of her neck is pulsing to release the most exquisite sound I have ever heard. I want to hear it again. I want to be the one to evoke joy from her gorgeous throat. When she tilts her head forward, I get lost in her mahogany eyes. Her perfectly human eyes…unfortunately, she's not the shifter Ryan has picked for me. I would gladly chase the woman with musical laughter.

Brilliant. I can use the guise of relaying Nate's message to learn the name of the newest resident to Strawberry. I nod to James and quickly approach his table before Ryan can send me on some fool's errand. "Nate says to save him a seat because he's coming in once they rescue Tommy," I stammer in his direction.

"Tommy's brothers decided to bury him and used a little too much snow. The adults are working hard to unearth him before he starts to cry." I sneak glances at the beauty between my stuttered words. She's more beautiful up close than across the room. Faint freckles dot her button nose in an adorable array while barely noticeable golden flecks brighten her eyes.

"Lucien, this is my Aurora and Alison's sister Betty," James says. "Ladies this is the Prince of Darkness, Lucien Von Popescu."

"Or as I say, Ryan's nephew Luc." My shy voice sounds nothing like Nate's modern speech patterns. I wish I had easy confidence like him or a booming voice like Grant to impress her with my presence. Being the sister to the pack leader, she must be used to powerful alpha male suitors or worse she could be here as Nate's date since James just claimed Aurora. Aurora is wearing a mating mark, so I guess the fight for her is over and James is the victor.

"Luc," Betty rolls my name over her tongue. "You have unusual eyes. Do you have distorted vision from them?"

At her words, I stiffen with indecision. My mouth refuses to function while my brain spits dozens of responses through my imagination resulting in a swirling mass of confusion. Do I fall back on the approachable vampire act? Do I act like Nate? I can't just be myself. Ryan will throw a fit.

I finally decide to imitate Nate and be funny. I can be funny. "If my vision were...*distorted*...I would be the last to know, since I don't change out my eyes for different occasions," I flirt, which sounds more like a sneer to my ears. "Do you have that talent?" Her smile falls at my words and a glare replaces it. *AH!* What possessed me to be funny? I have been in her presence for thirty seconds and already wish I were part of the decorations.

"Don't be a little bitch," Betty says, waving her drink at me. "I was curious. Now I'm bored." As she stands, she cracks her back. Her brash language hits my ears with the familiarity of my music. I often curse about the woes of my life, strengthening the emotions they evoke. Strong emotions she evokes in me. If her words were concocted to cool my heels, she shouldn't have used gasoline.

She sways her hips as she walks to the doorway to greet Henrik, prospective heir to the Strawberry shifter's pack. They embrace while she swings the boy around in a circle. Aurora makes some crack about her working for the chiropractor, but it flies over my head. The path Betty leaves, and the rhythm of her movement mesmerize me like a snake charmed into a basket. I wish I had my guitar. I want to play my songs and watch her dance. My mind conjures an image of her dressed as a belly dancer, rolling her hips in sensuality, smiling gently in my direction.

"You okay, Dude?"

"Yeah," I sigh with my daydream popping like a soap bubble. "I need some time off. I came straight here from the lab and I think my brain is fuzzy. All I want for Yule is some time alone in my house. See? The Vampire King is calling me over again. I need a night off from him most of all."

Why me? Ryan has oiled his way to where Betty is helping Henrik change out of his boots. Ryan is going to burst a blood vessel if I try to be funny again. I'm back to the Flamboyant New Orleans Vampire imitation only worse due to my failed attempt at flirtation moments ago. I'm so lost in my misery I almost get bulldozed by the Paulino boys crossing my path. The result is the splat of slush across my scrubs, instantly thinning them to tissue paper consistency.

I reach Ryan just in time for the arrival of pack leaders, Alison and Grant. The room erupts with applause as the leaders enter behind me in my nearly see-through scrubs. I pull my jacket tighter, but the action does nothing to lengthen it where I need it most. My wardrobe malfunction has my complete attention, so I miss Ryan's cue to bow to Alison and kiss her hand. Instead, his elbow connects with my wing slits sending a searing pain along my back. Doubling over in pain, my forward momentum from the initial blow throws me to the ground at Alison's feet.

"Oh no," Alison yelps as she kneels to help. "Have you hurt yourself?"

As she takes my elbows in innocent sympathy, Grant's baritone growl echoes in my ears. *Help me, Ryan.* Great, Ryan is flashing his fangs too. I wish I was no more than one of the red carpet's fibers. I get stepped on enough. I would be perfectly trained for the job.

"Only my pride is wounded Madam Commander. You are too kind to help me up. You must excuse my clumsiness. I am not worthy of such attention." Those are the words programmed to come out of my mouth. I really want to tell her to back the hell off before one of the alpha males behind her decides to eat me. If I'm going to get eaten, I don't want it to be for making alleged moves on Alison. Ryan is the predator, not me. Well, I am a vampire, but raised on bagged blood.

"Ally, your shoes," whispers Betty. "They are on the wrong feet again." Captivated by the sight of Betty on all-fours beside me, I hardly notice Alison's shuffling. Betty's hands replace Alison's locking onto my elbows to help me up which saves me from being the dinner of the alpha males posturing over Alison. The warmth of her hands seeps through my jacket sleeves, sending a glow through my entire body. Errant pictures of us snuggling under a quilt watching a snowfall flash through my mind.

"I hardly did a thing," Alison says as we raise to standing in unison. Grant's hand snakes around her back to rest on her hip possessively. "Have you been introduced to my sister, Betty?"

My chest rumbles as Ryan bows to Betty and kisses her hand as if I haven't embarrassed myself enough. I should feel delighted Ryan's attention is on her. If Ryan's infatuation with Alison would shift to Betty, then most of my problems would be solved. Ryan could secure the alliance with her, especially since she's not wearing a wedding ring or mating mark. Not that I was looking…I just noticed…when I looked.

Betty raises a delicate eyebrow at me skeptically when I repeat Ryan's gesture. A better man would take the hint to drop the act but I'm no saint. If Ryan's dog-and-pony-show has one perk, this kiss is it. Her hand is warm, strong but so tiny within my palm. Her fingers are soft as flower petals when I brush my lips against them, purposely missing the ring on her middle finger. *Bad form.* The primal vampire in me sniffs and dizziness floods my brain from the scent of the blood rushing under her skin.

"Yep, I met Luc before you came in," she snaps,

taking her hand out of mine and placing it back at her hip. Hearing "Luc" escape her lips fills me with unexpected pride. It overrides the terror of her usage of my nickname in front of Ryan. I try to hide my reaction from Ryan who is staring at me with glowing red eyes. Vampires' eyes only glow red when they are emotionally charged, usually with anger or lust, but Ryan's eyes glow when he has an idea to fulfill his lust for power. *Eff my life*.

****

I don't know who is more dangerous the Sluagh monsters that I thought were vampires or the devastatingly handsome jerk who is a vampire. When Luc's lips twist into a half-smile, I go weak at the knees. When his lips touched my fingers, electricity shot up my arm and singed my nervous system. I have always coveted a man's lips, but Luc's coloring maximizes their ruby contours. Too bad his cover is better than the book.

The last distraction I need in my life is another boyfriend with a competing addiction. Vampires are addicted to blood, right? No way am I going to be a supplier for a man again. I'm going to find a normal guy who loves me for me. No weirdos need to apply…including arrogant vampires. My guy will be a harmless accountant or maybe a nerdy scientist like my brother-in-law. Mr. Happily-ever-after will enjoy maintaining our lawn and falling asleep on the couch with golf playing on a nearby television.

"Yep, I met Luc before you came in," I say, placing my hand safely at my hip. His lip curls when I use his name as if it means something special. I may have a photographic memory, but I just learned his name five minutes ago. He either is surprised I'm astute enough to remember it or has such an ego that he believes I'm infatuated with him. My treasonous mouth grins in return instead of recoiling in disgust.

I quickly avert my gaze, so I don't engage with him and become ensnared by the glowing eyes of the Vampire King. The red eyes paired with the used-car-salesman smile are terrifying. Knowing my sister's eyes glow whenever Grant is mentioned, I surmise Ryan has dirty thoughts on his mind—ones I don't want to headline. Having a more social acuity than my sister, she probably doesn't even realize the danger or if she does, she's counting on Grant to save us. That strategy will only work for one of us.

"Let's not stand in the way of the boys serving the food, Ally. We need to find a table where your followers can greet you or start filling their plates." I lace one elbow through Ally's and my other arm around Henrik's elbows to march us toward Aurora's table. Nate already ate a Sluagh on my behalf. I doubt he would hold a grudge because I ran screaming into one of Ally's bedrooms. If so, I will have to explain I'm new to this paranormal lifestyle and hadn't seen her polar bear side yet. Between him and my snow monster sister, I should be safe from the plan Ryan is hatching. Right?

I drag my family to the table in time to watch James go down on one knee before his tablemates. *Oh God no*. At least he doesn't say the "m-word" but instead says, "Nate and Aurora, will you be my librarians?" He looks to them with love in his eyes and a panic attack blossoms under my ribs. I join Alison's hand with Henrik's so I can fade into the crowd behind them. I can't ruin what is probably the happiest day of Aurora's life by fainting. Never in a million years would I have guessed my best friend was receiving a proposal on bended-knee—my trigger.

My mind tumbles back to the Samhain before last when I ditched our family party for a special surprise date from Evan. We had been looking for apartments. I was going to announce I found the one I could afford by waiting tables. We would live together while he got clean. Evan had been acting cagy and I was certain he was preparing to propose. We had planned to meet at our old elementary school's playground, but I had to wait a few hours in the sprinkling rain before he arrived. He arrived high on drugs.

Back in Paulino's pizzeria everyone is laughing and applauding. I slowly clap and focus on breathing. My mind spins and weaves the past with the present. I have to get away from the happy trio. Evan plopped down on one knee like James just knelt before Aurora and Nate. Evan didn't speak of marriage either. He didn't speak at all. He seized.

I had seen many seizures in my clinical rotations as a nursing student. None of them prepared me for the sight of Evan's eyes rolling back in his head. It was at that moment he physically left me. The cops at the hospital informed me he had emotionally left me months before my special surprise. Evan hadn't been shopping for an engagement ring as he told me the day before, he was shopping for a speedball. The time I spent waiting tables, saving for our apartment was Evan's opportunity to find new dealers. The cops followed him from gutter to gutter as his dependency escalated from pills to heroin.

I am snapped back to the present by Alison's movement to hug Aurora. I hadn't noticed I was leaning on her until she stepped forward. The anxiety building in my chest expands until my festive velvet dress threatens to strangle me. Like a frightened rodent, I scurry from the dining room and down the entry hall of the pizzeria.

As I retrieve my bag and coat from the front closet, I send a silent thanks to Gran. She convinced Ally I needed to drive to the party separately. I explode out of the doors, dropping my coat in a pile of snow, and double over to put my head between my knees. A sound resembling one of Santa's reindeer surges from my belly into the frosty night.

"Wooo, wooo," I bellow into the night. Snowflakes perform a mocking polka around my ugly cloud of exhalation. My noises are more comprised of my pain at the loss of Evan than tension leaving my body. I claw angrily at the tears falling from my chin. I had promised myself I would stop crying when I left Ohio. I wasn't supposed to bring Evan's memory here. I was supposed to be okay. Supposed…supposed…supposed, why can't my heart heal?

Despite the change in location, my panic attack is not subsiding. I must leave before I can no longer drive home. First, I must loosen this dress. I twist and fight to place my fingers on buttons or a zipper at the back of my dress only to remember this one slides over my head. I wail in defeat as my tears crush the velvet across my chest.

****

I knew I shouldn't have followed her outside but the thought of her facing a Sluagh alone induces panic like I haven't felt in years. I can only hope Ryan didn't notice when we disappeared together. Perhaps I should have told him to follow her so he could play hero, but something about Ryan rescuing Betty makes my skin crawl.

I gently push the door open just in time to see her wrap her arms around herself in a tight embrace. A wail releases from the depths of her soul and echoes across the meadow toward Bergan Pharma. The sound of despair reaches inside me and tugs at my heart. The pain radiating from her surrounds me like an army battering my psyche with little swords of sadness. This is the type of pain that draws Sluagh, hoards of Sluagh. No wonder she was attacked the night of the invasion. I scan the skies before approaching her.

"Can I offer my assistance?"

"What," she yells while spinning around to face me. The quick movement causes her to sway on her feet. Keeping my eyes on the sky, I glide closer to catch her if she falls. "Did you really just offer to help me rip open my dress?"

"I…" *Oh my God.* That's what she was doing embracing herself. I am too mortified to finish my sentence.

"Look if you came out here to lord over me. Don't waste your breath. I'm at my lowest…so…leave me alone."

"I followed you because I am afraid Sluagh are going to attack. They are attracted to sadness. Your mournful call is bringing the cavalcade to our doorstep."

"Oh well, heaven forbid I ruin your party," she puffs between billowing breathes. She claws at her back as if she truly wishes to open the dress. She spins again and I am faced with the back of the dress. It hasn't a zipper or row of buttons to loosen it.

I take a deep breath and step against her. "Tell me not to rip it," I say with such trepidation that it comes out as a whisper. The wisps of hair on the back of her neck dance to my voice as the waves travel along her flesh. I tuck my fingers into the neckline of her dress, careful to only allow the backs of my fingers to touch her. Her skin is on fire and so silky I fear my callused fingertips will snag it.

"Release me," she sobs.

A strength buried inside me surges forward and my claws extend from my nailbeds. I dip their black tips into the collar of her dress and yank. The material gives way, revealing smooth creamy skin to her waist. I have a heartbeat to catch my breath before she whirls around and slaps me.

"You ruined it," she yells.

"You have enough oxygen to scream at me now!" I hold my cheek with one hand and her bare back with the other. "One, you were swaying due to lack of oxygen. Two, you were in hysterics trying to get out of it. Three, you said to release you from it."

"I meant to release your hands, Asshole."

Oh my God, I am still touching her. It felt so natural to spot her as she released her pain I must have reached for her subconsciously. I replay the events in my mind, but I was so focused on her I have no idea how my hands ended up on her. "Send me the bill then," I say dejectedly.

"Believe me, I will."

I bend down to retrieve her jacket and brush the snow from it. I offer it to shield her from the cold. Humiliating. I ruined her dress. *What possessed me?* As she slides into her jacket, I spy a small mole, no larger than a pencil eraser, between her shoulder blades. A second peeks at me from the bottom of the slit in the dress only to disappear in the black lace of her panties. *That's what possessed me.* I must stay away from her, especially if she's being hunted by Ryan. The comfortable role of Old World Prince recovers my dignity. "I can offer you entrance into Bergan for scrubs."

"Really, Bodice-ripper? Look as stylish as you? No thanks, I was going home anyway. You just accelerated my exit." She shoots daggers from her eyes in my direction with every word.

"I will notify Madam Commander of your departure if you would please send her a text when you arrive. With the Sluagh loose, she will be anxious until you are safe indoors."

"You do that. I will drive directly into the attached garage and text her. Are you going to tell her you tried to violently disrobe me, ruining my dress, or should I?"

"I will leave that to your discretion as it is your injury. I would prefer Ryan to be kept unawares unless I must explain why I am buying a tiny green velvet dress. However, I know the peril of living in a small town and Ryan will know eventually."

"Then maybe I will tell, maybe I won't." Her hair whirls as she turns back toward the row of cars. It fans over my nose and blasts me with the feminine scent of her shampoo. She enters a shiny red sedan with a slam of the car door. My claws press into my palms. It takes every molecule of fortitude I possess not to fly over her until she returns home safely.

"Don't be an idiot. She is not yours to protect," I say to the puffy snow clouds. A cold wind blast reminds me of my wet scrubs, and I'm left at a crossroads. Go back to Bergan and finish my project or go back inside to wait for Betty to text Alison. Since I am already outside, I am completely free from Ryan and the choice is mine.

Who am I kidding? I stomp back inside, pounding my despondence into the carpet all the way to the buffet line. I grab two giant plates and make a meal fit for a dress-ripping ogre. My logic is to eat slowly so I have no time for dancing or even better, eat until illness makes me useless.

"Betty is currently indisposed. She has retreated to your home, Madam Commander," I say on approach to Alison's table. The table is fully attended with Rosie, Frank Junior, Ryan, Grant, Alison, and Henrik sitting around it. However, I'm in the mood to be self-destructive. I plunk my plates between Henrik and Alison who meekly slide apart to make room.

From the bar, I snag a small glass and a large bottle of bourbon. I grab an abandoned chair from the next table and spin it backward at the table. Straddling the chair, I wedge myself between the occupants, glaring at everyone, and stabbing at my tortellini with violence. While loading my fork I take my first shot of bourbon neat.

The fiery liquid only momentarily distracts my body from the memories of the exchange outside. I don't need a woman like Betty in my life. They are too much for me. Too much drama, too much volatility, and in the end, too much heartache comes from a woman with more vitality than manners.

"Oh Grant," Alison says turning to her husband. "Do you think she will be alright? They could grab her as she walks to her car."

"I escorted her safely to her car and she spoke of an attached garage," I say with my mouth full. I earn a glare from Ryan, but I just lift my glass to him before draining its contents. Hopefully, Ryan seizes the opportunity to follow Betty so I can be without him for a while. A geyser of bile threatens my digestion as my mind pictures Ryan alone with Betty. No way. She would see through his antics and throw his ass out. That visualization brings a smile to my lips.

"Thank you so much. I am so relieved she is already through the most dangerous part of the journey." Alison won't be so grateful when she finds out about the dress incident or about my new nickname.

"She also promised to text you once she arrived," I say before stuffing an entire garlic bread slice in my mouth. I wash it down with another shot of the alcohol that I can no longer taste. I continue to eat like I have been wandering the Antarctic for days while staring at Alison's lifeless phone.

One of my plates is empty before Betty's text comes through and Alison reads it aloud. Relief floods my inebriated brain lifting the tension I wasn't going to admit was there. Even out of my sight, Betty has changed my plans for the evening. I'm not going to fly home. I'm not going to work on Grant's project. I'm going to stumble my way back to Bergan's bunks to dream of running my tongue over a pair of freckles partially hidden by green velvet tatters.

Chapter 4

"Happy Christmas to you, happy Christmas to you," Ally sings from the edges of my consciousness. Barely cracking my eyes open, I watch her skip around my room through last night's painted lashes. A tray is set on the bedside table with the clank of her expensive china. She throws open the blackout curtains allowing the low winter sun to assault my senses.

"Please Ally," I groan, hoping for sympathy. "I need to be nocturnal for when I start working for Dr. V. Go brighten someone else's day, an evil queen, a troll, an IRS worker, anyone else." I roll onto my stomach and bury my head between the giant pillows.

"That's why I let you sleep until dinnertime. In fact, I brought your favorite breakfast," she says in her sing-song voice. I love my sister dearly, but she was much more palatable when she was miserable. I'm about to throw her out when her words sink in.

"Carbs?"

"Oh yeah, herbal focaccia with extra garlic oil for dipping. A giant glass of iced green tea with vanilla syrup to wash it down. Also, the Yule gifts you left at the party."

I sit up enthusiastically, anticipating Ally's perfect baking, until the mention of last night. When I returned home, I cried over Evan. I sobbed, screamed, and released my pent-up anger to the empty walls of the giant plantation house. My wails of anguish echoed off the vaulted ceilings and swung on the chandeliers. I predicted nightmares of my final moments with him.

When I collapsed in a pile of tissues, it wasn't Evan's seizing face in my mind's eye. It was Lucien's face, tinged with pity and concern. *Lucien.* Lucien who followed me into the cold night to fight my dress and my bad attitude. The hostility to him was a defense against the magnetism between us.

Something inside me is drawn to him like a moth to a flame. Memories of him and the dreams he starred in last night haunt my psyche…all of him, but mostly his lips tilting into a shy smile, sipping at mine, and kissing me everywhere. Never has a man inspired so many fantasies after one poorly executed encounter.

"I'm sorry I left early. I wasn't feeling festive, but I didn't want to ruin the night for Aurora." The breakfast tray clanks onto my lap. Alison has shaped the focaccia into evergreen trees with flecks of herbs and balls of candied garlic as garland. A trio of cranberries floats in my green tea and a sprig of holly adorns the plate. "This is beautiful, but we don't celebrate Christmas. Why did you take the time to do this?"

"Because you are my sister and I'm your host." When I glare at her skeptically, she adds, "I wanted to bribe you into telling me why you left the Yule party. If you are sad or scared, I want to help."

"I'm a big girl," I whisper to my breakfast. As I choke back the tears, I scan the beautiful room I have been provided. I have the perfect refuge to shut out the world from the blackout window curtains to the matching drapes hanging on my giant state bed. I could even blend into the busy red and gold wallpaper with the right dress. The outrageous décor is more indicative of the era the house was built than my austere sister. It is the exact opposite of the tiny, plain house she left in Ohio. If this place can persuade her to enjoy the riches she deserves, then maybe it can transform me into a better person.

"Have you forgotten our deal so soon? We are going to share our troubles like when we were younger, no more hiding." The bed sags as she sits next to me almost spilling my tea.

I rip the first focaccia tree into bite-sized pieces while deciding how much to tell her. "James's proposing triggered a panic attack. It brought back the night when I thought Evan was proposing but he was really collapsing from…from…" I can't finish my sentence. The tears clog my throat and sting my tired eyes. Damn it, I thought I was finished crying.

"Shhhh, shhhh, I get it now," she whispers at me while smoothing my hair. "I should have been a better host to you at the party. I left you to fend for yourself, right from the beginning. I'm sorry."

"No, I was having fun hanging out with Aurora. It's not your fault. No one knew there would be a proposal. After all this time, I should no longer be mad at Evan. I have fewer triggers, but they are as much a surprise to me as to everyone else. I thought it best if I leave before I made an ass of myself."

"You left before I could give you the gifts from Grant, Henrik, and me." She hands me a stack of palm-sized boxes tied with a red ribbon. "I love the sweaters you gave me. I opened them at the party before I realized they were from you and you had left." She blushes light pink at her admission. Knowing Alison's child-like spirit, she was probably tearing through gifts as a woman possessed while hardly acknowledging their cards.

I use my tongue to simulate a drumroll while pulling the ribbon from the boxes. Her eyes sparkle with anticipation of my reaction. Inside the first box, sits an array of eight hair combs. They are adorned with tangles of colored wires of a multitude of colors. "They are beautiful," I murmur as I pick one up to study it. The one-inch comb is surprisingly heavy. Threading it into my hair, I love the sturdy engineering holding my thick strands in place.

"Josh made them out of iron like Aurora's earrings. They are designed uniquely for you as Sluagh weapons. One touch with the wire will burn them so if you are ever in danger…well, I feel better knowing you are armed."

I reveal larger clips to decorate my signature ponytail in the other two boxes. Each clip has a different colored cloud of wire topped with a black letter "B" in the center. Their beauty and the thoughtfulness of my sister is awe-inspiring. "Ally, these are perfect."

"It was Grant's suggestion. After Aurora proved they were effective weapons, Grant went to Josh to have them designed for you. I just went along with his plans…as usual. I wish you could have opened them at the party. It was tremendous fun sitting around a tree and opening presents."

"Ally, I would have ruined it. I am happier knowing that you, Henrik, and even Grant had a great Yule after having to miss Mom and Dad's party to fight the Sluagh."

"I should have at least driven you home last night. When I have panic attacks, I'm in no state to drive."

"Frankly, I am embarrassed at my lack of control.

Good thing the only person to witness my breakdown was bodice…bogus…that bogus vampire."

"Vampire? Lucien, that's right. Lucien walked you to your car. He was in rare form last night."

"Oh yeah?" She makes a face at me, so I raise my palms in surrender. "He was fine when I left him standing outside."

"He came inside in a funk and got completely wasted," Alison says with giggles.

"We thought you had worked your charm on him. He was so pissed off," bellows Grant from the doorway. "Sorry to barge in but Henrik wanted to be sure Betty got some of the bread trees before he took some of them."

"He can help himself to what is remaining on the stove. Betty has some pieces in here and I packed a few for her to take to work with her this week." Alison twists toward the doorway and I fade into the background, but it has always been that way when Grant enters the room. The difference this morning is the love reflected in his eyes. It is a relief to see my sister's affections reciprocated even if only in facial expression. He is as smitten as she is…for once.

"Be careful when alone with the vampires, Betty. They may look harmless compared to the Sluagh, but they have their own agenda, especially Ryan. I know they will be your patients with Dr. V but keep the relationship there," Grant warns. I can't help but roll my eyes.

"No surprise but I agree with Grant. Until we are certain whose side they are on, keep them at arms' length. There are too many questions. Ryan isn't being forthcoming with answers either."

"Believe me, one look at Ryan's red eyes and

dripping fangs was enough to put me off vampires for a lifetime," I quip.

Grant's eyes bug out when he asks, "his eyes glowed at you?"

"Yeah, why?"

"Glowing eyes means feeding or killing, I think. The last time I saw his eyes glowing, we ended up fist fighting in the dirt over Alison."

"What? How have I managed to piss off the Vampire King? We just met!"

Chapter 5

"Hey look! It's Mr. Sun bringing Christmas morning. Like Scrooge, the spirits must have given me another chance or there's a better chance that I will need to be given more spirits. My bottles are all empty, Planty." I slur to my new best friend, the holly bush outside of Bergan Pharma. We are having a grand time singing Christmas carols, philosophizing about life, and embracing the reason for the season.

"Lucien, are you trying to scorch yourself? Luc? Luc?" A vaguely familiar voice shouts over my head. Between the glare off the snow and the shouting, a killer headache grows between my eyes.

"Shhh, shhh, you will scare Planty away if you keep shouting. He's as fragile as a flower," I whisper between hiccups. I swat at the noise source over my head. A hand clasps my wrist and attempts to haul me to my feet. I swing my face upwards too quickly for my constitution and belch into the face of Brad, Bergan's CEO.

"Luc, are you still wasted from last night? I need to get you inside before it gets too bright," he says while swaying…at least I think he's swaying…and I'm on the ground again.

"No! I won't abandon Planty on Christmas. No one should have to spend Christmas alone, except for me. I always spend Christmas alone working in the lab. I'm always working in the lab." My voice pierces my ears and my brain.

"Well, today you get to sleep in the lab," Brad says, dragging me indoors by my feet. My head slams into the floor when I cross the threshold. My last coherent image is Molina and Ryan standing over me with matching frowns and glowing eyes.

My head is pounding. I clasp my skull between my hands to stop my brain from rattling. As the haze before my eyes clears, the bunks of Bergan appear. *How can that be when I forgot to grab my keys before the party?* Looking down, I inventory my bed contents: wrinkled scrubs, suit jacket, lab safety shoes, and giant holly bush. Slush and piles of dirt stain the sheets. I dreamt of my reenactment of the Dialogues of Socrates with a talking bush, but now I am having morning-after regrets. It could be worse. I could have awoken at Alison's house, cozy against the hellcat that threatens to turn my world upside-down just by existing.

Tick, ti-tick. There's a faint clicking, not rhythmic enough to be a clock. Pulling my head from the tangle of sheets, I fight nausea to locate the sound. Ryan is using a knife to pick under his nails while sitting at my bedside. Memories of my performance last night flash across my mind at the speed of light. I disrespected the shifters, pigged out at Paulino's, vomited it up on the village green, spent the night on the front steps of Bergan, took a plant to bed and all of it was triggered by ripping Betty's dress. Eff-my life, oh wait, I already did.

Thoughts of Betty stab between my eyes like an ice pick to a block. Perhaps Alison knows about the dress and has cast a spell on me to suffer migraines at the thought of her sister's creamy flesh dotted with sweet freckles. Unfortunately, none of their sweetness has diffused beneath Betty's skin. My cheek is still throbbing from her backhand, not that I didn't deserve it, but I suspect I will bruise. Oh well, her fiery temper is now Ryan's problem. A union between Ryan and Betty would be perfect. They deserve each other.

Maybe not…the wail I witnessed before the dress incident, rings through my head. I recognize the cause of her dissonance. I made that sound when my father died, the sound of loneliness, helplessness, and lost love. Perhaps her acidic personality is to neutralize the bitter hand she has been dealt. In that case, she needs to be protected, for Sluagh love to prey on the sad while Ryan loves to prey on the wounded.

"Are you awake and ignoring me or still plastered," Ryan asks while throwing a blood bag at me. It feels warm, *gross*. He probably let it sit out while I slept. I guess I should be grateful I don't have to drag my carcass up the three floors to the blood bank. I greedily tear the IV tubing from the bag and suck on the connecting fitting. As the red blood cells filter through my esophagus, my chest fills with warm satisfaction. My lingering hangover and consequent migraine will be cured by the end of the bag. I grunt to Ryan in appreciation. It is rare he helps anyone, let alone a lesser vampire who has displeased him.

"Lucien, please finish before trying to talk," he lectures. "I saw enough of the contents of your mouth last night. Your table manners were most embarrassing, and it was all under the nose of Madam Commander. Indeed, your Christmas spirit was certainly…spirited. My only curiosity is how much of it was by design, how much of it was self-pity, and how much of it was fueled by Alison's little sister. You were enchanted with her and then she suddenly vanished."

My suction on the bag slows to a halt to give me time to think. If I pretend, I engineered the whole ordeal to avoid his matchmaking, I will be scrubbing his floors with my toothbrush. If I reveal the bodice-ripping incident before Alison tells him, I will win honesty points. However, if he is already hunting Betty, I will have admitted to disrobing his queen. My only option is self-pity.

"Seeing James propose, I wasn't confident I could handle another dance competition with Nate. I must wait until he is mated before selecting a shifter to secure the alliance. I'm not as suave as he is." My lack of eye contact and proximity to the truth will push my lie past his radar. *Fingers crossed.*

"I will add stupid and inattentive to your list of attributes. James proposed to Nate. Two major competitors were eliminated last night," Ryan says while examining his claws. "You should have no trouble seducing Betty."

"What?! Who?!"

"If you are demoted, or heaven forbid replaced at Bergan, you need another tie to the shifters. A marriage to Betty would make the perfect bow atop the alliance gift to the rest of the colony in the Old Country. You do remember your sister stuck in the Old Country, don't you?"

At the mention of my little sister, Terika, my heart skips a beat. She was confined to her bed with illness the last time I visited home. Her skin was sunken and gray, but her eyes still sparkled with mischief, as if her brain was having a last stand against pneumonia. It is my dream to bring her to America so she can see Dr. V.

Choosing between Betty and Terika, I have more faith Betty can stand up to Ryan. "I will run to the lab to finish the projects post haste. I know what to do now. I can get back on track by working the holiday hours. Ryan, please give me a chance, if not for me, give Terika a chance."

"I am giving her a chance by ordering you to marry Betty."

"Marriage? Me? You have a better station than me and therefore, a better match for Betty." I can barely get the words through my clenched teeth. Deep in my heart, I know forcing a union between Betty and Ryan is wrong…because I want her for myself. Too bad guys like me get their hearts shredded by women like her.

"For the longevity of the colony I am embedding you in shifter society instead of me," he says with an eye-roll. "If I were to mate a shifter, it would only cement the relationship for my remaining lifespan. You have childbearing years left and can make an alliance lasting generations. Get to it so you have some babies, and your sister will have a long happy life, once Dr. V cures her illness. Besides I have a better alliance planned for myself as my birthright as king."

"Better alliance?"

"You would be best served by focusing on your tasks than inquiring about mine."

"Yes, sir."

"You will work the holiday hours to get microbiology back within the scheduled timeline and your department will never fall behind again," he decrees with finger-pointing. "You will be certain the new associate is your employee and not your boss. Furthermore, you will be having your stem cell injections in two days when Dr. V opens again. Not only does Molina tell me you are heinously overdue, but Betty will be working there. It will be a chance encounter where you will ask her to dinner at your house. Do I make myself clear?"

"Dinner at my house. Why my house? Why can't I invite her to the restaurant next door?"

"With your lack of charisma, you need to be away from any competing suitors. Being at your house, you have the opportunity to appeal to *all* of her sensibilities."

This can't be happening. A doctor's appointment and a dinner to go from being slapped to her bedmate. As if she doesn't already think of me as a sexual predator, I'm supposed to seduce her. My mind is spinning with excuses, arguments, pleas, and all the statements that will fall on deaf ears. More dejected than ever, I swallow my fate. "I guess I will go up to the lab now."

"No, you will clean up here and hit the showers. No one needs to see the aftermath of your disgraceful conduct. What would Reveca say?"

The mention of my mother makes my head throb again. My addled mind flashes back to my last visit home. My mother begging me to work with Bergan Pharma and Dr. V, to become the next Vampire King with control over the colony's resources, and to find a way to get Terika the treatment she needs. When Dad died, I used my inheritance to buy my house in Strawberry and our family house in Moldova outright, so at least my mother didn't have to use her allowance from the colony or the money she makes from sewing on a mortgage payment.

The colony put all their money together generations

ago and the king oversees investing it and allocating the dividends. Ryan has been a financial genius and the allowances have increased more than inflation in my lifetime. My entire allowance, as well as a large portion of my wages from Bergan, goes to Terika's doctors. While Ryan wants an alliance with the shifters, would he be comfortable with Betty knowing vampires get double salaries?

"My mother would be horrified and rightly so, sir. Mom depends on my allowance to pay for Terika's treatments. Wait…if I marry Betty, she will be privy to my finances. Do you want to risk the shifter's finding out about the colonies' money?"

"Molina forfeited her allowance when she chose Brad over her betrothed. Certainly, with your new shifter wealth, you would do the same."

"Are we certain there is shifter wealth? I have never seen Alison wear a single jewel."

"The shifters own every building in town. How could they afford that if there is not a stash of money somewhere?"

"I'm just worried about my family—"

"Then stop asking questions and get to it!"

"If I refuse?"

"Refuse?"

"This is not a guaranteed boon. If it turns out there is no shifter treasure, my family has to survive on less than they have now."

"Are you suggesting a deal?"

I inhale to puff out my chest. Standing up to Ryan is new territory for me. He could just decide to make me disappear, even though modern forensics would make it difficult. My family wouldn't have the money to search for me. "I will do this if you send my allowance directly to my mother. Therefore, it will be hidden from Betty and where it is needed most. Starting with the January allotment, I will confirm the receipt with Mom before proceeding." My heart pounds as we sit and stare at each other. To my delight, his brown irises do not hint at red. After an agonizing stalemate, the corners of his mouth lift into a smile.

"Sensible. You may be learning from me after all. You have a long way to go but decisions, where you put vampires first, are the first indications of the growing king inside you. Yes, you surprised me this morning Lucien. Clean yourself up so you look like the prince you are."

He leaves me with my mouth hanging open. New confidence illuminates my face. I got my deal with Ryan. The joy is short-lived when I realize I have a deal with Ryan. How could I be so naïve? I played right into his hands and now I have to pursue Betty who is currently not talking to me. What have I done?

Chapter 6

I should be excited to start my new job, especially since I almost sabotaged my entire career. Why aren't I leaping out of the car and skipping into the building? I'm still my depression's bitch, that is why. Emotionally shattered after more than a year of gentle healing, I am paralyzed in the parking lot, sitting in my car, and staring at the building. I owe my sister and Dr. Van Dijk big time for this opportunity. I can turn my life around if I just show up.

"Get up," I scream through clenched teeth at my car's interior. "Start your new life. Today is the first step to walking away from your mistakes." I slam my hands on the steering wheel until they sting. Tears threaten to ruin my third coating of makeup, as they washed away my first two applications. The guilt, sadness, and loneliness crush my chest until I remind myself, I already endured my punishment. I gambled and lost it all: my job, my parent's trust, and Evan. *Evan*.

No. Evan cannot continue to control me from beyond the grave. I slam my car door on thoughts of him as I emerge from my vehicle. Confidence swells my heart while a grin tugs at my lips as I step onto the curb. I'm moving on, one step at a time. I breathe in the chilled air and take in the stunning sunset. A slash of orange, rose, and magenta color the sky and reflect onto the thin layer of snow. It is a stunning contrast to the last time I stood in this spot, where the sky was a black void. Just like my insides are a black void.

A black void refusing Lucien's rescue. I probably owe him an apology for slapping him. I desired a physical person to lash out against and he walked into my vicinity at the wrong moment. He did succeed at distracting me though. I morphed from victim to fighter with one tear of my dress. His cold fingers rubbing my shoulders as he gripped the neckline of the dress still haunt me. A frozen caress that set my senses on fire, like the sizzle of dry ice.

Whoosh! Tonight's cold breeze intensifies lifting my skirt like a 1950s pin-up girl. Tendrils of frosty black fog whip around my legs and toss my ponytail around like a propeller. As I struggle to discipline my errant clothing, a blue blur flashes in my peripheral vision. The hairs on the back of my arms stand on end in terror. My brother-in-law's warnings of what lurks in dark parking lots drift across my imagination.

I dig into my soul to find the courage I have always used to defend Ally. Patting my hair to tame imaginary flyaways, I turn to see a woman…not a normal woman…a freaky woman with giant sky blue and white wings. She reaches a set of long black claws at me while pleading with her completely white eyes. Time stops for everything except for her. Black spittle drips from the corner of her mouth. She dabs it with her delicate translucent hand mindful not to touch her claws to her lips. She can't be a Sluagh, her long white hair and full lips would be gone.

However, she's advancing toward me in the same silent gliding motion as one. My eyes are locked on the tiny diamonds glittering in her mouth where her teeth have been reduced. I scream with every fiber of my being and thank the heavens I was blessed with a massive set of lungs. My sound echoes across the empty fields, long after I run out of air.

"Grrrrrrrr." *Now what*. Behind me, a chorus of growls resonating from the otherwise dormant pizzeria drowns out my screams. As if the sound was a forcefield the strange fairy-lady stops behind my car. Two wolves the size of extinct dire wolves cross in front of me putting themselves between the mystery woman and myself. A smaller wolf snarls at my side.

My escorts have arrived. Just inside the pizzeria door, with crutches in hand, is Matteo. He waves an impatient hand at me to move along but my feet have transformed into blocks of concrete. I wave back with nervous awkwardness. "Betty, move along now," growls one of the larger wolves. When I don't move, he bumps my hip with his flank, jostling me to awareness.

Seeing she's outnumbered, the silent banshee glides back until she hits the opposite curb. She lets out a small feminine shriek in surprise on impact before tumbling into the grass. She dusts herself off, flaps her wings, and turns to take flight, revealing the slushy grass stains along her backside. The image coupled with my fright sends me into a fit of giggles. The smaller wolf grins with tongue wagging while the larger ones are wearing shocked expressions. I'm laughing loud enough to echo when I reach the door to Dr. V's office.

"She's almost hysterical, Doc," says the leader wolf. "We were late, or she was early. Either way, she came face-to-face with a female Sluagh in the parking lot."

"Thanks, Junior. I'm sure she will be fine after a cup of tea," says Dr. Van Dijk. "Alison really appreciates you boys volunteering to monitor the parking lot. As a human, I thank you for your protection as well." The doctor pulls my elbow until I'm behind his bulbous belly. Dr. V looks like the type of man who uses the word "groovy" in his normal vocabulary but leads cutting-edge research into myelodysplastic anemia.

"Dad promised you would be safe here. We are proud to fulfill his wishes," Frank Junior replies before herding the wolfpack back to the pizzeria. Matteo waves, shaking his head at me, as he leans out the door to allow the wolves entry.

Turning to me, Dr. Van Dijk allows the glass door to slam behind him. "Good for you, getting the scariest part of the job over with first. The rest of the evening should prove boring after a run-in with the Sluagh. I will show you our hospitality center first where you can make yourself a cup of chamomile tea for the rest of your orientation.

"You will be in charge of making tea and coffee, but most importantly is keeping us stocked with all blood types in the fridge below the counter. You will have to call Molina at Bergan Pharma when it gets low and one of our patients will bring it over." We walk to the far side of the lobby to a simple kitchenette. Filling the water carafe, I shudder at the mention of blood as food.

"Some of our clients are picky eaters," he says with a chuckle reminding me of flaming-haired Santa. "They will only drink a certain blood type. Others starve themselves when they are working. They think they can squeeze in their appointment, get home, and eat before the sun comes up. They will come in gray-colored, swaying, sleepy, and slurring their words but insist they are fine. As their health practitioners, it is our job to convince them to eat in the lobby under the guise of saving them time."

"I get it," I say with a returning his wink. The water is already boiling, and I pour two cups adding chamomile to my own.

Dr. V. reaches a giant pudgy hand for black tea with orange. "My favorite. I usually drink three cups during the night to stay up and alert."

"I will keep your cup full," I say cheerfully. "I wanted to thank you for taking a chance on me. I know my references were not as flattering as you would have expected."

"Actually, I was more surprised at the number of positives," he says somberly. "They were all sorry for what happened to you. Your former charge nurse asked you to get in touch with her when you get settled. She said before you got in trouble, you were a brilliant nursing student, a hard-working intern, and a promising employee. She hopes with this new job, you are studying for the RN exam at the end of the month."

"My parents sent in the forms and fee as their Solstice gift to me. I got the ATT, authorization to test papers, the day I decided to come to Strawberry. Those papers were the only thing holding me in Ohio. I'm ready to start over," I say more to reassure myself than him.

"I look forward to a rewarding partnership. With your degree and certification, you can have a larger role than the hostess. Unfortunately, my Sweet Pea left the books in a mess which I further neglected when she disappeared. So, the first few weeks will be mostly cleaning, organizing, and making this place efficient. I don't even have a current appointment book."

"It will be a good place to begin anyway. I want to

know where everything is located before I start taking a more active role in the practice." The lobby looks like a tornado has blown through it. Stacks of papers and dog-eared magazines litter every surface. There's even an empty blood bag beneath the couch. The grey-speckled white walls, carpet, and space-themed furniture emphasize the lack of housekeeping.

"Most of our patients are visiting for stem cell treatments. Vampires have myelodysplastic anemia or hollow bone marrow, thus the need to drink blood. The stem cells build new bone marrow so the vampire can make their own red blood cells and platelets, reducing their blood dependence. They first get their injections in their knees, elbows, hips, and shoulders. Next, they wait out here until the cells filter into their spongy tissue at the center of the long bones. Finally, I give them chiropractic manipulations to clear residual stem cells from their joints to ensure the most cell implantation success."

"So, I should offer them blood and conversation during the waiting period?"

"Exactly," he says with a clap of his hands. "It is usually twenty to thirty minutes where they are stiff, irritable, and too light-sensitive for their phones. They also come in when they injury their wings, which is more often than I would like."

"Are all of our clients, vampires?"

"We are treating Henrik and Matteo for their injuries from November's Sluagh attack. Josh has injuries from the Solstice battle. Aurora will be starting Natural Allergy Elimination Therapy when she returns from her vacation too. They will require special scheduling since they are not nocturnal."

"Leave it to me," I say. "The Weston women are known for our organization abilities."

"Your sister has certainly transformed Strawberry, from the pizzeria to the pack dynamics. I'm confident you can evolve my mess into a well-oiled machine. I can't wait to see the transformation at the end of the night!" I gape at him before he shuffles to the patient rooms at the back of the lobby. His giant frame bounces his fluffy red hair, so it looks like it is waving at me. My first necessity is a pair of gloves to dispose of the blood bag under the couch.

"Sick," I whisper to myself as I crawl partially under the space-aged monstrosity. The bag I saw peaking out was only one of a legion of empty bags. Well, that procedure is changing right now. Twenty-five empty bags leave tiny brown splatters on the carpet. A forensic team would have a field day with this mess.

Next, I tackle the workspace in the hopes of clearing my way to the computer. Hopefully, Dr. V.'s daughter, who he refers to as Sweet Pea, has an electronic appointment book, patient database, or web-based billing system. The towers of papers yield piles of bills, test results, random notes, and used paper napkins.

I'm buried in paper scraps for seemingly hours when the bell over the door chimes. A tall thin woman is obscured by frosty fog as the door opens. "Sluagh can't open doors," I blurt out.

"Nope, they can't," says the woman in a silky voice. "Don't you remember me? I'm Molina. We met at the Yule party." Her shaggy black hair swings over her shoulders as she talks reminding me of an eighties rockstar. She is dressed in a blue pencil skirt with a matching blazer. The outfit displays her professional status but the sequined top peeking from beneath it gives away her fun side. Like the rest of the vampires, her tiny irises bounce merrily in large black rings at the center of her eyes.

"Molina," I say, rising to shake her icy hand. "Of course I remember you. I just had a run-in with a female Sluagh on my way in and I thought she was back to chat. What brings you to the office?" I vaguely remember meeting Molina at the party before my hasty exit. However, Ally told me about her performance. She danced the night away with her husband, Brad, from the foxtrot to the hustle.

"I injured my wing in the Solstice Sluagh battle, but it is not healing correctly. I hope Dr. V. has time to x-ray it to be certain it is not broken."

"You are the only visitor tonight, so you lucked out. Can I get you anything while you wait?"

"No thanks. I'm relieved he has openings. I visited him between the battle and the party, but the lobby was completely full."

"Starting tonight I'm going to be taking appointments. No more walk-ins. Could you help me spread the word around Bergan?"

"Absolutely and if you give me your blood order before I leave, I can have some delivered. Lucien is overdue for his stem cell treatment and I told Ryan to be sure he comes in tonight."

"Thanks." I turn to fetch Dr. V. and to hide my expression. A visit from a Sluagh, a wolfpack, and now Lucien the Bodice-ripper. It is just not my night. I'm going to need a stiff drink when I get home and it is only my first day on the job.

In examine room one, Dr. V crouches on the floor

looking at stacks of colored paper like a giant white cake sitting upon a confetti-littered birthday table. He has a laptop open with banking software displayed. Upon closer inspection, the colored papers are personal checks. He is using a magnifying glass to study one and doesn't hear me approach.

"Knock, knock," I say with a rap on the door. "Sorry to startle you but Molina is here for an x-ray."

"Oh no, her wing is still hurting?"

"Yes, she says she couldn't get in earlier because your lobby was full. Can I prep the x-ray equipment in exam room two or help with this?" I wave my hand over the multicolored mess to indicate his accounting issue.

"Both. Let's do her imaging together so you know the way I like my area prepped. I can teach you a little about vampire anatomy, even though it won't be on your nursing exam. Then we can figure out which of these are already cashed and which need to be driven to the bank in Louisville."

Back in the lobby, Molina sitting on the floor in front of the fridge. She is sorting the bags of blood on her skirt. "You have all the varieties if a vampire is willing to dig for them. I was placing the ones expiring soonest in the door. The laziest vampires reach in there, so they don't have to crouch down." She creates a cloud of dust when she stands and pats her skirt. *Hell, yeah, no blood delivery is required.* Lucien is under no obligation to stop by tonight. I will, however, need to spend some time with that refrigerator. I shudder at the thought of the last time it was cleaned out. *Gross*.

Once I escort Molina to examine room two, my nursing training kicks my psyche into gear. Turning to the sink to wash my hands, the soap dispenser is empty.

Of course. Increasing bangs and crashes resonate from the room as I discover each drawer is empty. "Just one moment," I say to a puzzled Molina as I rush back to the hospitality station. I steal the liquid soap from the counter and rush back to my waiting patient.

I stumble in awe as Molina has removed her jacket and opened her wings. They remind me of bat's wings in that they are thin flesh stretched over the second set of arms. They extend from wall to wall but are only as tall as her torso. A thick curved talon peeks out of the tip of wings with each breath she takes, hinting that they can be extended into formidable weapons. The skin over the wing is a tawny, healthier hue than her skin. When I have dried my hands, I move closer to inspect the bones looking for abnormalities. "Is it the top of your right wing?" I point to a dent in the top of the wing while asking.

"Yes, between the first and second joint is tender," she says pointing to the same area.

Dr. V emerges through the door and begins to wash his hands as well. "Do you have a full range of motion?"

"Yes, I can but it feels sore upon take-off."

"You may have a hairline fracture causing the soreness. You are officially grounded until the inflammation goes down and your wing-line appears straight again. Betty, our x-ray is a portable ray gun which I keep in this suitcase along with the aprons. You must log into the software before turning on the instrument for the Bluetooth link to establish properly. In the future, you can take x-rays without me present and I will upload them at my desk before greeting the patient. I can be doing injections or manipulations to save time."

"Sounds great," I say with more confidence than I

feel. I study his movements taking mental photos of each step. *Thank you, Mom, for the photographic memory.* When I entered nursing school, I never dreamed I would get to x-ray vampire wings. This new job is going to be an amazing adventure, the perfect therapy to repair my broken heart.

Chapter 7

"Yes, I'm back
Well, I'm baaaack, baaaack...
Well, I'm back in scrubs," I sing to the agar plates in my class II cabinet. Two days of yeast growth should provide the data to get this study back on track. Little beige colonies shine on pomegranate agar disks in various densities. I wish I had the data sooner but my mandatory presence at the Yule party derailed the project. My behavior at the party derailed the rest of my life and I nearly scorched myself.

My career would be scorched if I hadn't completed James's colony isolations before the party. He got the polymerization data to scientific before leaving for England earlier in the day. Unfortunately, James took Nate, the genius, with him on vacation.

Nothing can go wrong. I lack the confidence to fix it without Nate. Back in graduate school, my professors were so afraid of Ryan's retaliation for my failures, they hardly taught me anything. I felt terrible they couldn't control my lack of scientific talent or the temper of the Vampire King. I am more musically inclined than scientifically. I don't ask the correct questions or intuitively make the correct connections. Now I have a moderate education at best but expected to make cutting-edge biologics on Grant's impossible timelines.

Not that the day-to-day microbiology work is

difficult. Today I am enumerating plates, fancy science jargon for counting beige dots on a maroon background. Encased in my protective garb, I count the dots, write the number on the plate lid, and move the two hundred plus plates from left to right. The most difficult part of the job takes place after I remove my gloves.

I must transfer the data from the plate lids to the paperwork, remembering which stack is which column of data. Every nine plates are a different set of variables laid out in tables in my stacks of forms. If I had an assistant, they could write the numbers as I go along. If I could remove the plates from the hood or take the paperwork inside it, I could write the numbers myself. However, the paperwork would be contaminated and end up in my bleach bucket once inside the cabinet.

Two more stacks to go and I will cross the finish line when Ryan appears in the doorway to my lab. My night was going so well too. I loudly enumerate my plates in the hopes he will find me too busy to interrupt.

"How was your appointment with Dr. V?"

"57…58…59…" I keep working to convince him I am concentrating too hard to notice him.

"How was your appointment?" He yells directly into my ear, sending a ringing sensation through my brain.

"I…I…I didn't have an appointment so I thought I would stop by when this is f-f-finished. With these results, microbiology will be back on track. The project deadlines will be met, and Grant will be pleased. I have f-f-fulfilled my promise that I made to you on Christmas morning."

"Really? You have missed the mark again," Ryan replies with a shake of his head. "Your appointment is twice as important as the data."

"I will get everything accomplished. I am almost there," I stammer.

"It is nearly sunrise. It is too late to go to Dr. V. You missed a critical deadline. Is this your first night as a vampire? You are allergic to sunlight. You scorch instantly. Do I need to explain this to you like a toddler? You imbecile!" Ryan's tirade reaches a fevered pitch as he stomps around the laboratory. My agar plates jump and clatter in response. I scramble to maintain their lid assignments.

"Ryan," Molina says stepping into the lab. "Are you yelling at that poor boy again? He is here more hours than you." No one says a word until the heavy door clicks shut, blocking most of the sound from the gossip hounds lingering in the hallway. Being called a boy by Molina should hurt my pride, but any interference is welcome. If I can get this work finished during Ryan's tantrum, I can sleep all day in the bunks downstairs and dream of my free time—or my visit to Dr. V where Ryan thinks I can seduce Betty. *Now that's a nightmare.*

"He is the future king, and he is neglecting his fundamental duties," Ryan yells pointing at me as if I am an inanimate object.

Molina puts her hands on her hips and tilts her head to the side. "What are you talking about?"

Ryan stops cold. Well, this is a rare royal blunder. *Tee, hee.* If Ryan tells Molina of his plan to link the pack to the colony, she will be offended. She is married to Brad, a lion shifter, but female vampires are barren, so her alliance is weak at best. She also formally withdrew herself from the colony in the 1700s when she chose Brad over her intended husband. Ryan considers her an outsider even though her betrothed died more than two centuries before Ryan and I were born. Her true-mate status to Brad keeps her alive well past the normal lifespan of a vampire and makes her more sympathetic to the shifters than the colony.

"Lucien never went to the doctor tonight," Ryan sneers with a cold smile. "I'm afraid our little protégé is suicidal." Both vampires glare at me with flashing red eyes. I should have known Ryan would deflect this onto me.

"Lucien, is this true?"

"I'm just busy not—"

"You are going to the doctor first thing this evening," Molina says waving her finger in my face. "I will drag you myself if I have to. I promised your mother I would look after you and you are an absolute mess."

"Yes, Lucien, you are an absolute mess," Ryan echoes from behind her.

What can I do now? "Yes madam," I say with a nod in her direction. The motion cracks my forehead against the glass cabinet and I momentarily see stars. As I recover, they quietly exchange a few words before the door opens and shuts again.

"Looks like you do have an appointment now. Molina is making the call and I am escorting you there," Ryan whispers in my ear. "Lucien, don't. Let. Me. Down." Each word is punctuated with his fist pounding the cabinet glass. Lids eject from their plates and sail onto the floor while my hands grasp at the air in vain. Even the agar gel ripples and cracks beneath Ryan's onslaught.

"I mean it, Lucien. No more missed deadlines. No more mistakes." His loafers crunch over the shattered plastic as he exits.

His words don't penetrate my psyche as I survey the carnage of my enumerations. There is no way I can match the labeled lids with their matching blocks on the data chart. Half of them are lying in pieces on the floor. I can't even start over counting since the agar cracked giving colonies a place to hide within the maroon gel. I need to streak all new plates and let them grow for two days before enumerating all over again. My only question is which one to do first: boil more pomegranate to make new plates or tell Grant his timeline is ruined by at least three days setting his temper to boil? *Sigh*. I dump the remaining contents of the cabinet into a giant bleach bucket and sweep the debris into a biohazard bag. My last task of the morning is dumping my battered carcass into bed, protective gear, and all.

Chapter 8

"Hi Honey, I'm home," I call into Ally's kitchen. "My first day at work was great before you even ask. I think I am going to like working with Dr. V." My purse thumps on the giant oak side table. I turn the corner from her spacious atrium to the cavernous kitchen. Slumped in a massive kitchen chair is my sister, slowly stirring a cup of coffee. Beside her cup sits a pile of shredded tissues of the same size. Despite her bright sunflower dress, she looks drearier than the January sunrise.

"I know it is not Grant or you would be rage baking, so who am I beating up today?" I grab a glass of juice from the fridge and settle in a chair beside her. While I wait for her to speak, I gaze around her kitchen and sip my drink. The room is sunny yellow with butcher block countertops and white cabinets. It's a chef's dream. With large modern appliances and a rustic drying rack full of herbs, it has everything Ally could want. One good thing about Grant is that he has spared no expense in keeping her happy.

"It is nothing. Just my ego is hurt," she says to her cup with a sigh. "Anyway, I heard you had a run-in with a Sluagh on the way into work. I wanted to call you to check if you were okay, but I didn't…"

I finish for her, "…want to be like Mom? The Paulino boys scared the Sluagh so badly she fell and busted her ass."

"Yes, I swear Mom called me every day when I went away to college. It drove me nuts. I'm glad the boys were there to help you."

"Despite Mom's check-ins, you still managed to get in trouble anyway," I say elbowing her until she smiles. "Your accidental pregnancy used to be a sticking point between Grant and me. I think it all worked out as it was intended though."

"Ugh, bad pun," she replies with an eye roll.

"Come on, I'm just trying to cheer you up before I beat anyone up to fix it. Was it Rosie who bruised your ego? She's brash but she's your best friend, after me, so I'm sure you two could work it out."

"Rosie and the boys are great—"

"But?"

"Gran has chosen Henrik to copy her Book of Shadows. I tried not to be disappointed I was skipped because it is a great opportunity for him."

"That is a huge honor. A witch's Book of Shadows is her life's work. I remember Aunt Sarah begging our parents to let you copy hers. If you asked her, you could probably still copy it. Would that help you feel better?"

"Not really. Gran told me why she skipped me. She said I am a shifter first and a witch second. I need to focus on the needs of the pack and my mate, even over Henrik's needs."

"Mate meaning Grant? You have always put him first and managed to be a great mom. Does she know your past?"

"Yes, she a precog witch, remember? She knows most of our past, present, and future just by looking at us. She wants me to focus on Junior and Ray's intern placement, the success of Bergan Pharma, the integration of the vampire colony, and the eradication of the Sluagh. She says there's not enough time for me to study her witchcraft too. She needs full days of tutelage, starting now. She wants Henrik to stay with her this winter."

"Whoa, that's too much. What does Henrik want? He seems proud of being a witch. What does Rosie say about having another little boy living with her? Henrik's a high maintenance kid with all his medicines, therapies, and music."

"I would still see him daily when I homeschool the group so I could drop off his medicines already parceled out. Most of his therapeutic exercises he does on his own anyway. The only sticking point is the hyperbaric chamber. He would have to come back here every few days to use it."

"You still do that?" Henrik and Alison would sit in an enriched oxygen environment (HBOT) for eighty minutes almost every day in Ohio. It forces their bodies to grow more capillaries to deliver their medicines deeper into their tissues. The hope is both of them will develop more nerve cells to help their dampened senses. Alison has sensory processing disorder which enhances a lot of her senses, but she has terrible eyesight, a muted sense of touch, and limited vestibular control. Henrik's inherited these traits from her which contributed to his autism diagnosis.

"Sounds like you have it all worked out…"

"As long as I am in town. To secure the internships, I have to visit the Seagrass pack in Florida and the North Carolina pack. Grant wants to go too in order to protect me."

"Of course, he does," I snap. "He smothers you."

"I'm really scared though as this will be my first

leader-to-leader meeting. I will feel better with Grant by my side when I have to prove myself to them."

"As long as he is standing beside you and not stomping all over you. How will you prove yourself?"

"Rosie says they will ask for a partial shift and show of force."

"Well, you are terrifying in your polar bear form so I wouldn't worry so much."

"It is no big deal to born shifters but..." She trails off as her face turns a deep red.

"But what?"

"I don't get naked in front of an audience."

"Oh my God Ally," I say laughing out loud. I laugh at her until my sides ache while she fumes at me. "You are such a goodie-two-shoes. Just wear a sundress and partial shift your lower half before removing it."

"Betty, I will have to go to the meeting without wearing panties," Ally whispers with her hand next to her mouth.

"Don't be a baby," I say with an eye roll. "So that takes care of the internships. Grant will take care of Bergan Pharma because it is his life's ambition. Who takes care of Sluagh eradication? Are you going to storm the fortress?"

"It's warded too strongly," she says, tapping her coffee mug. "Gran suggests taking them out individually when they go hunting. They hunt alone so the odds will be in our favor."

"Are you sending out hunting teams?"

"No that would require sending out depressed people or witches as bait. Sluagh smell depression like freshly baked bread but it is a witch's soul they want most. I'm not sending Henrik, Gran, or a depressed person to battle Sluagh—"

"And let me guess, Grant won't let you hunt."

"No one in the pack will. I got voted down. It's not just him."

"So that just leaves integrating the vampires on Gran's Pack Leader Duties List. I can handle them since they are my patients with Dr. V. I will be getting to know them anyway."

"No way," she says, shaking her head so hard her red hair swings under her chin. "I don't want you going above and beyond their care. They can drain you dry without a second thought. We know nothing about them and while Ryan swore fealty to me, something feels off about him. My intuition says they are safe but until I know more, stay away. I mean it, Betty, be careful around them."

"Yes, Madam Commander," I say with a mock salute.

"I would be heartbroken if anything happened to you."

"I can take care of myself. I will also take care of Henrik's medicine schedule and HBOT dives while you are gone. No worries." I finish off my juice in a big gulp before leaning over to hug her.

"I know, Betty. You take care of everyone," she says into my hair.

Chapter 9

Since Grant and Patty are going to blow their tops when I get to the lab anyway, I am driving home to feed my cats. The aging felines, Bela and Christopher, were my last effort at obtaining friends when I moved to Strawberry. I think the feelings were mutual. I found them on the side of the road in an empty 12-pack of beer.

If only my friends at university could see my demise to lonely, cat lady. They'd laugh at my blundering attempts to date in Strawberry after I sowed enough oats to feed most of Europe. The vampiresses knew this doctoral candidate was heir to the throne and how I loved being surrounded by admirers. However, keeping all of Ryan's secrets and carrying out all his schemes made having friends in Strawberry an occupational hazard. I long for a time when I can be myself without losing my status. With my mother and sister depending on me, the fake Vampire Romeo act seems like a small sacrifice.

"Who is waiting to greet me?" I call into the dark atrium. The front half of the giant Tudor plantation home looks like a movie set from a cheesy horror film at Ryan's request. Christopher trots to me from behind a black velvet curtain, stirring up a cloud of dust. The fuzzy purr-machine rubs my legs lovingly and weaves his body between my steps.

"Christopher, where's your sister? Bela?" He jumps to butt his nose against my hand in response.

"Meeeee," whines Bela from behind the opposite curtain. She has been trying out new hiding spaces all over the house since I confined them. Black cats plus gothic décor equals epic hiding places. After the failed portal closing last month, Bela and Christopher are indoor-only cats to prevent them from becoming Sluagh food. Despite spending many days outdoors in the fields, my fierce twosome would try to snuggle with the demons. Christopher has been taking it like a champ while Bela is protesting.

"Good evening," I say in my best Bela Lugosi impersonation. Pulling back the curtain, I give Bela the opening she was awaiting. With claws fully extended, she pounces out of the darkness and onto the shirt of my scrubs. If they were as thick as regular clothes, I may not be bleeding from both shoulders.

"Touché, Madam," I coo to her. "I know you were expecting me last night…or was it the night before? However, Nate visited you before he went on vacation. He's not the only one you have to thank for clean water, food, and scooped box. I'm your primary caregiver. Who do you think buys the supplies?" I wrap my arm under her back and carry her like a baby into the kitchen.

Decked out in gothic black and purple wallpaper, my kitchen is just as ridiculous as the living room. I have two sets of dishes. Ones I use and black crystal ones to keep in my upper cabinets to perpetuate the myth that vampires do not eat. A myth Ryan decided to abolish as soon as Alison invited us to pack meetings with "family dinners". I wonder if I can get rid of them now, or smash them in the backyard, or better yet…

With a grinch-like smile, I fill two onyx dessert goblets with canned cat mush and two crystal bowls with kitty kibbles. "Dinner is served," I say with a bow to my roommates. While their snouts are in the crystal, I tackle the toxic waste in their litter box, while surveying my first floor for kitty surprises. As much time as they spend alone, the siblings have never missed the litterbox accidentally or in protest, but Bela's behaviors have me questioning if those days are numbered.

Pulling open the stainless-steel door, the cavernous wasteland that is my fridge makes my stomach growl. I brought home a cooler of blood which accounts for the tidy stack of blood bags at one side. I suck on a bag while perusing the rest of the space. In the center are ancient remains of a Paulino's take-out box. On the other side is a carton of unsweetened almond milk, which…is…NOT EXPIRED! *Hot Damn!*

Ten minutes later, I have steaming hot macaroni and cheese in a plastic videogame character bowl. I can just imagine Ryan's commentary about vampires and boxed dinners. "To grow into a king, you must eat like a king. You must immerse yourself in the vampire mythology to give your public the character they crave," I say in my best Ryan impersonation to the cats. Christopher, the smart one, ignores me as if Ryan may pop out from behind a dusty piece of furniture. Bela, my troublemaker, growls in agreement before turning back to her food.

The only person with more annoying vampire persona myths than Ryan is David. Technically, I outrank David as I am the Prince of Darkness but we are both department heads at Bergan so that is masked, much to David's delight. I let him have his fun, stomping on me because it is short-lived. David not only dresses like a vintage buffoon but also, he speaks like one—using words like "buffoon" almost daily. If he calls me a Vazey

Foozler one more time, I am going to cuss him out. I had to Google the name to figure out it was an insult. I'm not lazy and only clumsy when Ryan is physically pushing me around. If anyone is lazy, it is David who has six associates to review the data of three scientists. One of those scientists is me.

Followed by my wingman, Christopher, I move into the back of the house where I was given free rein. The dining room is worthless to someone who claims not to eat. So, I knocked out the wall connecting it to the family room and covered the walls with acoustic absorbing panels. I even wired sound equipment behind the panels to create a musical haven. During the summer months, I am stuck inside for many hours, waiting for the sun to set, which is perfect for construction projects. After a few instructional videos online, I built a stage. The result is my own Karaoke bar, where I can live the life I have always wanted.

Sitting on the stage, Christopher and I have a silent dinner date until Bela comes to join us. She moves slower than ever and plops down just within the doorway. "Why don't you join us, Sweetheart? You usually cuddle with Christopher. Why are you so distant?"

She glares in response. Putting aside my bowl, I traverse the room to pick up my forlorn female. She must have slowed down months ago because she is very heavy, maybe even heavier than Christopher. I gently arrange her next to Christopher, so he spoons her lovingly. I frown at Bela and wonder if she is angry or in need of a vet.

"Well, isn't this a pretty picture," sneers Ryan from the kitchen. "A lunatic in his padded cell with his emotional support animals."

"*Aaah!* The hell Ryan, how did you get in?" I nearly hit the ceiling at the sound of his voice. My wings automatically unfurl. My ancient DNA readies to launch me to safety like a Mesozoic mammal cornered by a dinosaur. Christopher takes the hint and launches himself away from Ryan. The cat slinks along the wood floor until he disappears under my bed in the adjoining room.

Ryan waves a garage door remote at me while running his tongue over his fangs. "You forget I supervised the garage door opener installation while you were at the lab. A lonely bachelor has no need for a second remote but perhaps I should return it? Your days hiding in here are numbered. How intelligent is it to hide in a soundproof room anyway? You never heard the garage open."

My boiling blood colors my face. I can hear my pulse thundering in my ears. How dare he. I can feel my fangs piercing the inside of my lips as I mash my teeth together. I play his games, but this is my sanctuary. On impulse, I step between Ryan and Bela, who has sat up in alarm but hasn't run.

"Calm down," he sneers. "I'm not going to hurt your little pussycat. In fact, I'm here to fix your life. We are off to Dr. V's office to woo your girl." He waves the garment bag in his other hand at me. I can only guess what the costume will look like: Shakespeare's most flamboyant actor, King Arthur's missing minstrel, or perhaps one of the founding fathers complete with a powdered wig.

Noooooo. I was more comfortable when I thought he was here to eat Bela. My only solace is the few bites left of my dinner. I grab my bowl and shovel in macaroni in the hopes I can finish it off while he lectures. He marches past the stage and into my master suite, while I follow at a safe distance.

"Shower, gel your hair back and for god's sake shave that scruff off your face," he orders. I continue to shovel cheesy elbows into my mouth. There's got to be more to it. Where's the pride of the colony lecture? "We don't have time for you to play imbecile. Shower, shave, hair gel, go." He walks behind me clapping his hands until I nearly fall into my sunken tub in the center of the bathroom. Feeling guilty that my cats are out there, along with a vampire king, I take the fastest shower on record.

I emerge from my cloud of steam to find Ryan harassing Bela. The murderous look on her face is accompanied by the occasional swat of her claws. "You know, they wouldn't hate you if you played with them or brushed them instead of taunting them. You are standing inches from one of her wand toys," I say with an adjustment to the towel around my hips.

"I am not amusing myself. I am trying to keep her from shedding on your outfit before you even put it on. I don't know why you insist on living with such creatures," he says, straightening his blazer and dusting its sleeves. "Instead of feeding the little urchins, you could hire a maid to dust in here once in a while."

"You were enamored with the idea of my having cats when the Paulino family ran the shifter pack because the wolves couldn't visit me without frightening them. It is because of the cats I have been able to reduce my number of visitors. With no one snooping around my kitchen, I could keep your secret about our eating until you reversed your decision. They also gave me something in common with Nate, the leopard shifter, so I could befriend him and receive help in the lab. If anything, the cats have been instrumental to our success." I may be bulldozed on many things but Ryan better not have a scheme to evict my roommates. We engage in a stare down until I notice the outfit laying on my bed.

Oh hell no. A predictable frilly white shirt lays beneath a purple velvet blazer with cut sleeves. The matching pantaloons and hose are just not happening. One look at this getup and Betty will fall out of her chair laughing. She already calls me a bodice-ripper do I really need to dress like one? I need a quick excuse to convince Ryan to select something else. "I never dress like this and she has seen me before so she will be suspicious. She's as smart as Alison so we must be careful about how I am presented."

"She has only seen you at the Yule party where you were dressed as a lab rat." He hands me the shirt instead of mercy.

"I am sure to be exposed as a fraud by other vampires at the office. I don't have a private appointment." Based on Betty's attire, she would be more attracted if I dressed as Robert Smith in his goth persona rather than Fabio. It would also be closer to the real me. Why can't the genius vampire king put that together? I step into boxers and put the tissue paper blouse over my head in disgust.

"Perhaps the pantaloons are a little much," he says to my elation. He wanders into my closet and rifles through my clothes, half of which are lying on the floor. "Don't you take care of anything? All of your acceptable clothes are hopelessly wrinkled."

"I have spent every waking moment at the lab getting two products off the ground in six months. I slept most days in Bergan Pharma's bunks. If I spent more time here…"

"You would waste it making noise in your padded room. I have heard your arguments before and we are on the same side, Lucien. You spend all your time in the lab making money for the colony so your sister can get medical care. I have half a mind to fly her here just to keep house for you. At least your relationship will be symbiotic."

"Terminal patients generally do not spend their days cleaning," I mutter just loud enough for him to hear.

A brief flash of humanity crosses his face. "I have never met a man who needed a wife more than you."

"I'm not marrying someone to do my housework—"

"No, you are marrying someone to keep your secrets and secure your power base, thus protecting your life. You may feel integrated into society, but you are a vampire. Never forget as the top predator, you are the most vulnerable to extinction." His cold stare drives the point home. As much as I hate to admit it, he's right.

If the vampires are ousted from Bergan, we are up a creek without a paddle. It acts as a front for vampire medical research and a supply line for Dr. V to treat us. Bergan not only funds the reserves but also supplies blood from a bank, so we do not have to feed on the source. I have been told feeding on a live human is exhilarating by those who feed on their human mates.

However, feeding on a one-night stand or stranger leads to a whole host of problems. If one person thinks of it as too kinky or heaven forbid assault, we are toast.

They will run to the authorities who will attract media attention and we are front page news. It only takes one feeding to go bad to exterminate the entire race. I sigh in resignation as I don the velvet doublet.

"I guess these will have to do," Ryan says holding up a pair of my skinny jeans with a disgusted look on his face. He's handling them like a bag of kitty droppings. The image is hilarious until I realize I will be dressed exactly like that douchebag vampire, the sparkly one, from the movies. *Oh my god*. I can only run my hand down my face in dejected amazement.

After a small spat over my footwear and a chauffeur experience that rivals "Driving Miss Daisy", Ryan and I arrive at Dr. V's office in record time. He even made me open his car door and assist him out of my SUV like a medieval page. There are so many places I would rather be. They fill my head as I trudge behind him, like receiving a horrific surgery with no anesthetic. Luckily for me, there is only Paul, one of David's peons in the waiting room.

"Welcome Gentlemen," Betty calls from behind her desk. Her gorgeous voice strikes me like lightning. I had forgotten its gentle timbre, much at odds with the riotous woman. I follow the contours of her shiny black hair over her small shoulders. She sits demurely between two towering stacks of paperwork, fingers poised over the keyboard. My lips tingle with the memory of kissing those fingers. I'm left standing at the doorway as Ryan approaches the desk and takes her hand in his. With a sweeping bow, he kisses the air above their clasped hands. Before I can control myself, I lean over to verify there was no contact.

"Betty, you look as dazzling as before. I am taking

care of Lucien while his family is in the Old Country. This man is so dedicated to Bergan he forgets to take care of himself. He is woefully overdue for his stem cell injections and has probably forgotten to feed. As a bachelor, he has no one to remind him of such things." Ugh really, Ryan? Being portrayed as a teenager is not a great start to seduction.

Judging by the look on her face, Betty is not buying any of it. Satisfaction bursts within me when she removes her hand from Ryan's and pumps a blob of hand sanitizer into it. She frowns at him while rubbing her hands together and I'm on pins and needles. Ryan is about to be served. The announcer in my head starts to narrate here's the wind-up and the pitch. "From my vantage point, he has a Mother Hen who is doing the job quite nicely," she says in a syrupy sweet voice.

Ryan looks so confused, I snicker. He doesn't know if she just complimented or insulted him. After a beat he says, "speaking of matriarchs, how is your beautiful sister? Fairing well, I hope?"

"I guess she's happy, but you would have to ask Grant. Having opposite hours, I only get to see her for a few moments before she retires to his bed each night. They do not usually emerge until after I am asleep for the day. You, of course, understand, being a vampire," she replies with batting eyelashes. Oh yes, Ryan has met his match. She has managed to throw Alison's happy marriage in his face. They are verbally sparring, and I don't think he even realizes the full extent of it. She is a champion I would love to have at my side…on my side.

"Yes, I can empathize," retreats Ryan. Point for Betty. As if noticing me for the first time, she swings her gaze and takes in my unfortunate ensemble.

"Ahoy Captain Bodice-ripper," she says, stifling a giggle.

"Argh wench, we be wantin' me appointment with ye ship barber-surgeon," I retort. I get rewarded with her high-wattage smile that causes my heart to stutter. I'm careful not to laugh with her to encourage more of Ryan's matchmaking. He is looking at me with eyebrows raised to his hairline as it is.

"Well, Captain, your ship has docked too early. Your appointment, the one Molina made on your behalf, is not for two days. Please limit your plundering of our town until then," she says, returning her focus to the computer screen.

"You could just squeeze him in before Paul," Ryan says while leaning over her desk.

"I could but I won't," she snaps. "I am enforcing the policies put in place before I started this job. Everyone must have an appointment, arrive at their appointment time, and have payment arrangements cleared during their appointment. No exceptions."

Ryan straightens and crosses his arms over his chest. Poor Betty, she's in for it now. "Thursday, I shall return. I will keep my pillage restricted to areas out of your sight," I say with a bow in her direction. I am behind in my injections, but it is not worth a confrontation to wait two more days. On Thursday I can hopefully slip away to return without Ryan, maybe even in my regular clothes.

"Here's a reminder card to help you keep the appointment. Maybe it will alleviate the need for a babysitter," she says with an index card extended to me. On the front is the date and time of my appointment within the confines of a form but on the back, she has scrawled the message, "10 petite Rebelvixen". I study the message, pondering its contents, while the two continue their banter.

"This is unacceptable. I demand to speak to Dr. Van Dijk," Ryan says to the beat of his tapping his toes.

"He is with a patient," Betty replies coolly.

"You will just have to interrupt him."

Paul and I watch the exchange with our mouths hanging open. Only Grant has ever stepped in Ryan's way before. Our heads swivel back and forth with each verbal volley. Ryan's eyes are glowing, and his fangs are elongated. Betty doesn't seem to notice, and I fear I may have to rescue her if he attacks.

"This is not an emergency, so no I don't *have to* interrupt him."

"Do you know who I am, little girl?"

"A pain in my ass about to be escorted out?"

"That's it," Ryan says slamming his hands on her desk. The paper towers to sway like palm trees. "I am the Vampire King and no one's time is more important than mine. Paul leave. Your appointment is now on Thursday. Lucien, come with me. You are getting your injections." Ryan steps past Betty's desk toward the exam rooms. He beckons me with a hand gesture, but my feet are rooted where I stand.

"Temper tantrums will get you nowhere," Betty says with a frosty demeanor. "Paul, he has no authority over you here. Ryan if you open that exam room door, it will be a violation of that patient's HIPPA rights. I will be dutifully obligated to call in the authorities to have you removed and trespassed from the premises."

"You wouldn't dare."

"I have multiple phones on my desk. Do you doubt

my ability to use them? Don't make this a bigger issue than it needs to be. I'm not asking anything from you I wouldn't ask any other person who steps through that door."

"But I am not like any other person who walks through that door," Ryan rants.

"To our office policies you are. Now be gone before someone drops a house on you." She turns back to her keyboard and begins typing loudly in dismissal.

Ryan's entire head turns crimson before he surprises both Paul and me to our toes by storming out of the building. In the frigid weather, he stands fuming against my car. Feeling a small act of mercy is in order, I use the key fob to unlock the doors remotely. My horn beeps loudly alerting everyone in a five-mile radius we are leaving. Dr. V emerges from the exam rooms and invites Paul to his appointment leaving Betty and me alone in the waiting room. If only Ryan had calmly waited a few more minutes…

"Are you going to let him freeze in the car while you wait in our lobby until Thursday?" Betty asks without making eye contact.

"No, I…I…" Come on brain get it together. "I was hoping to take advantage of a rare moment without Ryan to ask about your coded message on the appointment card." I am ecstatic not only did the words come out of my mouth but also, they have a smooth lilt to them.

"It is the size and manufacturer of the dress you ripped. Do not mistake my silence to Alison and Ryan with the evidence you are getting away with it. You will replace it as you promised."

"Of course, I will. Are you feeling better?"

"Better than ever," she says stopping to stare at me

in a challenge. Oookaaay, that door is closed. Her body language says she has moved on, but her eyes are still filled with the sadness contained in the haunting wail she released on Christmas Eve. Deep seeded sadness makes her a magnet for Sluagh attacks. I wish I was close enough to her to suggest she talk it out with Alison or better yet, with me.

"Great, I will be going then," I fumble. "See you Thursday unless…"

"Unless I see you first?"

"Unless you join me for dinner tomorrow night at my plantation. We could dine under the stars." My words sound resolute but the blinding change in the topic of our conversation scrapes at my psyche. I must sound so awkward to her. I turn to leave, glad no one else heard my bungled attempt at my princely duty.

"I do love to eat. I open here at 10 pm so it will have to be between then and sunset. What time?"

WHAT?!

Chapter 10

With Grant and Alison on a plane to Florida and Henrik at the Paulino house, I have only a few moments to spare before my covert operation at Lucien's plantation. The only question I have is where does Lucien live? He is so damn arrogant that he assumed I knew. I haven't lived in Strawberry for more than a month. Unless he has a neon sign reading "Castle Darkness" over his home, I have no hope of finding it.

In fact, I have a list of people who would know but I can't ask without them reporting back to Alison. I still don't understand why she is so adamant I don't get involved with the vampires. Society doesn't know they exist, but social media makes it impossible to erase someone. It is not the Dark Ages where they can suck me dry without law enforcement discovering whodunnit. Well, too bad, what she doesn't know won't hurt her.

I grab my phone and punch a text to Aurora since she's my closest friend besides Ally. We bonded as soon as I arrived in Strawberry when I cut her hair and pulled her out of her shell. "Lucien forgot his jacket at Dr. V's office. Do you know where he lives so I can return it before work?" I set my phone down to primp for my big date with the not-so-scary Prince of Darkness. I hope Aurora is not flying to England with her phone in airplane mode.

Half an hour later, I receive a reply with his

plantation marked on a map. "It is a huge creepy house surrounded by empty fields. There is nothing around it for miles so you can't miss it. Good luck and let me know if he has any ghosts hidden there." She ends the instructions with a laughing emoji and a ghost emoji. *Perfect.* I send back a slew of emojis in gratitude.

Driving on one-lane unmarked roads is a scary experience but no comparison to the giant brick home fit for a slasher film. The only other houses are dots on the horizon. Aurora wasn't kidding when she said Lucien's plantation house was surrounded by empty fields. Not only is there no place to hide but also no one will hear me scream if this goes pear-shaped.

The house is covered with tentacles of greenery just waiting to pull it down to hell. A scary proposition if I hadn't been raised not to believe in such a place by a long line of witches. The grimy windows, cobwebbed gables, and swinging shutters convey a haunted house or lazy bachelor owner. If Lucien is royalty, why doesn't he hire a lawn crew or at least repairmen to keep his property value up? Even if the vampire needs the scary-factor to feel at home, the practicality of protecting his investment should be enough to persuade him to do the basics.

Remembering Ally's worry over the secrets of the vampires, my spine hardens to steel and my courage rises to the surface. I may not receive another chance to solve this mystery. Some ancient pompous ass in a crumbling neglected house is not going to frighten me out of helping Ally. I step out of my car and slam the door with a resounding bang. The staccato of my stilettos heralds my arrival like battle drums.

Lucien surprises me by stepping out onto the doorstep before I can knock. He bows with stiff posture and I'm in trouble in a way Ally could have never predicted. His hair, usually slicked back like Bela Lugosi, flops over his forehead as he leans over. Why am I compelled to reach up and smooth it for him? He then swings his head in a small gesture to replace the errant strands while simultaneously showing off his angular profile. His eerie eyes meet mine and a small smile forms on his lips, obscuring his fangs, which are probably monstrous. My common sense kicks in at that moment. *Sigh.* I am caught ogling my enemy.

"Good evening," he says. Really? Is he going to do the Dracula impersonation all night?

"Hi, you startled me when you stepped out."

"Forgive me, I heard your music as you approached."

"Music is one of the few pleasures I have left since moving in with Ally," I say with a shiver. Frigid air of Sluagh whispers around my shoulders or perhaps it is Evan's ghost. I don't know which is more frightening: being attacked by one of those demons or crying in front of Lucien because of a memory that has no right to my heart anymore. That assumes Evan had a right to it in the first place. Confusing emotions churn my insides as I fight for control. I need to pull this off for Ally, damn it.

"You must be chilled, and I am being a poor host. Please follow me." He walks around the side of the house. It's so strange he doesn't invite me inside despite his words affirming I am cold. *Weirdo.* I'm so ridiculous I just called my vampire host a weirdo. When I'm old and grey I will put that in my memoir.

"You said we were eating under the stars, so I wore layers." Our steps crunch over the snow to a gazebo containing a dressed table. Four heat lamps cast a red glow over the tablescape giving it a creepy appearance despite the romance of the flowers at its center. Black crystal goblets glitter photons of red over the snow around us. Silver cloches cover two place settings which smell faintly of garlic.

"I put out the heat lamps so jackets will be unnecessary. Since I come out here in the night cold, I installed heat lamps to permit me to enjoy my land. May I take your coat and entice you to sit beneath them?"

"Only if you promise not to rip it off," I say in an attempt at humor. I can't believe how stuffy he acts. Unfortunate because he smells as amazing as he looks. I bet his cologne is French and costs as much as my car. Over my shoulder, I watch a faint blush form over his elevated cheekbones.

"My goal tonight is to prove to you I am a gentleman. Please grant me the opportunity." He hangs my jacket on the gazebo and pulls out my chair.

I sit so daintily my mother would be proud. My dress drapes over the sides but the chair is tall enough my hem doesn't touch the ground. Ruining two dresses in two encounters would put Lucien on my short list of people to avoid. Not that I don't have plenty of reasons to avoid him like the fangs, the stuffy personality, and Ally's mistrust of him. "Pity, I have no need for gentlemen in my life," I quip.

He grips the wine bottle with white knuckles and freezes. Oh come on, my comment wasn't that scandalous. Aren't vampires supposed to be naughty masters of seduction?

"It smells amazing. Do you cook?" With his reversed pupil and iris configuration, I can't read his eyes. Is he offended or laughing at me? Either way, I need to get my info before I tell him to shove his attitude up his stodgy ass.

"Yes, when I have time. Alas, I spend too much time at Bergan."

"You and Grant—that place seems to be life-consuming."

"It is Grant's timelines that entangle me. I do not wish to be the scientist holding back his vision for the company." He pauses to lift our cloches. "Tonight, we have filet mignon and garlic rosemary potatoes. I decided against a vegetable since you are accustomed to Alison's winter garden. I am a poor competition for her."

"A green witch does have the best produce this time of year," I say while placing my napkin on my lap. He resumes opening the wine, stopping to sniff the cork and pour a tablespoon of wine into my glass. We just stare at each other. Am I really supposed to judge his wine selection? Feeling awkward with him standing at my side while our food cools, I sip the offering.

"Sweet enough?"

"Yes, thank you," I reply just so he will sit down. "I'm not much of a connoisseur. My parents are teetotalers and until I moved in with Alison, I lived with them. Their dinners were more family-style than fine dining."

"I'm surprised the shifter royalty is treated so poorly," he says finally sitting down.

"Alison grew up as a witch, not a shifter. Our family has middle-class happiness, so don't knock it until you tried it. Even with all of Grant's riches, Alison still prefers a happy home like our parent's house. He offers her designer clothes, jewels, and fancy cars all the time. We may not have grown up as royalty, but we learned what is really valuable in life."

"I do not mean to be obtuse. I find your family a fascinating enigma. I have been treated with reverence since Ryan announced his succession."

I busy myself cutting my steak before I reply. If I explode, I will ruin this. However, my insides are starting to simmer. I can't decide which is more insulting, that he wants to study me like a bug pinned to a board or that he judges our family for being middle-class Americans. We are simple people who grew up in a fly-over state. So what. He's a Kentucky resident too.

"Well, for all your royal manners, we ended up in the same social circle. You can lighten up without losing your status in Strawberry." I take my first bite of the delectable potatoes before I give him a piece of my mind.

"I have mortgaged my lighter side to be the next vampire king. As king, I can modernize the colony but until then I must play by Ryan's rules—"

"If you hate me so much then why did you invite me over for dinner?" The words take flight from my mouth before I can stop them. His over-the-top performance is irritating to the point of insulting.

His lips twitch with amusement before he replies, "if you thought I hated you, why did you come?"

"You are Ryan's shadow. Alison is finally happy with her husband in check and Ryan is going to ruin it. Grant is a possessive man and he's going to blame her eventually. I'm here to stop the bat bastard." I fork another fried potato into my mouth. A burst of garlic and rosemary makes me yearn for a bigger purse to take them home with me.

"So, the plan is to use me to get to Ryan? I am wounded you think so little of my feelings," he says before lifting his wineglass to his lips. As he rolls the liquid around his mouth, my eyes are glued to his candy-apple lips.

"Seriously? You are what, four times my age? I would never fall for a reanimated corpse, and neither will my sister, as much as she loves fresh soil. No thanks, decomposing is not our type." I wave my fork at him for emphasis.

"Ryan, as our king, has the duty to put vampire interests first and secure our colony. Alison is the Shifter Pack Leader of this area, so it is natural he tries to create an alliance. Besides after the rise in popularity of paranormal romance novels, all women love a sensitive vampire from a romantic bygone era." He punctuates his sentence with a smug dab of his mouth with his napkin.

"So, he doesn't even like my sister? Ryan's just a political gigolo. And no, not every woman wants to be a vampire's juice box."

"Do not misunderstand, he has confided his lusty thoughts of Alison, but one cannot help but notice her…well, she…she seems," he trails off, looking down at his plate.

"She's strange," I finish for him, leaning on the table in an aggressive posture.

"Thank you, I didn't want to offend —"

"Oh, I am offended but you are not the first to point it out. Everyone back home saw her as odd except Grant, so Ryan can't break up their marriage. Besides, there is an alliance. They joined the two groups together to fight the Fae, isn't that enough?"

"Apparently not, because here we are," he says, lifting his wineglass again. Is it my imagination or did his eyes roam over my skin with that remark? I feel scorched from ponytail to stilettos.

"As I said, no corpses need to apply." I pull my sweater shut, suddenly aware of how much cleavage my dress is showing.

"What makes you believe I am a corpse? I can assure you I eat, sleep, breathe, move and reproduce as living beings do," he purrs.

"The stuffy speech, tired fashion, prison pallor, and advanced age all smell of Night of the Living Dead."

"Perhaps you can be enlightened with a little physical evidence. Wait here." He is rushing into the house before his sentence is finished.

"No way," I whisper to myself while rising to follow. I burst into the house to find a small stage, littered with instruments and Karaoke equipment. I slowly spin in awe as I take in the life-sized posters of punk bands, from the Dead Kennedys to Millencolin. I lightly touch the life-sized poster of my favorite band, the Living End, marveling at the scribbled autographs at the top.

"No use gawking at the scenery when you don't seem to be able to hear," he says with lowered brow and a dangerous countenance. His face looks stormy with rage to my amazement. Finally, I get some real emotions, instead of the plastic expressions he held at dinner.

"You are secretly fun—" I say, waving a finger at him "—like Area 51. On the outside you are another boring government building but inside is a funhouse of the unusual and fascinating. You are holding all this back, why? Afraid of being ostracized for not being an asshole?"

"I am Ryan's apprentice and the future king. I have the opportunity to learn how to lead. How I dress, how I speak, where I work, what I do, and who I marry is all part of Ryan's plan for colony survival." He bobs his head in fury. His earring glitters in the moonlight with each movement.

"I should have been clued in by this," I say as I flick his earring. "This pirate bauble is a dead give-away you are more than Ryan's puppet."

"A pirate has traded his responsibilities for freedom and my boat is firmly chained to the dock. I'm not more than what Ryan has molded me to be…I can't be," he stammers. I find myself liking him more and more as his veneer fails to stay in place.

"Uh-huh so you say, but my favorite candy is chocolate-covered cherries. Do you know why Luc? When you reach the inside no one sees, you get a burst of sweetness. How about you act like yourself when we are alone, and I won't squeal your secret when we have company."

"Why?"

"Because I'm bored in this hick town. Ryan is my only problem and since you are going to help me stop him—"

"I never said—"

"You didn't have to. Your eyes glow when you are excited, and they glowed when I mentioned candy. You are already inside my web. If you struggle, then the threads are only weaving themselves tighter," I say with more confidence than I feel. If we can convince Ryan to back off Alison, then she may have a chance at happiness.

"Well Black Widow, I came in here to show you my birth certificate. Proof positive I'm not as old as you think." He hands me the piece of paper in his hands.

"Wait…If we are practically the same age, then why do you speak and dress like an extra from Masterpiece Theater?"

"Ryan's orders, besides a suit is the most comfortable way to conceal my wings," he says with a shrug.

"Show me," I say. I am fascinated by the vampire's ability to fly and their beautiful wings. Sure, my sister is magic, but she doesn't have wings.

Lucien turns bright pink at my request. "You really know nothing about vampire culture, do you? Ryan thinks it is an act, but no one would knowingly make that mistake."

"Are you calling me stupid?"

"I hope you are," he says with a smirk. "Asking a male vampire to show you his unfurled wings is like a man offering beads to a woman at Mardi Gras."

Now my cheeks are on fire. "Guess I'm going with stupid…keep the jacket on…please. Back to my original question: why did you invite me here?"

"Part of the secret, you sweetly promised to keep," Lucien whispers. He waits until I nod in compliance before continuing. "Ryan has tasked me with seducing you to secure the alliance, even though you are only human."

"Then you should have serenaded me with Cheap Trick, instead of the stuffy vampire dinner routine."

"Cheap? I, err…Ryan doesn't see you as a harlot. He just tires of competing with Grant and wants the matter settled."

"Maybe he isn't completely clueless after all. What does secure the alliance entail," I ask with gestured air quotes around his words.

"Sex is not on the table—"

"No shit Sherlock—"

"I'm sorry I have been incredibly rude—" He walks away from me. "I don't know what possessed me…"

"You don't do anything unless it is at his request, even hiding all this," I say in disbelief, waving my hand at the room. Someone I thought was manipulative has turned out to be trapped. What type of leverage does Ryan have on him? *Have his brown eyes always looked so sad and lost*?

"Hiding it is different than getting rid of it, there are limits to what my conscience will allow." His melancholy smile says more than his words.

"No biting me, ever. I don't want to be a vampire. I like games but not that one—"

"Look. I'm sorry I told you. Humans can't be turned into a vampire. That's a Hollywood myth. The Bergan Blood bank is right next to my office at work. I have no need—"

"Lucien, if…"

"Betty, please, I can make up something. I will just say you are a shrew—"

"I'm in."

"WHAT?" He reels around with glowing red eyes the size of stop signs.

"I will do anything for my sister," I say with my heart pounding, "even pretend to be the mistress to the Prince of Darkness."

Chapter 11

The smell of fear is back. Betty's scent of overwhelming despair, which masks almost everything else, including our dinner, cannot disguise the fear within her. No wonder Ryan fell into her traps when they sparred at the Dr.'s office. A vampire has to sort emotions beyond all the sadness to read her current one. It was fear when she arrived, followed by irritation at dinner and then I got the sweet hint of happiness when she entered my studio. My rage at being discovered almost blinded me to it. Once she agreed to team up with me against Ryan, the fear came back. The rotten stench combined with the sadness would be a cocktail of ecstasy to a Sluagh. I'm not surprised she has already been haunted.

What does surprise me is my reaction to it. I'm not as scent savvy as some other vampires but hers reaches to my soul. I enjoyed making her happy. I'm stunned how much I want to make her happy again. Being a people pleaser is ingrained in my DNA, thanks to my generous mother. My reactions to Betty's sadness are probably just an extension of that.

"Let's talk terms. No feeding. No sex." She counts her demands on her fingers. Despite the fear and sadness swirling around her, she is confronting me. The scenting of emotions must be another secret kept from the shifters or at least Betty. The shifter's pack would be proud of this delicate human. Standing strong in front of a creature from her nightmares with fear rushing through her, she negotiates terms on her tiny, pink-tipped fingers.

"Not yet," I say, grabbing her hand. "I have something to show you first. Will you join me for dessert?"

She looks at our joined hands in horror but doesn't remove hers from my grasp. She continues to stare as if she is acknowledging she has two hands for the first time. Her hand is so warm it heats mine. An anemic man could get used to having a source of warmth in his life, even one who fears him.

"I don't really like sweets—"

"—I bet you like surprises. This is a dessert you have never had before, even living with Alison." My insides coil with anticipation. This masterpiece came to me in a dream. I dreamt of surprising a girl with a dessert buried in snow but had not made it a reality until tonight.

She bites her lip in contemplation. She is trying to figure out how she will end this date. She weighs the temptation I present until I cannot wait anymore.

"Come on, dessert is outside." Like a kid on Christmas morning, I lead her through the door and steal a glance as I shut it. Her small smile barely crinkles the edges of her eyes. I can do better than that. I lead her to the snowdrift created by clearing the gazebo and hand her my discarded shovel.

"I said a mistress, not a gardener. Maybe I'm not the only one with a listening problem," she snaps.

I grip the shovel with her and bat at the snow. Revealed are my two crystal goblets standing in two-gallon bags. "See perfectly sanitary," I say handing her a bag. "I bet you have never had something like this—"

I am caught off guard by the expression on her face. She eyes the dessert with uninhibited desire. The scent of curiosity and pleasure fills my nose at odds with the sadness lingering around us. "I buried vanilla panna cotta with cherries to crystalize in this snowdrift. The result will be part ice cream, part panna cotta, part granita, and every bite unique." I don't hide my glowing eyes. She knows my tell so it is too late to be embarrassed by our shared excitement.

"I normally do not have a sweet tooth, but ice cream is my kryptonite. Thank you." The gratitude in her eyes is as addictive as is the sweet smell of happiness seeping from her. When she smiles her eyes crinkle and freckles ripple over her nose. I stare as long as my manners allow.

"My pleasure," I say with a bow. I wish I had the confidence to tell her how much pleasure it is to make her happy or at least less sad. No vampire act, no mutual exploitation, just the desire to cheer up someone else.

We sit for the dessert course. Her hands dance over the plastic as she greedily unwraps hers. Before she even picks up her spoon, she is laughing. Not giggling but the full-throated laughter I heard at the Yule party. I school my face to cover the goofy grin I can feel emerging.

"I'm sorry," she says wiping her eyes. "I just unearthed buried treasure with the Dread Pirate Bodice-Ripper." She continues to laugh at her own joke, and I'm captivated by her sound. "Oh no, I'm not making fun of you. Well, I am, but it is not you. It is Ryan's version of who you should portray."

Come on, brain. I need something witty to reassure her I am in on the joke. I want to hear her laugh again. I want to be the one to make her laugh. My brain stutters while the smile fades from her face. The moment dies, along with our temporary camaraderie. Damn it, why do I do that? I'm pulled out of my fog by her clearing her throat.

"So terms, what at the top of your list?" Her question hangs in the cold air as I anticipate her spoon reaching her mouth. I just want to watch her eat, not discuss business. If only my social anxiety had allowed a response before her joke fell flat.

"The first one is trying the dessert before I burst. I lucked out by picking cherries but—" When the spoon disappears behind her lips, my body freezes more firmly than the ice cream. Her eyelashes flutter. The spoon glides out followed by a subtle mew. She, who doesn't like sweets, is swooning over my dessert. When she sees my mouth hanging open, I earn a glare.

"I'm glad you like it as much as I enjoyed preparing it. I like creative surprises and games too. My terms are simple: do what it takes to fool Ryan without telling my secrets, blackmailing me, or arguing over everything. Oh, be nice to my cats too," I add before dropping a cherry into my mouth.

"I don't have a problem with pets. I mean, come on, I live with bears," she says, smiling at me. "I will keep your secrets and not blackmail you, because you could blackmail me too. Alison doesn't know I am here."

"She doesn't?"

"She is visiting other shifter leaders and I am housesitting. So there— We are even until she gets home. How do you propose we fool Ryan?"

"DNA evidence is where I want to start. If you don't mind, I have an extra toothbrush and hairbrush you could use before you leave. I will drop hairs on my pillow, so he thinks you are sleeping here during the day."

"That seems simple enough. I can leave the makeup I have in my purse as well. If you leave it out in your bathroom, it will be authentic. I live in makeup and Grant yells at me for leaving it everywhere on a daily basis."

"Thank you, that's a great idea. Would you mind spending some time here on your days off? I will leave you alone if you wish or I can cook for you, but Ryan will be watching for your car."

"Yeah, since he is my sister's neighbor, I can't hide there. However, I will have to be careful when Alison comes home in a few weeks or when Grant comes back to check on Bergan. I doubt he will be able to stay away. I'm not ready to explain this to them." Her goblet is empty, but I am full of pride. I managed to do something right…for once.

"I will leave it up to you when the time comes. You have been more than reasonable about our arrangement."

"If we are in agreement, then I will leave my DNA and head over to Dr. V's office," she says standing up. "Thank you for dinner. I enjoyed my first buried treasure dessert."

My heart screams for her not to go but my training overrules it. "Please follow me," I hear myself say. We leave the temporary magic of the gazebo for my spartan master suite. At least she will see my decorating style isn't haunted house chic. In the bathroom, she admires the sunken tub while I rummage through my cabinets. "You can use the tub when you visit."

"I will have to bring my bathing cap," she says with a soft tilt to her lips. She takes the brushes from me and prepares for her workday. A glow warms my chest when her toothbrush is placed next to mine in the holder. She places her fingertips on the counter as she leans forward to apply mascara, leaving tiny prints on the black marble. She places the mascara tube in the crevice between the counter and backsplash as if it has rolled there accidentally. Lastly, she folds all my towels on their racks, so they hang in straight lines like sentinels.

The transformation is astonishing. In less than ten minutes, she has made a bachelor's bathroom look like it belongs to a couple. It feels so comfortable to be part of a partnership even if it is a complete farce. I didn't realize how lonely I was until smacked with the image of what my space would look like if I shared it. If this image were real, I could live an honest life without pantaloons, or phony accents.

"No woman would put up with mismatched towels, at least no Weston woman," she says to my reflection in the mirror. "We are known for our organization. So, if you want to be authentic, you need to purchase a robot vacuum and mop too. How do you think Alison keeps her palace neat as a pin when she spends all day outside?"

"Noted. Anything else?" My pride is a little wounded at her assessment of my housekeeping. However, I'm a spooky bachelor, not a family man.

"Your appointment is tomorrow at the end of the night," she says fluffing her hair once more. "Have Ryan drive you over from Bergan because I am driving you back here. It will tell him we are together without being obvious about it."

"You think of everything."

"I have practice at lying and hiding from living in my parent's house for nearly thirty years," she says with a failed attempt at humor. The sadness in her eyes matches the rising intensity of it in her scent. One step into the master suite, Ryan will recognize it. As much as I have enjoyed her set up of the ruse, it wasn't necessary with the depression she carries.

"If you want to see living a lie, then follow me," I say to steer the conversation back to the present. I lead her toward the front of the house and into the mausoleum I call a living room. The cobwebs, gothic furniture, fading wallpaper, and gaudy décor look even more absurd than usual.

"Whoa," she says with wide eyes. "Shoplifting isn't my thing so I must ask how you managed to steal a whole Halloween-decor aisle. Was it all at once or in multiple trips?"

"I just stuffed the items in my frilly shirt sleeves."

"Dread Pirate Bodice-ripper, no damsel or supermarket decorations are safe," she says sharing my joke. "Maybe you need two robot vacuums." She heads to the door and I am reminded she can't stay here all night.

I take her jacket from her and our eyes lock. Dammit, I can't kiss her. She will slap me…again. I hold her coat open and she slides into it. Feeling bolder than usual, I wrap my arms around her to close it tightly. Her hair tickles my chin, and her warmth thaws the parts of me forever frozen by my disease.

"Thank you," she whispers, tilting her chin upward to look at me. She doesn't step from my embrace and I don't have the fortitude to let her go.

"You're welcome," I whisper back. The spell holds us captive until the grandfather clock in the corner chimes. Startled, Betty jumps and I must step back as to not get knocked in the face. I open the door with another courtly bow, and she steps through it.

"Until tomorrow night then, goodbye." She waves and I wave back silently. The riot of emotions must be under my control before I open my mouth. Something stupid like "give me lift to town" or "call off work tonight" will escape, so I get more time with her.

"I may be a romantic or an idiot, but at least I am consistent," I say to myself as I grab my keys. I lock my door and unfurl my wings. With a burst of power, I take to the skies leaving the mess of our candlelight dinner for another night. Just high enough to dodge the sparse trees along my farmland, but not high enough to grab a motorist's attention, I fly over her car as it speeds to Dr. V's office. I'm just warning away Sluagh, I reassure myself. I'm just enjoying our mutual taste in music like the rest of Kentucky. There is no way I am stalking my own mistress.

Chapter 12

My sister is trying to drive me crazy. On only four hours of sleep, due to her constant frantic phone calls, I have hit my breaking point. "Yes, Ally, I have Henrik in the hyperbaric chamber now. Before you drill me with questions, it is at four psi and ten percent oxygen. He knew how to set the parameters—even without your six pages of instructions. He has thirty minutes to go so I have time to pack his medicines for the next few days when he's at Rosie's house."

"Thank you for taking care of him. As pack leader, I had to go to Seagrass Island for the intern swap negotiations, but maybe I should have waited until the spring. I feel terrible being away when our first giant snowstorm in Kentucky is tonight. Maybe I should come home—"

"Don't you dare. You would disappoint Rosie by jeopardizing her oldest son's internship on the beach—plus piss her off that you don't trust her to take care of Henrik. Your best friend is counting on you."

"You are right," Ally says with a sigh. "I'm just being overprotective of Henrik, I guess." I can imagine her twisting her fingers, stretching the hem of her dress.

"He's from Ohio like us. We are used to snowstorms. It will be fine as long as you quit sending beach pictures of you frolicking in a tiny bikini to my phone. I'm dying of jealousy," I say with a smile. The pictures of her having fun with Grant are just short of miraculous. My sister, who cries at the drop of a hat, wears a gigantic smile in all of them. I've never seen her so happy, and it gives me relief.

"Let's plan a vacation here. You would love it."

"Maybe after the nursing exam. I signed up to take it in Louisville at the end of the month so I'm using every free minute to study."

"I know you can do it."

"Piece of cake when I inherited Mom's fantastic memory."

"It does make school easy, doesn't it?"

"Take care of yourself and don't worry about frozen Strawberry. We made sure your babies are safe. Henrik already put tarps on the exposed bushes and plywood on the greenhouse base. I will help him pack his bag and drop him off with Gran when I go to work."

"Be sure to visit Rosie when you drop him off. She made a care package for you in case you are snowed in alone for days."

"How did she know to do this?"

"I may have called her freaking out when you didn't answer once today…"

"I was in the effing shower. I called you right back. Gawd, you are turning into Mom."

"I am a Mom, just wait until you have kids."

"I won't hold my breath—"

I get interrupted by her giggles, "—because you can't swear at me without inhaling first!"

"Okay, you are too happy for me. I'm hanging up to prepare for snow-pocolypse. Go inflict your sunshine on your grizzly bear."

"Love you, sis."

"Love you too, Ally." I end the call with just enough time to line up Henrik's pill bottles before the air concentrator shuts off. The hyperbaric chamber is a three-foot by twelve-foot soft plastic cylinder held in shape by a stainless-steel frame. It is flanked by the oxygen concentrator and pumps to force ambient air into the chamber, creating an atmosphere with more oxygen than the air in the rest of the house.

As the chamber depressurizes, I wave at Henrik through the window. As he motions for me to move my head out of his light, I laugh at how much he has turned into Grant. When the pressure gauge reads zero psi, I pull the double zippers open. Henrik hands me his bucket of supplies before batting my hand away when I offer to help him emerge.

"I got it. I just need to hold the frame for a boost. I can't hold my books at the same time," he grouses.

"Your books? How about your snacks? Ally mentioned you take gummy bears in there to pop your ears, but you have one…two…three pounds in this bucket. If I didn't know you were a cherub, I would say you are taking advantage of my sweet nature," I tease.

"Mom has never limited my gummy bears."

"Uh-huh, your secret is safe with me, champ," I say before directing him to pack a bag of clothes and toiletries for the next few days. I inspect the bag according to Alison's instructions, add his pills, and sneak a bag of gummy bears inside before securing it in my car. I pack my own bag of supplies to give to Lucien to strew around his house.

The sun is hidden by a thick layer of puffy snow clouds that resemble scoops of ice cream when we head into town. What was once slush has now frozen along the narrow roads of Strawberry. My car creeps along the slick passages at a snail's pace. I may be a wild child, but I don't dare use the gas pedal with Henrik in the car. Thank goodness I have Dad's sensible sedan instead of Alison's deathtrap to drive in this weather. It takes twice the usual time to reach Paulino's and I'm pretty sure I taught Henrik a few new swear words along the way.

"Don't be too good over there or Rosie will think you are a pod person." I squeeze Henrik until he squirms out of my hug to disappear inside the dark hall.

"Are you sure you want to be alone in that giant house? I have room for you here," Rosie says with a step outside.

"No, you don't. This place is bursting with boys!"

"I will miss them when they move out. They grow up quickly, you know," she replies with tears in her eyes. She pulls a dingy wad of tissue from her pocket to wipe feebly at her nose.

"Yeah, that eight-year-old has one foot out already," I quip.

"You will understand when you have children."

"You are the second person to say that to me today. One more time and it becomes a hex."

"Don't make me get my mother-in-law."

"Noooo thank you," I say waving my hands in front of my face. Gran is a witch who probably has the power to create immaculate conception. With the magic of that magnitude, no one messes with Gran—even me.

"Smart girl, I have often wondered if my circumstances are a fertility spell gone wild. Since you seem determined to rough it, I packed some supplies. In this bag are breakfast pastries, freshly baked bread, and jars of olives, peppers, sun-dried tomatoes, and burrata.

You know, oil-packed mozzarella spheres. That should last you a few powerless days without having to open Alison's refrigerators."

"Thank you so much. Your food is my favorite part of Strawberry," I say, wedging the parcel into my canvas bag.

"I thought it would be the shifting man-candy," she says with a waggle of her brow. "I noticed Miles looking at you at the Solstice party. If you wanted to meet him, I'm sure I could arrange a chance dinnertime meeting here at the restaurant."

"Doesn't he shift into an alligator? I don't mean to discriminate but I really detest reptiles, especially ones with large teeth." Is she really trying to play matchmaker with me? It is on the tip of my tongue to brag about my farse with Lucien…until I remember she is Ally's best friend. If only I could use my arrangement with Lucien to keep Rosie from setting me up with random shifters but ensure she doesn't pass the info onto my sister. I file the conundrum away until I have some peace and quiet to think about it. I need distractions if I am going to survive being snowed in alone with only my anger at Evan to keep me company.

"It is those large teeth that can keep a woman safe," Rosie says with another waggle. *Ugh, she doesn't let up, does she?*

"I don't know how much Ally has told you about my past, but I live with her because my boyfriend overdosed at my feet." There. That should shut her up. Most people shrink away from the girl who dated a druggie and watched him die. Too bad Rosie carries as much death in her heart as I do, so she doesn't even skip a beat.

"Your heart could be complete again. Frankie told

me to move on in his dying breath and we built a life together. If I had the time and flexibility, I would be actively dating. Love will find you if you look." This is too much and my veneer cracks.

"Thank you for looking out for me, Rosie, and I'm glad you are open to love."

"But?"

"My heart is complete. I am whole on my own." I hug her while the shock settles and walk to Dr. V's as fast as my heels allow on the icy sidewalks. The clicks echo in the night as a warning to anyone who tries to get close to me. I will play the game, but I will never fully engage again.

Chapter 13

"So am I still waiting
For cells to do their mating
Can't find the right price,
To have to do this twice," I scream-sing my parody of Sum 41. I jam all the agar plates into the incubator with a resounding *thunk*. They will live there happily during the snowstorm threatening Strawberry over the next two days. This incubator is special not only because it is in George's lab instead of mine but also it is on the company's generators. Although Ryan has ruined this data collection twice, I don't have to worry about Mother Nature adding to my misery.

My singing is interrupted by the drum solo of my ringtone. "Hey Mom," I answer while strolling to the bunks in Bergan Pharma's basement.

"Hello Pumpkin, are you busy?"

"Come on, Pumpkin? I'm in my thirties, Mom. Oh, never mind. I have a few minutes before I see Dr. Van Dijk for my injections. I'm fine before you worry, and he is going to keep it that way. How's Terika?"

"Oh...about the same." There is a strange timbre to her voice. I bet if we were in the same room, I would smell a lie. I am grateful she would try to protect me, but I can't fix what I don't know is happening. I push my way into the men's locker room and check I am alone.

"I have some good news. You shall be receiving

more money directly from Ryan. It is no big deal. My cut is going directly to you that's all. Have you received a check from him lately?"

"Yes, and I called him immediately," she snaps. "Lucien, what are you thinking? An arranged marriage for money? You will not go through with this even if I have to come there to put it right."

"Mom, wait," I stammer. "It is not a marriage. It is more of a trial dating period. You do not need to come here when Terika needs you overseeing her care."

"What more can I do for her? She is on her deathbed, Lucien. She says she is ready to join your Dad."

"Don't let her give up! That's what you can do!" I whirl around and slam my fist into the locker beside me. My knuckles explode spraying blood like a Jackson Pollock masterpiece. The locker doesn't even dent in response to my abuse. *Damn that hurt*.

"Lucien, don't tantrum. I taught you better manners than that," she commands. "This call is about you. I have two children to raise and at the moment, both seem to be throwing their lives away."

"I'm not throwing my life away, Mom. I—"

"—If you don't marry for love you are! I don't care if I have to fly there to tell the king to his face. On this issue, I will not budge."

"Right now, you sound just like Betty." I roll my eyes to the lockers for sympathy.

"Who?"

"The girl Ryan has picked. She's feisty and argues with him all the time. She's a nurse with Dr. V, doing the regular stem cell treatments so he can work on complex cases like Terika's."

"I'm not arguing with you over Terika—" she huffs

in exasperation. "However, Betty sounds like a good friend for you to have. Anyone who keeps you from compromising yourself on Ryan's behalf is a friend, I approve."

"When you bring Terika here, you will meet her."

"Lucien," she says with a sigh. "You are impossible. Go to your appointment."

"I will. Love you, Mom—"

"Love you too, Pumpkin." The connection clicks after her small sob and it feels like the final nail in Terika's coffin. My hand is throbbing, so I head to the showers and get cleaned up for my appointment.

"When was the last time I went for my injections?" I ask my locker mirror as I comb my freshly washed hair.

"Seven weeks ago," says Ryan's reflection in my mirror.

"Aaaaah, do you only sneak up on me or everyone else too?"

"I came down here to see if you were hiding—" he snorts "—but pleasantly surprised to see you showered."

"I'm glad you are here. I need a lift over to Dr. V's."

"Why? Where's your car?"

"I left it at home. Betty suggested I get a lift from you and we just drive one car back to my place." I get immense satisfaction as the sneer falls off his face. It is replaced by a look of surprise. Betty's plan to notify Ryan of our farse has thrown him off-kilter. I reach deep into my locker to retrieve my cologne, so my face isn't reflected in the mirror. I need a few seconds to wipe the evil grin from it.

"Yes, well," he says. "I was planning on leaving early to avoid the snowstorm. It will be no problem to drop you off."

A bitter wind carrying plump snowflakes greets us as we step outside. A thin coating has already covered the salted walkway. Squalls of wintery powder swirl beneath the parking lights. Vampires scurry to carpool to their homes. Those who flew into work at the beginning of the night must bum rides off coworkers with the commonsense to bring their cars. Thankfully, Brad canceled the shifter's dayshift until further notice, so the parking lot does not have two-way traffic. His message was followed by a message from Grant reminding everyone to bring their laptops home and maintain document timelines as long as we have internet capabilities. Leave it to Grant to overrule Mother Nature.

The drive to Dr. V's is a two-mile circle around the village green. In the ten minutes, I have seen my life flash before my eyes five times. Ryan's giant Mercedes is rear-wheel-drive more suited for racetracks than snowy roads. It is designed to create a controlled slide using traction to turn at higher speeds. There is no control because there is no traction on the ice. The result is a ping-pong effect where his car slides sideways until he corrects, causing it to slide to the other side. Narrowly missing trees, road signs, and other cars, his courtly manners are reduced to those of a common, potty-mouthed sailor. When I catch my breath, I will laugh at him and I repeat the experience to Betty.

"Thanks for the lift," I call, stepping out of the car. To my surprise, he exits the car as well and follows on my heels into the office.

"I need to stretch my legs before tackling the impossible trip to my home," he replies while holding the door open for me. My breath hitches. He's testing my lie about going home with Betty.

"Lucien", Betty says breathlessly. She stands from behind her desk and rushes toward us. I am hit by the scent of amusement underneath her usual sadness. Anyone believing the farse will think she's happy to see me, but I know the truth. She's amused Ryan thinks he can outsmart her. When she reaches us, I get the shock of my life. She throws her arms around my neck and kisses my cheek.

"You need to hold me too for this to work," she whispers in my ear. I hesitantly place my hands on her waist and enjoy the embrace more than is appropriate. She leans back to speak but I cannot seem to command my arms to let her go.

"I am so glad you made it. I am anxious to leave with the weather picking up." Wisps of truth and anxiety float around us. Of course, only an idiot would want to be out in this weather.

"Yes," Ryan says, looking outside as if seeing the snow for the first time. "I have successfully delivered him, so I best be going for my estate is much farther out. Were you going to Lucien's or the Luther residence?"

"It is much more sensible to be at Lucien's house since it is closer." Truth scents her sentiments again. She is so careful not to answer as to our whereabouts. I need to take lying lessons from her or at least give her a chocolate statuette for her performance.

With a curt nod, Ryan leaves abruptly. "He must be fooled we are really together," I whisper to her.

"Then you can ease up on the death grip you have on my waist," she says with a giggle. I jump back letting my hands fall to my sides. My eyes are glowing, so I keep them downcast with the hope she doesn't notice.

"Lucien," Dr. Van Dijk calls from an open exam

room door. "I am so glad you decided to visit before the storm. I have been worried about you being so overdue for your injections."

"I have been busy at the lab, Doc. I have no complaints though. I haven't experienced any joint locking—even in flight." I clasp his hand and pat his shoulder.

"Betty, you can lock up while I am with Lucien. I want you out of here and off the roads since you are so determined to drive home instead of staying with me." He addresses her loudly before turning to me. "You take too many risks with your health, Lucien," he says with a somber countenance.

"What's life without risk?"

"Ryan is not going to live forever, and you are his hope for the future. I can only do so much. I need you to make seeing me a priority. I will even write doctor's notes if Grant is standing in the way."

"That's not necessary. Grant doesn't do all the pushing at Bergan. I wanted to speak to you about what has been driving me. I need your help." The closing door gradually obscures Betty's face as she strains to hear our conversation.

Chapter 14

Damn automatic doors. Lucien was about to divulge some good dirt and all I get is a door in the face. Could it be connected to Ryan's hold on him? Far-fetched tales spin in my brain as to what help a man in his prime would need from Dr. V. I wash the coffee pot and used cups of the evening on autopilot while cataloging my facts about Lucien. He was so weird about my seeing his wings that I bet his condition has to do with them. It is probably a deformed wing…or a missing wing…or instead of a wing, he has a third arm. A man with three hands opens a playground of possibilities. That ruse about a man's unfurled wings was probably a stab at my pride, like an inside joke vampires play on humans or a successful diversion from his ailment.

The most surprising part is my reaction to the secret. Why do I feel a tightness where my cold heart lies? I thought I closed it off to keep everyone out. This feels like more than professional sympathy. The sooner I drop him off and get to Alison's house the better. I don't know which is more dangerous: the snowstorm outside or the storm brewing in my heart.

Mundane tasks like powering down the computer and locking this evening's files in their cabinet are not enough to keep my brain from returning to Lucien's medical dilemma. Too bad vampire-specific diseases were not part of my nursing education. If I had a crystal ball when I was choosing career paths, I would have double-majored in nursing and mythology. The entire office is cleaned and shut down while he still hasn't emerged from the examining room. Stem cell injections take ten minutes tops with the joint manipulations taking the bulk of the appointed hour. What the hell is keeping them?

With the delay, I call my sister and do some pre-emptive damage control. *Hell yeah*, straight to voicemail. "Hey Ally, it's me. I just wanted to call and let you know I made it home safely from work. It is really snowing here. If I don't pick up my phone, it is because the power went out before I could charge it. No need to worry though because Henrik is safe at Rosie's house and I am here. Enjoy the surf!" There. That lie will hold her for a while.

Locking the front office door, I trip over my bag. It is stuffed with supplies for Lucien's house and goodies from Rosie, still lying beside the desk like a speedbump. I better put it in the car before I forget to separate Rosie's goodies and Lucien doesn't get them by accident. Medical problems or not, my fake boyfriend has no claim to my carbs. My arms are overloaded so I use my key fob to unlock my car before leaving my keys and purse at my desk.

I shuffle into the cold night, stopping only to wedge my shoe in the door. Light from the streetlamps glitters over the shoe to guide my return inside from the building blizzard. Crossing the parking lot with one high heel and one bare stocking might not be my brightest idea, but too late now. Snow cocoons around my foot soaking my tights with each step. Large flakes embed in my mascara obscuring my peripheral vision. I pull my hood tighter to block the howling wind from my delicate ears. If only I had left my hair down to protect them.

Please don't let me fall. I toe at the curb or at least the drift I think is the curb to verify there is a step buried here. A cold blast wraps around me like a vise and oh shit, I never checked for black fog before opening the door. Fingers of black fog wrap around my legs chilling me to the bone. I bend to brush it away only to watch it thicken to block the falling snow.

Without lifting my head, I spy three Sluagh through my frozen lashes. They are gliding toward me but still have to traverse the parking lot from the village green. Pretending to study the snow, I absently reach into my hood to pull out my iron hairclip to defend myself. I'm grateful Ally drilled into my head I need to wear a weaponized accessory every day.

The movement tilts my head to the side, revealing another two Sluagh approaching from the end of the sidewalk. These two are twice the size of the ones in the parking lot. Giant egg-shaped heads leak black ooze from lipless smiles. Instinctively, I swing my heavy bag to block my chest from impending danger. My heart rate accelerates but not enough to induce a panic attack. In a small town, a resident is never alone. They have to pass the doors to Paulino's pizzeria before they get to me. With any luck, the miniature wolfpack will jump out.

"Oh damn! I forgot my shoe again," I yell into the night. Anyone listening would certainly hear I am outside. As much as I bitch about the townspeople watching my every move, I hope someone with claws is eavesdropping. My free hand bops my forehead like I'm an idiot. Hopefully, my tiny stature and performance will convince them I can be overpowered by an individual. If they attack as a group, I'm toast.

If this were a movie, they would start fighting over me and I could slip away, but somehow, I don't think I am that lucky. The three in the parking lot have fanned out so the five have collectively formed a semicircle around me. A brick wall stands firmly three feet behind me. My only option is to slowly slink back to the office and get into the doors before they attack. Ally says all the buildings and homes of Strawberry were warded as they were built so Sluagh cannot enter them without an open window or door. Looking to the office, I also remember Ally saying Sluagh only possesses one functioning eye so they must attack from a certain direction. *Was it the direction of the office or the pizzeria?*

Dammit all, I'm such an idiot. Not only have I placed myself in danger, but I have invited them into Dr. V's space with my shoe ala fairytale princess. If I draw their attention to the office, then I put Dr. V in danger. My only option is to fight. I plant my feet, bring up my weapon, and lower into a fighting stance. A high-pitched screech wails into the night but I don't take my eyes off the Sluagh. That sound would incapacitate Ally's senses, but I hardly notice it. *Sorry demons, wrong sister.*

"Throw your voice all night while I kick your asses one by one," I yell at them. Each Sluagh diverts their attention to my side, at the source of screeching sound. Their expressions turn from menace to fear. I would take credit for scaring them but I'm too busy backing against the wall. As soon as my back thuds against the brick, my view of the Sluagh is blocked by a black leather jacket with wings protruding from it. Not Sluagh wings with their kaleidoscope of colors, these are tan wings covered with tiny black hairs. Giant wings reach from my waist to high over my head. Their span shields my escape route.

Not to waste an opportunity I run the length of the wings to the door. I yank and pull with all my might. *No!* My shoe is lying helplessly on the doormat inside. When my winged hero emerged, the moron dislodged my shoe inside locking us out. With the Sluagh between my car and myself, an escape from this nightmare is dependent on the owner of the wings.

I mumble as my mind swirls with panic. "Please be a friendly shifter…Please be a friendly shifter… Please be…Lucien?"

The man I love to torment has transformed into the scariest monster I have ever seen. *That's because he's not a man. He's a vampire, Stupid.* Long curved claws extend from his wingtips and hands. His chest billows as he makes the screeching noise drawing the attention of the Sluagh. Canines extend from his mouth and curve along the sides of his face, while his other teeth lengthen into mouth-filling points. Compared to the Sluagh surrounding us, he is the nightmare on the block. The most formidable image is his glowing red stare. I recognize his clothes, his cologne, and that's about it.

Chapter 15

"It's always a pleasure to help, Sire," Dr. Van Dijk says as he escorts me into the lobby. "It sounds like your sister's infection may be antibiotic-resistant, but here in the States, we still have other options."

"It's Lucien and I can't thank you enough—" I shake his hand with both of mine. "—I'm really excited about the prospect of IVIG. If we could teach her body to fight it, we would be strengthening her for anything else that comes her way."

"You just need to bring her to Strawberry. I don't have an IV line long enough. Seriously, I can't diagnose and treat someone on another continent. Even with her records and a video chat, I wouldn't be able to assess her lung function."

"That's my goal, though I doubt she has the medical tests completed in the records you seek. They don't utilize the modern medical options in the Old Country in favor of discretion. The service you provide for the vampires of Strawberry is lifesaving."

"I like feeling useful, that's all. The pack is very gracious in their protection and inclusion of this lowly human as well. I'm going to secure the cell bank and log your injection lines. Just hang out here with Betty and tell her when your joints tighten. I'll loosen you up early so you can get a head start before the snow."

"Thanks, Doc." I head to the mini-fridge for a blood

bag of A positive. He waves as he disappears behind the automatic exam room door. Where is Betty's sarcastic greeting? I wonder what she will call me in my usual outfit—scrubs and my aging leather jacket—instead of one of Ryan's costumes. Seconds blink by with no comments.

Her desk chair is empty but her phone, purse, and car keys still adorn it. A quick scan proves she's not in the lobby. Creeping across the floor, I quietly open the second examination room door with the plan to jump in and spook her. "Boo! Betty?" Automated lights flicker in the tiny room signaling a previously empty room. Silence.

My heart pounds. *Oh God, she's outside*. The most damning piece of evidence is the glittery black shoe wedged in the door. My blood boils with terror causing my elbows to lock and the newly injected cells to grate inside my ankles. A dull ache settles into my knees and hips as I force my body outside, with only my fear blocking the pain. Step. Step. I must reach her…just in case.

At the doors, I sag on the frame with relief. Betty is in one piece about six feet down the sidewalk. Eyes alight with ire, she scowls at something perpendicular to the building. I can only hope it is an overprotective Rosie, an annoying Ryan, or any being other than a Sluagh.

Throwing the door open, five Sluagh are in a ringed formation. They are closing in and Betty doesn't stand a chance. The commonsense of texting Ryan or shouting to Dr. V to call for backup leaks from my brain as my instincts take over. Within seconds my body transforms from mild-mannered microbiologist to monster, complete with pointy accouterments. An ear-piercing screech rips from my chest usually reserved for a defensive male in the Old Country with others encroaching on his territory. My father made this noise often for my mother is a legendary beauty, but I have never had the urge.

My shriek stops all five phantoms, and they swing their attention to me. "Throw your voice all night while I kick your asses one by one," Betty yells at them, completely ruining my diversion. I have no choice. I leap to shelter her against the wall in the hopes my body language is enough to convince the Sluagh she's mine. Other vampires, who have earned my wrath, think I'm as terrifying as the Vampire King, but Betty doesn't seem phased. She runs along the length of my wings to office doors pulling their handles in vain. The glittery shoe wasn't a sign for me to follow but a doorstop. *My bad*.

Betty mumbles as she turns to face me. "Please be a friendly shifter…Please be a friendly shifter… Please be…Lucien?" Eyes round with shock, the fierce warrior loses all the color from her cheeks. My signals to her that I am on her side fail. It hurts to see her frightened of me. The Sluagh closest to her takes the opportunity to advance toward her, so I push my feelings aside to be analyzed later. If the flock is trying to decide how far I will go to defend Betty, good luck, I am just as shocked by my own instincts.

With an unnatural hiss escaping through my teeth, my wing crashes into the pursuant demon and sends it hurtling into the darkness. The shadow disappears into the snow squalls with a dotted line of black acidic blood leading to its landing site. Tatters of the demon's robe and ribbons of its decaying flesh hang from the claw at the tip of my wing. Its buddies in the parking lot hesitate to move forward as they compare my wingspan to their remaining distance. Sluagh are maniacal creatures but they recognize a fellow predator.

Growling, I stare down the rest of them. The testosterone that fogged my thinking began to clear once I had Betty within my wingspan, so I attempt to logically assess the situation. I have fought Sluagh to their death without fear, but in this instance, I am outnumbered. If I engage in combat with three of them, there is no guarantee I can keep Betty from being snatched by the fourth. There is also the Sluagh I threw away. Did it have a hard landing or is it lurking on the village green? If he is calling the other seven demons in the fortress, we are doomed. Retreat to the office...nope. Flee to her car...nope.

The two larger phantoms on the sidewalk glide toward me. "Feeling lucky, Batboy? We will find how many of us you can take at once and when you are a pile of bloody bones, we will find out how many of us your girl can take at once." Their cackles elicit a whimper from Betty.

Enraged, I shriek in response. My fully-extended fangs block my ability to form words. In all my battles with Sluagh, I have never wanted to tear one to pieces so badly. Satisfaction pumps my ego when the remaining Sluagh cover their ears and cower at the sound.

The temporary diversion gives me just enough time to wrap my wing around Betty and push her into the safety of my arms. "Erhold onerm," I whisper through my fangs in the hopes she can decipher my monster-speak.

Her terrified gaze turns into one of confusion as she

stares into my eyes for a split second before she complies. With a flap of my wings, the swirling snow is sent into a vortex around us. My knees creak and protest as I leap straight up. At the apex, we take flight. If I weren't trying to race the Sluagh to my house, I would savor the feeling of Betty's death grip on my shoulders. Her legs wrap around my waist as she tries to crawl into my skin to stay aloft. Hair whipping around us like a forcefield, she buries her face in my chest with a small cry.

Sluagh wings are much more delicate and take a few flutters just to lift off the ground. They are also built for the mild climate in the Fae Realm not the throes of a Midwestern Blizzard. They will be soggy in minutes and weighed down with ice. These factors add up to a fifty-foot head start for Betty and me. A victorious smile spreads across my face as I gloat, "they pose no threat to us in the air" which comes out as a jumble of grunts.

Over the miles of cleared farmland iced with white sparkling snow I soar, calming my blood pressure to a manageable level. Hooray, my fangs retract. As much I love having Betty snuggled firmly against me, it would be dishonest to let her continue out of fear. Large flakes dance around us as the winds push us farther away from the town's center and her face is still buried against my chest.

"You are missing the enchanting view of Strawberry," I whisper into her ear.

"You can talk again." She lifts her chin peep at me from the folds of my jacket.

"My fangs extend with surges in blood pressure. Look around at the scenery and hopefully, it will calm you too. Trust me. I would never let you fall."

"Lucien, once you get to know me, you will realize I don't fall easily."

The wind and snow continue to beat at us. The cold stings my wings as the frigid temperatures take their toll. Stem cells threaten to solidify my joints with every flap of my wings. I can only hope I get us home in time.

Chapter 16

I'm just cowering against him because I'm scared, right? It isn't because he just saved my life or he smells good, right? Turning my face from his embrace takes a colossal effort and I am rewarded with snow prickling my cheeks. The snowflakes against the barren skyline of rural Kentucky look like stars suspended in outer space. Our speed has them whizzing past as if someone turned on the thermoboosters of a science fiction rocket. With Lucien's coaxing, I muster the courage to look below us and I am blown away by the majesty of the countryside.

The usually boring landscape is transformed into a wonderland, but I am having trouble focusing on it due to my proximity to Lucien. White snow glitters like a magic carpet as far as I can see. Trees, coated with a silvery glaze, dot the blanket, scattering the faint moonlight into tiny rainbows on the ground. Being this close I sense his whole body fighting gravity to bring us to safety, in the beating of his heart, his steady breathing, and the rhythmic motion of his powerful wings. The whoosh they make is the only sound lending to the feeling of intimacy I am trying to ignore. Cradled in his arms, I feel secure, almost cherished, and a myriad of other emotions I have no right to feel.

In the distance stands Lucien's haunted house, complete with icy spiderwebs. Leave it to a snowstorm to make that monstrosity look inviting. Piles of snow act as a slipcover over the neglected landscaping and creeping vines, in an obvious upgrade. *Almost there.* A sudden drop in altitude has me climbing Lucien like a frightened cat. "Are we going to have a bumpy landing?"

When he doesn't answer, I turn to glare at him. His face is contorted into a grimace of pain. He grinds his molars and squints his eyes at the sight of his house. I must be too heavy for the distance we have traveled. Guilt crashes down on me in waves. Does he need rest when he morphs back into himself, like when Ally returned to herself from her polar form?

Another drop and we are skimming his land, less than four feet off the ground. His porch bangs against my shins, and I clothesline myself. Lucien folds his wings just in time for us to hit the concrete in a tangle of limbs. Lying with my belly against the snowdrift, I feel cold for the first time since leaving the office. Panic looms as I whip my head around to check for following Sluagh. Luckily for us, we weren't followed closely, and our hard landing is not our demise.

"Red topped key," Lucien says between gulps of air. He tosses his key ring to me and I flip through it to reveal his house key. When the door opens and a blast of hot air welcomes us, I let out a sigh of contentment. Stepping over the threshold, I drop my bag and wait for Lucien to get up. Prostrate in the snow, he doesn't move.

"Lucien," I say, crouching down in the entryway. "Luc? It's open. Let's hide before a Sluagh finds us. Lucien, are you okay?"

Slowly he lifts his torso and seal-walks on his hands into the house. His legs drag lifelessly behind him, smearing snow on the antique rug. I lift his feet and walk them to the side until his entire body is inside, perpendicular to the door. He drops his torso with a grunt. His eyes are closed, and his mouth is open as he gulps for air. I take the space between heartbeats to worry about him before my nursing training takes over.

Securing us inside with the deadbolt is my first move, followed by a trip to the kitchen for a blood bag and a touch of the "ARM" button on his security system. Back at the doorway, he has flipped to his back and both of his cats are licking his hands in concern. His chest continues to billow with each heaving breath. "Don't worry Furballs," I coo at them. "Betty is going to save your master. He saved me tonight so I kinda owe him."

At the sound of my words, Lucien opens his eyes slightly and a smile curls at his lips. "Welcome back." Why is my voice a husky whisper? "I wasn't sure if you passed out or just collapsed with exhaustion."

"Neither. My joints lock with the stem cell injections. I need the material to be moved into my bone marrow."

"I brought a blood bag because I didn't know what was wrong. Will it help to sit up and drink it?"

He nods as I wrap my arms around him with a professional hold. I lift his torso and have to coax myself to let go when he is leaning against the door. "Pull off the IV plug and I can suck it out like a straw," he instructs.

"Where's your phone? I'm going to call Dr. V and have him talk me through the joint manipulations."

"Oh no, you don't have to—"

"Tell me or I will frisk you to find the phone," I say in my no-nonsense nurse voice. He pauses with a smirk on his face. A small flash of red alights his eyes, but it is gone as fast as it arrives.

"Left jacket pocket," he says, gingerly taking the blood bag from me. He waits for me to root around in his pockets until he adds, "inner left jacket pocket." *Asshole*.

"Thanks," I mutter dryly before tapping the office number into the device.

"Chiro," Dr. V answers on the second ring.

"It's Betty—"

"Thank goodness, girl. When I saw your phone and keys left behind, I thought you were another guest to the Sluagh fortress."

"No, Lucien flew me to Alison's and he's going to shelter at Ryan's next door once his joints recover—"

"He flew…carrying you…all the way to Alison's…is he conscious?"

"I'm right here, Doc," Lucien calls over my shoulder.

"Betty, he's in tremendous pain," Dr. V whispers. "What have you done so far?"

"Given him a blood bag?"

"He needs much more than that. Are you up for this? Would you feel more comfortable putting Ryan on the phone? Betty, this treatment gets intimate quickly…"

"He saved me from a group of five Sluagh in the parking lot."

Dr. V exhales a loud puff then says, "remove his shoes. To give him the most relief in the shortest time, we will start with his feet."

"I am putting you on speaker," I say when the phone slips onto the floor. Lucien's eyes round to saucers as I unlace his boots and remove them, followed by his socks. I wrap my hands around his cold left foot and rub circles on it, as described by the doctor. I massage until the long narrow foot is warm. I repeat the motion at his ankle and run my hands along his calf to reach his knee, feeling his lean muscles without looking at his face. He makes a noise as I rub behind his knee. It is easier to keep my distance if I picture him as another vampire. An old vampire. A Nosferatu-looking vampire.

"Now, erm," Dr. V clears his throat before saying. "Next repeat the circles at his hip." *Oh my God*. I run my palms over his frozen scrubs tracing his quadriceps. I focus on my own hands instead of how his bare legs would look like a dancer's, lean but powerful. I stop at his leg socket to push and rotate his hip joint, in the most impersonal manner as possible. His swift intake of breath startles me into looking at his face. What I see there, accelerates my heart rate more than the Sluagh attack.

"Have I hurt you?"

"No" —he says around his blood bag— "I feel relief." The lie is written all over his face, but I am not ready for the truth, so I let it go.

"Once he indicates the crystals have finished clearing, you do the other side."

"She's ready to move, Doc," Lucien says while burning me with the lust in his eyes. I get scorched by his gaze as I massage his frozen right foot, ankle, and knee. I keep my Nosferatu image locked in my forebrain to stay impersonal. Dr. V instructs me to rub his right hip to complete the cycle. The backs of my fingers brush his hip flexor muscle. He twitches before I realize where I'm staring. I push, rub, and rotate in clockwise circles until my field of vision is tinged with red. Oh my, Lucien's eyes are glowing fiercely. I get relief when he closes them, and I assess my own vitals. I am breathing heavier than a prank caller, with sweaty palms and a racing heart. This experience will feature in my fantasies for decades.

"Hands next," Dr. V squawks from the phone on the floor. Thankfully, it pulls me from my lust-fueled downward spiral.

"Gotcha," I call back with a voice shakier than I would like. Hopefully, Dr. V takes it as nerves. I clasp Lucien's hand in both of mine. I puff into the cocoon to warm it, causing his eyes to fly open. I continue to blow as he smiles at me and Dr. V barks instructions.

Next, my hands follow a painfully intimate path to his elbow tracing hills and valleys of lean muscle. As I massage into the base of his bicep and triceps, I hold the image of his monster persona firmly in my mind to keep my libido firmly in check. Picturing the fangs curving from his upper lip to his chin is enough to spoil any amorous mood developing between us.

The shoulder manipulations are so intense I must raise to my knees to reach over his body, one hand on his elbow, the other on his opposite shoulder blade. My arms barely reach across for his shoulders are deceptively wide for his narrow frame. It isn't until I have been kneeling for five minutes, that I check my alignment against him. Sure enough, my breasts have been swinging across his nose with every movement. His eyes are closed now, but were they the entire time?

"When the creaking noise in his shoulder stops, you can switch sides," Dr. V says through the crackling connection.

I stop massaging long enough to yell into the phone, "Is that the end?" All I get is static in response. The storm clouds must be too thick for cell signal or a tower has been damaged. My lifeline to Dr. V and civilization has been severed. I end the call leaving the sound of the grandfather clock as our only ambient noise. We are alone.

"That's the last of the manipulations. In fact, I bet I can do the other side myself. The pain is tolerable because my left side is loose. Thank you for your expert care," Lucien says with a small formal nod.

We just survived a Sluagh attack, a flight through a snowstorm, and his joints solidifying. Now he thinks to switch to his fake formal demeanor? I'm practically straddling him, and he wants to be emotionally distant? My pride is wounded as I thought we were becoming co-conspirators. I thought he was the friend I needed with Ally gone. An image of Evan's mocking sneer flashes across my conscious reminding me I deserve this. I can't escape the memory of the man I killed while trying to love him.

"What kind of nurse do you think I am? I would never leave my patient only half-healed to fend for himself. When I took you into my care, I intended to see it through," I snap. He smirks at my mini-tantrum. I push his shoulders back against the door before climbing to his other side. I massage the opposite hand, a tad rougher than the first one.

"I thought I could show my gratitude with manners. I don't have much to offer at the moment." I stop manipulating his knuckles to look at him. The honesty in his eyes is breathtaking. I stare for what feels like hours and build the defensive walls of ice around my heart to keep from developing feelings for him.

"Right now, you could offer your vehicle to get to Alison's house. I don't sprout wings," I say to his wrist. I pretend to focus on it as if it takes my brain's capacity to rub in circles.

"The roads will not be plowed for days. The state

doesn't clear the roads out this far. Tyler, the grocer attaches a plow to his delivery van and clears roads. You will be sheltering here."

Oh, I will be? For days? "Once it stops, I guess I will be shoveling," I grouse.

"Guess so."

My eyes snap to his with alarm. Lucien's driveway is over a mile long. A bodybuilder couldn't shovel it manually let alone a carb-lover who is less than five feet tall. Those Old Country manners faded quickly. My temper builds until I see his tight smile. A small chuckle escapes in response. "You got me," I whisper while shaking my head.

"Too risky. Ryan would drain me like this blood bag if he saw you shoveling my driveway. He would know I have forgotten to equip my SUV with snow tires and chains."

With the tension released into the stuffy room, I position myself to rotate his shoulder. This time I am cognizant of my body placement, keeping my curves to his side instead of dangling my assets in his face. I rub, turn, and push creating a rhythm of creaks that echo through the silent house. When the noise stops, I fold my knees to sit beside him. My hands slide to his elbow, but I can't find the motivation to lift them completely. I can't sit here staring at him for the next few days, or perhaps I could and that's the problem.

"Well, I bet you are as tired as I am," I say nervously. "Will you coordinate the sleeping arrangements?"

"After massaging my body for the last hour, do you really think it is wise to ask me about going to bed?"

Chapter 17

I'm having a nightmare. Did that fly out of my mouth? When I need to be polite, this woman throws me so off-balance my mouth can't form words. However, the treasonous organ has no trouble doing so when my subconscious decides to embarrass the hell out of me…and that's not even my most treasonous organ. Even the replenishing blood bag doesn't supply enough to my brain, because it is all pooling at my groin.

Starting with the vision of her undressing me and ending with her nails scraping at my shoulders, I have been treated to pieces of a reenactment of my most recent wet dream. The only piece missing is her consenting scent of desire. She was the impersonal professional she claims to be throughout the entire ordeal. Then she has the audacity to give me those sultry eyes and innocently ask about going to bed. Maybe a better strategy would be a confession to being a pervert and get it over with.

While my brain sputters with self-recrimination, she climbs the stairs to claim a guest room. No need to move from my restful pose against the front door. She's in for a rude awakening and I brace for impact. 5…4…3… She opens the door at the top of the stairs and steps back in shock. She sees…an empty room. 2…1…

"There's nothing here," she calls down to me. Yep, she's a sharp one. I wait patiently as she checks the other three bedrooms are just as empty. Now she's furious. Her wrath is being released on the floor above me. The stomps of her stocking feet are impressive for someone with such a petite figure. The tympanic cadence continues as she descends the stairs to stand in front of me with her hands on her hips. Has anyone notified her as to how attractive she looks when she's about to unleash a tirade?

"Your entire upstairs is empty," she accuses.

"Yeah." There is nothing else to say but the truth. "Empty guest rooms discourage guests from staying too long. They can only sleep on the floor for so many days." I shrug and meet her gaze. Her eyes sparkle as the fire cools within them. Then she laughs and her beauty shines in my direction. My ears delight at the sensation of her twinkling music bouncing within the eaves of the atrium. She throws her arms in the air with exasperation giving me an unfettered view of her throat muscles. They shake and contract to release my favorite sound. I catalog the image in my brain for a time when I'm alone.

"You really hate everyone, don't you?" Her question doesn't register as I picture myself nuzzling my face against her throat. She takes my silence as agreement and it is just as well. What am I supposed to say? My most frequent visitor is Ryan who lives to torment me.

She lifts her bag from my side and stalks back toward my master suite. She's going to sleep in my bed, my subconscious cheers…but no, without me. The question as to where I'm going to sleep motivates me to my feet and I stumble after her. "Wait, what's the plan?"

"Oh, I never asked if you sleep in a coffin. Perhaps that is why you only have one bed in a five-bedroom plantation home?"

I am shaking my head before she says the word coffin. "No, and I don't burrow into the ground either," I mutter between clenched teeth. I pull the blackout curtains closed to block the minuscule daylight penetrating the snowstorm before I am accidentally scorched.

"Pity—" She opens my dresser drawers. "—We are just going to have to be adults about this." She lifts out one of my t-shirts and holds it up in front of her body.

"You…you…" I stutter and stammer while pointing at her.

"What? Fake or not, mistresses steal their man's clothing and sleep in their beds. We need to think of it as playing roles. We stick to the terms of the agreement and tackle our living arrangements with clear heads in the evening." With that she walks to my bathroom to change, holding her arm outward to navigate the darkness. In shutting the curtains, I forgot her human eyes cannot see in the dark.

"I can do that," I say to the empty room. Why do I feel deflated? Of course, I can host her in close proximity without touching her. I must do it with my glowing eyes shut. She can't sleep in the red-light district. Not wanting to get caught with my pants down, I strip to my boxers and get in the bed on MY side. She took my clothes and half my bed without permission. I won't give her a chance to steal the better side with the pillows I prefer. Hearing the covers ruffle, Bela and Christopher hop onto the foot of the bed. What will Betty's reaction be to having live foot warmers?

She's so tiny my shirt hangs almost to her knees. Her hair is down and creates a rippling black curtain against the bright white fabric as she scurries across the room.

The make-up, the jeweled hair clips, the hose, and the singular high heel are gone. While she climbs between my covers, I receive a rare close-up of her face. Without the obtrusive make-up, her freckles stand out against her alabaster skin. She is natural, raw, and absolutely exquisite. I shut my eyes tightly and think of my ugliest vampire professor. I have a feeling I'm going to have the old bat in my thoughts all night long.

"G'night Luc," she whispers and rolls over to lightly kiss my lips. Then she rolls back to her side and snuggles into the covers as if we have been sharing a bed for years.

"G'night Betty." Old bat professor. Old bat professor. Old professor, old college, old habits. In college, I would have never laid here respectfully with the hard-on from hell. There was never a shortage of vampiress social-climbers willing to do anything to be queen. Since Ryan was already in America, I was an easy target, but the females were easy too. Should I be proud of my maturity that I'm letting Betty sleep or disappointed I'm losing my touch? *Touch, ugh.*

One day, I can do this. I bet she's suffering too. She must have some attraction to me...so much for that thought. Her rhythmic breathing has turned into a tiny snore. Through squinting red eyes, I risk a glance at her sleeping form and instantly wish I hadn't. Her little fists are curled under her chin as she clutches my bedspread tightly. Long lashes form crescents on her rounded cheeks giving her freckles a curtain to play hide-and-seek. Her lips are slightly open giving the impression that a gasp is about to fall from her mouth, a gasp of surprise, a gasp of rising passion, a gasp...at what a creepy pervert I am. I can't watch her sleep all day, so I shut my eyes and start to count sheep, drifting slowly into a thankfully dreamless sleep.

Pounce! *Dammit, Bela!* I must have moved my feet suddenly in my sleep because Bela has sunk her claws into them. The nearly twenty pounds of fuzz bounces repeatedly as she hunts and kills my toes. What is wrong with this cat besides an intruder at my side? *Pounce, scratch!* Reaching toward my feet, I scoop the she-devil cat into my arms and place her on my pillow above my head. I curve my arm up to lightly stroke her fur. This is her usual spot. She should have crawled into it hours ago, at least what I hope was hours ago.

My clock glows noon in the darkness. Bela licks at my hair, while Christopher continues to snore loudly only to be echoed by the tiny puffs of Betty. Dammit, why did I look over again? Her pose is the same but now a small smile has formed on her face. She looks like a young girl dreaming of a new pony, a frilly ball gown, or her first kiss…and my smutty thoughts take that south along with most of my blood. Old bat professor. Old bat professor. How long can I sustain this erection? Old bat professor. Old bat professor with an erection. *AH! NO!*

"Dammit," I hiss into the darkness. Being practical, I will use my free time to brainstorm where I will sleep tomorrow if we are still snowed in. I have never wished more for soft furnishings in my life. Blizzard means same-day delivery is out. Twenty-year-old me would be horrified I'm lying next to a bombshell, in my own bed, contemplating the best way to evict her.

Got it, clean up the gothic sofa from the living room. Wait, it is not long enough for my six-foot lanky frame. It's not very chivalrous but her tiny body would fit easily. I could make it quite cozy to coax her. I will move it to the stage so she's in the warmest part of the house and away from spiderwebs, *and close to me*. I swat at my errant thought and concentrate on the task at hand. I can load it up with blankets and pillows. I will provide her a little nest.

A memory of Grant's voice floats uninvited through my head. He's brainstorming with James in the hallway at work about James's Christmas gifts to Nate and Aurora. James is asking about how to show not only love but commitment. You would think he would be whispering about such a private matter, but Grant never whispers. "That's how I show Alison, I love her, James. I provide her with a little nest to feel secure." That's not what I am doing. I'm reclaiming my bed. I'm just so tired. My thoughts are borderline delirious.

This is why schemes never work out for me. I get cornered, my heart invested, and my body committed while everyone else involved is unaffected…or at least seemingly unaffected. Possessed by a sadistic impulse, I look over to Betty again. She has turned to lay on her stomach, her hair fanning over my pillows. My eyes travel down her curves until they reach her widely stretched legs. Oh, the pleasure to be found with her in that position…

"Dammit." The word flies out of my mouth and right at her face. Prayers and pleas fill my mind that she sleeps through my agony. She twitches restlessly with a little mew. How will I explain watching her sleep for hours because I'm a sicko? Her shifting movements become more animated, and I fear the worst.

"I will take care of you," she says in a dazed sleepy whisper. She shifts closer to me and reaches a slender hand to my opposite shoulder. She cuddles into my side and lays her head on my heart. My arm has a mind of its own. It lowers from beneath Bela to hook around Betty, my palm landing on the curve of her ass. We fit. God help me, we fit perfectly.

Chapter 18

Floating between wakefulness and dreaming, Evan's arm tucks around me. Security flows into my bones as I nuzzle into his side. It was all a nightmare: shapeshifters, Sluagh, vampires, drug dealers, and cops. It was all a figment of my imagination and I am cuddled with Evan, waiting to start our lives together. I will go to work at the nursing home while Evan looks for work. We will build a new life where he is clean, and I am his.

Doubt clouds my soap-bubble fantasy as my rising consciousness brings too many questions to my frontal lobe. When did Evan bulk up? He's the right height but when he started living on the streets, he lost so much weight. It felt like hugging a skeleton. Not anymore, the man I am holding is a landscape of lean muscle. Where did Evan get the money for expensive cologne? While I'm glad he is spending money on something other than drugs, we will need to pay for utilities sometime this month. He smells so good. I rub my cheek against him like a cat. Why is Evan so cold? His skin is cold to the touch like he's…he's…dead.

Evan's final seizure plays out in my head. Whose body am I spooning? Evan's dead face stares lifelessly toward the ceiling, foam seeping from his mouth. Evan's arms tighten around me as I start to fight the corpse. Hands reanimate to smooth down my limbs and caress my body. I can hear myself screaming in the distance as

I imagine clawing at the dirt.

"Betty, Betty, Betty," a man calls in the distance.

"I'm underground. I'm trapped in Evan's grave."

"What? Who is Evan? Betty, you are dreaming. Betty, wake up," the voice calls as it inches closer.

The corpse's hands push me into a sitting position. I'm jolted awake. I'm in bed with Lucien, not Evan. Not just sleeping on my side of Lucien's bed, but cocooned around him like he was Evan. *I hate you, Evan.* My heart stutters and my face colors with humiliation. "I'm sorry I had a nightmare."

"You dreamt you were in a grave. I thought we already established I am not a corpse." His silhouette sits up beside me in the darkness. It is just as well. If pity clouded his countenance, I would be tempted to punch him.

"No, I mean…yes, we did and no you are not." How do I tell him I wasn't dreaming of him? Would he care one way or the other? A simple case of mistaken identity. It happens all the time, right? "You weren't the corpse. Oh eff-me, it was…"

"Evan?"

"Oh god." I pull the blanket over my face. "Was I calling for him?"

"You were trapped in his grave and I think I was your rescue." To my horror, he places his hands over mine and lowers the blanket to stare directly into my eyes. The brown pieces in his black eyes roam my face without pity but another more dangerous emotion.

"Evan is a corpse in real life. His grave is in Ohio by my parent's house. He died just over a year ago. I don't know why I'm telling you this…"

"I'm not going to pretend to understand the

workings of your subconscious but let me guess." I let him pull me back into his arms like a child seeking comfort. We lay down in our initial position. "The Sluagh feed on distress and sadness. It calls to them like the song playing from an ice cream truck. Your depression has been luring them to you and one of these times, they are going to hurt you. Subconsciously you know it and the nightmare is an act of self-preservation."

"Ally warned me, and had Josh make iron hairclips as my Yule gift." Being snuggled against him dissolves the terror from the dream, the humiliation of talking about Evan to him, and some of the wall I have built around my heart. I don't deserve this tender moment. If Lucien knew Evan's death was my fault, he would throw me out into a snowdrift.

"Maybe your dream was a reminder that you are putting yourself in danger by not going through the grieving process fully—"

"I'm not the type of girl to sit and cry—"

"I didn't think you were," he says with a chuckle. "However, you need to talk about him to turn his memory from a nightmare to just another memory…when you are ready."

"I'm not sure if I can because I am still so pissed at him for leaving…"

"I lost my dad and miss him every day. When I'm struggling, I ask the stars why he's not here. I still get angry and his passing was over a decade ago." We lay in the darkness lost in our memories.

The grandfather clock ticks in the distance. We are isolated…almost. The cat splayed out at my feet decides to stand and stretch. His ears vibrate while he arches his back causing Luc and me to chuckle in the darkness. The depression lifts off my shoulders to a merciful level. The cat paws his way over the hills and valleys of the covers to stand on my chest. He walks in a circle and sits nose-to-nose with me. With a little puff, he tucks his face under my chin. "Which cat is this?"

"That's Christopher, my sensitive guy. The Sluagh aren't the only ones who can scent sadness."

"A life-saving vampire, a head-shrinking cat—"

"Aren't you the one who called this Area 51?"

"Yeah, guess I did," I say to his profile, "you don't look like an alien though…well…only your cheekbones."

"The better to house my fangs, my dear. Where did you think I kept them?"

"That's right. I forgot you can make a Sabre Tooth Tiger face." Christopher stirs at the jostling of his perch and kneads my chest. "Damn, those little claws are sharp."

"Betty, none of my pointy bits are little."

"Not you. Christopher."

"Here let me take him." He reaches over me to lift the cat. Christopher slips from Luc's grasp, bounding to the floor with a thud. Luc's hand falls to the opposite side of me. I'm staring into his eyes and caged by his body. The peace I am beginning to associate with his embrace wraps around me like cotton batting. I am quickly becoming accustomed to his security and silently wish the covers weren't wadded up between us.

"You kissed me goodnight and I never kiss you back. You must excuse me," he whispers while brushing our noses against one another. "I forgot my manners and I'm about to do it again." I hold my breath as he tilts his chin. His eyes search mine for protest. I flutter my lashes closed to consent to whatever he offers.

A teasing kiss feathers over my lips. He pulls back but I give chase to extend the magic. The compassion, the security, the feeling of having someone look after me is too much to resist. I don't care if it is real or fake, I just want to feel less sad. He lifts his head out of my reach and smiles down at me. A smile spreads across my face in response before I can regain my thoughts.

"I'm going to shower and brush my teeth before I get myself into trouble," he says, brushing our noses again. "Help yourself to the coffeemaker, fire up my laptop, or just lounge here with the cats."

I can only nod in response as he climbs out of the bed. I stifle a groan as he stretches at the bedside. He is only wearing boxer briefs and… *Good Lord.* As he pulls back the blackout curtains, his nearly translucent skin glows in the moonlight encasing miles of lean muscle. In his clothes, he looks too thin to be powerful, but I'm treated to a glimpse of the strength he keeps hidden from the world. My wandering eyes confirm there is not a soft spot on his body.

"It is still snowing but the flakes are smaller," he says to the window. Thank goodness he hasn't caught me staring. I couldn't claim modesty, fake romance, or anything but the blinding lust at his questioning. "There isn't a chance of plowing, erm, snow plowing. Grocer Tyler or the Paulino boys won't start clearing the snow until it stops falling. Looks like you are a temporary resident of Area 51, so let me know what you would like to do today when I return."

With that, he turns and glides into the bathroom. My eyes follow the rippling of his back muscles from his wide shoulders to his unfurled wings. They look like twin silken curtains as if he's wearing a parted tan cape. According to him, he just flashed me, and I can't stifle my giggle. He throws a heated look over his shoulder turning my giggle into a gasp. His glowing eyes indicate he did flash me…intentionally. I let him see my eyes roam over his wings to his buttocks and back up to his face. The smug satisfaction I find there is more endearing than arrogant.

He closes the door, and I am left alone with my smutty thoughts. Unable to resist, I put his pillow to my face and inhale his scent. If only I had the forethought to bring my vibrator with me. That man is intoxicating in every way. I would love to have a one-night-stand but that would severely jeopardize the plan to use him to keep Ryan away from Ally. This partnership with Lucien must work so I must keep my hands, eyes, and lips to myself. Besides, that's why I was blessed with ten talented fingers. I close my eyes and engage in play that will not get anyone hurt.

Chapter 19

Her lust diffused through my bedroom like the aroma of a homecooked meal. I had to get out of there before I ruin the trust we are building. I lean against the bathroom door to catch my breath. Already acting out of character, I flashed my wings like a teenager on prom night. The scent of her desire intensified not only signaling she doesn't fear my vampire status but also, she liked what she saw. *Awwwwesome.*

My nose tells me she hasn't moved from the bed and her arousal level is not lowering. She wouldn't…I bet she would because she doesn't know I smell emotions. Stepping into the frigid shower, my libido doesn't cool in the slightest. I must get my mind out of the gutter if I am to survive this night unscathed. She is mourning another guy for god's sake. Is this Evan a brother, a friend, a former lover, or something more? Who is to say it is not his head on my body that fills her mind? That thought cools my loins more than the shower so at least I can finish my hygiene routine.

Wrapping up in my robe, I do one last check in the bathroom mirror for glowing eyes, hairs out of place, or spots in my teeth. I square my shoulders and open the door to reveal Betty, spilling crumbs into my bed in the soft lighting of my bedside lamp. She has moved my laptop from my desk to the bed and is surfing the web with a pastry in hand. Her guilty smile is so adorable the anger over the crumbs dissolves.

"Where did you find that?"

"It is a gift from Rosie. A welcome one at that." The temptress waves it at me. "Your cabinets are empty. I thought you said vampires eat like everyone else just with blood to wash it down."

"My cabinets are empty because I work too many hours to grocery shop and eat the food before it spoils. I found I could live on carryout from Paulino's after Ryan allowed shifters to see us eat. You can verify this with Rosie next time you are collecting gifts. She's fed me for two months."

She nods while taking a large bite of the pastry. Red filling spills onto her chin. A delicate finger sweeps it between her lips. As she licks her finger, her eyes flutter closed, and I contemplate returning to the cold shower. "I was mad Alison asked her to make a blizzard care package for me, but Rosie outdid herself. This one is cherry."

My stomach growls in response. "How many do you have?"

She stops mid-bite to narrow her eyes at me in suspicion. "I, and I do stress I, have two more of them."

"I will arm wrestle you for one."

"Eff that, not happening after I saw your Prince of Darkness monster. I'm wise to your tricks," she says with her finger outstretched in my direction.

"What's your price?"

She nibbles while faking contemplation. She smells like she knows exactly what she wants but not how to ask for it. *Doesn't that make a man feel good?* Not a wisp of her usual sadness lingers in the room and I can only hope she realizes she can find happiness again.

"I couldn't find any tea. I don't suppose you have a secret stash?"

"I keep Earl Grey over the fridge for visitors, but I am a coffee drinker."

Her face reminds me of a child trying broccoli for the first time. "No thanks on the Earl Grey. You need to have bags of green tea if you are going to fool Ryan into believing I'm living here. I drink it all day long. Hot on wintery days like this but iced the rest of the year. He has watched me drink it from his balcony. Do you believe that asshole watches my sister with binoculars?"

Unfortunately, I can. If Betty were my neighbor, I would be next to him.

"A bath," she replies before taking another large bite.

I look to my bare feet before my eyes can give me away. I picture us in my sunken tub in a cloud of steam and bubbles. Betty's body presses against mine as she feeds me pastries, licking the spilled filling from my chest. Her hair is piled on top of her head so when I feel the urge, I can lean over and sip...

"You do have hot water, right?" Her question flies through my thoughts, clearing out the steam.

"What? Yes, I can draw you a hot bath in exchange for breakfast."

"One bath for one person in exchange for one pastry," she articulates cautiously.

"It's a deal." I must be a worthy co-conspirator for her to continue to broker deals with me. The resourceful little wench has everything I desire...including breakfast. I make good on my promise by returning to the bathroom and activating the taps.

"I don't have any fancy bath salts or bubbles, but I

have plenty of hot water. How hot do you like it?"

"Scorch me." Dragging her giant bag behind her, she enters the bathroom. "Oh, and I don't require the fancy stuff. Just use your shampoo. It will be enough foam for me."

"I lugged that bag all the way from Dr. V's. What's in it, bricks?"

"Add the shampoo before the water level becomes too high," she says with a regal wave at me. I glare at her the entire journey to my shower stall. Her eyebrows disappear into her bangs as she watches my pouty performance. Adding a generous amount of my shampoo into the bath, I turn to her for approval.

"Wow, that tantrum was the most royal thing I have ever seen you do." The gentle twinkling of her giggles fills the room and wraps around me like a ghostly hug before I laugh along. I would throw the entire bottle in the tub if it would make her laugh. I'm grinning like a loon when she starts speaking again. "This is a bag of stuff I wanted to leave here for Ryan to find. It has the usual girly odds and ends that I would bring as a regular visitor. Plus, it contains Rosie's bag of provisions. That's why I'm not letting it out of my sight."

"I am wounded you think me a thief when I have opened my space to you." She turns to me with remorse, and I almost get away with it. My best puppy-dog eyes lay it on a little too thick. I get a playful slug in the shoulder for my theatrics.

I clutch my shoulder while I give my best impression of the melting wicked witch. As I lower past her waist, I wrap my arm around it and drag her into my lap. She swats at me without ire, while laughing the entire journey.

"Unhand me, Captain Bodice-ripper!"

"Giving me a wound at the side of your bath was a big mistake," I say reaching to shut off the taps before the tub overflows. "I will have to avert my eyes while you undress…"

"Oh no you don't,"—she scrambles off my lap— "I bartered for a solo bath fair and square. Out, out, damn vampire!" She tugs my arms and my treasonous velvet robe slides easily on the tile floor. I tumble into my bedroom at the changeover to the carpet. My journey is completed with the shove of my door closing. That tiny woman just threw the Prince of Darkness out of his own bathroom.

I sit at the door laughing, shaking my head at her audacity until the door is cracked open. A slender hand reaches out at my eye level holding a large pastry on a slightly used napkin. "Thank you, m'lady."

Bela and Christopher climb onto my lap to rub against me. "No way, urchins. I had to earn this meal. Let's make sure you are topped off with dry food." The robot vacuums she suggested I buy arrived before the storm. Once I set one up, could it run on my bed? My plans for the morning are kitty food, coffee, and de-crumbing my bed—probably not in that order. Hopefully, it will be enough to keep me distracted from the scene unfolding in my bathtub.

An hour later she emerges in a puff of steam smelling of serenity and faintly of my shampoo. Male pride rises in approval of the hoodie she has stolen from my closet. My hoodies are larger to conceal my wings, so the band's logo hangs almost to her knees. I wish it didn't conceal her neck. She's wearing her hair piled on top of her head identically to my earlier fantasy. Maybe

I should have taken a page out of her book and masturbated in the shower but knowing me that would make it worse.

"Feeling better?"

"Yes," she says with a small smile. "Thank you. I wasn't sure where you collected your used towels, so I hung mine over the shower door."

"I can collect them for laundry once I clear the snow from the dryer vent, I guess. You would be proud I am taking care of the front room. I have a vacuum working on it and I am assembling the robot mop as we speak."

"I am proud of you. You are almost like a grown-up."

"Hey now—" I point a screwdriver at her— "don't be too generous with the compliments. I will suspect you are after my kingdom." Her jaw drops open to argue with my remark until I wink to let her in on the joke.

"I bet we could spend the whole day cleaning and not get it all finished."

"Or we can let the robots work and play video games…"

"The Prince of Darkness plays video games in his spare time?"

"The key to that sentence is spare time or time spent here before your brother-in-law moved to Strawberry." I hold up the finished mop assembly and earn a slow clap. In the kitchen, I fill the mopping robot with water and set it to go. Cats scatter like shattered glass as the new invader wheels after them. Returning to my room with two steaming mugs, Betty is obediently perched at the end of my bed. The picture of her reaching for me is one of comfort and home. I shake my head to clear it.

"Let's play," she purrs.

This is fake. This is a farse and I have to remember I am only a co-conspirator to her. My stone-cold logic cools the warmth glowing in my chest. Handing her a controller, we sit in comfortable silence while the gaming system boots. The level begins and we intuitively work in tandem. Without formally defining roles, we cooperate through the scenes achieving milestones at a record pace. "Did you and Alison pay a lot of videogames growing up?"

"No, she can't watch screens for long periods of time and first-person shooter games give her vertigo. I mostly played with my brothers. Did you play them with siblings growing up?"

"No, I discovered them in college. My parents were very old school."

"I can imagine royal vampire parents would be."

"Yeah, my sister never developed an interest in them. I don't have any brothers obviously."

"Why obviously?"

"Because they would be trying to assassinate me to get the throne."

"Seriously?"

"That's how it works in the Old Country."

"Where is that, by the way? Alison couldn't tell me where to find it on a globe."

"Butuceny, Moldova. It is a small peninsula by the Raut river, a picturesque place full of old cathedrals and vineyards. Hence my embarrassingly large wine collection—"

"—And the stuffy wine tasting act at our candlelight dinner."

"Hey, I thought that was classy. Don't roll your eyes! I can see your reflection in the TV screen." I elbow her hard enough to mess up her jump, killing her character.

"Why did you do that? We are on the same team!"

That statement should not have sent a flutter to my heart, but I'm falling harder by the minute. "Older brother habits die hard. Even though Terika and I only played card games together, I still found ways to torment her."

"Terika is your sister?"

"My only sister. She's living with my mom in the Old Coun—in Butuceny. We are ten years apart."

"Same with Ally and I. Our two brothers are a lot younger. That's probably why we are so close. Do you miss your sister? Do you wish she was in Strawberry?"

"I want Terika here more than anything. We have been saving for her relocation for years, but it has been difficult with her continued medical expenses." *Oh shit.* It felt so good to talk to someone about my problem that it just flew out. Ryan will be pissed if Betty suspects vampires have a weakness to be exploited. That is…if Betty tells him.

"Between us…mistress to vampire…female vampires are usually sickly. I want to bring Terika here to see Dr. V, not me. Our females cannot have children and have shorter lifespans. Molina is an anomaly since she mated a shifter. Her ability to stay young and healthy for an extra two hundred years is another reason why Ryan pursued your sister."

At my admission, Betty puts down her controller to stare at me. "If females vampires are infertile, then how did you get here?"

"My mother is as human as you. The vampire genes are dominant or at least co-dominant enough to wipe out the healthy bone marrow of a hybrid. There are some lesser vampires without wings. They have a lower status in Moldova. There are those who own the vineyards and those who work the vineyards. The human intellectuals ran during World War II and many of the older vampires wanted isolation over education."

"No wonder you left."

"Actually, it was Ryan who left Moldova first. He may be an asshole in the US but to them, he is revolutionary. He is the one who first invested the colony's wealth in the stock market and grew it enough for every member—winged or wingless—to get a cut. Despite his not-so-charming act, his leadership style is very close to your sister's pack dynamics. Ryan requires the mannerisms of the Old World to appease the ancient vampires but brings in the capital, so everyone is fed."

"Fed? Wow, high standards Luc."

"It is a step in the right direction. When I am King, I can take more steps like convincing Dr. V to train professionals in Moldova and creating scholarships for those vampires outside of the ruling family to have access to education. The colony has a fifty percent literacy rate."

"I had no idea. No wonder you let Ryan puppet you around like an idiot. You have a vision." I want to risk a glance at her face but I'm afraid she is mocking me, and about to release a zinger. Instead, I inhale and fake a giant sigh. My nose scents surprise, admiration, and contentment.

"My vision is bringing Terika here for treatment. That's it for now."

"I understand because of my relationship with Ally. Having a witchy sister with SPD was difficult without a colony to hide her. I'm grateful Grant found Strawberry for her and I guess, I'm grateful she found Grant."

"Everyone at Bergan is jealous of their romance. They are like Brad and Molina."

"Ally had it rough before settling here so don't let their goo-goo eyes fool you. I had to dig Ally out of lots of scrapes from childhood on up."

"You have always put her needs first."

"Yep, that's what siblings do."

"Does she put you first?"

My question darkens her expression slightly and a faint odor of disappointment floats to my nose. "How could she? I never had bullies, therapies, medical treatments, or sensory issues. You understand how weird it is being a healthy sibling. You can't complain because you are playing in the lobby not performing tricks for doctors."

"Did you spend a lot of time playing in lobbies? I couldn't because we didn't have the specialists to see Terika."

"Don't make it sound like a chore. I knew every time Ally was going to have to endure something horrible because we got matching new toys the day before. Blood draw? New dresses for our dolls. Ally got a green one while I got a pink one. New feeding therapy for Ally? New Lego houses. Ally would get a farmhouse while I got a townhouse. My parents gave both of us toys to keep it even. It made me wish I had medical procedures so we could get double the toys." Her hollow chuckle is as haunting as my living room. I envision two little girls with their Lego houses playing on a hospital bed, one with IV lines and the other with a long black ponytail.

"Your parents probably just wanted to keep the

peace."

"No, they honestly felt bad. One time only Ally got a gift, and I threw a fit. I was older, nearly twelve, so my dad sat me down and explained Ally's disability. He thanked me for loving her anyway. He was trying to make me feel better, probably so I would act like less of a brat, but it only made me feel worse."

"What happened?"

"You don't want to hear my silly tale…"

"Why not? Our level has ended. We earned more stars than I would get on my own." I brush my fingers under her chin to coax an answering smile. If this moment were real, I would kiss her. This is a farse. Why does this feel like more than a farse?

"Okay, but no telling Ally…or Ryan…or Grant. She would be so embarrassed she would turn into a beet."

"I will file it away in our pact." My fist thumps over my heart.

"Ally was scheduled for an electrotherapy sleep study. Her night terrors were keeping the entire house awake, especially me since we shared a bedroom. My brothers were toddlers, so they were cranky all day and making my mom crazy."

"I can imagine it was difficult sharing a bedroom with someone who experiences night terrors."

"Ally started seeing sleep specialists and a few days before the study, my dad took us to a wig store. You can imagine the fun we had as middle schoolers while trying on all the outrageous wigs. Ally and I were all smiles and laughter when dad let us pick wigs for him as well. At the end of the trip, Dad told Ally to select a wig, much to our amazement. They were so expensive. We weren't royalty so each dollar was stretched amongst the four kids."

"You mentioned you weren't royalty but were you poor?"

"No, middle-class. Enough for the good times but struggled through the hard times. Mom says the ups and downs are what make life worth living."

"So why the wigs?"

"Wig, singular, was the problem. Ally and I had picked out matching magenta wigs. My parents decided the expense of one was justified but not two. It was the first time I saw a real difference between Ally and me. I was pissed."

"I can imagine." A vivid image of a preteen version of Betty, fuming over the loss of a silly pink wig, makes me chuckle.

"Ally got to take the pink wig home while all I got was my sour attitude," she says with an answering chuckle. "I held onto my mad until the next day when I went to school and Ally went to the hospital…again. I stormed off the school bus, whipped open the front door, and found Ally crying in our room on the floor. She was clutching clumps of her hair in her fists."

"You're shitting me…"

"Nope, they had to shave parts of her head to put the electrode receptors on her skin. The wig was to cover the bald patches. My parents either didn't warn her or she didn't tell me. I had no idea she got a wig instead of a dress because she would lose some of her hair."

"I'm sure she was devastated but how did that affect you?"

"I felt like pond scum, of course. Luckily, I am the vain sister, so Ally got over it quickly. The pink wig helped with the kids at school too. She had a few days reprieve from the teasing. Whoever came up with that idea was a genius."

I am overwhelmed with the urge to buy Betty a pink wig. Why am I such an idiot? Ryan would say a king would look beyond a girl's desires and use it to conquer the women in which she resides. I guess I'm not ready to be king because the notion turns my stomach. I cannot fulfill her heart's desires either, at least until I can figure who Evan was and why she still weeps for him. Just the whisper of his name causes my claws to push through my nailbeds. The ones on my wings puncture my hoodie.

"Mom and Dad knew fairness meant giving the neediest child the most resources. I'm strong and self-reliant because of them."

"I admire your bravery, strength, and independence. However, you don't seem to let your guard down. Do you ever wish for someone to take care of you?" *Bull's eye.* My question drains the color from her cheeks and the scent of longing fills the air. Whoever Evan was, he didn't cherish her as she deserves…like I would. She rebuilds her walls with a deep breath while my heart slips inside them.

I need a manual on how a vampire is supposed to court his own mistress. Ryan would be so disappointed. I was supposed to seduce her, but she bewitched me. The only saving grace is she doesn't have a clue. If I can keep my feelings to myself, I will survive until Alison comes back.

"Since we are sharing secrets today, how about you play for me?"

"What?" My mind flies into the gutter. I envision myself stripping out of my clothes to bad techno music. In my mind's eyes, I prance around the room while getting drunk on desire emanating from her.

"You all but bragged about being able to play all those instruments. Your ego even had a stage installed for you to give concerts to it—"

"Had it installed? I built a sanctuary with my own two hands," I yell, letting my wounds hang out. All my bottled aggression is unleashing in an honest tirade at the wrong person. "My ego, as you call it, keeps me company because I have to lie to everyone else. Don't you wish the lies would stop? Do you realize how much easier life would be if I could be myself? Well, I don't just think about things. I do what is necessary to make it happen, even if it means I only get to share it with my ego…and my cats."

My final words are stated from beyond the doorframe. My body has a mind of its own as it carries me to my stage. Pride sends electricity shooting through my veins. She is dangling too many temptations under my nose. To have someone to share my secrets, someone to sing to, someone to sing about, someone on my side is my deepest desire.

A desire so selfish my sister would die for it and the colony could fold. It is customary the royal vampire males have vampire queens and human mistresses for breeding only. I would love nothing more than to place a crown on Betty's head whether in her silky black hair or on a pink wig. That would cause an uproar and a mass of challengers ready to fight me to the death.

To abandon the throne to marry Betty would leave Terika's fate and my vision for the colony in the hands of an unknown challenger. I don't have a distant cousin I can trust to govern fairly. I have faced challengers for the throne since college and I am the only one still alive.

I pick up my guitar and plug it in with an angry jab at the amplifier. I rip at the strings while singing my own creation. It starts fast, whines hard, and has more cuss words than a rugby field on match day. To my delight, Betty bounces into the room without a word. She jumps and runs around the floor to the music in a solo mosh pit. The sight of her spinning into walls only to push them away, like obtrusive dance partners, has me in stitches. I tumble over my own words, skip lines, and jumble the verses with my laughter. The song becomes instrumental until…she begins to sing.

Chapter 20

"Dressed up in pantaloons
Kept like your pet baboon,
I let you make a fool of me
Just to protect my destiny.
My place in our family tree
Is not all that defines me.
In your claws, I sit and wait
For the day I change my fate.
Stack the plates, Count the dots,
Keep your secrets, guard the locks.
Today I let you control my life.
I shut up through the pain and strife.
I listen to who I should be
But when you're gone, I'll just be me.
My words will ring true and strong,
Long after you're dead and gone.
I will be a better king, you'll see,
Being who the hell I want to be.
Mortgage fates, unravel knots,
Pay your debts to lead your flocks."

Abruptly as he started, he stops playing. His jaw drops while his eyes glow a slight crimson. The hell, Dude, I thought we were having fun. Are you so possessive of your songs I have managed to piss you off just by singing with you? Unable to contain my annoyance, I turn to him and sneer, "what gives" while throwing my arms in the air.

"How were you able to learn my lyrics so fast?"

"When I say I have a photographic memory I'm not joking. You sang the same lines five times already. However, it is only short-term memory so you don't have to worry I will become a songwriting sensation overnight. For me to permanently memorize them, I would have to see them written down. My visual memory is much stronger than my aural memory."

"Incredible. I'm not worried about piracy, remember? I am the Dread Pirate Bodice-ripper."

"You are too much." I giggle more out of relief I haven't pissed off my host than his attempt at humor.

"I bet your memory makes life much easier."

"I wouldn't know the alternative. Actually, having a great memory is a curse. I can fixate on my every mistake, lie, and heartbreak whenever they float to the surface. I don't have the escape route of forgetting."

"Perfect, I won't have to try so hard to be unforgettable. I'm glad I went low-maintenance when choosing my fake mistress." As he leans over to put his guitar away, I get a glimpse of his perfect backside encased in his gray cotton pants. He turns to a laptop sitting on the amplifier and pecks at the keys until a vintage punk band plays loudly from surrounding speakers. Like a Rockstar, he leaps down from the stage and stalks me with predatory eyes. "Mind if I join you?"

"I don't tango, ancient one."

He releases a bark of laughter while tilting his head to the ceiling. Then he catches me off-guard by shoving me lightly. He bounces in a large circle joining me in my pretend mosh pit, his hoodie revealing a band of porcelain at his waist each time he raises his arms. My eyes focus on the tiny patch of hair below his belly button and refuse to let go. I freeze in the center of the room grinning like an idiot. Hopefully, he takes it as innocent enjoyment of the music, or I will be mortified.

He has joined in my fantasy as another concert-goer. What would he think if I told him he belonged on the stage rather than in the crowd? He's the type of guy a girl would put on a pedestal easily. *He has spent the past decade being groomed to be a king, stupid.*

The bass picks up to a driving beat signaling the imaginary crowd to jump in unison. Driven by my subconscious, I jump in place. Lucien makes his way to jump in front of me and grabs both of my hands. He raises our hands and lowers his head, letting his hair swing over his eyes.

He has the most tempting candy-apple lips, and I am lucky enough to have felt them more than once. He is absorbed in this experience and I am a forgotten observer. How can someone have such talent and obvious love for a profession and completely ignore it at the bidding of someone else? Could Lucien love his sister so fiercely he would push all this aside?

The memory of my discovery of his music room floats through my mind. *"Hiding it is different than getting rid of it," he had said with a melancholy smile. "There are limits to what my conscience will allow."* I swat the desire for him to love me with that level of loyalty like a parasitic mosquito. It is the need to be loved by any man not that he's absolutely amazing, right? Guys like him deserve trophy wives with bouncing hair and boobs, who will curtsy when appropriate and get on their knees later. I smile at him and genuinely hope he finds her.

"Wait here," I say at the end of the song. He opens his eyes to reveal a look of confusion…and hurt? It can't be hurt. I run into the bedroom and yank the bedspread off the bed. I grab Rosie's bag of goodies and return to my forlorn vampire. He hasn't moved from the center of the room with his head hanging. I yearn to smooth back his hair to look into his eyes with an intensity that brings me skidding to a stop.

"Surprise! Let's have a picnic." I borrow the singsong voice of my sister. Anything to perk him back up. He lifts his chin to meet my gaze and we stand transfixed. "I want to take care of you," flies out of my mouth. My eyes widen and my face heats to roasting. I hold my bounty with white knuckles while I await his reaction. *Oh my God, save me from myself.*

A small smile curls at his lips as he saunters in front of me. Taking the blanket, he lifts my hand to his lips. He kisses my fingers with a courtly bow, honed with decades of practice. "I would be honored." The words breathe pure sensuality over my knuckles. I can only stare like an idiot as he kisses them again. When he turns to spread the bedspread on the stage, I'm still frozen. Thank goodness he has no clue as my body readies itself for a man it cannot have.

He returns to me to take Rosie's bag. "Are you sure you want to share? I'm prepared to negotiate terms," he says with a half-grin that has me choking on my own lust. I bite my lower lip to keep from asking for too much without conscious thought.

"No parlay needed, pirate." I am delighted when my feet cooperate, and I climb onto the stage. He ushers me to the blanket with his hand branding my lower back. My temperature soars and I push up my sleeves for relief. Sitting in the center, I turn to reach for the bag. *Wow*, Lucien sits way too close to me. My shoulder brushes his chest, and my lungs fill with his scent, not the cologne he displays for the world but the man underneath. *Holy hell,* he is intoxicating on every level.

"Too bad. You have a lot to offer. I was looking forward to sparring with you for it. You know I have a sword set, right?"

I laugh while placing the jars Rosie provided on the blanket. Lucien opens each one in a masculine gesture that reminds me of Grant taking care of Alison. *Oh no, don't go down that road, stupid.* When I unwrap the bread from the parchment paper, Lucien groans.

"I know, right? I must dream up a gift to return the favor to Rosie."

"At least I can add wine." He jumps up and trotting toward the kitchen.

"Bring a knife too."

"That sounds more like my girl— Not that you are my girl…you are fully grown…I am sounding stupid…oh hell's bells."

"—A large knife for cutting the bread and a small one to dig olives and burrata out of their jars, please." Whether he calls me a girl or woman doesn't matter, for his kisses have shown me he knows the difference. As for him calling me, his? I'm not touching that with a ten-foot pole.

"Gotcha."

The banging of drawers and the rattle of silverware precedes the jingle of a cell phone. "Be back in a flash." He hands me the knives without breaking his sprint across the room.

"Didn't your mother ever tell you not to run with knives," I yell after his speeding form. He doesn't look in my direction as he disappears into his room, pulling the door closed. The obstinate door bounces off its hinges and drifts open a few inches. It is just enough space for me to listen in without being seen. I convince my insubordinate heart this is a fact-finding mission for Ally not a soap opera episode. At the end of the storm, I need information, not songs or kisses.

"Hey Little Girl, are you feeling better?" His voice is warmed with affection. My movements freeze as I anticipate his next words.

"Oh yeah, you heard Betty in the background. We are snowed in." I can't help but feel smug at his having to admit he's alone with me.

"Yes, she's pretty like you." *You are just a mistress and a fake one at that, stupid.* Stomach acid eats my insides as jealousy tears through my system.

"Oh Terika, she is everything you will be when you come here. She speaks her mind. She has a degree and a profession, and…" My shoulders sag as the tension releases. He's talking to his sister. I shake my head to clear out the remnants of possessiveness I have no right to feel.

"No, she's not betrothed. They don't arrange marriages in the Strawberry shifters pack. You will be able to marry for love here. Maybe not right away. I want you to find yourself first but…" A painful realization floats through my head. Is Lucien betrothed? If he was, why would Ryan push for a human mistress? *You are simply a breeder, stupid.*

"Terika, please hold on to hope. You will live here. Stay well so you can meet her," he pleads into the phone.

He sniffles My heart cracks. I helped grieving families in the nursing home. Losing Ally would destroy me and Terika is so much younger than us.

"I think I do, Terika." Dammit, I lost the thread of his conversation.

"You are coughing again. Does Mom know you called?" More sniffles and the hush of a tissue being pulled from a box. "Listen to them so you can get well enough to travel. Promise me, no more risks."

"Love you too, scamp." His phone clatters against a surface and he blows his nose. I can't take much more of this. Rising to my feet, I slip into his room to find him standing with his back to me. His head is lowered to his hands and his shoulders are rounded forward in defeat. I wrap my arms around his waist and lay my head on his wings. We stand in silence listening to the music.

"Did you hear it all?"

"Just your half." A piece of me reaches out to him and I want to hold onto him forever, even though he is not mine to hold. He reaches an arm behind him to tuck me into his side. We emerge from the bedroom together where he leads me back to the picnic.

"Good." He plops down and grabs the bread. He cuts it into slices signaling he doesn't want to talk. I take the hint and retrieve the wine bottle, opener, and glasses from the kitchen. I open the wine before returning to his side. I pour myself a full glass and place a tablespoon in his glass.

"Thanks." He sips it absently. When he finishes, he frowns into the glass as if the rest of the wine has run into the stem. At my giggles, he turns to me and says, "Okay, that's payback. No more stuffy sommelier behavior. You're not impressed by it."

"Yeah, lighten up." I refill his glass.

"Funny, that's what Terika was telling me. She wanted me to focus on being happy and having fun."

"She's smart. Here start by enjoying this." I pile olives and cheese on a piece of bread. I hold it to his mouth, and he opens obediently. He gives me an impish smile that zaps electricity to my toes. I build a second bruschetta and pop it in my mouth.

"Hey, I thought you were an admirer, feeding me to gain my favor. That was mine."

"No way."

"Good because you would suck being my slave."

"You bet I would," I say before I can catch his double-entendre. My face starts to resemble a tomato while he barks with laughter at me. At least my humiliation has brought him back to life. I can't remember the last time I succeeded at cheering someone up.

We eat in comfortable silence, listening to his music shuffle through punk songs. He lifts olives to his lips and sucks them into his mouth in a gesture unique to him. My smutty thoughts envision each olive as my nipple. What is wrong with me?

Once the food is gone, he lays back on folded hands and closes his eyes. I feel compelled to pounce on him and roger him senseless. Why is my libido out of control after taking care of business earlier? Perhaps I require a sample his goods with a one-night stand. If he becomes less of a mystery, I won't yearn for what I can't keep.

The music changes to the next song, a slower ballad, and he gives me the brightest smile like the joy of a child with their first ice cream cone. "I promise not to waltz."

He pulls to me standing and leads me to the dance

floor. He places one set of our joined hands at my waist. The action bends me backward slightly, squishing my breasts against his chest. I hope he doesn't notice my pebbled nipples.

"No minuet either, captain," I quip to hide my embarrassment. "I am not wearing heels."

"I would offer to fetch them when I change into my pantaloons, but you only brought one to the ball. I'm a little put out my party was second, so I didn't retrieve the shoe you left behind in Dr V's lobby. I only hope your first choice of prince is smaller than me or at least has an A-positive blood type."

I can only laugh in response. He has stolen my words and removed my armor. When I have quieted, he pulls me tighter against him resting his chin on the top of my head. If he announced he has hypnotic powers, I would believe him because I become docile in his arms. Surrounded by his fortifying cocoon, I release my troubles to his care.

How can a man who produces so little body heat make me feel so warm and protected? My libido cools as I realize this man probably doesn't have one-night stands. His hidden personality screams he plays for keeps. I'm in trouble and this song feels like the longest one on record. Who rescues damsels from their rescuers?

"Perfect," he whispers in my hair.

"What?"

"Perfect…the snow…it looked like it had stopped snowing earlier, but it has picked up again," he stammers. We watch the flakes fall in giant cotton balls as if the clouds are having a pillow fight. Lucien surprises me by wrapping his arms around my shoulders as he stands behind me. I melt into the embrace at his silent command.

"Looks like you are stuck with me for a little while longer," I whisper, confused by his dry comment.

"I have the ingredients from the last time I made a snow frozen dessert. Would it please you to have it again?"

"Singing, dancing, ice cream? Your hosting would make my sister proud."

"She is our Madam Commander, but I don't care. I want to please you." He leans over my shoulder to look into my eyes. Gone is the geeky scientist whose awkward conversation has entertained me and, in his place, stands a confident man who takes my breath away.

I throw caution to the wind and kiss him with all the passion brewing between us tonight. He kisses me just as forcefully and spears his tongue into my mouth. His hands turn me to face him to gain better access to my lips, or so I thought. I'm shocked, from my ponytail to my bare feet when he grinds my pelvis against his erection. Our tongues duel while my hands roam over his shoulders and biceps. I groan into his mouth giving him permission to make his next move. He gathers my hoodie to my waist, baring my legs and panties. I shiver at the breeze wafting over them or is it at the way his hands grip my butt?

I cling to his shoulders when he lifts me off my feet. I squeal in delight and wrap my legs around him in an effort for balance. Our new position places my burning core over the tent in his pants. He moves us as a unit to the wall and presses me against it. The posture frees his hands which immediately removes our hoodies.

They join his shyness on the floor. I have unlocked a hidden side of him which burns with passion. I'm not naïve enough to believe he waited to give his all to me, but I'm honored to witness the real Lucien. Not only are his hands roaming everywhere but his filthy whispers threaten to set my ears ablaze. He's not the stuffy vampire with a fondness for tired fashion but he's not the wilted pansy who hides behind Ryan either. I wish I wasn't so attracted to the alpha male emerging from him because I won't just give him my heart; he will take it. Something has changed between us. It's like a lost piece has clicked into place. I pull out from his kiss to verify I'm with the same man and my brains haven't completely scrambled.

"I thought you promised sex wasn't on the table."

A feral smile curls his lips making me cower like prey. "Darling, I would never have sex on a table. I don't trust their integrity. One would collapse underneath us."

Chapter 21

Crushed between our panting bodies, her pale cleavage has stolen my sanity. With each heave of the white mounds, I become more possessed. I have been hypnotized by their dance since Betty started jumping to the music. I slam her against the wall with more force than I intend but when I release her lips to apologize, my lower one gets bitten.

The shock of her desire for rougher play wears off when she resumes our feverish kissing. My hands trace her torso while the tips of my claws score her skin. She arches her back as far as our position allows and the last of my manners out into the snow.

"You must tell me when to stop," I say between gulps of air. "I don't want to take advantage of you. I don't want to ruin what we—" I stop talking when she covers my mouth with her hand, and I swirl my tongue in the center of her palm with defiance. *Is there an inch on her body that doesn't taste like ambrosia?*

"Luc," she commands, "take me to your bed."

At least I didn't embarrass myself by running. I'm lucky I didn't trip over anything as I watched her breasts sway more than where I was going. I drop her on the bed and slide her panties down her legs. I lie on my side to memorize her curves until she tries to cover her belly with her hands.

"No—" I pin her wrists above her head with my left

hand "—I love to admire art. I will not let this chance go to waste. You look like a Rubenesque portrait come to life. Darling, you are a masterpiece."

"So, I am to lay back and keep quiet?"

"The opposite." Her eyes widen as possibilities swirl in her brilliant mind. To put her at ease, I add, "your laughter at the Yule party beckoned to me from across the crowd. I had to find the source of the music. Now that I have you, I am going to enjoy every gasp…" I place a small kiss on her lips.

"Every sigh." I kiss in the hollow of her throat.

"Every mew," I add with a flick of my tongue to her nipple. "Every moan." I nibble her other nipple. Her eyelashes flutter and her lips part.

"Until I get to listen to every pleading scream." I run my tongue from her ribcage to the bottom of her chin, my rough stubble rasping audibly against her the entire journey. Her back arches with what I am learning is her sign that she is pleased. She squirms until her eyes open to meet mine. I hold her gaze while I lower to her breast and its cherry awaiting me.

"You—" I cut her off by putting a finger to her lips. The seductress draws it into her mouth, and she sucks at it greedily while her eyes smile at me.

"Shhhh, I'm learning you." My lips experiment with tugs, flicks, nibbles, and lashes until I master her code. Her breathing increases to ruffle my hair. The twin to my test subject receives identical treatment. The motions double the cherry's size rewarding me for knowing the correct combination.

She's a feminine shade of pink from nose to navel. I lean back to stare at my handiwork and gain control over my body. I need this to last long enough to burn it into my brain. My memory is not instantly photographic like hers, but this moment is one I will treasure. My eyes drift over her form until they reach the black hair at the junction of her legs. *Mine.* The dangerous word materializes in my psyche and Betty opens her legs as if she has heard it. I am moved to tears at the portrait she has sculpted with her pose.

A tiny mew escapes her lips while her hips sway in blatant command. "If you want to bind me so you have both hands free, you can. I don't mind if it makes you feel more confident."

Ugh, she has mistaken my time of worship for a lack of confidence. Why does my brain lock onto beauty while the rest of the world wonders what is wrong with me? It is obvious she has never been with a man who has taken the time to appreciate her body. An oversight I will rectify right now. She may mistake me for an inexperienced kid now, but not for long.

"Have you been tied up in this manner before?"

She shakes her head, and her eyes widen. Is it with fear? I draw in the scent of her heightened desire to my nose. No, my tiny warrior is not scared of being dominated. She craves it. If I can get past her preconceived judgment of me, I can ensure she gets the master she wants.

"Stay." I push her wrists further into the mattress as I stand. I calmly walk to my closet, proud of my controlled stride. I turn to her before entering the alcove, pleased she has obeyed. What a gift she has given me to reveal her secret fantasy. I will not squander this opportunity. I pull a trunk out of the back of my closet and throw it open to reveal all my college toys. I return to my bedside with my arms loaded. *Inexperienced,*

Betty? Good thing I am not.

I carefully place my last clean bath towel, two satin scarves, two sets of handcuffs, a tube of lube, a blindfold, a ball gag, and a condom next to her. Her eyes widen with shock as each item is revealed. I use my advanced sense of smell to decide which to use on her. I would never gag her, as I love the sounds she makes, but I'm drunk with lust when the sight of it unnerves her. Most couples mistake the acts of using toys as true domination, but the anticipation is what drives the desire higher.

I link the anticipation to me by asking, "are you still willing to play with me?" Her eyes dart between the offerings and my gaze. She is so excited small mews escape her lips with each exhale. I have barely touched her and sense her opinion of my confidence is changing. Her adventurous soul is calling to mine and I answer it with a commanding kiss, forcing her lips to open wider than is comfortable. Our teeth hit and our tongues duel in a violent mating. I pull back abruptly, and her head falls back to the bed.

"I stop to stare because you are gorgeous, sweetheart. I don't think you hear how beautiful you are as often as I would like," I purr against her belly. "I want to watch your sweet arousal change your body. I want you to blush for me. I want you to burn for me."

"I am blushing from my ponytail to my toes, Luc." Her belly quivers beneath my chin.

I shake my head slowly at her and she swallows, drawing my attention to her throat. I can't bite her. No matter how far she lets me go with our playing, she will never consent to my feeding. I can't mess up. Not when she's calling me Luc and not Lucien. I center myself with a deep breath to release some of the tension holding me painfully erect and get to work. I open the towel and spread it over the center of the bed.

"On your knees, princess." I release her arms and push at her hip. She takes a second to comply but demurely turns to her hands and knees. Using my hand between her shoulder blades, I push her face to the pillows before stroking her cheek. The other hand is busy opening a set of handcuffs and wrapping their elongated chain around a decorative cutout in my headboard. I secure her wrists while she watches my face with glazed eyes. I am forced to recall the image of my old bat professor to keep control of my senses as I run my hands down her body to her hips. I pull them so high her knees nearly lift off the bed and her shoulders drop. An adorable little "omf" escapes her lips.

"So pretty," I whisper while pushing her knees apart. She is remarkably flexible as her hip joints release and her treasures are unveiled. Light touches do not elicit a response from her, so I caress her with open palms followed by rasps of my claws. I alternate the sensations to keep her focused on my hands. I find the little mole at the base of her spine that I spied within her torn dress at our first meeting. I kiss it lovingly. Her muffled moan is not the only sign she enjoys my touches. Her legs open further.

"That's a good girl. Open for me. Let me adore you." I tie each of her knees to her elbows while she watches with a confused countenance.

"Not tied to the bed?"

"Why bind your legs together when they look gorgeous spread apart? I have my work cut out for me if you can still speak so coherently." I run my hands over her hips while she squirms either to test her bonds or out of anticipation.

"Oh Luc, take me." *Oh God, she is tempting.* I move behind her, so I am not lost in her dazed expression. I must maintain control to impress her. *Why does that matter so much all of a sudden*? I have never wanted to impress a bed partner.

Sitting between her knees I let my legs drape beside her. I want her to see my feet and calculate how close my face is to her core. I want her to ponder how she is bare, open and I am still mostly dressed. My playmate is brilliant, and I want to pleasure her mind as much as her body. I reach my wings over us to tease her with their tips to remind her she is being pleasured by a vampire…*her vampire*. No, all thoughts of ownership must be tossed aside to enjoy her gift of this one day to me.

"Stay still, I need to study you more." Not that I need her still, but I want her to focus on keeping her body still. To cement my place in her fantasies and erase anyone who has ever touched her from her photographic memory, engaging her mind is paramount. My plan works when her hands clench my pillow and squeeze into fists.

I draw lazy shapes on her skin with my fingertips avoiding where she needs me most. I paint the marks left behind my ministrations with the slow glide of my tongue until she squirms for more. "Still, sweetheart. Let me focus." I slap her flank and let the whack, along with her gasp, echo throughout the room. "So musical," I say and add a slap to the other side. I sit still for a few ticks of the clock, enjoying the pleasure-pain of my sex confined inside my pants.

Allowing my fingers to dance over her intimate

parts, she surprises me with obedience. She groans loudly into the pillows and my chest swells with masculine pride. I give in to my baser urges to taste her and bask in her heat. How did she seduce me being tied so tightly she can't touch me? I must be bewitched.

It takes all my fortitude to pull away but she is tightening like a bowstring. I have brought her to the edge and now it is decision time. I can bring her to orgasm and risk she is done, completely driven to her limit without a release for myself.

"Please," she whispers. *Groan.* If she is the one for me, she will be worth the wait. She is worth it. *Dammit.* When did I start asking if Betty is the one? I want to watch her release, drive her up, watch her release, and continue until she is boneless with exhaustion.

"Please," she begs a little louder and I switch from master to slave. Her hips sway to collect what I provide.

"That's it, sweetheart," I purr. She stops rocking her body to isolate the movement to her hips, achieving a breaking pace. She moves so violently the bed is vibrating.

With a scream that shakes the walls, she clamps onto my fingers like a vise. I swivel to lay stretched out beside my quaking lover. I soothe her into a gentle rhythm, so she glides back to earth. Nose to nose, I watch in fascination as she gulps for air, her face a portrait of rapture. If I had any artistic talent, I would paint her this way. As I slowly withdraw my digit, her eyelashes flutter as a herald to the arrival of her bright brown eyes.

"Welcome back, beautiful." I rub our noses together. I get a shy smile in return that causes the ache in my balls to intensify. I rain small kisses on her face in gratitude for the expressions she gifted to me. She chases my lips until we connect, and the fireworks start all over again.

"Will you help untie me, please?"

I kiss her between words. "No, even though you did ask so prettily." I take advantage of her pouty countenance and bite her lower lip in retaliation for the bite I received earlier.

"What if I want to please you?"

"You have already, princess." Her smile widens and her pupils dilate with this nickname. She wants to be a princess. *She will be my Princess of Darkness.* I blink away the thought of commitment and return to my baser self.

"I have reached an orgasm and you haven't." I wondered how long she would stay docile or maybe this is part of her play as well. Time to test my limits. I stand up beside the bed and wait for her eyes to drift down my body. When they seem to be crotch level, I drop my pants to the floor to step out of them. Her tiny pink tongue moistens her lower lip giving me an idea.

Taking her, and frankly myself, by surprise, I swing my leg over her outstretched arms, so I sit between her elbows and the headboard. "Thank you," I say curtly. "Now suck it."

Moment of truth. Will I receive an acidic quip or only a glare? The last action I expected was delighted compliance. It isn't until she moans with pleasure that I relax enough to enjoy the experience. She could have bitten me. Instead, my job is to simply hold her hair out of my view and massage her scalp.

My eyes lock with hers and I am encouraged by the warm emotions I see there. I feel confident in her permission to loosen the grip on my pending climax.

With my pulse thundering in my ears, I am held captive by the care she puts into bringing me down to earth.

After releasing a few years of celibacy, I will have the control to give her the thrill of a lifetime. She will be able to gross out her grandchildren with the story of her night with the Prince of Darkness. No, the story will be of her *first* night with the Prince of Darkness as my addiction to her is growing by the second. The sweetest mew escapes her lips when she lays her head down on my thigh. The picture she creates sends an arrow cruising into my heart.

"Rest Princess." My fingers run through her hair with gentle strokes. The knot keeping it off her shoulders has completely unwound because of my greedy tugs. I smooth it into a curtain over her shoulders like a security blanket.

"Tied up?"

"Yes," I say with a kiss to her cheek. "You didn't think that was all I had in store for you, did you?" Her desire roars to life and her scent smacks my nose. She must be used to someone who doesn't plan ahead or someone with an inferior appetite to hers. My heart tightens as I dare to hope I am a match for her but only time will tell.

Confident I firmly implanted curiosity in her mind, I pull myself from the bed and put on a clean pair of pants from my dresser. With each movement, I can feel her aroused stare burning into my body. Her mind is spinning with possibilities, completely focused on my every movement. It makes a man feel like a god to have such an intelligent woman decipher him like a puzzle. In this moment, I am the only one in her universe. To add subterfuge, I gather the dirty clothes from the floor and the stage to start a load of laundry.

Alone in the kitchen, I top off the cats' food bowls. As I bend to the floor to present their dishes, I sneak a glance through my bedroom door. Betty has stretched her bonds taunt to watch me. We lock eyes but she doesn't cower or show a modicum of guilt. I blow my warrior princess a kiss and immediately admonish myself for calling her mine. Even in this intimate space, she would fight my possession of her to her last breath. She may be wearing the physical bonds but the ones she has placed on my heart are stronger.

I chastise myself for falling for a fake relationship ruse I had a hand in setting up while making a second batch of my snow-frozen cherry panna cotta. Would she be disappointed to know this isn't meaningless sex for me?

Donning a giant snowsuit and boots, I carry the plastic bags into the night. My vampire senses flare into the darkness to scan for Sluagh. Even though there is no one close, I shut and lock the door behind me. I have left Betty practically gift-wrapped, so I take zero chances of someone else getting inside. *Mine*. Using the snow blocking the dryer vent to bury the desserts, I kill two birds with one stone and I'm back in the house in a flash…unless you are tied up, left to imagine what happens next.

I must prepare my fiery princess for my cooler body invading her most intimate place. She probably has a clue of the temperature difference from her luscious mouth, but women can be unnerved by their temperature decreasing with penetration instead of increasing. Some of my former partners hated it so we parted ways. Having such low blood pressure produces a much lower skin temperature, everywhere on a vampire. Unlike a human erection, which is produced from mostly increased blood pressure for a small amount of time, a male vampire is constantly semi-erect, produced by tendons woven together in a lattice. The weave expands with blood pressure requiring less pressure to gain greater size. Size without added heat.

I grab two bowls from the cabinet with as much noise as possible just in case her mind has wandered or if her rest has morphed into sleep. One bowl is for hot water while the second is filled with loudly clinking ice cubes from my fridge dispenser. My last accessory is my softest kitchen washcloth.

I am welcomed to my bedroom with a glare of defiance. My princess doesn't like being left out of the planning. The sight of her fuming makes me chuckle which I do not dare allow to escape. I will get bitten, and her temper will detonate when I enjoy it. "Miss me?" I can't help but poke at her. She has flushed a warm pink from cheeks to cheeks. It is no surprise to me when she clamps onto my lower lip when I kiss her. If I had her consent, I would bite her back, *sigh*.

"We're going to play a game. Tell me the temperature—"

"I haven't played hot or cold since I was a child."

"But you never played my way…and if you have, let me believe you haven't." I settle between her knees, placing the bowls to my side and the washcloth submerged in the hot water.

"Your role is to be still enough we do not knock over the bowls while concentrating on the temperature difference you feel. Can you do that for me?"

A breathless "yes" floats to the ceiling from her

while I wring out the washcloth. I rub it over her with more love and care in my palm than I would admit to anyone. She moans loud enough to receive answering calls from my cats hiding in another room. The primal call to signal all animals on earth of an impending mating. The sound stops my breathing and causes the hairs on my body to stand on end. It is on the tip of my tongue to tell her how hard I have fallen for her, but the words catch in my throat. Tears form in my eyes as it hits me how long I have waited for the sound of her surrender.

"I will take that sound to mean hot," I say instead like a coward. "How about this?" I pop an ice cube in my mouth with the intention of lightly teasing her. She takes control by leaning into me, forcing my icy tongue to meet her with more aggression than I intend. A strangled cry rings out and I feel like an ass. I jolt away and slosh water on the bed while quickly returning the warm washcloth to lessen the shock.

"Again," she commands in a husky voice.

"Yes, Your Highness," I say around the ice cube. I reposition myself with my focus on pleasuring her. When she begins to pant with each swing of her hips, I shoot the ice cube from my mouth. She screams and quakes as her orgasm melts the ice. All my other plans fly out into the snow and I shuffle to my knees, dragging my pants to my down with claws.

"Nooo, fill me, Luc. I need you, Luc."

"I've got you, princess," I growl. I align our bodies and glide home.

"Yes, yes, yes!" She chants and I feel ten feet tall. She wiggles, squirms, and pulses around me greedily to dissolve my control. One slam into her has more force than intended and freeze with the fear I have injured her.

"More, Luc. Do that again. If you don't start moving—"

Her threat is cut off by resumed thrusting. She is my perfect playmate. The headboard slams into the wall at the tempo of my pistoning hips, along with the most beautiful melody I have ever heard — her cries of ecstasy. The harmony of our connection pulls the raging burn of my release along my spine. It is only when I flood her that it dawns on me, we are bare to one another. *Fuck.*

"This doesn't change anything," she says between pants.

"Of course not." I fail to hide the trepidation in my voice. After withdrawing, I reach for the washcloth and clean her thoroughly before removing her bonds. She tucks her body into a ball and sighs with contentment. The forgotten toys fall to the floor with a clatter and the bowls of liquid splash before I move them to the floor. I snag my spare down comforter from under the bed. Lifting my arm to drape the bedspread over us, I inadvertently invite her to snuggle. To my delight, she rubs her backside against my hip giving me the option to spoon her through the daylight hours. Nothing has changed. She's still playing a game while I am playing for keeps.

Chapter 22

I could wake up to this every day. Wrapped around a hard male body with a delicious soreness between my legs, this is how bliss feels. Luc's profile is barely visible in the darkened room. His mouth hangs open slightly and I feather kisses over it. "Forever," he grumbles, deep into his dreams. I shiver at the connotation of that dangerous word. He must have been shouting in his sleep to have woken me up. Too many years forcing myself to sleep during Ally's crying, nightmares, or screaming fits has conditioned me to shut out the world.

A crash out the window notifies me Luc wasn't the being who woke me up. I sit up in the dark. Bela and Christopher sit up as well. "So, you heard that too? Well, sic'em kitties," I whisper loudly in the hopes of waking the Prince of Darkness. He doesn't even move. I huff in disgust at myself for cowering behind a man, even if he is a saber-toothed, winged monster at times.

The house is freezing compared to Luc's embrace under the down comforter. I scamper to the closet to grab another hoodie. A stop at his dresser yields a pair of socks and mile-long sweatpants. Bundled up in my cotton armor, I sneak to the kitchen to peek out the window. The sweatpants hang over my feet muffling my steps on the hardwood floor. The grandfather clock tics as it stands at attention and the security system still glows as armed.

"Sluagh can't open doors," I reassure myself in a hissing whisper. The hairs on my neck stand on end. Would Gran have warded the vampires' houses? Could a vampire enter a warded house? I guess they could because they are patrons to Paulino's which houses the source of the wards. I crouch under the closest window to listen like an idiot. Sluagh glide or flutter upon approach, both motions make no sound.

Using my courage to stand at full height, I pull back the blackout curtains and poke my face between them. The gentle hills and fields look desolate now that their wild beauty has been smothered with a fresh blanket of snow. Lonely trees stand at attention over Luc's property in their glaze of ice, frozen limbs pointing in warning to those who dare to go outside.

The sunset reflects pinks, purples, and oranges over the snow. The snow is disturbed in a ring around the house with piles formed under all the windows as if someone or something has been trying to get inside. I scan the horizon repeatedly to catch a glimpse of the would-be intruder. The hairs on the back of my neck stand when a roaring sound emanates from the front yard.

Dammit. I left my hairclip weapons in Luc's room. I skid and slide to the front door. I grab the black gauzy curtain covering the window in the door. *One. Two. Three.* Yanking back the curtain, I come nose-to-nose with a golden-eyed polar bear.

"I'm here to rescue you." Her growls fog the glass between us with condensation. A furry paw reaches out to wipe it off with a high-pitched screech, like nails on a chalkboard.

"Stop it Ally or you will wake up Luc," I scold. I

hold up my index finger to her and return to the security panel. Hell yeah, the system is an older simple model with a simple "DISARM" button to disengage it.

"Don't worry Betty, I—"

"Get in here, and stop being so loud."

"Oh, is he prowling around? Stand behind me and I will eat him."

"Don't you dare, Ally! He's not my captor. He's my rescuer. Can you change? I'm getting creeped out talking to a bear with a red ponytail." The bear rolls her eyes and slips a pack from around her neck. Fur recedes, claws retract, and her snout shrinks. Her joints pop and crack while her skeleton adjusts to the change in species. All that's left in Luc's atrium is the shaking form of my hero-sister.

"Could you get my dress from the bag?"

I hand her the plain gray cotton dress which she pulls roughly over her head. I rummage through the bag to check her other supplies to find a rope, her cell phone, bottles of tincture bound together with vines, bandages, a utility knife, and a box of my green tea. "Oh Ally, you did rescue me," I whisper while throwing my arms around her. "Luc only has Earl Grey, so I have been drinking coffee. Let's go to the kitchen and make tea. I have so much to tell you."

"Perhaps you would like to start with why you are here and why you are dressed like a slob. That's my job." Ally tugs at the sweatpants dangling from my hips. I yank her by the arm to the kitchen and set a saucepan of water to boil on Luc's stove.

"These are Luc's clothes. I think my clothes need to go into the dryer. He started a load last night but got distracted before it was time to change it over." I sigh at the mental replay of my fantasy night with a vampire. Glowing brighter than the sun, I can't wait to debrief Ally on how the vampires are normal people who play video games, care for their pets, and make ice cream in the snow. Yes, they have a disease which makes them drink blood but they are not the creatures of nightmares Ryan hypes them up to be…if you ignore the five-inch fangs.

"I don't believe how at home you seem," Ally says as an eyebrow climbs to her hairline.

"Oh, Ally. I feel as fresh and new as the bright, white snow outside. As the flakes fell down, my depression lifted. In this house, I received over twenty-four hours of happiness."

"Happiness?"

"Yeah, Luc has been a great host since saving me from the Sluagh—"

"That's the second time you have called him Luc, Betty. What's going on?"

"We are kinda kindred spirits. I needed a distraction from my misery, and he needs a feminine touch…to his home…his house needs a feminine touch."

"It does resemble a carnival's haunted house in here…"

"Don't you know it. He docsn't even own a kettle or teapot."

"An oversight I will remedy as soon as you select one," rumbles Luc's sleepy voice. He saunters into the kitchen with his bathrobe hanging open and a pair of sweatpants matching my own. I sigh with longing at his adorable appearance from his bare feet to his bedhead. Ally turns to me with her jaw on the floor.

"Madam Commander, please excuse my

appearance," Luc says with a bow to my sister. "I wasn't expecting company and you have awoken me from my slumber. Thank you for bringing Betty's tea and staying to have a cup. She has been most helpful in educating me on robot vacuums, self-propelled mops, and other accouterments to make this haunted house into a home."

"No need to be formal," Ally says with a dismissing wave. "I should apologize for barging in here. Grant insisted we stop home before leaving for North Carolina so he could check on Bergan. When I came home to an empty house, I called Rosie who had Betty's empty car in front of her restaurant. She called Dr. V who had Betty's keys, cell phone, and a wild story about you flying away with her."

"So basically, you fueled the town's rumor mill by calling everyone I know," I grouse.

A distant rumbling startles us but puts a look of terror on Luc's face. "It's my garage door opener. Ryan took one of the remotes and will use it to visit unannounced."

"Well, that stops today," I snap at him.

Luc gives me pleading eyes, "can we trust her?"

I turn to Ally and beg, "if you want to return the favor for my beating up your every bully, this is it. If you really want to rescue me, please play along. Go with what Luc says and let him handle Ryan." I extend my pinky finger between us in our childhood symbol of sisterhood. She coils her pinky around mine without hesitation and nods at me.

"W-W-We can't lie to him, he'll smell it," Luc sputters.

"What?" I ask while Ally calmly asks: "can vampires smell lies?"

"Yes, it comes from smelling the emotions behind the words." He slaps his hand over his mouth. Rounded eyes stare at me with guilt.

"Let him come in. We can handle this."

Luc shakes his head. "I don't let him in, he just—"

"Well isn't this a pretty picture," Ryan says while entering the kitchen with outstretched arms. "The two most enchanting women on the planet and the Prince of Darkness can't even pull on a blazer." He drops a large bag and the garage remote on the kitchen counter.

"Good evening, Ryan," Ally says cheerfully. Her bright smile pulls Ryan like a magnet giving me the perfect opportunity to slide his remote into my hoodie pouch. *Thanks, Sis.*

"My dearest Alison," he says with a loud kiss to her hand. "I have a confession to make to you. When I saw you leave our grounds on foot, I was so worried. When I inquired to Grant as to your whereabouts, he became irate and mentioned a possible rescue here. I immediately followed to serve as a mediator between Lucien and yourself."

"You told Grant? Oh no, I snuck out." She grabs her phone from her pack and taps at it furiously.

"We were most confused as to why you would call it a rescue mission as you can imagine. He didn't know you were leaving, and I didn't know Betty needed to be rescued." The warmth in his eyes melts as he swings his gaze from Ally to me. It becomes murderous when he looks at Lucien.

My blood boils, bringing confused looks from both vampires. "How dare you barge here and—"

"Barge in? I was bringing Lucien blood," Ryan says pointing to the bag on the counter. "He is quite in need of someone to look after him."

"You see Ryan," Ally says calmly while still looking at her phone. "Betty is a monster when she has a caffeine headache. She drinks green tea all night long and Lucien was trying to get her to drink Earl Grey which is too bitter for her. I was on a rescue mission. I was rescuing Lucien from my sister's attitude. Betty, is the water boiling yet? Because you are unbearable. See what I did there?"

Ryan laughs too loudly at my sister's bad pun before saying, "for a moment, I thought you didn't approve of Betty being his mistress."

"I never asked her permission. She's not my mom. She's my sister," I blaze at him. My aggressive pouring of the hot water into mugs becomes a performance to drive Ally's story home.

"She's the leader of the shifter pack, isn't she?"

"Do I look like a shifter to you? I don't belong to any pack or anyone—"

"Except for Lucien, correct?"

I can only blush in return. I freeze with the memory of being tied to his bed and how much I enjoyed belonging to him. We must get rid of our rescuers and talk. He lied or at least omitted to tell me about his ability. My sting is my own fault. If I hadn't forgotten about our deal, then I wouldn't have considered myself close to him.

We will end up getting hurt if we don't clarify our boundaries. Is Ryan asking if I'm Luc's mistress because he is supposed to marry another vampire? Not that I have developed deeper feelings because he's great…masterful…in the sack, but I would like the one-night stand to be more than one night. In fact, a no-strings-attached mistress sounds like a title I wouldn't mind having for a while.

Both vampires inhale loudly until their chests puff out. How can I hide my stupidity for developing feelings for Luc if they keep breathing them in? The emotions they smell are ones I wish to remain hidden. I don't give my consent, but no one asked. Luc has a goofy grin spreading over his face while Ryan looks like he's trying to solve a rubrics cube.

"Interesting," Ryan says slowly. "It would seem we are too late for the permission phase."

Mortification blazes in my chest, traveling to my cheeks. They are reading my private thoughts with their noses. I feel violated with their every inhale. Another sniff and my feelings of betrayal hit Lucien's nose. He looks at his feet and shuffles them around. I continue to stare until he meets my gaze. His grief-stricken expression tells me everything I need to know.

Vampires stick together. This affair is just an affair because I will never compete with his bond to the vampire colony. I will always be just a breeder or worse, a source of food. No human builds a life with their food, except for maybe my sister the green witch with her garden. Perhaps the unhealthy connection is in our DNA which is why I was susceptible to Lucien and his games.

Alison slices the tension with the diplomacy of the leader she is. "Thank you, Ryan, for escorting me here, but as you can see, no one is in danger. My sister and I are going to catch up over a cup of tea if Lucien would be so gracious as to find a private place for us."

"It would be my pleasure," Lucien says with sagging shoulders. Hearing the word pleasure escape his lips stabs my heart. I sink into myself while depression pounds at my brain. I should be accepting my punishment from Evan's memory. Lucien is the first man I let close to me and look how it turned out. *He's not a man, he's a royal vampire, stupid.* I conveniently forgot vampires are notorious for seducing human victims. I deserve to be played for letting my guard down. One of these times, I will learn a soft heart crushes easily.

Ally grabs the two full mugs from the counter and turns her back on Ryan and me. "Show me the way, Lucien," she commands. My sister did rescue me. Rescue me from humiliation but a rescue all the same.

Lucien leads us to the living room, pushing a dust-coated vase to the far side of the coffee table. "I don't suppose they make robot dusters." I can't even look him in the eyes. He can't see my hurt right now. Not that it matters, he can smell it.

"In this case, you could use your dishwasher," I reply curtly.

"This is fine. Thank you, Lucien."

"N-No problem. I can understand the need to escape Ryan."

"No, I mean thank you for taking care of my sister. She's more delicate than she is willing to admit. You sheltered her while I was away, and I will never forget it. Any favor you have of me, please ask."

"Thank you," he says with a formal bow and my heart sinks. He earned a political favor. I plop into a chair with the plan to hide under it until he adds, "but I didn't shelter her for the pack. I wanted time with her…by ourselves. My motives weren't pure." His cold palm grasps my shoulder firmly so I cannot ignore him. "You cannot smell it, to verify its authenticity so I'm telling you, Betty. I have enjoyed every second of your company."

"Well, I will be sure to reimburse you for any extra expenses."

"Great, I ask to be paid with time. After you are finished with Alison, I want a conversation with you before I head to Bergan." Oh God, he sounds like he's saying goodbye. This is going to hurt.

He bows to Alison but kisses my hand. I get the familiar zing of electricity up my arm and tears prick at the corners of my eyes. He rushes out of the room as if it is on fire and shuts the door with a clap.

"Sit and spill it quietly because they hear as well as we do." Ally sits delicately on a couch which calls a cloud of dust to envelop us. *Hiss!* A cat dashes across the room causing Ally to screech in response. I open the door to let Bela escape before shutting it tightly again.

"What was that?"

"Lucien rescued two cats, Bela and Christopher. You evicted Bela from her latest resting place," I say, returning to my tea.

"He rescues cats…and then names them after Hollywood vampires…"

"Bela Lugosi." I smile at Luc's self-deprecating joke. He could have an ego the size of Kentucky but doesn't.

"And Christopher Lee," Ally says smiling in return. "I'm glad he isn't as bad as I thought. That's actually sweet and funny."

"I took bags out to my car and got locked out of Dr. V's office. Five Sluagh encircled me. Lucien scared them off before I got hurt. He picked me up and we flew here. He hosted me during the snowstorm, that's all."

"That's all?"

"No, but it is a show for Ryan," I say, pulling her head closer to mine. "We made a deal to fake a relationship while you were away to fool Ryan into leaving not only Lucien but you alone." I take a big gulp of my now lukewarm tea and feel the rush of the caffeine.

"Me? Why would you do that?" She takes a drag on her own mug and rolls it around her mouth.

"—To keep the peace between you and Grant."

"Oh Betty," she says with a fierce hug. "You are too brave. Let's get you out of here."

"It is too late, Ally. I had sex with him and can't just run away." I throw back the rest of my tea with a flourish.

"Oh, Betty…"

"Totally worth it. Lucien said he wants to talk so I'm sure it is to amicably part ways."

"Knock, knock," Ryan says opening the door. Lucien is behind him with a sheepish expression on his face. "I wanted to offer my escort to Alison before I depart. Lucien's car is still snowed in. Perhaps you would like to fly with me?"

A look of disgust flashed across Alison's face before she smiles sweetly at Ryan. "I do love the snow. Will you fly over me while I run? I need your protection as much as I need to feel the snow under my paws."

Ryan's eyes flash red before he answers, "it would be my pleasure."

"Is there anything you need before I go?" She asks me the question while standing and handing her mug to Lucien.

"Shoes, if you brought shoes to change into, I would like them. I only brought one shoe with me." Lucien turns red when Ryan turns to him incredulously. *Good.* It is time for him to share in the embarrassment.

"I can't help but only because I didn't bring shoes. When have you ever known me to wear shoes, let alone carry an extra pair?"

"I forgot Dirtball." At the use of her childhood nickname, we hug tightly. I can dissociate from Lucien because I will have Ally to lean on. Well, in Strawberry, I am never alone. The feeling is more comforting or at least less annoying than when I first arrived. I guess it took me a while to understand the magic of this town.

"If you don't mind, I would like a few seconds in the atrium to change," she says to the vampires before shutting us in the living room. Lucien and I look at each other with matching frowns. The need to be alone with him is raking at my heart. It burns that we will not have what the honest intimacy of during the snowstorm. That magical moment has passed. It is time to move on.

Ally scratches at the door and Ryan opens it to reveal the large polar bear. He puts his palm on her back with ownership and her fur bristles. He nods to me while Lucien bows so deeply, he nearly knocks his forehead on the coffee table. As the leaders leave the house, the door slams like a judge's gavel.

"Here, Lucien," I say, returning his garage remote. "I got it back from Ryan. Hide it."

"I-I want you to have it. C-Can't it still be Luc, not Lucien?"

"After you played me? I thought we were co-conspirators or even friends."

"I'm sorry. There wasn't a moment…no wait…that's a lie too," he stutters while running his fingers through his hair. "Dammit, I got addicted to the confidence of knowing you liked me too. No anxiety, speech impediment, or awkward silences. I liked being able to read the real you. I'm not sorry I liked being the one who knows you best."

I choke on the words I want to say. I want him to know me better than anyone else and that scares the hell out of me. I want him to gain confidence from his time spent with me. He can rise from Ryan's shadow. *What the hell—I fell for him.*

"I smell shock just so you know. You can compare that with your feelings to gauge how sensitive I am." I can only stare at him with wild eyes as memories of our time together flash through my mind at a rapid pace. *When did I fall for him?*

"Look, you don't have to reply. When we are alone and I smell an emotion, I will ask you about it okay. I really screwed up, didn't I?"

"Yeah, but the pieces still fit."

"The emotion smelling is not all. We were unprotected when we…last night when I…dammit…I don't know how to ask…"

"I am not on the pill…Luc," I say to put him out of his misery.

"That's what I thought. I swear I'm clean. Oh God, I sound horrible. I have been celibate since moving to Strawberry and I was tested when I entered the country, not by the authorities, but by Ryan and Dr. V."

"Luc, stop…"

"Back to Luc"—he sighs of relief— "Thank you for taking me back." He pulls me into his embrace. *Stupid vampire,* he never lost me…I mean he never had me, right?

One inhale of his rich scent and I am a goner. I lift my face to receive his kiss. This kiss is tender enough to coax the tears from the corners of my eyes. His lips pull at mine with tiny nips until I open for his tongue. Our kiss becomes a dance of mouths saying much more than either of us is willing to admit. He pulls me closer and the waves of emotion within me calm.

"I can fix this. I promise. Molina has been experimenting on the morning after pill to learn about vampire contraceptives. Come to Bergan and she will give us one of her pills discreetly."

A lump forms in my throat. If I'm pregnant, he wants to get rid of it. "I never thought to ask what happens if a human is pregnant by a vampire." It is safest if I stick to the practical issues of a possible pregnancy. I push my feelings in the deepest recesses of my heart in the hopes he doesn't smell my disappointment.

"Human-vampire couplings always produce vampire offspring but don't worry. Molina is experimenting with hormone therapies used for human fertility or infertility advances. She is trying to build a vampire fertility drug."

Do I really want to vampire baby right now? I have the nursing exam, my new job, and Sluagh chasing me. Guilt crashes into me like a runaway train. I am contemplating carrying Luc's baby when I should be building my life and getting over Evan. *Evan*. His name floats through my mind without the usual sadness. Our story was tragic, but it is over. My anger toward him has dissolved. He chose drugs but I can choose life. I mentally shut the door on that chapter and smile up to Luc, the vampire who set me free.

"You don't have to worry about any of that. I will be more careful…if…that is if…I would never presume," he stammers while waving his hands behind my back. It is as if he is trying to draw out the words with invisible strings. His pale skin turns pink and he closes his eyes. I stand on tiptoes to brush my lips on his ear.

"Luc, I'm going to bang you again." The air shoots out of his lungs in a *whoosh* at my words.

"I made more ice cream," he blurts out. "Oh my God, that was not the appropriate response but that's what my brain elected to tell you. Why do I sound brilliant in my head but like dumbass outside of it?"

"It is part of your charm," I say before kissing his nose. "Lead me to the ice cream."

One more quick kiss and we are running to the back door of the house, laughing, and shoving each other into the walls. The sound of the cats skittering over the wood floor accompanies us. Real or fake, my heart doesn't care. I am his mistress.

Chapter 23

I marvel at the difference between our first and tonight's flight. Betty stretches her arms out and leans into the wind. Legs wrapped tightly around my waist, she trusts me implicitly to carry her twenty feet in the air. Her face is glowing with happiness. She smells of euphoric bliss. "I'm freeeee," she screams, pulling laughter from my belly. As scared as I was when Ryan disrupted our dream existence, I have laughed more tonight than any of my previous nights in the US.

Our first stop is Dr. V's office where Betty retrieves not only her keys and wallet but also her missing shoe. Dr. V greets Betty with a hug. "Crazy kids, I was so worried I would be called out to Lucien's haunted mansion to repair injuries. Thank you so much for keeping in touch, so I had updates for Alison. I wasn't the only one worried."

"She barreled through the snow, fueled only by her worry, to his house in her polar form." Betty's musical laugh softens her scorn at her sister's antics. Dr. V fades into the background as I stand captivated by her. She tells the story of her rescue while painting me as a white knight and my heart swells with pride. How do you tell a woman you rescued her because you want your life filled with her laughter?

Especially when that woman has panic attacks triggered by displays of commitment like James's proposal? If I got down on one knee, would she pass out? Not that I am planning on it, but... I wonder if I could ask Alison about the trigger of the panic attacks without Betty exploding at me, or if Grant would know.

My daydreams release me when Dr. V pulls at my elbow. "You did a great job, Betty. He doesn't have any residual crystals in his joints. You should thank your lucky stars she was the one you rescued. I hope you rewarded her," Dr. V says manipulating my shoulder. I send a conspiratory smirk to Betty as I picture her sprawled out on my sheets. Sheets that I won't wash until I have a guaranteed date, she will return to them.

"He makes ice cream with snow. He made it for me twice so I would say we are even," Betty chimes in. I love how her quick thinking saves me when my brain sputters. I have just enough time to recover.

"I am grateful for her expertise and your instructions. I cannot say how much of an asset you are to the vampire community, my family, and my plight." How one man could extend the life expectancy of the vampire community twenty years or more is incredible. Without the stem cell injections, I would be dodging infections and probably headed for my last rites.

"I like being a contributing member of the colony which keeps me safe. It's quid pro quo," Dr. V. says with a clap on my shoulder.

"Any word on the IVIG?" When I ask the question, Betty turns to me with a puzzled countenance. I can practically hear her mind churning out possibilities. "I hope to have Terika here by the spring," I add more for Betty's benefit than Dr. V's clarification.

"I'm set up whenever she can make it. The immunoglobin infusions are available online but I need her weight to calculate her dose. If we try to do too much too fast, it will risk her kidney health."

Betty is about to burst with questions. "Does Terika have a high viral load? Or an antibiotic-resistant bacterial infection? What else has she tried?"

"Terika has pneumonia and the healers in the Old Country are using treatments from the Dark Ages. Dr. V came up with the idea of boosting her immune system as a whole since the infection seems to be antibiotic-resistant. It has been my intention to bring her here since I met Dr. V. Now I fear she is running out of time." Tears clog my throat and give my voice a croaking quality.

"What has held her in the Old Country for so long?" Betty asks the question with defiance radiating from her.

"Mostly money, but also Ryan has to approve the transport of vampires. We can't risk discovery by using commercial airlines. If I were king, I would invest in a private jet to bring patients or better yet, vampires who wish to set up satellite offices to continue Dr. V's work over there." Dr. V nods while I speak and Betty's eyes light up.

"You will be the king who brings life to the colony, literally."

"That's what I am working toward, with the assistance of Dr. V and you." I rub my hair in frustration. My wrist hits my earring, and I am reminded of my father and his too-short reign.

"Speaking of assistance, I want to walk next door to thank Rosie before she closes for the night. Her food bundle saved us during the snowstorm."

"Better hurry then," Dr. V replies as he ushers us to the door.

I step into the deep snow, relieved she is wearing

two shoes even though they are glittery heels instead of sensible boots. I add a pair of tiny boots to my mental shopping list. Having an extra pair of shoes at my house only makes sense, I reassure myself. *Right*.

"Betty, I'm going to run down to Josh's for a sec. Could you wait for me at Rosie's?"

"Wait for you?"

"You didn't think we were going to part ways before dawn, did you?"

"You said you have to work."

"I will show you the lab and you can keep me company. That is…if you don't have somewhere you would rather be," I say, losing my nerve.

"I will drive us over." My chest inflates and I beam back at her. She opens the restaurant door, and a crowd of werewolves nearly topples out onto her. It would seem the rumor mill has sent spies to learn of Betty's activities. I can't resist. I place my hand firmly on her ass while grabbing her chin with the other hand. I plunder her mouth for the loudest gossips in Strawberry to see. *Mine*. The word typifies my posture, my gesture, and my deepest desires. When I withdraw from her, she stares with a dazed expression and swollen lips.

"I won't be but a minute." I open my wings with a whoosh that echoes over the village green. The flight is only four shop fronts, but I have always loved putting on a performance. The werewolves cower at my display of strength. Giddy with excitement over the dream in my head, I must talk to Forger Josh, not Auto Josh, but Betty doesn't need to know that yet.

"Lucien! Y'all the only vampire without a bill to settle and y'all the one I see," calls tall, willowy Auto Josh while throwing his arms in the air. His fingertips brush the ceiling. How many times has he smacked it? He stands behind his case of chocolates placing cellophane bags of hearts on the shelf. Josh's artistry is incredible and a contradiction to his occupation as the gas station owner.

"You know if you hit up Ryan, he will settle all the bills of the colony. I hate that they take advantage of your kindness. Having the ability to get gasoline after sunrise is invaluable to us," I say after shaking his hand. I am just over six feet tall and considered slim, but Josh has got me beat. The giraffe shifter must be close to seven feet tall with the same weight load.

"I will have to email Ryan. David's bill is outrageous."

"So is David," I say with a knowing smile.

"What brings you in, if it is not a bill to settle?"

"Forger Josh, is he in?"

"Yes, but I didn't think vampires needed weapons when they have more claws per pound than anyone in Strawberry." His suspicion lifts an eyebrow to his hairline.

"I had my father's royal ring converted to an earring when he died. Now I want to design another ring with it." I look over my shoulder like a teenager buying contraband. I don't want many residents knowing of this, in case they mistake it for a coup to take the colony from Ryan. I take the silver-encased ruby from my ear and squeeze it in my hand to channel my father's strength. Dad won Mom by being the consummate romantic. He would be so happy I am doing this.

"Josh will be ecstatic—"

"Ecstatic about what?" A second Josh approaches the counter, wiping his hands on a towel. I guess the two would have a cleanliness agreement to keep chocolates next to the auto bay.

"I would like you to convert this to a ring." I drop my earring into his outstretched hand. "It was once my father's royal ring, but he is no longer with us."

"It's a gorgeous ruby. What kind of ring were you thinking?"

"I had hoped you could melt the silver into wires and weave it with iron threads over the stone like a two-toned basket."

"Sluagh repellent?"

"Yes, but also a symbol...I want the basket to be heart-shaped..." My words freeze both men. I have managed to shock them both. It doesn't help that my face aches from stretching into a wide grin. My brain vacillates on the correct words while they dare each other to ask the recipient of the ring.

"Vampire bride, Lucien?"

I look at them but picture Betty in my mind. My image of her asleep in my bed, wearing my shirt with her freckles uncovered by makeup, warms my heart. "Yes, but she has no idea. If you could hold that info close to the vest, I would appreciate it. I mean...even...Ryan doesn't know."

"Well, it is an honor. Your father's ruby? She must be special. Do you have her ring size?" Josh studies the earring with the excitement of a child on Christmas morning. His enthusiasm for jewelry design dissipates my nervous energy and I feel confident in my decision.

"I don't but you made the leafy ring for Alison's Yule gift from—"

The smiles fall from both men's faces as they assume defensive postures. Hostility radiates off the two men, stinging my nose. Forger Josh allows me to see his inner feline by sprouting claws around the earring in his palm. "What does this project have to do with Madam Commander, Lucien?"

"N-N-Nothing to do with Ryan, Grant, or Alison. I just…Betty is the same size as her sister," I stammer.

Forger Josh's claws recede, his shoulders droop, and his smile turns thoughtful. The once hostile scent evaporates. "Are you proposing to Betty?"

"I think so…" My smile increases ten-fold. An image of me singing to her in the moonlight in my gazebo flashes across my mind. The heat lamps will shine off her skin as she glows pink with happiness. I will slip the ring on her finger and she will be not my mistress, but my wife.

"When?" The question pops my daydream like a soap bubble. Is this too soon? Will she panic over a proposal from me? Should I ask Grant or her parents first? Panic squeezes my chest as the magnitude of this decision weighs on me.

My posture must have changed because Josh rescues me from my thoughts. "I can email you a group of sketches later tonight. When you select your favorite, I can have it crafted in two days. Take as much time as you necessary to use it," he says and puts his hand on my back in support.

"Thanks. This is fast but it feels right," I say to reassure the feline shifter as much as myself. I leave the auto shop with a box of condoms in my pocket and emotions swirling around my chest like an angry swarm of bees. I get halfway down the sidewalk when Betty steps onto the ice. She wavers when her heel missteps. Without my usual hesitation, I open my wings and fly to her aid. As she lands in my arms, I memorize how perfect. She turns toward me and her shock melts away.

"You have magnificent timing," she whispers. I gently set her back on her feet aware of the blinds flapping inside the restaurant. It is not a question of the wolfpack watching us in order to report to Alison, but rather a question of how many werewolves are watching to report to Alison.

I hope she's right. A hasty proposal could signal the end of us. I will pour my creativity into asking; no sappy poetry on one knee for my princess. I can't risk triggering her panic attacks. If only I had the courage to ask for their story. She talks about her life before Strawberry with such fondness, I can't glean their source. The only person she doesn't open up about is the mysterious Evan from her nightmare. All I know is that he's dead, but a dead what? Boyfriend or more? My brain sinks into murky territory. How do I measure up to him? She's perfect for me but was he the one who was perfect for her?

Chapter 24

"I'm the Head of Microbiology, not as powerful as Grant, but I have an office, a budget, and a lab of my own. I'm excited to show you my lab. Nate is going to work for me plus a new microbiologist," Luc gushes. His enthusiasm is adorable but if he knew the source of my nervousness, he would back off. Too bad I am not honest enough to change his opinion of me yet. Part of my growing fondness for him stems from Luc seeing me as a good person.

If Grant catches me at Bergan with my legal issues, he will blow a hole through the roof. Strawberry seems like a fairytale and unfortunately, I got carried away with its charm. Someone actively being investigated for drug dealing has no business stepping foot into a pharmaceutical company. How do I convince Luc to allow me to escape without letting on about my troubles? I would hate the warm feelings in his embrace to cool because of my status as a person of interest.

Oh, Evan, why? From beyond the grave, Evan's evil deeds have managed to hold me captive. How could I be so stupid as to believe I could move on? I may never be free. I must tell Luc before he gets in trouble. He could be fired. Terika needs him to fund her trip to America, for medical treatment. I can't jeopardize all his dreams for a tour of his lab.

"I smell nervousness but don't worry, you will be

there with me. I thought we could stop by the grocers and try cooking together tonight…if you want…if you don't have anything more important," he stammers when I have navigated around the village green.

"I wish I could, but I have to study my NCLEX books. The exam is at the end of the month and I need to be ready." We pass Tyler the grocer clearing the roads and Miles, the reptile shifter, who is clearing the Bergan parking lot. The plowing of snow is a reminder. Our fairytale arrangement was temporary, and this is a day of reckoning.

"I thought you said your memory is photographic."

"I have to see it to memorize it, but I'm pleased you are put out. You may even miss me," I tease. The remarks sound hollow to my ears. Who am I kidding? I would give anything to rush back to his place and hide in our fantasy. My heart sinks as this situation goes from bad to worse. "If Alison is back, then Grant is too." I point to the flashy BMW parked by the front door.

"You don't want him to see you?"

"More than anything." I park on the opposite side of the building. Ever the gentleman, Luc comes to my side of the car to help me cross the parking lot in heels. I cling to him like a security blanket while goosebumps break out along my arms. My fear is diffusing from my skin like a fog machine and sadly I know he smells it.

"You get along with him, right?" His claws emerge and his fangs extend to defend my honor.

"Not really, oh it's not like that so put the stabbers away. Luc, I…I…" My stammering sounds just like his. If Aurora heard me now, she would die laughing. She is always teasing Ally about acting more and more like Grant. She has a hypothesis that mates start to fuse personalities and copy each other's mannerisms after a while. Not that Luc and I are mates, although we are here to get birth control.

"Are you making fun of me?"

"Hell no," I say with recovered bravado. "I just don't know how to say I don't belong inside Bergan."

He takes both of my hands in his, using his foot to prop open a side door. "Betty, I want to remind you that in vampire society, an unmarried vampire's mistress belongs at his side. If this is going to work, this is where you are required to be."

I'm not sure how to take that. I want to be with him in a larger capacity if my history with Evan will allow it. *You can only be a breeder, stupid, but at least you are good at that.* Never in my wildest dreams would I ever think I would wish to be something other than human. Feelings aside, Luc is right. For our ruse to work, I must be seen with him…just not by Grant.

"We can ascend to the labs from here. Since the blood bank is on the third floor, it is a vampire hangout. Grant's office is on the second floor with Brad's staff and most of the shifters. He won't come up unless he's looking for data. I'm hoping to collect a bunch tonight to lay on his desk. I will keep him busy for you."

Perfect. I sprint up a couple of stairs pulling Luc by the arm. "Stop, dammit stop," he says, catching me by the waist. A whoosh of his wings and we are at the top of the stairwell. He activates the door with another thumbprint scanner.

"That's an incredible trick." I am shaking like a leaf but when has that ever stopped me? I look to Luc for security. Pathetic how I have come to depend on him like this.

Creeping into the hallway, I am assaulted by red lights. An HVAC system on steroids drowns out the usual sounds of an inhabited building. This floor would make a great setting for a slasher film. Luc grabs my hand and pulls me down the hallway. I try to peek into each door we pass but they are blocked with mirrors. Placing my fingers against one of the mirrors, there is no gap between my finger and its reflection. These are two-way mirrors to warn of intruders. What intruders would get into a lab with a fingerprint scanner but not break open the lab doors? No wonder the shifters are suspicious of the alliance with the vampires.

"That darkened lab is Molina's. She usually doesn't get here until after midnight because she arrives with Brad…And this is the blood bank. Come in, princess, we have time to kill. See I don't need you to be a food source…unless you ask sweetly." He kisses my hand before letting go to sign out a couple of bags of blood. For such a happening hangout, I have yet to see another vampire. I look over my shoulder as if Grant is going to jump out from behind a refrigerator. I must get my wits about me. Grant has the stealth abilities of a garbage truck.

"You know, you didn't need to take out your earring. I made fun of it because I liked it," I say to release some tension. I guess Luc is the last one on earth to realize how sexy pirates are.

"Oh…I…thanks, I don't wear it when it is too cold," he says pulling on his ear. "I don't like the shock when it hits my neck."

"Funny, a vampire that doesn't like a prick on the neck." He smiles in return and my insides turn to goo.

I wander around the blood bank remarking on how

the glass-front fridges look more like vending machines than the hospital fridges. Bags of blood of uniform type hang in each fridge. The labels above the hooks display attributes like "Zero percent caffeine", "Lightly Caffeinated", "Regular" and "Ultra Caffeinated". There are similar levels displayed for nicotine, THC, naproxen sodium, estradiol, progesterone, alcohol, and diabetic ketones. Dr. V warned me of picky eaters, but this is hilarious.

"To my lair, princess," Luc calls from the door. He holds out his hand and I am compelled to his side. He tucks it in his elbow and hangs a blood bag from his lips. I get swept through the door like a Victorian lady and become a part of the now bustling hallway. It must have been too early when we arrived because it is wall-to-wall vampires with matching scrubs, black hair, and eerie eyes.

Every pair of reversed-pupil eyes judges me as they greet Luc as "Your Highness" or "Sire". Being so comfortable with him, I forgot he is royalty in the vampire world. He is the pinnacle of his station as the vampires fall into each other to bow to him. No one dares to ask who I am, but they will gossip once a door closes behind us. This is exactly what we need to continue to fool Ryan. I just hope Grant is as anti-social at work as he is at family gatherings.

At the door at the end of the hallway, Luc activates a third thumbprint scanner. "Not every vampire has access and certainly not Grant." *Well, hot damn.* We may get away with this after all.

"Wow, Luc, you keep your lab like your house." I step around piles of science debris to enter the disaster area.

"This mess is a genius at work." He lays his empty blood bag on a pile of trash.

"Aren't you afraid of the interviewing microbiologists seeing this? Grant will have cubs if he sees your genius covered with…Ewww, gross. I thought it was liquid on that stack of papers, but it has hardened to agar. Luc, there are colonies on it! You may have an outbreak on your hands."

"Emily from HR will require my attendance on phone screenings first so I will have up to a week's notice before they visit."

"Aren't you scared of an FDA inspection? Your ass is grass if one of them were to see this filth." I slowly spin around to take in all of Luc's mess.

"The FDA inspections provide an agenda the day they arrive so I will have enough notice to clean this up—" He pauses to fold his arms over his chest. "No one can get in here besides Ryan, Nate, and myself. The FDA would have to make special arrangements to enter at night because Nate is in England."

"Not forever. You gather your work stuff, and I am going to clean up your pigsty. Really, Luc." I grab a giant pair of gloves from the dispenser by the door and snap them on with a crack. He grumbles about Ryan being right about something while grabbing a cart from under a teetering pile of binders.

"I'm going to fetch my plates from George's lab." He pulls a lab coat over his clothes.

"Will you give a secret knock, so I let you in?"

"No," he says with an adorable look of confusion. "I will use the thumbprint scanner." So much for us being like Bonnie and Clyde, my Clyde would miss half the hand signals. I hide behind a pile of books at the door opening until it clicks shut. I start bagging trash on the opposite side of the room in case I need to hide in the aggregate again. It takes thirty minutes for Luc, clad in scrubs, to return with a crash of his cart into the class II cabinet. Stacks of agar plates sway precariously on top of the sagging cart.

"My God, Luc, you have hundreds of plates."

"Ugh, don't remind me. I have tried to enumerate these dilution stacks of plates twice already. The rest of them are for DNA isolation and PCR verification. I'm counting on you to keep me from being disturbed so I can get these numbers once and for all."

"Those three experiments will take more than one night. How do you plan on getting all of it done?"

"I guess that's why I practically live here. I need a manager to space out the experiments into manageable chunks. It was feast or famine until Grant started driving the projects."

"What is it like working for Grant?"

"Like drinking from a fire hose," he says with a chuckle.

"If you have smaller PPE, I will jump in and help."

"Every room is supplied with small, medium, and large PPE per OSHA regulations. Mine is just buried under the pile of lab coats by the door. How are you at counting dots?"

I give him a side-eyed smile before digging through the pile to a plastic apron, face shield, and Tyvek sleeves. He freezes in loading plates into the cabinet to watch me garb up. "What?"

"You don PPE like a pro. Only someone who has worked in labs for a while can double glove over double sleeves that fast."

"I'm studying to be a nurse, dumbass. You wouldn't want me to be slow getting on my own protective gear, would you? Oh, I'm sorry sir if you could die a little slower, I need to glove and gown first." My words drip with sarcasm. Luc throws his head back with laughter and resumes lifting a bucket of concentrated bleach into the cabinet.

I dump a stack of lab journals and computer printouts on the floor to reveal Luc's desk chair. I wheel it to the hood and sit before the glass sash. "Where should I start?"

"I don't know, hold on"—he rifles through a stack of papers— "I must check the method between steps. Improvising the protocol is an automatic deviation which is Grant-speak for a buttload of paperwork, meetings and administrative pain."

"Why do you keep it across the room if getting out to check it requires new PPE?"

"I can't hold it outside with one hand and do my work inside with the other." He swings his hair back before treating me to an eye-roll.

"Okay Smarty-pants, then you should realize your class II cabinet is attached to your fully-wired glovebox."

"Yes, so I can pass work back and forth between them without exposing the room to whatever I am growing. I cannot put the paperwork in the glovebox. It would require decon to come back out."

"You also haven't grounded your metal structure so while electricity flows horizontally, a magnetic field coils around the beast."

"So?"

"So,"—I pull my hairclip off my ponytail and grab

his paperwork out of his hands— "with a piece of metal, you can attach your instructions right in front of your nose. No mess, no fuss." I place the papers against the cabinet and use my hairclip to anchor them in place.

"Ta-da!"

"Neat trick, you have already saved me the time I take walking back and forth." Luc steps aside to dock his phone into a speaker system. Vintage punk music rocks through the lab. "I am so appreciative I may even serenade you."

"I can't believe you never used that shortcut in college. I took one year of microbiology and I learned that trick from the older students. You must have wasted tons of time on your dissertation…"

"What dissertation?"

"Your Ph.D.…." I stop when he shakes his head.

"I am next in line for the throne. Professors fell over themselves to get their names on my transcript. Everything I know about Micro I have learned here, on the fly." He busies himself opening bags of plates with shaky fingers.

"You know what? I respect you more for it. Most royal brats would be content with a desk job, taking credit for the work of the little people."

"Thanks, little person. Here's a marker. By royal decree, count the dots."

I count dots for hours, singing to his playlist. I write the numbers on the plate lids and place them in an array at Luc's instructions. He isolates the colonies required for digestion and DNA extraction before joining me in enumerating. When we are finished the entire three-foot by six-foot stainless-steel cabinet is covered with numbered lids.

"Almost there and I can't believe—"

"Shhhh, it's Patty and Ryan approaching."

Fear dances down my spine. Patty is Grant's right hand and Ryan has access to this room. If he lets her in, Grant will know about my visit. I quickly de-garb and step behind my favorite mountain of microbiology magazines. Lucien secures the plate he is counting and withdraws from the cabinet as well. I look to him to save me, but his brain seems to have short-circuited. He stands like a statue listening to the increasing argument. My heart pounds in my ears.

"I don't care who you are, Ryan. This is my first project and I'm not going down in flames because Lucien can't count dots on a plate. Grant trusted me to get this ANDA out the door before the momentum on our other projects kicks up and I'm going to kick vampire ass until that happens," yells a female voice from the door. I assume it is Patty's voice, but I hardly heard her say a word at the Yule party. The quiet, plain, ornithic shifter sounds like she's ready to peck Lucien's eyes out.

"My dear, don't fret—" Ryan's voice is approaching at a rapid pace.

"Don't you patronize me. This doesn't concern you. I just need you to open the door to his lab, which by the way is a violation of personnel controls. We need accessibility for QA internal inspectors to lead the FDA through there. As long as my project is going on in there, I should have access," she rants.

"I have a plan," I whisper when Luc joins my hiding spot. I pull off my hoodie and pants to toss them to the door.

"Consider this payback." I tuck my fingers into the collar of his scrub top and rip it open. His chest tints pink with the glow from his eyes. It is covered with a matrix of scars.

"Perfect. I can keep your eyes glowing." Despite the urgency of the situation, I kiss each scar. I smear my lipstick down his chest creating a line to his waistband. Loosening the laces, he is forced to hold his pants up with curling claws.

"I can't let Ryan walk in and see your undergarments."

"Credibility, my dear," I whisper along his neck. He unfurls his wing to wrap around me while coaxing my arms around his neck. Someone standing at the door would see my bare arms and exposed straps, just enough to get the point. Luc lowers his head to capture my lips as a few gentle beeps herald the arrival of our visitors.

To my elation, Ryan enters alone and slams the door behind him. "Lucien, I hope to God you have something to give to Patty. Where the hell are you? Why aren't you working? Oh…"

"Pssst, Ryan over here," I whisper. "You can't let Patty catch us."

"I should say not," he replies with an evil twist to his lips. "A little scandalous, even for you, Lucien. Do you have anything I can give Patty to get rid of her?"

"The DNA isolates are ready to be taken down to George's lab on the cart. They can have PCR results to her by the end of the day. Those plates in the cabinet are her enumerations. I will have the data to her shortly."

"Perfect, I will give you some privacy," Ryan says with a punctuated snap of gloves. He grabs the rack of test tubes on the counter and heads for the door. I shrink into Luc's wingspan as it opens and shuts. I strain my hearing to listen through the doorway.

"See my dear, you are on schedule and Lucien will drop enumeration numbers to you tonight. He is working diligently—"

"I'll bet. Tonight. I need my data tonight, Ryan, or I will have to bring in Grant. I wish Nate was back from vacation to push Lucien along," Patty says with a cooling temper. Their footsteps fade into the background of the noise in the hallway and Luc's sudden laughter.

"Oh my God! You are wild," he says while spinning us around. "I can't believe you did that!"

"What? Use Ryan's master plan against him? It only worked because of your horrible reputation."

"A reputation I'm about to earn." He retrieves a box of condoms from his jacket pocket. He takes one out of the package and presses it firmly into my palm.

"Luc, we can't. You promised her data—" My words are cut off by his aggressive kiss. His wings enfold us in a cocoon, and he sways to a slower song. His wings block out the light, the lab equipment, the mess, and the outside world. In his wings, I can release my past without consequences. For the second time tonight, he has given me freedom while balancing it all with the serenity he provides.

Having my arms around his neck exposes my entire torso to his busy hands. My bra seems to jump off my body at his touch. He cups my breasts and kisses down my throat. His tongue swirls with each inch of movement, teasing, asking for permission to bite. I'm thrilled at the sensation that would have scared my socks off a week ago. I guess I needed time, or close proximity in order to build trust. No, it is not building trust. It is discovery of the hidden Lucien. I was scared of the plastic vampire who only lived in books, movies, and nightmares. Lucien is a man, an honorable man.

His lips trace across my collar bone to latch onto my nipple. I forget where I am and groan with abandon. Lucien lifts his head to chuckle at me. "Princess, you are going to make Ryan's job of keeping gossips away difficult making noises like that. I will have to save your favorite moves for the next time you are in my bed." He loses hold of his scrub pants so they puddle on the floor.

"No need to play then. I'm ready for you." He hisses when I roll the condom over him. Beyond the red glow of lust is another emotion, could it be love shining back at me?

His hands lose their finesse as he roughly grips my hips, lifting me off my feet. I wrap my arms and legs around him like a life preserver. He turns me to the nearest wall, using his wings to cushion my back against it. We moan in unison when his cold member glides inside of me. Luc swivels his hips to touch my core at several angles. The temperature change with the varied pressure on my pleasure sensors has me seeing stars. The waves of my orgasm hit by his third thrust followed by a possessive growl from Luc.

"That's it, princess, come apart for me. Let your body ripple, dance, and love me as you fly in ecstasy." As I cling helplessly to him, he finishes with a muffled growl buried in my hair. I rain tiny kisses on him as I slide down his body. When my feet hit the floor, he topples forward onto the wall behind me with exhaustion.

Crash! Clatter! Luc folds his wings to reveal our retaining wall was the side of the class II cabinet. Plastic shrapnel coated in fruity agar litters the floor. "Dammit, shit, effing dammit! This is a repeat of Christmas Eve just before the Yule party. Only this time I sabotaged myself instead of waiting for Ryan to do it. I will need another four days to redo these results when Patty is currently waiting for them." He hangs his head in defeat.

Chapter 25

"Do you need those colonies for further experiments?" Her beautiful voice lifts my spirits from their downward spiral. If I'm going to prove to her, I am not a waste of space in this lab, I must do it now.

"No, I need the numbers written on the lids. I need to know which lid corresponds to each dilution. Patty is going to kill me." Plastic crinkles as I bang my head on the cabinet.

"Not necessarily, maybe I can save you." I hang on to her words as she calmly washes her hands and grabs a printer test sheet lying haphazardly next to the sink. She flips it over to draw an array of circles on the back.

I busy myself pulling my scrubs together and disposing of the evidence of our liaison. I cocoon my arms around her shoulders. I'm dying of curiosity, so I ask, "what are you drawing? A bull's eye for me to wear on my back?"

"Silly vampire," she says before kissing my nose. "My magical powers are more useful than yours in this case." In each circle, she writes a number, and it hits me like a bolt of lightning. She had memorized the placement of the plates in the hood.

"You are magic." I kiss her ear because I can't resist. She closes her eyes and waves the pen in the air before scribbling a cluster of numbers. She has three spots empty when she stops to look at me. Her mahogany eyes entangle my emotions into a snarl of tenderness, gratitude, and reverence.

"I'm not sure about these last three numbers—" Her eyes turn glassy with frustrated tears. Could she really be upset that she hasn't saved my data completely when I would have been up a creek with a paddle without her?

"I'm amazed. I'm grateful. I'm fascinated." I pick her up and swing her around with joy. "We can recreate the arrangement now. It is not a total disaster but a matter of filling holes, which if you believe my reputation, is my specialty."

My self-deprecating humor earns me one of her melodic set of giggles and a fierce hug. We are quite a team. "I wanted to save you," she says against my shoulder.

"You have, princess. I save you from Sluagh and you save me from myself." I put her down begrudgingly and we recreate the plate's array using Betty's plate map. In less than half an hour, the numbers are recorded, and the plates are soaking in bleach for waste disposal.

My phone dings with a series of text messages from Forger Josh. His drawings of the ring designs are stunning. I choose one with a braided band that reminds me of a crown for my princess. The braid continues over the ruby to hold it in place, wrapping around it several times. I text back my selection with the giddiness of a mad scientist. Betty raises an eyebrow at me, but I can't give away my surprise. When it becomes obvious I am not sharing, she lets out a little huff. At the adorable sound, I transfer the money to Josh to start making it. Betty continues to straighten and tidy the room while softly humming to herself.

I settle behind my newly cleared desk and begin the

tedious task of calculating dilution concentrations based on colony counts. I average the identical plates and multiply them by the dilution ratios to get a master concentration. If all goes according to plan, all the dilutions will agree on the same master concentration. This master concentration is the number needed to calculate the initial volumes for the drying columns and the amount of powder placed in each pill capsule. Too many colony-forming units, lovingly called CFUs, will give the patient a run for their money…or should I say the runs for their money?

I wish to share my gross pun with Betty. She is leaning against the counter, reading a forgotten journal while twirling her hair around her finger. *My God, she is enchanting.* Feeling my eyes memorize her, she looks up and blushes. "That's why I always wear a ponytail. I twirl my hair when it is down and look like I'm stupid."

"Then you are safe to do it around me. Your brilliance has saved my bacon repeatedly since we have met."

"Thanks, my family focuses on the intelligence of Grant and Ally. They gush over my sister's big house and big-shot husband while I'm just a nurse to them. I thought I would get more recognition at the nursing home, but nurses are taken for granted everywhere." This confession is as raw as her freckles beneath the heavy makeup. It is on the tip of my tongue to offer her my title and mansion if only to impress her family.

"I'm honored to be the one to remind you that you are as smart as anyone in this building, probably more than most of us. A nurse is not a janitor or coffee hostess. You are a multifaceted professional who has saved my life and my career in two different crises in the same week." She goes back to reading and I go back to work. However, whenever I catch her gazing at me, I swear I see the love shining in her eyes. Maybe commissioning Josh to make the ring was a stroke of genius.

"We did it! Let me find a folder." I dig through my desk with both hands. My rummaging is interrupted by Betty clearing her throat. She holds a folder at the end of my nose with a smirk on her lips. "Thanks," I say, stuffing my report into the pockets. "We can drop by Molina's office, drop this off to Patty, and then I will have only one more task for the night."

"What's that?"

"Convincing you to bring your study materials to my place," I say with more courage than I feel. I'm like a toddler wanting to stay up a little later. I can't help but whine for more time with her. My life seems so much better when she is around. The thought of her slipping through my fingers causes my chest to tighten in panic.

"If I bring my books to your place the only attention, they will get is from the dust bunnies."

"Ouch! Watch your claws," I say with my hands over my heart. She laughs at my theatrics. I am doomed to be a slave to her laughter for the rest of my days. Good thing she can't read my thoughts or smell my emotions. *I'm such a sap.*

"It's close to sunrise so we better hurry if you don't want to end up stuck here for the day."

Grabbing her hand, we head for the door to face the gauntlet of my nosy vampires. A crowd has gathered around Ryan just outside our door, proving my hypothesis that the entire US portion of the colony is talking about me. *Good. Let them gossip.* Let each of them realize I am off the market so it will not shock them when I wed Betty. It is a tradition for the king to marry a vampire queen while having a human mistress, but my family has a tradition of its own. My father didn't hand over the throne to Ryan because he was dying. He abdicated when he married my mother. The norm of human mistresses should have been put to pasture during his reign. It will be his legacy when I abolish it in mine.

"Lucien, what a pleasant surprise to see you not working," Ryan says with growing agitation.

"I am looking for you, sir. I have the enumeration report completed for Patty and I was going to give it to you for review. If it is to your standards, perhaps you would like to present it to her." The sneer falls from his face to be replaced with an evil smile. No doubt he will spin a tale to Patty about pushing me along. He may even take credit for half the work. If the calculations weren't in my handwriting, he would take credit for the entire package.

Does Ryan even suspect his lies are often exposed by paperwork? GMP regulations require handwritten initials for every hand calculation and signatures for every step of a method, so whatever story Ryan tells Patty is immaterial. With the king appeased and the curiosity of the masses peaked, Betty and I knock on Molina's door.

"Lucien, Betty, this is a surprise," Molina says as she opens the door for us to enter. She slams the door on the mass of vampires hanging onto our every word. Molina was formally cast out of the colony before Ryan was even born. She chose to stay with Brad in America instead of taking her place as Vampire Queen. Choosing love over duty must be in my family's DNA. Despite her extended lifespan as a shifter lifemate, she has always treated me like a close aunt instead of an ancient relative.

"Thank you for seeing us, Aunt Molina," I say, hugging her. "I need your help." It stings when I compare her lab to mine. You could probably eat off her floors. Bookshelves are filled from floor to ceiling with periodicals and books arranged by size. Her class II cabinet is empty with the stainless-steel surface gleaming at me. No wonder Ryan thinks I need a wife and Betty thinks I need a janitor. I might as well oink instead of speaking.

"Of course," she says with a hand motion to sit in the chairs by her desk. They are separated by a small table with blank paper and a cup of pens for guests. She adds to the comfort of her office by wheeling her chair to our side of the desk and sitting.

"I need one of your Plan B pills," I blurt out. *Nice going, Shakespeare, you have such a way with words.* "I-I-I meant to put that more delicately, I…" I bury my head in my hands.

"Getting to the point will make this less awkward. It's okay," Betty says. She infuses her strength through a rub to my shoulder, fortifying my reserves. I must do this for her. She has plans and dreams that don't include a family right now. She will make a kick-ass nurse and give Dr. V the help he needs to take his practice to the next level. If I want to help my people, they need Betty's attention and skill set.

"No problem, as long as you are sure," Molina says. Ugh, she is fishing. I wish I could show her the ring and tell her that I am a decent guy. Betty has gone pale. She must hate the idea of caring for a vampire baby but who could blame her. Nursing a vampire requires giving it blood and milk at the same time. She has made it perfectly pellucid how she feels about biting.

"I'm sure," I say as I grab Betty's hand. "We rushed into this and want to take the time to get to know each other. Betty has a nursing exam and a growing role with Dr. V. I am bringing Terika here for treatment so I will be taking care of her too."

"That does sound busy and ambitious," Molina says more to Betty than me. I inhale a noseful of Betty's scent: nervousness with a tinge of sadness. If I had prepped her with Molina's history with the colony, she would see Molina as an ally. I certainly wouldn't make this request of Ryan or any other vampire.

"So, you can see—" I can't even finish my statement. I'm so flustered.

"Lucien, I was young once too. You don't have to explain to me," she says with a wistful look on her face. Anyone who has watched her with Brad knows she is a hopeless romantic. After close to two hundred years together, they still act like teenagers. Stories swirl around Bergan of catching them being indecent in closets, locker rooms, and showers.

"I knew you would understand," I say with a puff of relief. Betty is strangely quiet during this exchange. I expected her to boil over with feminist comradery with Molina. She gives me a half-smile when our eyes meet.

Molina grabs a key from her desk and gloves from a dispenser mounted to the wall. Going to a small cabinet beside her glovebox, she removes a pill bottle and places it on the countertop. As she places one pill in an orange bottle, my gaze wanders to the papers hung on the glovebox with heart-shaped clips. *I'll be damned.* It seems everyone with real scientific expertise was in on the magnet secret.

"If you are sure…" She hands the bottle to Betty. Betty takes it with trembling fingers and holds it tightly in her palm as if it is a grenade.

"Of course," she replies and tucks it into her hoodie pocket. It is my sweatshirt but how did she put it? Memories of her rifling through my dresser drawers bring a smile to my face. *Fake or not, mistresses steal their master's clothes and sleep in their beds.* Perhaps when I get home, I will clear out a drawer in my dresser. I have a few things of hers in my dryer. I can't wait to see her face when she opens the drawer to commandeer more of my stuff only to find her own clothes.

"Is Dr. V's open tomorrow? I will come over and check on you," Molina says to Betty.

"That's too kind but I'm sure I will be fine." Molina surprises all of us by grabbing Betty and hugging her tightly. Is it my imagination or is she whispering to Betty?

"I have a feeling we are going to be close friends."

"Same here. My first vampire bestie." *Perfect.* These two would be powerful mentors for Terika. Molina will guide her through vampire politics. Betty will teach her to be a modern woman. I must call Terika. I'm sure the added excitement will boost her desire to fight her illness.

We leave Molina in triumph and head back to the stairwell. Unable to resist, I scoop Betty into my arms as soon as the hall door closes. Unfurling my wings, I lower us as softly as a feather drops. How can I prolong my time with her? "Please tell me you have reconsidered my offer. Please say you will accompany me home."

"I'd love to, but I can't. I have responsibilities. In Molina's office, you reminded me of them. I need to balance our time together with all the others in my life."

My temper blazes like a forest fire at the mention of others. I want to monopolize her but that's not feasible. She's right. She hasn't spent time with Alison since she has returned, and she hasn't seen Henrik for days. "Then I am just going to have to miss you." I kiss her with all the passion I possess. I wish I could brand her with my scent like a shifter.

"I will miss you too." She takes her first step out the door before I can stop her.

She navigates the ice until her heel skids on a larger sheet. She wavers and I push the door open to rush to her aid. The first rays of morning sun scald my knuckles and sizzle my wrist. I recoil into the safety of the building. She doesn't need me anyway. With extended arms, she steadies herself. As much as I wish to be her champion, she is a hero in her own right.

Just as she warned, I overscheduled my duties and I am trapped here. I can only watch her drive away from behind the protective glass and appreciate that she has the freedom to escape. One is royalty but the other is free. I know which one I would rather be.

Chapter 26

I drive back to Ally's plantation on autopilot. Tears flow freely down my face as Luc's words swirl in my head. Of course, we have lots of responsibilities, but I thought I was proving to be an asset to him. I perceived my quick thinking as being a valuable half to the partnership.

I would have died with embarrassment in Molina's office if she wasn't so compassionate. I am genuinely happy to have Molina as a friend if I am going to integrate myself into the vampire community. Intuitively, she knew I thought of carrying a baby, not a burden. She could smell my mortification and offered counsel, whispering Lucien was being dense, not damaging. Why couldn't he smell my emotions when I needed him to do so?

Reapplying my makeup in the garage, I step into Ally's house with a plastic smile. "Honey, I'm home," I call into her sunny yellow kitchen.

"Hey, Sis," Ally greets me with a loose hug. She can't stand the feedback from being hugged but right now I don't care. I hug her tighter than I hugged Molina and sniffle. "Hey, Hey, Betty, are you okay?"

"Overtired from too much fun." I chicken out on seeking her support. She peers at me through squinty eyes. The vines of her magic reach out to read my insides. Vampires smelling my emotions. Witches trying to read my insides. Can't a girl get some privacy?

"Not buying it. Go to your room, young lady. I will bring up breakfast and we are going to solve whatever is bugging you. If you need me to eat someone, just let me know."

"Thanks, Ally," I say, stealing one more hug. I drag my carcass across her mansion to my ostentatious room. The gaudy red décor never looked so inviting. I could get lost in a sea of ruffles and no one would ever find me. I dump my bags on the bed and head to the bathroom to splash water on my face.

I better take Molina's pill before Ally gets up here. That would be fun to explain to her what is bugging me. Hey Sis, I want a vampire baby and I'm too scared to admit it. I guess the first step is to admit it to myself. The next would be to admit it to Luc. *Fun times in hell.*

Pulling the pill bottle from my pocket, I fill a cup with water and open the jar. The little white sphere looks so innocent nestled against the wall of the bottle. I sink down to the floor and curl into a ball while staring into the tube. Water splashes from the cup onto Luc's hoodie mixing with my tears. This is the right decision. This is a responsible decision. Why is this so hard?

"I will close your blackout curtains so you can sleep. When Aurora is back from England, we will meet for dinner at Paulino's before you go to work. It will be just us having a girl's night as the restaurant will be closed." China clinks as Ally sets down a tray, no doubt with heaping piles of goodies. Next, are the chimes of the metal curtain rings sliding down the rod.

I need to pull myself together or she will freak out. I can't seem to stop crying. Sadness and indecision glue me to the floor. The door flies open and Ally gasps in shock. The smile falls from her face as she crouches on the floor beside me. She slowly reaches out to pat my shoulder as if I am a wounded animal. I rock toward her to lay my head in her lap. She lets me full-on ugly cry for a few minutes before speaking.

"Who broke you?" The question comes out in an angry growl that sounds more bear than homeschool mom.

"No one can break me but myself, Ally," I say with a whimper to her tear-soaked dress.

"Don't shield that vampire," she snaps.

"I'm not. He's doing everything right and that's the problem." I sob while her fingers comb through my hair.

"Do you need to get clean? Is that what is in the pill bottle?"

"It is not narcotics. I promise." I sit up to show her my eyes are clear. It stings that she would jump to drugs. I thought she was one of the only people on earth who believed me when I said I never did drugs with Evan. I guess she's not.

"You get clean with other medications."

"It's a morning-after pill, Ally," I snap.

"Oh my, I guess I owe you an apology then."

I wave a hand to dismiss her. I'm used to being under suspicion. As far as I run, Evan is always with me. I just wish I had someone to counterbalance all the sadness he brings with the resurfacing of my past. Someone to brighten my future. Someone who is mine without all the death and sadness attached.

"Ally, Luc is my Grant." Her eyes round with shock. Ally fell for Grant, both literally and figuratively, the day they met. Within a semester, she was pregnant. I helped her through her pregnancy, took turns getting up with newborn Henrik at night, and watched him while she attempted to stay in school. If anyone can understand what I want to do, it's Ally.

"You fell for a vampire?"

"He's not just a vampire. The vampires are regular people with myelodysplastic anemia and genetic anomalies, except Luc, he's extraordinary. Don't make that face."

"Yep, with your eyes twinkling like that, he's your Grant. Are you asking me to flush the pill?"

"I'm asking myself to flush it." I wipe my eyes on my sleeve, take a deep breath, and start to sob on the exhale. "He got the pill from Molina. We went to her office together. He had all these rational reasons to get rid of our possible pregnancy, but I wanted to strangle him. Is it so bad that I am willing to raise this baby alone?"

"Never alone, I will be right here," she says, grabbing the bottle from my hand. "Besides we don't know if you are pregnant, what's wrong with letting nature take its course? Sometimes we must be humble and remember Mother Earth knows more than we do."

"You, mom, our genetics. Ally, we are one shot, one kill," I say with a sniffle. "It is too soon to know if I am pregnant, but our family history says I need to knit some booties."

"If you are, the baby is half-Weston. We will love it to pieces." I can't help but smile in return at her naivete.

"Vampire genetics are dominant. My baby will have wings, glowing eyes, a thirst for blood as well as milk…" I leave out that the baby could have candy-apple lips, musical talent, an honorable heart, cooking talents, a messy disposition, and softness for abandoned cats. My growing smile says it all as I nod with Ally. She gets it.

"Good thing you work with Dr. V. If there is a doctor appropriate for helping you through a vampire pregnancy, it is him." She grabs my hand, curls my fingers around the bottle, and holds them with her fingers. "I am here to give you anything you need, Betty. Let me return the support you gave me all those years ago."

"If I get a positive pregnancy test, Dr. V is the first person I am telling."

"He better be the second."

"Okay, the second person." I lift our joined hands over the toilet. The pill tumbles out and sinks to the bottom. *Please don't hate me, Luc.* I dump the water from my drinking cup to act as a chaser. The pill kicks up in defiance before disappearing down the hole. "I hope he's not mad. I don't want to hurt him."

"He still has a choice. These aren't Victorian times, and you are not a fallen woman of no secure means. We have more than enough love, money, and babysitters. Don't think for one minute that you have trapped him. If he tries to bully you, I'll stand up for you."

I laugh at my pint-sized sister. She has never stood up to anyone in my presence. Residents of Strawberry have a legend of her saving herself from the Sluagh fortress and eating two of the demons, but I am still highly skeptical.

"Thanks, Ally, right now I just need your secrecy. As you said, I don't even know if I am pregnant."

"But our family history—"

"Zip it."

"Okay, well you are now my patient until I see a negative on a test. So, you shower while I put your pajamas in the dryer to warm them. Then it is breakfast, sleep, and in a few days' fun with the girls," she says, ticking items on her fingers.

"Thank you, Ally."

"I will always be here for you. That's what sisters do."

Chapter 27

In Bergan's bunks, nightmares of unwanted pregnancies, rejected proposals, throne abjection, colonist revolts, and Terika dying plague my slumber. Why in the world have I put so much pressure on myself? It seems every decision I make paints me deeper into a corner. My problems aren't new, so I search my foggy sleep-deprived brain for the true reason I am unsettled. My sheets have been at war for hours. The fitted sheet released the mattress to join in the fray. I am entangled in cotton, a victim of friendly fire.

Betty's face in Molina's office flashes across my imagination. She looked nervous but on introspection, she seemed more disappointed. I assumed aborting the pregnancy was what she wanted because she is ambitious with a bright future. Did I ever ask her? I must have asked her. Being decisive isn't my strong suit.

I yearn to hold her and she's sleeping happily at Alison's house. Even my skin lost her scent with the shower I took before bed. On to the next best thing: hope for the future. I grab my phone from the floor under the bed and dial my mom's number. "Hey Mom, are you busy?"

"Never too busy for my kids. How are you Pumpkin?" *Ugh, Pumpkin.* Maybe calling her wasn't the best idea.

"Never better, how are you and Terika?"

"I'm doing okay but you don't sound like you are better than ever. I can't smell emotions, but you are a rotten liar, Pumpkin."

"I am questioning some of my decisions, Mom. That's all." I wad my pillow into a ball so I can sit up straighter. Just hearing her voice reminds me of my station and why I put up with Ryan's antics. My family is depending on me. Betty has a large Weston support network while there are only three of us, four if you count Molina.

"Did you make them with love in your heart?"

"WHAT?"

"That's what your Dad always used to say. He never regretted a decision he made with love in his heart. Terika tells me she thinks you are in love." Memories of my parents together dance across my psyche. They gave us the consummate example of what being in love should look like. My dad never tired of finding ways to make Mom happy. I can't help but smile when my addled brain transposes Betty's head and my head onto my parent's bodies.

"We grew up watching a fairytale with you and Dad. No wonder Terika is in such a hurry for me to find love."

"Terika didn't know much about her. Will you tell me more?"

"Terika is too young to be talking about love. She needs to be formulating her career plans while focusing on recovery. You know, Dr. V is doing some amazing work and I know he can help Terika. The girl Ryan has set me up with is working with Dr. V on the regular stuff so he can do novel research. Betty's a modern nurse with cutting-edge training, not the blood-leters over there."

"Betty is the nurse you mentioned last time we

talked…"

"Yes, a good one. She's smart, organized, and professional. She even has a photographic memory. But she's more than her profession. She grew up in a big family who put happiness over riches, so she puts everyone else first…and her laugh…wow."

"Hearing you are happy warms my heart, Pumpkin. I can't wait to meet her."

"I don't think it can wait. The bottom line is you must bring Terika here."

"Lucien, Pumpkin, she no longer wants to come there. She said she already said goodbye to you. She's talking to your dad in her sleep. She has been day-to-day since Christmas."

"No," I whisper. I sink into my covers in despair. "Should I book a flight home?"

"You know you promised her that you wouldn't," she says with a stifled sob. She's right. When I left the colony to move to Strawberry, I promised Terika I wouldn't return to watch her die.

"Remember me this way, Luc. When I am about to die, I don't want you to see me. Promise me. Luc, please promise me," she cried, gripping my shirt. It was the first summer day when she hadn't gotten out of bed. She always had her nurse set her on the hill over the vineyard to watch for the blossoms. She loved being the first one to see them open. This summer day was different. My ego thought it was sadness at my leaving but now I know, it was the day her lungs filled.

"Sure, I will promise, only because it doesn't matter. I will find a way for you to come to Strawberry. We will see each other there," I had joked in a boasting way only a big brother can pull off to his little sister.

She hadn't answered me then. She had coughed instead. Coughed and coughed. I see now that she let me believe we would see each other here. She had known she was too sick to ever make the journey but had the heart to let me believe.

"What do I do Mom?"

"Live. Live, Pumpkin. Live every second with gratitude while you still have the chance."

"How do I live? I have lived under Ryan's thumb to get her here for how many years? Her recovery was my motivation. That bastard killed her…"

"Lucien, stop it. Ryan didn't give her pneumonia. That's not fair."

"He delayed and deferred her transfer to get more out of me. Was it to punish us for Dad's loyalty to you over the colony?"

"Ryan has cherished every moment being king so no he's not punishing us. Don't you dare blame the man who stepped in when your father died. You would have turned out differently without the king's generosity."

"Different? Probably better, and it is all for nothing," I say between sniffles.

"Lucien, you will be a kind, warm, progressive king. The colony needs you like they needed your father. Ryan made them rich. You have a gift to give too. Terika would want you to concentrate on that…and having a family. Your father, your sister, they live inside you. Just because they are not on this earth to tell you doesn't mean they aren't proud of what you have become."

"Thanks, Mom. What will you do? You have been her caregiver her whole life." I use the sheets to wipe my eyes.

"Terika wrote a list of final wishes. I am going to

fulfill those and then evaluate my seamstress business. I have more clients than I can handle. Maybe it is time for a partner and possibly a storefront. I don't know, Pumpkin. I'm taking it one day at a time."

"Then I will take it one day at a time too. I love you, Mom."

"I love you too, Pumpkin." She severs my connection home. I burrow into the twisted sheets and sob. My little sister surrendered to her disease while simultaneously telling me to live. I cry for the little girl who watched flowers bloom for fun. I cry for the things I could have shown her, the places we could have gone, and the people she could have met. My grief gives way to a day of dreamless sleep with no promise of relief.

Chapter 28

"When you requested a chocolate cake for Aurora's welcome home party, I bought the test," Ally says through the stall door. "You have eaten nothing but sweets since I got back from Florida. You don't even like sweets, especially chocolate."

"I'm depressed and sugar cravings go hand-in-hand with depression," I grouse from inside a bathroom stall of Paulino's pizzeria. If only my sister would leave me alone. Days have passed without a peep from Lucien. So much for him maintaining his mistress. If our relationship were real, I would have dumped him by now. I replay our parting ad infinitum and I can't figure out what happened.

"Chocolate cravings mean you are pregnant with a boy. You crave spicy food with a girl, sweets with a boy. Don't you remember when Mom was pregnant with Calvin and Donnie, she would eat a cake for dinner? The rest of the table had a slice of cake for dessert, but she had a cake to herself with no dinner required."

"Yeah, well, I also remember you trying to get Dad to give you a cake for dinner when you were pregnant with Henrik—"

"Ha! Proved my point," she says in her sing-song voice. She pulled me in here by my ponytail and barricaded the door until I peed on the stick for her. *Little Tyrant.*

"There. Happy now?" I can't help but be grouchy. Finding out the outcome of the test will be heartbreaking and exhilarating, no matter what the results read. If it is negative, then I have time to focus on my career, but I lose a tie to my time with Lucien. If it is positive, I get a baby to love but I have to reveal to Lucien I flushed his pill.

"Getting closer," she says while I wash my hands. "I will be happy when we get the answer and can start planning. I have been researching what vegetables to feed you to maximize each phase of your pregnancy with recipes. If you only eat cake, then you risk gestational diabetes."

"Torture via veggie puree? Pass. Mom never got gestational diabetes. Did you find vampire pregnancy on the internet too? If the test is positive, I listen to Dr. V—but only Dr. V."

We emerge from the restroom to find Rosie decorating the dining room with streamers and balloons. Ally had made a "Welcome Home" sign for Aurora which is now proudly hanging over the bar. "About time you two got back to helping me decorate. Maybe if one of you stands on the shoulders of the second, you could reach high enough," Rosie calls to us. I make a rude gesture in response that she laughs off.

A dressed table in the center of the room is loaded with Aurora's tomato-free favorites and a fudgy chocolate cake. Ally places the pregnancy test gently by her purse on the table. The box stands proudly next to it for all to see. At least my sister has agreed to say it is her test, but could she use a little more stealth? *Geez.* Puffing with all of my anger and embarrassment, I blow up balloons at the speed of light.

"Whoa, we only need four balloons," Rosie says.

"It's your fault for assigning her the perfect job. Betty has enough hot air to heat the building," Ally jokes from atop a chair.

"Hardy, har." I'm still sulking when the door chimes herald Aurora's arrival. She runs down the gauntlet and bursts into the dining room.

"Surprise," we yell. She runs to Ally to sweep my sister off her chair and spin her around. Next is a giant hug for Rosie.

I get my hug last, but she keeps her arms around me when she addresses us. "I'm so happy to be home. England was everything I dreamed it would be, but Strawberry has captured my heart. I can't wait to tell you all about it."

"We are so happy to have you back and want to hear all the stories," Ally says.

"Especially the dirty ones," Rosie says, making us all laugh.

"I don't know, Rosie. I do things that can even make you blush," Aurora says with a wink.

"I can't handle that on an empty stomach." I try to be as light and happy as possible. In truth, my body feels like it is digesting itself, even after I snuck cookies on the way here. We sit at the table with Aurora on my right and that damned pregnancy test box to my left. I am still fuming at my sister for not hiding it. The test is on her side to further the ruse that it is hers. However, the bastard box blocks my view of the results portal.

Aurora follows my gaze to the box and squeals, "Oh Alison, you think of everything! We traveled around England, so I never stopped for a test. We have been so busy since getting home. James and I moved most of his apartment to our new place while Nate slept. Well, James moved most of it. I was only allowed to load and unload boxes. Nate is at Bergan tonight while James is packing his place." She grabs the box and jumps out of her seat to hug Ally.

"Wait for just one second, miss," Rosie says in her Mom-voice. Aurora slowly steps back to the table. Rosie reaches in the box and opens the plastic wrapping on the remaining test before giving Aurora a nod.

"Thank you for thinking ahead. I still struggle with opening packaging after my amputation. Why everything needs to be individually wrapped I will never know."

"Thank goodness Grant isn't here to tell you the long boring story of how individual packaging came to be. He has so many regulations memorized, I bet he could rattle off the legal parameters of packaging your innovative medical device," Ally says.

"Innovative medical device," I say in my best impersonation of Grant. The table erupts with laughter while I get a swat from Ally. With everyone distracted I sneak peek at my test. A plus sign peeks back at me. Holy shit, I'm carrying a vampire fetus.

"Alison, is that a plus sign on your test?" Rosie's eyes are the saucers while her mouth is stuck in O-ring formation. Ally twists her fingers as if her anxiety builds within her like volcanic ash.

"No, Rosie," I say, giving her my meanest glare. "It is a plus sign on my damn test."

Ally drops her shoulders and lets out a whoosh of air. I didn't realize lying to her best friend for me would have been so hard on her. I file that away for a more private time to thank her. Rosie continues to stare at me while her mind calculates whether or not to congratulate me. I take the test and place it back in its wrapping before shoving it in my purse.

"No one else is going to know until I get my bearings." I glare at my friends while issuing my demand.

"I am beside you every step of the way. If you want it to be a secret a little while longer, Rosie and I will help you do it." Ally takes my hand and squeezes it in hers.

"I hope you are happy. Every baby is a blessing even if it is Evan's baby and you wanted him out of your life. The baby isn't necessarily a chip off the old block." Rosie walks to my side of the table and hugs me fiercely. The support of these women—or my riotous hormones—brings tears to my eyes.

"It is not Evan's baby," I whisper in her ear. She jolts upright to stare at me with renewed surprise. It is on the tip of her tongue to ask who the father might be when a shriek erupts from the bathroom.

"Aurora," Ally yells as she leaps from the table and sprints to the bathroom.

"No one left a door open for Sluagh, right?"

Rosie doesn't answer me but bounds after Alison instead. She shifts from a homely woman to a sleek black wolf. Her thick coat gleams in the fluorescent lighting as her fluffy tail bobs after her. I am left alone in the dining room with only her flowered housecoat to keep me company.

"Pregnant! I'm pregnant, baby," Aurora yells from the bathroom. She skips back into the dining room with Ally and a wolf following her. She sets her phone down on the table to spin around. "I can't believe it. I'm so happy I could burst. We wanted to have a baby right away, but I was skeptical I could get pregnant so fast."

"I'm so happy for you. I can't wait to plan a baby shower," I say with a hug of genuine affection. Having a family after the death of her parents has been Aurora's dream since I met her. She is glowing with the news.

"We have a little confession," Rosie says, looking to Alison. Her wolf form wriggles into the crumpled housecoat before she changes back to human. She needs to give my sister lessons on that, so Ally quits flashing everyone. Of course, a super-sized polar bear would be harder to wedge in a petite dress.

"Remember that rose-hip lip-gloss we made for you?" Ally twists her fingers in her dress until it wrinkles.

"Yes, I loved it. The winds in London were brutal. It was nice not to get windburn. I was pissed when it was empty. James loved it too and I suspect he's the reason I ran out."

Rosie bursts out laughing while Ally looks horrified. "We stole Gran's Book of Shadows to make a fertility potion. It came out like a paste, so we gave it to you as a lip gloss," my sister confesses. She looks so guilty I can't stand it. My laughter rocks my body until my sides ache.

"It didn't look like the description in the book so we weren't sure it would even work," Rosie adds, and Ally's guilty blush deepens.

"Did Nate ever use it? I want to take leopard versus rabbit bets," I say while Ally's jaw drops in horror.

"It will be the baby of *all three of them*," says Rosie sternly, "but put me down for the baby's first words being 'What's up Doc'."

"You two are too much," Aurora says. Thank God she's laughing. "Just don't tell my guys…and make another tube for me next year. I want a house full of babies."

Fettuccine alfredo with Cajun spices is piled on our plates with Rosie's homemade bread. The other ladies tuck in while my stomach revolts. My fangy fetus wants cake. Really wants cake. Would my baby like the blood-laced chocolates Josh makes at the auto shop? My stomach rumbles and I plan a date with my baby batman to get some bloody chocolates after work.

"Be careful what you wish for," Rosie says, waving a fork at Aurora. Rosie's six sons range from rambunctious to hellions. We laugh harder when she describes the trick Gran pulled on her when she was first married. The in-laws switched bedrooms with the newlyweds to give them more space. Gran confessed after three babies born in four years that she had saturated the room with fertility wards. The young couple had three more babies in the next set of four years before vacating the room.

Ally puts her hand over mine which had drifted to my belly. She caught me smiling at my midsection while daydreaming of sweets. Good thing Rosie and Aurora are in a deep conversation on shifter pregnancies. Ally and I smile at each other. I'm happy, surprisingly happy. I have Ally's support, so it doesn't matter if Lucien is involved or not. I'm strong enough for two parents. I try to exhale the pain settling over my heart. *Who am I kidding*? A vision of Lucien holding a bundle wrapped in a blanket, singing nonsense words, floods my imagination. I push the errant thought away to make room for the tears I need to contain.

Bang! The front door slams open and shut followed by the thundering of heavy boots. James skids in the dining room followed by Nate in his snow leopard form. The two guys are yelling, weeping, and jumping around. Aurora leaps into James's arms and kisses him fiercely while Nate licks at their faces on his hind legs. The trio members are all talking at once, laughing and celebrating.

"Congratulations everyone," Ally says from her seat. James stops and bows in a gesture vaguely reminding me of Lucien. Nate shows submission arching his back to lower his head to the floor. Amazing that ferocious creatures bow to my humble sister. When I first met Nate, he was in his cat form and scared the hell out of me. *Wow, was that only a month ago?*

"Thank you, Alison," James says. He can't take his eyes off Aurora while she bends down to stroke Nate's fur. The love passing between them is so sweet I've lost my appetite, even for cake.

"I thank you for the party but we..." Aurora looks pained as she chooses between her friends and her guys.

"Go celebrate with your men but you are coming back some other night this week to tell us all about your adventure," Ally says with a wave of her fork. Hugs are exchanged and the happy family trots out the door. They take the air from the room with their departure. Their laughter trails through the window as they cross to their apartment over the library.

"I'm sorry, Betty," Alison whispers, still holding my hand.

"Why?"

"That must have been hard to watch," Rosie says, reaching across the table for my other hand. Her compassion is almost my undoing. Damn hormones, I'm going to lose my hard shell if this continues.

"Not really," I say with care to hide the quiver in my voice. "Aurora loves babies. Why wouldn't I be happy she's having one?"

"No one congratulated me with Henrik …well, only you. I will never forget how you stood by me. Remember Dad calling Grant to scream at him?"

"Well, Dad isn't calling Lucien. I am telling him myself."

A clamor echoes through the dining room as Rosie drops her fork in shock. "Wait, what? You are carrying the second in line to the vampire throne?"

So much for that secret, dammit.

Chapter 29

"Time to wake up, your highness," a voice calls from the farthest reaches of my consciousness. I am poked with a stick…or fork…or stake. Someone is trying to stake me! I jump out of bed to face the mob trying to assassinate the Prince of Darkness…to find I am at Bergan Pharma, in the bunks, facing Nate, in full vampire form, with no clothes. *Oh my God.*

"Sorry, man. I haven't been myself lately," I mumble while ripping the sheet off the bed to tie it around my waist. *Breathe*, I must encourage my fangs to recede.

"Yeah, I heard you haven't left this bed in four days."

"Four days?" Why hasn't my mom called to let me know when Terika has passed? I have ignored Betty for four days. She must think I have ditched her. Come to think of it, why hasn't Ryan come down here to berate me? I get down on my hands and knees looking for my phone under the bed.

"Yeah, four days. If you need someone to talk to, I have listened to James's complaining for years. Now that he's happy, I don't know what to do with my free time."

"Thanks. Do you remember me talking about my little sister Terika?"

"Yeah, she still sick?"

I shake my head and choke on a sob. "She's gone."

It's all I can say and even those words grate on my throat upon release. I give up on the phone and stand, pushing my hair to stand straight up.

"Dude, I'm so sorry." His manly embrace does little to soothe my broken heart, but I appreciate the sentiment. I pull myself together, wiping my nose on my bedsheet train.

"Well, I guess I just used my vacation time in the worst possible way ever."

"I think you have to leave the building for it to be counted as vacation time. I would lobby for family bereavement time. But get dressed first, I don't think you are Grant's type," Nate says with a snicker.

"Thanks for the hint," I say, slugging his shoulder. "Why did you revive me anyway?"

"Grant has been showing a microbiologist candidate around. She is a highflier from New Jersey, a human with tons of experience getting drugs approved."

"Why is she interviewing in Strawberry?"

"She talked about the greed of large corporations in her phone interview. She wants to get back to making miracles over making money. Even though a miracle worker came to clean your lab while I was gone, I thought you would want to prepare to meet her…uh…in the flesh," he says with a chuckle.

"Yeah, thanks. Meeting future employees in the nude is frowned upon by HR, I bet. I'll shower and meet you upstairs in twenty minutes."

"You are the boss." Nate gives me a mock salute. If only. The only reason why I'm head of Micro is Ryan's insistence. Nate is a genius who doesn't want the limelight, so he allowed me to keep the title. If this new professional is a highflier, then she will want control over the lab…especially when she learns my degree is a fake.

Where is Ryan when I actually need him to smooth this over? He wants vampires in positions of power on the third floor. *Wait.* He no longer has leverage over me. Sure, he can name a new heir but that doesn't change my living conditions. It is his fault Terika never got over here. He prevaricated to prolong my servitude. *Eff-him.* If this newbie becomes the department leader, I have less stress, more time alone, and less facetime with Grant and Ryan. Ryan can set his sights on seducing her instead of pushing me around.

With a clean set of scrubs, and contact lenses to camouflage my eyes, I meet the entourage in front of my lab. Nate, Grant, and Patty are fawning over a tall, willowy blonde. She must be the candidate. She has thick black glasses perched on her nose but otherwise a pretty face. Her suit is a course polyester mix hinting that it is not tailored to her but rather from a mall. Either the east coast cost-of-living is a struggle for microbiologists, or she doesn't believe in spending money on clothes. Nate says something ridiculous and the candidate laughs. It is a nasal gaff ending in a snort. *Yikes*.

"Dr. Lucien Von Popescu, this is Dr. Kimberly Parker. Lucien is our head of microbiology and would be overseeing your day-to-day operations."

"Hi, it's Luc," I say shaking her hand. Her hand tremors in mine as does her smile. She's terrified, according to my nose. Why would someone living the fast-paced life on the east coast want to be in an isolated town like Strawberry? A place to hide. Luckily for her, this scores more points with me than the four-page CV I found rumpled in my sheets. She reminds me of Bela and

Christopher on the day I found them.

"Thanks, Luc, I'm Kimberly. Thank you for the opportunity to tour your beautiful facility. I'm excited to see the lab," she says in her thick east coast accent. Nate had mentioned she worked in New Jersey, but I bet she was born and raised there as well.

"Thank you for accommodating my odd hours. I've been nocturnal all my life but that is what keeps Bergan ahead of the pack. Nate works the second shift while I work the graveyard shift. Your hours would overlap with ours so there would be at least one microbiologist in the building at all times," I say with a small bow before catching myself. Without Ryan's hold on me, why do I need to bow? It's time to blow the lid off this Old-World charm charade.

"That's not a problem. I will be relocating to Strawberry and I don't have a family to support. I mean, I have family, just not kids or a husband, a not current husband. There is no one who dictates my schedule."

I use the thumbprint scanner to open my lab. *Betty*. Her influence is everywhere, from the clean countertops to the lingering scent of her arousal. My fangs tingle and threaten to drop until I reassure myself, I am the only vampire in the room. No one else has the ability to smell her but me. This interview needs to end, so I can at least text Betty to explain. *Damn, I miss her*. Memories of her laughter haunt the room. Kimberly is walking around like she is in heaven, but I hardly notice. Instead, my mind puts Betty in every corner, flipping through a journal, sitting at the hood, digging through my PPE, and coming apart in my arms.

"So, I would get all this space to myself?" Kimberly's question nearly flies over my head. She's looking at me to answer but I am stuck.

"The three of us share this lab but you will have bench space in Scientific or Molecular Toxicology if your work requires their equipment. With our rotating shifts, you will get a lot of time in here by yourself. Only a few of us even have access to this room via the thumbprint scanner, fewer people than those who have access to this floor," Nate says.

"Then I will be safe in here," Kimberly says with a sigh. "In my current job, there would be twenty scientists stuffed in a space this large with competing agendas. The sabotage of projects is commonplace, even though we work for the same company. Competition is encouraged over cooperation." Nervousness blooms from her and its putrid stench fills the room.

She is running scared from New Jersey and not from competing scientists. Good thing Strawberry is a haven for misfits, even ones whose laugh sounds an asthmatic pig. I would love to hire a runaway with real microbiology skills who is afraid of taking the credit for the department.

"Bergan Pharma supports everyone in town," I say, earning a glare from Grant. "Cooperation is our business model. We never create the generics of our own products or perform counter-research outside of fail-safes. We have three products in the FDA pipeline right now, but they are addressing widely different ailments."

"Would we be assigned certain products or how do you manage the lab?"

Good question. My current style is to do everything to make Ryan happy until I screw up the project and then have Nate bail me out. "I will manage all the projects until you are settled," I say, leaning on the class II cabinet with mock confidence. "I break down the submission package into smaller reports with Standard Operating Procedures, the usual lab SOPs. Those have been converted to forms for you to populate. We are GMP/GLP certified so unfortunately most of it requires paper signatures and data entry. I will provide a folder of your part in the project and look forward to your report."

"Wow, you are both Good Manufacturing and Good Laboratory Practice certified?"

"We want to keep our options open for the good of the company. Being able to manufacture our own products as well as R&D, gives us room for expansion," Grant interjects.

"And I would get full autonomy? Just here's your assignment and give me your report?" I inhale at her questions and get a noseful of hope. She may be the perfect fit for my department. I understand wanting to be left alone more than she realizes.

"Yes," I say with what I hope looks more like a gentle smile than a fangy sneer.

"Like these, Luc needs to get this data to me," Patty says, pulling a group of papers off the cabinet front beside me. Betty's hairclip clatters on the floor to land directly between Grant's feet. He picks it up and drops it in his pocket while my horror chokes my airway. Patty and Kimberly are going over the paper trail while all I can do is stare at Grant. With Patty and Kimberly standing between us, I can't catch a whiff of him. However, the glare in his eyes tells me he knows the origins of the hairclip.

"Well, what do you think?" Nate asks before his phone rings with a shrill. "Excuse me I have to take this. Whaddup Buddy? She's what? We're what? Oh my God, where are you guys? I'll be right there." He's shouting into his phone with the rest of us staring. He turns to us with a smile splitting his face. "I'm going to be a dad! I'm going to be a dad!" He bounces around the room more like a storybook tiger than a leopard.

"Congratulations," Grant says with a hug when Nate passes him.

"Fantastic news," I say, getting an uninitiated hug. He grabs both Patty and Kimberly in a combined hug before bouncing out of the room. "I am sorry if he stepped on your boundaries, Kimberly. He was a little excited to be a first-time father."

"First-time father but a life-long dream," Patty says sourly. Jealousy bites at my nose. She never did get over the Yule-party-that-shall-not-be-mentioned. *That's not fair.* As a changed, non-witch shifter, she is as barren as a female vampire. Hopefully, she is over Nate and lamenting missing out on motherhood.

"If you have no more questions for Lucien, the local Italian restaurant delivered dinner. Patty, if you will take Kimberly to get Emily from HR, I will meet you downstairs. I must talk to our Head of Microbiology before I eat," Grant commands. Was that flash of fangs directed at me? Bring it on, Pooh Bear.

If he wants to take issue over Betty's hairclips with me, I have a few concerns of my own. Betty's fear over him seeing her was overwhelming and I'm not standing for that, not when she currently resides in his house. That's another thing I'm not allowing. I'm going to assess her situation there and if it isn't satisfactory, she is moving in with me.

Hell, without Ryan's mandates, I'm asking her to move in with me tonight. I am picking up the ring. I am free to take what I want and all I want is to listen to Betty's laughter.

Our stare down is so intense I hardly notice the women exit the lab. When the door clicks shut, Grant reaches into his pocket and holds the hairclip at the end of my nose. "Shall you talk first, or shall I?"

I want to blow up at him. No, I cannot show my cards. Grant would suspect Betty ran to me for help if I let on that he scares her. He would automatically be suspicious because Betty doesn't run to anyone. People run to her for help. A vision of my pint-sized warrior in her fighting stance before the five Sluagh floats in my mind. Yeah, she would never run to anyone.

My stuttering brain gives Grant room to start his tirade. "She either gave this to you or she was here. Watch it, vampire. Don't try to cover up Betty's involvement because I designed this clip with Josh for her Yule gift," Grant says between the fangs of an elongated muzzle.

"I brought her here, so what." I puff to my full height. I can barely contain my own fangs and wings. "You aren't her keeper."

"No, I wouldn't want that job. Believe me," he says, shaking his head. "I am Bergan's keeper. Hosting a person of interest in an ongoing narcotics investigation is not in this company's best interests. Betty is in a world of trouble that threatens multiple certifications and licenses for Bergan."

The air is punched from my lungs with his words. She wasn't afraid of him. She was afraid he would share her secret. "I misjudged you, Grant. I thought you were trying to keep her out for another reason. I'm sorry." My heart sinks as Grant shakes my hand. Betty played me.

Damn it, I thought I was on her team. I thought we were deceiving everyone else. *I'm such a fool.*

"She's not hiding a drug problem if that's putting the sour look on your face. Damn Luc, you look like I kicked your puppy. It's more complicated than that." He spins a chair from the cabinet and sits in it. The chair groans in response to his bulk.

"I know it is not your story to tell, but I am worried about her. We met because she ran out of the Yule party with a panic attack. Was her panic due to legal issues?" I fold myself into the second chair at the cabinet.

"Alison said James's proposal set her off. Evan, her piece-of-work boyfriend, had a seizure proposing to her and died at her feet a year ago."

"Oh my God…"

"Yeah, the asshole had been using her nursing credentials to steal drugs in her name. Not that she was a sweetheart before him, but the guy did a number on her. He isolated her from her family, screwed her career, and messed with her mind."

"Her mind? How did he do that?"

"He pretended to push her to take more clinical side jobs under the guise of supporting her. It got to be, so she only worked to please him. In reality, he was pushing for multiple places to steal drugs to lessen the risk of getting caught. Even after it was all exposed, she took multiple jobs waiting tables instead of going to class to pay for a love nest where she was going to get him clean. While she worked, he ran a drug den from the place."

"Did she ever get arrested?"

"No, thank God, that would have devastated her parents. The last straw was when she ditched their Samhain party. Frantic, they sent her siblings and me to scour the city for her. Alison and I found her with the paramedics as they took his body away. Evan died before she came to the realization, he wasn't the one for her. She's scarred, deeply scarred, Lucien. Do you know what it is like to rearrange your life for someone and then they die on you?"

Unfortunately, I did. Terika gave up on our plan before I even moved here. I've been pushing Betty, manipulating her at Ryan's request, for Terika's benefit. Terika is dead and I have fallen in love with Betty, despite it all. "I had no idea," I murmur to the floor.

"No one does and no one else will. She may act tough but she's down to her last hit points. Just don't hurt her and keep her out of this lab. Okay?" Grant hands the hairclip back to me and pats my shoulder.

"Did she love him?"

"Of course, she did."

I let my head fall into my hands when the door clicks shut behind Grant. Betty's hairclip pokes me in the forehead with defiance, drawing blood at my hairline. It is like her spirit is punishing me from afar. Maybe she has latent genetic magic after all. I deserve to be slapped by her…again. She was at her most vulnerable when I prayed upon her. I should have realized her wail of despair at the Yule party was a deeper wound that wasn't close to healing. Yet I manipulated her love for her sister to get close to her. Like the predator I accuse Ryan of being, I hunted her.

Even when she had a nightmare of Evan, I continued to pursue her. The nightmare probably was a voice inside her telling her that rebounding to me wasn't a good idea. She had a nightmare because she wasn't over him but sleeping beside me and I let it happen. No, I engineered it to happen. I could have circled back to Dr. V's office, but I kept her in my house. Good thing I'm ditching my gentleman manners. I was never a gentleman.

To compound her pain, I have ignored her for days. Love her and leave her, all while she's nursing a broken heart. *Nursing*. She came here for nursing opportunities and saved my life. To repay her, I seduced her and ditched her. She deserves freedom from my toxic behavior. Now I just have to be man enough to apologize and let her go.

Chapter 30

"Betty, I don't know how you can eat that stuff. It is so gross," Ally says scrunching her nose. Rosie offered me a bowl of the risotto with scallops and butternut squash, but my fangy fetus, Little Batman, didn't want anything to do with it. Just sitting at the table while my sister and her best friend eat it is turning my stomach.

The only thing I am keeping down is the blood-laced chocolate from Josh. I just hope he continues to believe the lie that I am picking it up for my new best buddy, Molina. Perhaps I should call Molina and let her in on my lie but then again, I would have to tell her about Little Batman. If any vampire deserves to know, it is Lucien. Too bad I am not speaking to him until he contacts me, immature behavior or not.

"At least it doesn't smell. Ryan mixes his bagged blood with hot water when he dines here," Rosie says. "It reeks to high heaven. It even drowns out the smells in the kitchen on a busy night. Of all the vampires, Ryan drinks the most blood in public. He must have a king-sized appetite."

When our laughter at Ryan's expense dies down, Ally raises her glass. "A toast to Betty. A toast to congratulate her on completing her NCLEX exam today."

"Here, here. Here's to you for getting it done before the kid is born. They will consume your life you know,"

Rosie says with her glass raised.

"Yes, I learned from Dirtball's mistake and got my schooling out of the way. I will still need continuing education here and there. Hopefully, I can find stuff online."

"Well, I was happy to drive you to Louisville for the test and I will be happy to do it again for any reason— education or nephew stuff."

"Little Batman and I appreciate it—"

"You call your baby, *Little Batman*?" Rosie is turning red with her inability to hold in her laughter. Ally's mouth hangs open and horror lights her eyes.

"It feels like a boy and he's a vampire so yes, for now, my baby is a little batman. Go ahead and laugh. You will be gushing over it when I show you the comic book nursery décor I have picked out."

"Awwwwww," they coo in unison.

"Rosie, do you think Gran would know about vampire pregnancy? Dr. V is going to deliver the baby at the office but if she has any tips, I need them."

"I'm scared to ask. Gran hasn't left her bed since the Yule party. She is drinking broth and tea, so she has the energy to bark orders at Henrik. Otherwise, she just wants to sleep. I'm really worried she's leaving us."

"Oh Rosie," Ally says with tear-filled eyes, "I'm so sorry. I wish to make my peace with her, right now. I was so angry she chose Henrik over me to be her apprentice."

"Go on up," Rosie says motioning to the stairs to her apartment. "It can't be too late at night for visitors when you sleep all day."

Ally bounds upstairs, leaving us in the dining room. I pull out another chocolate sculpture from my purse and use the handle of my knife to smash it into bite-sized pieces. Loudly crinkling the cellophane, I unwrap it before slowly lifting a piece to my lips.

"Gross," Rosie says from behind her outstretched hand. "Now you are just being disgusting."

"That's what the preggo is good for—substituting repulsion for despair." The words barely leave my mouth when the bells over the door jingle.

"Hello, hello? Your door was open, so I assumed someone was in here? Hello," a feminine voice calls out.

"You two sit. I will investigate. Gran was asleep anyway," Ally says, crossing the dining room. Short black claws have sprouted from her hands and feet. Her flowered sundress strains over her increased bulk as she battles the need to change into her polar form. "Hello, Come on back. We can help you," she says when she rounds the corner to the entry gauntlet. Her offer to help is not a comfort to the visitor but a sign to Rosie they are not Sluagh.

A beautiful woman in a full-length red leather coat towers over Alison as they enter the dining room. Her black hair is piled on top of her head in a network of pearled clips while her makeup looks professionally done. She removes her matching gloves to reveal manicured nails. *Fabulous*.

The Strawberry welcoming committee looks shabby in comparison. I don't know which is the worst. Rosie in her curlers and housecoat. Dirtball in her flimsy sundress with dirty bare feet or myself in the scrubs I found on the floor this morning. I nominate myself for best dressed because my ponytail is smooth and I'm wearing makeup, even if it is of the drugstore variety.

"I'm so sorry for barging in. I'm just at the end of my tether," she says with an eastern European accent. "I have been on planes for days only to arrive in Louisville, not Strawberry. I couldn't figure out the heat in the rental car, so I have been freezing for hours and then it got dark. Not that I am afraid of the dark, I have been nocturnal for forty years, but I ran out of streetlights. Half the time I wasn't sure if I was driving on a road. This is the first commercial square I have seen for over an hour."

The mention of being nocturnal has me checking her eyes for the sign of the vampire. She is too far away but Ally does a minuscule headshake to indicate the visitor is human. "I'm Alison Luther and you could say I'm the mayor-of-sorts of Strawberry." Ally shakes the woman's hand. "You are freezing. Please come and sit with us to warm up. We were celebrating with a late-night dinner for my sister."

"Hi," I say with a wave when they approach the table.

"—And this is Rosie, the owner of Paulino's pizzeria."

"Gracious, your fingers are icicles," Rosie exclaims. "Do you like risotto? I find myself with an extra bowl. It's yours and it will warm you right up." She disappears into the kitchen after giving me a face at not eating her risotto.

"Thank you for your hospitality. I have been so lost...I'm Reveca, by the way," she says, shaking my hand before sitting beside me.

"Here we go, piping hot risotto and ginger tea. It will revive you in no time," Rosie says, plunking a plate and mug in front of our guest.

"You are too kind. Thank you so much. I hope I'm not intruding. I was hoping for directions." Reveca eyes her bowl like a hawk about to snatch a rodent.

"Don't think another thing about it," Rosie says, swatting the air.

"It is not safe to be driving around alone at night. You are lucky you found us." Ally sinks back into her chair with what we are all thinking written on her face. If this woman were caught by Sluagh, she would be destroyed. Aurora was able to survive the captivity of two Sluagh until her rescue, but this woman seems delicate while Aurora can kick ass.

"Oh, I'm not afraid of vampires," Reveca replies before scooping a heaping spoonful of risotto. "I must pay my respects to Ryan for entering his territory, but he knows me so well, a delay shouldn't be a problem."

We freeze and stare at each other. How is this woman related to the vampires? Why aren't they escorting her through Sluagh-infested territory? "Well, Ryan swore fealty to me, so consider your respects paid." Ally punctuates her sentence by shoving a spoonful into her mouth.

"Where are you from, Reveca?"

"Moldova, I have lived in the colony since I was a little girl— "

"Your English is fantastic for someone who lives so far away," interjects Rosie.

"Thanks, learning English was a royal decree from Ryan. I know to pay my respects to him but he's not the one I'm visiting. Do you know Lucien Von Popescu?"

My heart skips a beat at the mention of his name. Of course, this gorgeous woman is a friend of Lucien's from the Old Country. He told me repeatedly of his conquests there. Why didn't I realize his sudden silence heralded the arrival of an old flame? He only needed me to tide him over while this cultured bombshell was being delivered. "I know him quite well actually," I say. Rosie and Alison look at me with expressions of pity. Once we are alone, I'm going to knock them silly for that. "Were you looking for his estate or visiting him at Bergan?"

"Silly me, I thought Strawberry was so small I could drive to the town center and a vampire could show me to Ryan who would shuffle me to Lucien's house." Reveca nerves thicken her accent. Her cheeks stain pink in a sweet, innocent way. It is like her every gesture has been practiced before a mirror. Every quirk of her lips draws the eye to them. Wait…those lips…

"Strawberry is small, but we have acres of farmland to separate the buildings. Lucien's haunted house is quite a distance away from here," Rosie says.

"Haunted house?"

"That's what everyone calls it because he doesn't maintain his property. It is a joke and even he finds it funny," Ally says, going to the window and pulling the blinds open. "If you are ultimately looking for Lucien, you need to go to Bergan Pharma across the village green. My husband, Grant, is in the final push on a big project. Lucien is part of the team working to meet the deadline."

"That's her sweet way of saying Lucien is working his hands to the bone," Rosie says with a snicker. Ally glares at her friend, earning a laugh from Rosie and myself.

"You are more than welcome at my house while he's working. I have plenty of guest rooms and then you can visit Lucien tomorrow evening. The deadline is during the day tomorrow so I doubt he will come home tonight. Besides, I am Ryan's closest neighbor. If you still want to visit him for admission to his territory, I can walk you across the yards."

"I couldn't impose like that."

"Take her up on the offer," I say, swallowing my pride, "because Lucien's guestrooms are without furniture."

"What?"

Rosie's eyes bug out before she says, "that makes his house even more creepy. You mean he has four to five empty bedrooms?"

"Now you must stay with us."

"Yep," I say with a pop of another chocolate in my mouth. "If you slept there, you would have to share his bed."

"That will never do. What grown man would want to sleep next to his mother?"

Cough! The chocolate shard lodges in my throat threatening to decapitate me. I sip my tea to stifle the coughing. *Little Batman, if you can hear my thoughts, listen up and meet your grandmother. Your dad gets his perfect lips from her. I hope you inherit them too.* I chug the rest of my tea in an effort to melt the chocolate. Ally reaches over to smack my back with her brutal shifter strength. "Okay, okay, I'm good"—I swat her away—"You hit me one more time and you are going to leave a bruise. Keep your super strength to yourself."

"Alison, you must be one of the shifters, Pumpkin…I mean Lucien told me about."

"Pumpkin, eh?" Rosie has a devious twinkle in her eyes. Lucien's mom calls him Pumpkin? Well, now so does everyone in Strawberry. I would feel sorry for him if he hadn't ditched me.

"Yes, I am the pack leader of the Strawberry shifters

and a ferocious polar bear," Ally replies. "Well, I am," she adds to us when Rosie and I laugh at her. A pouty frown forms on her face and makes her freckles droop.

"Believe it or not, the ferocious flower here succeeded my husband as Strawberry's leader. I'm the leader of the Paulino wolfpack only because I have a house full of sons."

Reveca looks to me for explanations. "Oh no, not me, I'm not a shifter. I'm much more feared than a big animal. I'm a nurse," I say with my mouth full.

"A nurse? Are you Betty by chance?" Her eyes are shining with tears. *Well, shit*. This can't be good.

"Yes, Betty is my little sister," Ally answers with her claws poking the tablecloth. Good God, Ally put those things away. She's not going to attack me when she knows you are a bear and Rosie is a wolf.

"I have something for you. I'm so excited I found you so fast. I've been carrying this around for hundreds of miles. I didn't trust the checked baggage," Reveca says jumping up. She clacks out of the room with staccato taps of her heels, leaving her coat behind. The rapid tempo continues down the gauntlet before the doorbells chime.

"I better watch her so a Sluagh doesn't jump her," Rosie says, walking in Reveca's wake.

"So, Lucien's mom came across the ocean to find you. Are you okay with this?"

"Do I have a choice? I just hope she doesn't have a cyanide pill for me."

"She will love you. You are carrying her legacy…her little pumpkin," Ally says, launching a fit of giggles.

"Be careful, he's the Prince of Darkness."

"Pumpkin of Darkness. The Dark Pumpkin except when you are around," Ally says before laughing harder.

"Why not when I'm around?"

"Because then the Dark Pumpkin rises!" I glare at her laughing face until she snorts and turns red.

Reveca returns carrying a giant white paper box. I've seen that shape before. It looks like a bakery box. My heart leaps as my little batman sends signals for a cake, more specifically a giant sheet cake. Could she smell my pregnancy? She's not a vampire and claims to be human but I never checked her eyes for metallic stars. Could she have the mark of the witch, like Ally and Henrik?

"This is for you," she says, choking back tears. *Damn, it's not a cake if she's tearing up.* I push the chocolate to the side to make space for the box on the table. She lifts the lid as her first tears fall. The air flies from my lungs when she embraces me fiercely, crying on my shoulder.

"I'm so happy and I hope you know Terika was happy too. Had she been well, Lucien wanted her to be just like you," she sniffles.

I peer over her shoulder to the contents of the box. A red dress with a black lace overlay sparkles at me. Black jewels and pearls dot the lace, like stars. Below the ornate bodice is a full red skirt that shines like waves of silk. In the corner of the box is a small bag containing a small strand of black pearls, jeweled black combs, and…and… I start to hyperventilate. In the bag is a black lace veil.

"I gave it to Terika, first, but she didn't live long enough to wear it. It was her dying wish that I pass down my wedding dress to you. I had to pay respect to Ryan, and I wished to check on my son, but I came to America to deliver this to you."

"I don't know what to say," I reply while she hugs me tighter. I doubt she wants to hear how I'm totally fucked.

Chapter 31

"I know Bela. It is almost over," I coo as she births her fourth kitten. I stop home to feed two cats to find them multiplying under my bed. Cats don't get that pregnancy glow, I guess. I wish for help as I wipe kittens with towels while avoiding Bela's claws. Christopher paces just outside of the bedroom like an expectant father. He looks at me as if I have two heads when I call him into the bedroom. Three of the kittens are bright orange, exonerating all-black Christopher.

"Bela has kittens." I type into my phone only to be deleted. Who can I text? Ryan hates the cats, and I am supposed to break it off with Betty. If I text anything, it should say—have a nice life…without me…because I can't hurt you again. *Ugh*. After staring at my phone for what feels like an hour, I text Betty, "Want to talk tonight?"

"Well Christopher, what can I name them? Terika, Erika…no that's stupid. I don't know if they are boys or girls. Pumpkin, Bumpkin, Lumpkin, and the little black one is Nod," I say to Christopher. He grooms himself in approval.

A pang of longing hits my chest. I'm a Vampire Casanova turned into a Lonely Cat Lady. However, the knowledge Betty will have a house full of family, complete with a husband to watch over her as she grows old, is worth it. Her life shouldn't be a series of burials.

I refuse to add to the list when I join Terika too young.

"Office is closed, but I am still working. Stop by whenever," says the reply text from Betty. My heart sinks. I would rather she be pissed than indifferent. I guess it could be worse. Her reply could be full of love and hope—that I am about to crush. This fake relationship is like a runaway train.

My dark mood matches the black clouds hovering over Strawberry. Snowflakes swat at my car as I drive in silence. I don't want to contaminate any of my music with this horrendous event. It is bad enough every song I heard in her presence will remind me of how much I love her. I can't risk reliving our breakup repeated with the music that usually cheers me up. The good news is that I only have ten to fifteen years left to suffer.

I stop at Josh's auto not only to fill my car but also to clear my head. I stand outside in the dark, frigid night and rehearse my speech to her. I practice sounding convincing as the gallons drip into my giant SUV. My Princess is sharp even if she was never mine, to begin with. Who knows which of her narratives were true and which weren't? *Good.* That burning lava of betrayal is what I need to fuel my argument.

"Luc," whispers a voice behind me.

"Josh, I'm sorry I was daydreaming I didn't even see you approach."

"I snuck around the back. I wanted to give this to you in secret. I got your PayPal days ago, but you never responded to my messages about pick up. It is a miracle I got it to you without Betty seeing." I take the velvet bag from Forger Josh and peek inside. A stunning ruby ring twinkles back at me with a mocking promise of commitment.

Go Scorch Yourself

"You have outdone yourself. My father's ruby is in a work of art."

"Put it away before you spoil the surprise," Josh says before looking over his shoulder. "I don't know how long Josh can keep her occupied with free chocolate samples. Betty will be out here any second."

"Not here," I huff. I can't smash our relationship in the town center with who knows how many shifters watching.

"I know a gas station isn't romantic, Lucien, but she's right there. Come on, there's a field behind the building. Propose under the stars." I allow Josh to lead me behind the building to a field devoid of footprints. The pristine snow sparkles in the moonlight with no evidence of anyone hanging out in the shadows. It is perfect...for a breakup.

Betty emerges from the shop carrying a giant bag of chocolates. Her cheeks are rosy from the cold and her nose matches her red coat. Snowflakes hitchhike in her hair creating a crown. I will always remember her this way, a small smile on her lips as she watches her boots sink in the snow.

"Hey Betty, look who I found," Josh calls before elbowing me. She turns our way, and the air gets trapped in my lungs. Her dress flares out with her movement showing off her shapely legs. Her ponytail fans around to adhere to her cheek with newly-fallen snowflakes. I stand slack-jawed as her delicate finger caresses her cheek to push it away. I would kill to have the job of pushing errant strands from her cheek. Cheeks speckled with freckles that she hides from the world. I consider myself part of an elite few who have been close enough to her to see them.

"Go get her, man," Josh whispers and trots back into the shop.

"Why the silent treatment?" She thunders the question at me as soon as we are within shouting distance. I guess this is starting off on the correct foot. Why do I feel like crying already? It is Dad's ruby. I can feel it burning a hole in my pocket. His spirit pushing me to love her more than myself.

"I needed to grieve for Terika—"

"I could have been there for you—"

"I know...I know the whole Evan story now."

"You don't because I wasn't the one who told you. So, whatever you think you know is bullshit."

"That's the problem with a web of lies, isn't it Betty? You lose sight of which ones are affecting which people and they spin out of control when you aren't managing them. Here's a word of advice: Strawberry is a small town. Limit the lies because everyone talks to everyone else."

"You know what? Fuck your advice and fuck you," she says poking my chest with her finger. There. Is she mad enough to cut our ties for me? Mad is more palatable than sad. If she hates me then she won't miss me.

"You wanted a public breakup, so anyone listening: your drama has been served. I'm done. I don't have time for this."

"Really? Does Ryan have another errand for you instead? No wonder you mope around. You never do anything to improve your situation. You don't have the balls to be happy. For once, I would love to see you stand up and do something just for you," she yells with ire. The faint golden flecks in her eyes flash like lightning.

"Actually, with Terika's death, he no longer has

leverage over me. My first order of business was to get rid of you and the lies that complicate being around you." Droplets fall from her eyes along with my heart to the ground. I can hardly breathe. I need to finish this or I'm going to fall to my knees to apologize.

"So, you assumed, I still love Evan because you are mourning Terika. You equate your sorrow over her loss with my loss of Evan. You never asked me how I felt about him. You never asked me how I feel about you. You never took the time to—"

"I think I already stated I don't have the extra time to play your games." That feels closer to the truth, so it rolls out of my mouth a little smoother. It is not that I don't want to be the one who helps orchestrate her lies. It is that I don't have time—I don't have a full lifetime.

"Why would you do this to me?"

"Because I'm dying, Betty."

"The stem cells will keep you alive. Look at Ryan."

"You know why he pushes me so hard? The pantaloons, the m'ladies, the bowing? Because he has months to live not years. He is fifteen years older than me, and he's got months to live. He hasn't come out and told me, but it's as plain as the nose on my face."

"What?"

"The stem cells are not implanting in him anymore. Hell, Dr. V has injected enough cells in him to make a whole new Ryan. I've been to most of the appointments. He consumes blood at the rate we drank back in the Old Country. He never built enough marrow despite the treatments and what he had is dissipating. It's over for him and soon it will be over for me. Two-thirds of my life is gone. I'm on the downward spiral. I'm not taking you with me."

My strategy changes before I know it. Truth bombs drop out of my mouth at an alarming rate. All of this will get back to Alison and I don't care. I don't want the last words between us to be lies. It is on the tip of my tongue to tell her I will love her from afar because that is all I can offer her.

"Why not? What about your precious colony? Am I only good for a fun time but not good enough to continue your royal bloodline?"

"You don't get it. If the purity of my bloodline was so important, do you think I would have been allowed to plow half of my college population? No. The elders were hoping for an accident. They were hoping a mistake would make an heir. You know what? If you were there, I would have made that accident happen, but you weren't."

"You can't blame me for not being born in your country."

"I can blame fate though. It didn't happen and now it won't happen. Why can't you be like Alison and find a shifter to love you? You could live for hundreds of years."

She steps back as if I have slapped her. The tears turn from mascara-coated droplets to blackened streams as my cruelty pierces her heart. The love that has grown between us shatters with my caustic words. "More like my sister…"

"You should aim higher than a charity case. You should be looking for true love. I can't give you that."

"What if I already gave it to you?"

"You don't know how to love. You think you do because of the pain when Evan died. Don't you see I'm just like him, just as sick, just as close to death? I would use you for end-of-life companionship just like he did. He didn't love you, you didn't love him, and you don't love me."

"You can't stand there and tell me what I feel!"

"No, but I can tell you the truth. You collect broken birds. Alison was the first and when Grant took over her care, you were pissed at being replaced. Evan took advantage of your misplaced jealousy. He was so broken, he died too soon to completely destroy you. I walked into your life with a death sentence that made me irresistible to a bleeding heart like you. You don't love me. You love the idea of taking care of me. An incurable genetic disease? I am the most broken bird you can find. Your kryptonite."

"That's not true," she chokes between sobs. Her makeup slides from her face onto her coat. Her freckles gleam at me in the moonlight, imploring me to make this stop. Dammit, I'm not enough to give her the happy life she deserves.

"Prove it by walking away. Prove it by living happily ever after. Prove it by finding someone whole to love," I choke through my developing tears

"You don't mean that."

"It doesn't matter," I say, unlocking my car doors. I leave her there before my tears begin to drop. I drive away in the hopes my memories of her are enough to finish out my short lifespan. For once I did the right thing and let her go. I just hope she finds someone to love who will grow old with her.

Chapter 32

"Hi honey, I'm home," I call into Ally's yellow kitchen. "I'm going to make some chamomile tea and go straight to bed. I'm fine but this creature needs her black lagoon." The cheery kitchen assaults my senses. If I hadn't met the very human Reveca, I would think a vampire pregnancy could transform a person into a vampire.

"Chamomile, coming up," Ally practically sings. "I already have water boiling. Reveca and I were having some black tea to start our day."

The two women look like opposite ends of the self-care spectrum. Ally is barefoot in a pink sundress smudged with dirt despite the frigid temperature and snow-covered ground. Reveca wears a set of pearls over her pink cashmere sweater set that matches the combs holding her black hair on the top of her head. Whether it is makeup or winning the genetic lottery, only her conservative clothes hint at being Lucien's mom.

Oh God, I can't face her, not when I want to eviscerate her son. Maybe I will survive this conversation if I force Ally to talk about herself. "How was the pack meeting last night?"

"Lucien wasn't there is that's what you are asking," Ally says, handing me a steaming mug. "It was so embarrassing to introduce Reveca to the pack without him in attendance. Ryan was acting out of control without Lucien's influence too. Betty, I wish you had been there to keep the vampires in line."

"Oh yeah, did Ryan try to kiss you again?"

"Not even on the hand."

"Whoa, that is odd. Do you think it was because she was there?" I point to Reveca who raises an eyebrow at Ally.

"No, he addressed the pack at the end and said some strange stuff too. He was going off about sending a delegate to the Fae realm during the May Day parade. He wants to broker a peace deal with the King of the Fae. Even the other vampires thought he was off his rocker."

"How did you respond? Do you think he will try to align with the Fae against you?"

"He never gave me the chance to question his motives privately. He piled a bunch of food into a bag and left. Betty, I think he was saying goodbye. He's planning something but I can't put my finger on it."

"I have known Ryan since we were teenagers, and he has never acted like that. He is meticulous to a fault and last night he looked like he had taken a stroll through a carwash. I'm worried he lost his mind to stress," Reveca says with a shake of her head.

"I know Lucien wasn't there because I got cornered at the gas station. He was filling his car when I was filling up on chocolates."

"Oh Betty, did you tell him about his mother being in town or any other new business?"

I look from Ally to Reveca in horror. My damn sister couldn't keep a secret if her life depended on it. "No," I say with my most aggressive glare.

"Is Lucien coming over tonight?" His mother looks so hopeful, it is my undoing. *Damn pregnancy hormones.*

"No," I say with mascara-tinted tears falling. "He is done with me. I didn't get a chance to tell him about your visit before he ended things."

"Oh no," Ally says, hugging me from behind, "he can't mean that."

"He does Ally. Lucien isn't my Grant after all," I say between hiccups. "Grant has always loved you. Lucien never loved me. We were a fixed arrangement from the beginning. I'm the stupid one. I fell in love when he didn't."

"That's not accurate," Reveca says, grabbing my hand. "He told Terika he was in love with you. That's why she willed my wedding dress to you."

"I broke his trust. He's done but it doesn't matter. I require sleep and then tonight I will plan my new life. The dress is here if you wish to take it back."

"I will be right here for you," Ally says. "Anything you need, just ask."

"Thanks, I want to be alone." I pull away from them. I need to grieve, and I can't do it with an audience. I get as far as the front staircase before my strength gives out. Sitting down to sob, I run my hand over my stomach. *I'll never be alone again, right Little Batman? You will love me even though I am unlovable.*

"I wish vampires had a smell test like shifters," Ally grouses from the kitchen.

"What do you mean?"

"Shifter females smell like garbage to males unless they are destined mates. It is like the powers that be knew they needed a little nudge."

"Vampires have the ability to flash from place to place. They can only do it alone or in the arms of their one true love. Didn't Lucien try to flash with Betty?"

"I wouldn't know," Ally says before the clicks of Reveca's heels approach my stair.

"Well, did my idiot son ever flash with you?"

"I don't even know what that means," I whine. Their appearance energizes my body to climb the stairs. I would walk back to Ohio to get out of this conversation.

"You embrace, link thoughts, and snap! You have traveled a distance instantaneously," Reveca says with a clap of her hands. "Did my son ever try?"

I throw my arms in the air and ask, "how would I know?"

"The three V's of vampire failure: vertigo, vomit, and vacillating thoughts. If he tried and failed, then you would be sick for hours," Reveca says, ticking them off her fingers.

"Then no, he didn't care enough to try."

"Alison, I need your help," she says, grabbing both of my sister's hands. "My son is making the biggest mistake of his life."

"Stop right there, Thelma and Louise." My voice shakes with volcanic fury. "I didn't tell him about Little Batman because I don't want to guilt him into being with me. I don't want to wonder if he really loves me or is secretly trapped. I need someone to love me for me, not because of a fucking flash prophesy."

"Terika knew you were his one true love. He deserves the opportunity to flash with you."

"She was isolated until her death. Did she even date? What would she know?"

"Female vampires do not have the gift of childrearing but have another gift instead. Terika could read thoughts. When I say she knew he loved you, he didn't just say it. He believed it."

"That may have been true at the time but—"

"My Lucien, his father, believed love was more important than anything else on this planet. He would roll over in his grave if he knew his son was throwing his chance away…his chance to be loved by you," she says, pulling my hands to her face.

This is too much. I tried to save Lucien the aggravation but at the end of the day, this is between him and his mother. Let him explain what happened between us. I'm too tired. *I'm too broken.*

"Well, it's over. Believe me. If you want to waste your time convincing him to do a flash test, then fine. I'm nauseous all the time so it won't be a big loss to me." Lifting my foot to the next stair takes the strength of a construction crane.

"Ally, you can't blab to him though, I will never forgive you." I send the warning floating down the stairs without turning to face her. She knows I am relying on her and it doesn't feel comfortable. It would be so easy to let them pamper and pity me. It would also keep them in the house. What will Lucien say when the cavalry approaches his doorstep?

Chapter 33

Sleep. I need to sleep. Researching kitten parenting online while Bela instinctively keeps everything under control has eaten the day away. At least I didn't do anything stupid like cut the umbilical cord, based on what I have seen in the movies. Each kitten is a hairless bean with folded ears and closed eyes. Every few hours I check for a pulse because they look more like ceramic statues than pets, except maybe naked mole rats. Bela is the consummate mother, going beyond the call of duty by drinking their urine after stimulating them to go. *And people think vampires are gross for drinking blood.*

My stomach growls and twists as I wander to the kitchen with the hope there are leftover bags of blood. *Hot damn.* Two bags are chilling with a breakfast pastry between them. A pastry left behind by Betty for me to use to torture myself. Nuking the confection in the microwave, I have a last meal to say goodbye to a relationship that could never be. *Ouch, effing thing.* The rebellious pastry is a testament to its owner and burns my fingers as I remove it from the microwave. I drop it on a plate and watch it smolder like I would love to watch Betty smolder.

Visions of her dance through my head. A divine providence puts a pen in my hand. I compose my feelings for her on a paper towel. I scribble letters, notes, and feelings at a fevered pitch. She may never be my wife, but she will always be my muse. My breakfast scorches the inside of my mouth with each bite fueling my memories of the woman who scorched my senses.

Bang! BANG! Betty? Could it be? Would she visit me, even if it is only to scream obscenities? I throw open the door without verifying who is on the other side. I wait on the balls of my feet until they step inside so I can emerge from the shadows. An irate Alison comes into view and my hopes fly to the sky. Is Betty with her? An apology formulates in my head as the other figure walks through the door but turns to the living room.

"Welcome, Madam Commander, to what do I owe the visit?"

"Goodness Lucien, do you always answer your door in your boxers? Put on some clothes," she snaps. She puts her hand over her eyes and blushes pink.

"Many pardons, I am handling a crisis and I have forgotten my manners—"

"At least you acknowledge being taught them!"

"Mom? Mom, you are here?" I shut the door and enter my mother's embrace. Tears collect in the corners of my eyes. "Is Terika in the car, Dr. V's office, or a local hospital? How did you get Ryan to agree without my knowledge? When I didn't hear from you, I assumed she was passing."

"Oh Pumpkin," she says, taking my face in her gloved hands. "She did pass. I brought her urn for you. She wanted her ashes with you. I came to fulfill her last wishes."

"Mom, I need your guidance more than ever."

"I know that's why I had Alison bring me. Go get dressed and we will meet you in the kitchen."

I nod with sniffles and lead them to the kitchen.

Alison fills a pot with water as I disappear into my bedroom. Questions float through my head as I don a pair of jeans and a college sweatshirt. How did my mother become acquainted with Alison? Has she been staying with Ryan long enough to be introduced to Alison? Did Betty meet her? I bet they would hit it off…I shake my head. They have no reason to hit it off. I'm their common link and I broke that to save Betty. It was the right move, right? Mom will know.

Lost in the jungle of my thoughts, I trip over Christopher in my entrance to the kitchen. I fall like a pile of bricks. Alison rushes to my aid. "I was going to scream at you until I was blue in the face and my claws were showing. Now I see that you are suffering as much as she is."

"I have one crisis after another. I'm not myself," I say to the floor. It hurts to look at her. Her face is too similar to Betty's. Alison is like a haunted version of her. Where Betty's eyes have hints of golden magic, Alison's eyes radiate with knowledge and power. My soul is stripped bare with all its tatters shedding onto the floor.

"Certainly not. I thought the years with Ryan would have hardened you into cold royalty," Mom says with clipped tones. She sets the last of Betty's tea bags in two cups and my heart jumps. I don't want them used. How stupid is that? It's not like I would drink it, but I can't lose another piece of her.

"Mom, please—"

"I'm glad Ryan failed," she says putting her hand up to stop me. "I'm looking at the mirror image of your father. It is like he has risen from the dead." Tears flow from both of us and Alison returns to the pot on the stove. I embrace my mom once more and experience the flood of strength only a taste of home can bring.

"I ask myself what Dad would do all the time. I never wanted to be like Ryan. I have always had my own plans."

"I know Pumpkin," she says, smoothing my hair. "Dad's taking care of Terika now so I can devote more time to you."

"Mom, I need your help."

"You bet you do," Alison snaps. "My sister is crying her eyes out and won't give me any explanations that incriminate you. You drop her and then hide here. I ought to slash you to ribbons."

"I have extra responsibilities. Look." I lead them to my bedroom and peel back the fallen bedspread to reveal Bela's nest under my bed. She hisses on cue and puts a limb over the snuggled kitten-beans. "I got a taste of fatherhood without the months to mentally prepared. I haven't slept since delivering them, just done constant laundry."

"Well, that's practice at least," Alison mutters under her breath.

"Kittens! You have kittens but not furniture?" My mother scolds me with a manicured nail waving in my face.

"I found the cats on the side of the road a few years ago and they have been my companions. Wait, I have furniture," I whine like a recalcitrant child. "You mean upstairs? Wait, how did you know my upstairs is empty?"

"She met Betty at the same time as she met me. She came to Paulino's looking for directions. I took her in when Betty clued us into your decor problem," Alison answers.

"She's as wonderful as you told Terika she is."

"She's grieving the death of another, Mom. She's not for me."

"That's bullshit," Alison snaps. I have never heard her swear or sound so much like Betty. I'm losing it. My sleep-deprived brain is sensing Betty around every corner.

"Alison, Ryan would tear me to shreds if he knew I told you, but vampires are not immortal monsters. We are sick. We die young. Betty doesn't need another dying man in her life. I owe her an apology but not for leaving her. I owe her an apology for not caring that she already lost someone. I ignored it for my own benefit— being hers for a little while."

The fury in Alison's eyes extinguishes, leaving pity in the ashes. "I had no idea…"

"Do you really think Betty is so weak? I barely know her, but she seems tough as nails, Pumpkin," Mom says with her hands on her hips. She turns back to the kitchen to fill the mugs and hand one to Alison. Then she leads us to the living room like the consummate Queen Regent she is. I force my body to trudge after them and plop into a chair.

"First of all, my sister is not grieving another. Her last boyfriend died, yes, but she's pissed at him," Alison says before blowing on her tea.

"Yes, Grant filled in the gaps of Evan's story."

"My Grant? No wonder you are confused. I bet he left out all the feelings," Alison replies with an eye-roll.

"I asked him point-blank if she loved Evan and he said she did."

"Two things. First, that ended when she learned the extent of his lies about getting clean. She was oblivious to his crimes in her name until *after* his death. Without his influence and cops gathering evidence, she couldn't ignore the fact she was used. You know my sister. She was irate."

"I can imagine."—a vision of Betty kicking a headstone floats through my mind—"but that doesn't change the fact he died at her feet."

"It also doesn't change the fact the terminated relationship has nothing to do with you," Mom says with a glare. I shrink into my seat like a five-year-old. Mom's temper was as legendary as her beauty in the village growing up. I still have phantom pains from her switch.

"Secondly, she was over it when she left Ohio."

"No, I will have to contradict you there. I met her during a panic attack. It is only because she needed help out of her dress we ever spoke—"

"You what?!" My mother's poise slips and shock shoots tea from her lips onto her blouse.

"It's not like that, Mom…"

"Are you sure? When you have a reputation with the ladies, it includes *all* the ladies, even your mother hears the stories eventually."

Oh my God. If I shrink any lower, I will be a puddle under the table. Alison snickers into her teacup while Mom's glare darkens to the edge of violence. *This has got to be a nightmare.* I pinch my elbow in vain. *Nope.*

"It may have started as Ryan's plot, but I messed it up as usual. I couldn't use her because I fell for her. So, I ended it for her benefit. I'm not a jerk." I sound like a child whining to his mom for an extra dessert. If I live through this, my dignity will need a major overhaul. Spending the rest of my life as a hermit is sounding better by the minute.

"Did you consider she may want to make that choice? Do you think she's incapable of thinking for herself? If you call her stupid, do you know how she would respond?" Alison fires questions with increasing tempo.

"I want to protect her—"

Alison cuts me off by throwing her head back with laughter. The sound echoes ominously through my empty house. When she recovers, she leans toward me to place her transformed paw on my edge of the table. "Betty protects others. She's protecting you not the other way around. You need her much more than she needs you."

I stare at her incredulously. Everyone has strong and weak moments. My brain whirls with the conclusions falsely drawn by Alison. No wonder there is so much pressure on Betty to be invincible. Could it be that she showed me a softness even Alison doesn't acknowledge? No one can be expected to be strong for everyone else.

"We will have to agree to disagree there," I whisper after a long pause. The table stays silent while both fuming ladies sip their tea.

"Lucien, do you remember the story of your father's courtship of me? He didn't want to die before me either. He tried to push me away, which was easy since humans were second-class citizens in the Old Country. Everyone thought I had too much power as a mistress—"

"He married you."

"Not right away, pumpkin. He vowed never to take a wife years before he married me. He said I would make a terrible widow," she says, laughing through tears.

Alison gets her purse from the atrium and we wait for Mom to dry her eyes before continuing. "I had to convince him having the years together was worth the loss. He made me promise repeatedly to carry on after he left this world. I told him I would have you kids and that would be enough…enough reason to live through the heartache. He never really understood leaving me would feel the same as dying. Gone is gone, Lucien."

"Mom—"

"This is not about me. I had my love story, and I wouldn't change a minute of it. Lucien, did you try to flash with Betty?"

"No, I—"

"Why not?"

"It started, progressed, and ended so quickly. I…I took our time together for granted I guess." My explanation sounds stupid to my ears.

"It doesn't have to be over," Alison says.

"She isn't ready to kick my ass?"

"Yes,"—Alison shrugs— "but her anger burns itself out quickly."

Hope fills my chest like a balloon. Could I have her back? Seeing the look on my face, Mom pats my hand. "You must try, Pumpkin. You want to be your father's son—go try to flash with her. Don't pass up a chance at love. His legacy is putting love first."

"It's daylight. I'm trapped," I whine before I can catch myself. Dammit, I'm the Prince of Darkness, not a schoolboy.

"Get some rest, Pumpkin, while we clean up this pigsty. I can't have my sister living in squalor. Leave your phone with your shopping app open. We are going to order some furniture for Reveca's guest room," Alison says dryly. *Great. I'm going to be Prince Pumpkin forever. Thanks, Mom.*

"Betty bought robot mops and vacuums. I have had them going constantly since they arrived," I say in defense.

"Do they climb onto furniture?" The question comes from my treacherous mother's grinning lips. My fearsome reputation is going to be forever changed by her visit. Somehow, that feels awesome.

Chapter 34

"You came into my life at the perfect time,
Stole my heart in one fell swoop, mastermind's crime.
How did I come to need you so?
To fall for you? When you don't know…
I live to make you laugh, I need to hear your sound.
Twinkling bells fill my house when you're around.
How did you turn me inside-out?
To love only you? When you have doubts…
Temporary partners in an unraveling plan,
I learned that I just want to be your man.
What do I need to do?
To be the one? For you to love me too?"

As if I'm in a cheesy eighties' movie, Luc's song carries into my window. I peek through the blinds to see him on my sister's front lawn with an electric guitar and amplifier plugged into his SUV. His leather jacket shines in the moonlight as much as his boots. He sings while looking from window to window as if he's trying to guess which one is mine.

Somewhere in the vast house, there are beeps of the security system disengaging. Ally must have turned it off from her bedroom so I can answer him. I pull and wretch at the window, but the damn thing won't budge. I run my fingers around the frame to locate a lock or a weak point to push. The window refuses to give up its secrets, so I open the curtains fully and turn on the bedroom light.

The light shines onto the snow catching Luc's attention. As his smile brightens his face, I press my palm to the frosty glass. He continues to strum his guitar absently as we stare into each other's eyes. There is so much to say but I don't know if I want to hear all of it. I would rather freeze this moment where he came…he came back for me.

"I love you, Betty," he yells, putting his guitar in his car before cutting its engine. I resume my fight with the window in earnest. He has to hear I love him too.

"Oh no, you don't," Grant thunders as he emerges from the front door. "There has been nothing but crying and misery in this house. It's all *your* fault. I told you not to hurt her and that's the next thing you did! Get out of my yard before I take you out!"

"Noooooooo," I shriek at the window. Grant's upper half morphs into a giant grizzly bear. His shirt disintegrates as his body expands past the limits of the stitches. He grows a snout full of fangs, matching his black claws, and thick brown fur. Not to be outdone, Luc has transformed into his vampire monster complete with a saber-tooth face. The two men square off and circle each other.

****

Anger radiates from Grant in waves. I wish I could tell him I am on his side. We are both protecting the interests of the Weston sisters. However, my fangs have descended beyond the length where I can speak. A garble of mismatched growls and syllables emanates from my mouth. I transformed to defend myself or I would be bear food for Grant's grizzly form. Even my monster persona doesn't feel evenly matched. I fight the urge to fly away. I need to prove to Betty that I am the one to protect her… that I was wrong about us…that I deserve the beating I am about to receive at the paws of Grant.

"No, Grant no," Betty screams as she explodes through the door. She wears flannel pajamas and long swinging pigtails tied in red bows. She runs barefoot across the snow, her tiny stature fitting under his raised fists. She launches herself into my open arms. She wraps her legs around my waist before turning back to Grant with an outstretched hand. "Don't fight him for me. Grant back off. I need him more than you know." She lays her head on my shoulder and cries.

Grant's snout recedes first as he lowers his fists at her command. "I hope you know what you are doing, kid." His body shrinks and the fur is sucked under his skin. The sound of a car approaching brings down my blood pressure enough to retract my claws and fangs. I concentrate on holding Betty close. I have missed the perfect fit we have together. The realization of what I lost hits me with the force of a tornado.

"Grant, it's okay," Alison calls from her car door. I hold my breath as Grant walks past me to get into the passenger side of the car. He's transfixed by Alison's presence. My mother must have stayed at my house because otherwise, the car is empty. The car crunches over the snow and disappears into the garage. Alison leans out to throw a puffy red coat at me.

"Thank you for everything, Alison," I call over to her. She waves in return and shuts herself inside the garage.

"How is it I never have shoes when I am with you?" The muffled sound from my shoulder is music to my ears. We laugh together as I spin around in the moonlight, and my heart soars.

My soul pleads to my mouth and brain not to blow it…again. "Shhh, you will sabotage my trick of holding you in my arms as often as possible."

I carry her around the house to Alison's gardens. Ryan's house looms over them like a monster from a black and white movie. All the lights are on, but his figure is not visible in the windows. Walking amongst the hoop houses, I find a snowdrift at the back of the greenhouse and settle into it, sitting on the ground. The heat escaping from the seams between the glass panels will keep us warm. I open my jacket and coax Betty to curl into a ball on my lap. I create a cocoon for us with the puffy red coat.

"Warm enough?"

She just nods and snuggles under my arm. *Oh my God, she feels so good.*

"Why did you come here?" Her question is whispered against my throat and gives me goosebumps that have nothing to do with the frigid temperatures.

"I misjudged you. I tried to ruin our lives for your benefit…I came over to apologize." I rain kisses onto her freckled cheek before asking permission. She sits statue still but doesn't slap me.

"You knew that comparing Alison to me would push me away. Why the change of heart?"

"I thought you were still in love with Evan, and I was a rebound. I'm dying Betty, not today but I have fifteen years at most with you. If Evan broke your heart after a year, I thought I had the power to destroy you. I didn't have the full story and I acted before I asked you about it. I wanted to save you from grieving for me because...I love you. I've been a fool trying to protect you but doing more damage in the process."

"I was over Evan before I met you," she says, pushing herself upright to look into my eyes.

"Then why were you panicking when we met?"

"I was triggered by the memory of him seizing at my feet. The feeling that overwhelms me is not lost love but helplessness. Even though he didn't love me in the end, he loved me in the beginning. I hate feeling helpless. I will probably have that reaction whenever anyone gets on one knee to propose. I will fear they are going to die and there is nothing I can do to save them."

"I'm sorry. My genetics limit my time with you. There is nothing you can do besides the maintenance of stem cell injections." I lift her chin to look into her eyes.

"I'm working with Dr. V to rejuvenate your bone marrow. In your case, I'm not helpless. Besides, my triggers will fade with time."

"I don't want the memories of our snowstorm refuge to fade too. You can torture me forever if it means staying with me. Take me back, if only to punish me until the end of the world for comparing you to Alison. I just want to be in your life." I brush my lips across hers and she opens them slightly. I deepen the kiss and collect the sweetness inside her mouth. The cutest little mew escapes her throat and I swallow it greedily.

"I'm not going anywhere," she says breathlessly.

"I need to feel certain of that." I pull out the ruby ring and slide it onto her finger. "Marry me. Be my princess for as long as I live." Betty turns white and her jaw drops in horror. I frown as I had hoped for a slightly better reaction, but hey, she hasn't fainted.

"Heeeeeelp me, heeeeeelp me," howls a female

voice. The source of the high-pitched wail is over my shoulder. It comes from a Sluagh advancing across Ryan's yard. Wait...she isn't like the monsters I have fought in the past. She has a nose for starters. The Fae banishes their worst members to Earth when they exhibit signs of becoming Sluagh. Don't fairies transmute to Sluagh the moment they land on Earth? There hasn't been a portal since solstice so she couldn't have landed recently.

The Sluagh female wears a long white dress partially camouflaging her in the snowy landscape. She would blend in completely if it weren't for her blue and white swirled wings. We scramble to our feet and I push Betty against the greenhouse. I open my wings to obscure the Sluagh's view of her.

"I need your soul to go home. Please have mercy on me," she begs. Black tears fall from her eyes sizzling as they hit the snow. She extends her black claws toward me and I hiss in return. My body expands and my fangs drop. I'm going to tear this bitch limb from limb.

"Mine." My growl stops her from advancing.

"Please, she has the soul of a witch. If you give her to me, I can pay you. I'm wealthy," she says pushing icy blond hair over her shoulder. How could she withstand the transformation from Fae to Sluagh for the six weeks since the invasion?

"Mine," I growl louder and swipe my wing at her. A claw at the tip slices at her outstretched arm, leaving a gash across it. An arc of black blood splashes onto the snow as she pulls the hand against her chest.

"You needn't lash out at her," Ryan says, dropping between the Sluagh and me. He folds his wings with leisure before plucking flakes of snow from his jacket as if we are in the hallway at work instead of facing a soul-sucking Sluagh.

"I need the girl behind him." The Sluagh stomps of her foot at him.

"Orchid, we will talk about her later," Ryan snaps at the Sluagh.

"Orchid? Do you know her? Ryan, what the hell is going on?"

"She is none of your concern, Lucien. Leave Betty to us and go home," he says in his condescending tone. He puts his hands on his hips as if annoyed.

"No." Newly found confidence hardens my spine and power surges through my muscles. I'm not sure if it is Betty's warmth at my back or my mother's words ringing in my ears but Ryan is about to get a rude awakening. My eyes glow red with wrath. He is not going to sacrifice Betty to a Sluagh, unless it is over my dead body. Whose side is he on?

"What do you mean no? Have you forgotten who I am? *Just leave.*"

"No," I growl again. I want to tell him to fuck off, but my fangs are in the way. Perhaps I should just rip the smug look off his face with them. I take a deep breath to lower my blood pressure slightly. My fangs raise to my lower lip. I still look monstrous but at least I can speak.

"Tsk, tsk, Lucien, what will your mother say?"

"She will be p-pissed when I tell her you are trying to sacrifice Betty." I watch the blood drain from his face. "Oh, you don't know? M-Mom brought Betty her wedding dress."

"You are just like your father—weak. I raised you to be stronger. I groomed you to be a king. You were finally making progress toward being the king the colony needs to survive."

"You didn't need to make the next king. I-I was b-born to be h-him."

Ryan throws his head back and laughs. It echoes across the snow-covered fields as I glare at him. "You were b-born with a soft spine and even softer b-brain. S-Soft, s-soft, s-soft—"

"I don't see my tender heart as a detriment. Compassion is sometimes warranted when ruling. If you had more compassion, then less of our kind would be dying young—"

"Don't you lay their deaths at my feet." Ryan flashes to the end of my nose. He spits in my face as he yells. "I took the throne when your father selfishly threw it away. I was the second son destined to have a life of leisure and my vampire bride had just died. I wasn't groomed to rule. I was thrown into it. Why? Because your tender-hearted father chose your mother over our entire race! I never threw that in your face even though, your existence ruined my life." His tirade echoes into the night.

"Give me a break, *sire*," I say without flinching. "You love the fame of being king. You love the money you make as a king…but most of all…you love controlling everyone around you. You couldn't have that power if you weren't king."

"I made the colony *rich*. Look at your home, your car, your education. My investments paid for all of it. I made investments when I was half your age that now fund our race," he yells with his arms waving like a madman. "You are just like your father—"

"Good! That's all I ever wanted to be."

"I was proud to give you the throne. I thought you had earned it."

"Exchanged Terika's life for it, you mean? Earned it with my servitude since we came to America? I don't need you to give me anything. When you die, the colony will crown me. You cannot control me any longer."

"Luc, we can fight later," Betty says with a muffled voice against my back. "Please take me out of here. Please save me."

"Please save me, Luc," Ryan mocks Betty with a chipmunk voice. "Yeah, Luc, just flash her out of here." He cackles at me while my brain fumbles for other options. If we are going to get out of this alive, the teleportation has to work. "Why hesitate? Oh yeah, because your relationship was engineered by me. Betty, your Luc is a gigolo who beds who I say." Ryan ends his taunting with another evil laugh that stands the hairs on my wings on end. My fangs descend again as I boil with rage. My brain flips from escape routes to scenarios where I kill him and his Sluagh.

****

The fallout between Ryan and Luc must end before Luc is permanently damaged. This man practically raised Luc and now he's throwing their relationship away as if it was only blackmail that kept them together. Deep inside, Luc thought of Ryan as a second father. My heart breaks for the pair until Ryan mocks me. My eyes may not be glowing, but I am seeing red.

"You are such a fossil you don't realize I know all about your deal. These aren't the Dark Ages where leaders align with marriages. My sister's pack couldn't care less who I go to bed with so Go. Scorch. Yourself. Ryan," I yell from under Luc's wing. I am so done with the damsel in distress role. I fight through the wing folds to face Ryan. "He told me at the beginning. Luc is honest no matter how hard you tried to corrupt him."

"Then you should know there is no escaping. Step to us and we will let your precious Luc escape. Your little nest has backed you into a corner and the Luther's are giving you privacy. Why else would they have closed their blinds so early?"

"Please let me have her, Ryan. She is our ticket for travel," the Sluagh begs.

"Orchid, is it? Listen, Bitch. I'm not going anywhere with you." I give her a rude gesture over Luc's wing. "Call this off Ryan or my sister will hunt you down and eat you. Hear that Orchid? My sister loves to eat your kind." The glow of pride warms my face when Orchid gasps and puts her hand to her mouth. So, she has heard the tale of Alison the Sluagh-eating polar bear. Who told her, was it Ryan or someone in the Fae?

"I no longer need your frigid sister, not on your life. Oh, but it is betting on your life, isn't it?"

"I will defend her with my last breath," Luc growls through his fangs.

"Oh yeah, she's that great between the sheets, eh? Go on then. Flash with her. Save me, Luc." Ryan's last words mimic my voice with a squeaky cadence.

"Luc?"

"Please be real," he whispers as he turns to me. Time slows down as he retracts his wings and wraps his arms around my waist. My arms entangle his neck on their own volition. He closes his eyes and I follow suit without knowledge of his plan. He better have a plan—

Chapter 35

"It worked," I say with a sigh of relief. Betty allows her arms to slide off my shoulders and takes in Alison's kitchen. Alison stands at the stove with her spatula suspended in midair. A pan of vegetables sizzles at her side while Grant sits wild-eyed at the counter. Betty walks in a circle with no signs of vertigo. I feel giddy with the knowledge she was always meant to be mine. My father's ruby ring sparkles at me from her hand.

"To flash through walls, you must hers," Grant says, nodding at me.

"How do you know?"

"Ryan," he says with a shrug. "He could flash alone but not with me when we were rescuing Alison. Looks like you two are stuck together for a while."

"Luc, what is Grant talking about?"

"Princess, we flashed—"

She turns to me with the brightest smile I have ever seen. I lift her off her feet and spin her around. *Crack!* I whack her legs against the table in my excitement. "Oh, I'm sorry, I know I had to be more careful with you—"

"What?"

"Betty, have I hurt you?" I pat her to test for injuries. I feel like an imbecile as if her limbs will crumble under my touch.

"What did you say?"

"I need to be more careful with you," I repeat. The

smile falls from her face and her eyes fill with tears. As if a curtain is lowered, her expression flattens and the tears dissolve.

"She told you. That's why the flash test worked," Betty whispers. My addled brain whirls again to ascertain how I managed to anger her. "The baby. You talked about the baby."

Alison, Grant, and I exchange confused glances. I need to get control of the situation, but I don't have enough information. Grant shrugs at me while the sisters square off like cats about to pounce. My heart pounds clouding my brain with added blood pressure. If only I had flashed her to my house, where we would only face the wrath of Bela…oh.

"There is not one baby, there's four," I say after a moment of silence, grasping at straws. Her stare changes from rage to bewilderment as she turns to me. "There is only one when there is something wrong with the mother. With the amount of weight gain and terrible attitude, I knew that wasn't the case. On first look, I knew it was four."

Tears fill her eyes as her jaw trembles. Are those tears of joy? I had no idea she loved animals as much as I do. Beneath her tough exterior was a softer heart but she has surprised me by being the chocolate-covered cherry she claims to love. She cuts off my next sentence by asking, "Ally how could you?"

"Well, she saw it first. If I wouldn't have pushed you away, we would have found out together." She doesn't even hear my words as she sizes up Alison. The look of panic on Alison's face alarms Grant and he stands beside his chair. What the hell is going on?

"Don't bother." She removes my ring and hands it

back to me. "I don't want to trap you. You had me fooled with the flashing stuff. You created a very tempting fantasy." She continues to talk while I struggle to process. My eyes are focused on the ring with my brain following suit. What did I say?

She can't be offended on Bela's behalf because I called the cat fat with a bad attitude. How is Alison involved? Questions fight for my attention as thoughts muddle my overloaded circuits. If only Betty would stop talking, so I could think. I get my wish when she leaves. Just leaves. My brain spins to connect the dots but she leaves me no time to ask questions.

The image of Betty at the gas station appears in my foggy thoughts. The snow falls over her red coat as she delicately steps into the snow. She watches her boots sink with each step. One hand holds a bag of chocolates while the other...rests on her midsection. She wasn't smiling at her boots...she was smiling at her belly...*oh my God*... Can it be true?

"I have a feeling Betty wasn't talking about Bela's kittens," I mutter.

Grant and Alison look at each other instead of answering.

"Alison, there's something you must know. We flashed here because Ryan—"

"Lucien, I don't like females crying under my roof. You have to the count of five to fix it." *Fantastic, I may get my ass kicked by Grant after all.*

"Ryan has a Sluagh in his house. They are working together—"

"Lucien, if Ryan's betraying the pack for the Fae, we will deal with him as a pack. My sister comes first. Are you going upstairs to tell her what happened or am

I? We can raise the child with or without you."

"Five," Grant growls when I hesitate.

"I love her more than words can say. We will be a happy family, I promise."

"I know, Lucien, but she doesn't." Alison and I exchange teary half-smiles. Grant's jaw threatens to grind his molars to powder when he spies his wife's glassy eyes.

"Four," Grant says with a chin flick toward the steps.

Ornate rooms dot the hallway with two closed doors at the end. I'm about to knock on the door at the terminus when the door to its right flies open. "That's Henrik's door. Please don't wake him," Betty whispers. Her eyes are swollen, and her cheeks are stained pink with fresh tears. I advance toward her and she backs into her room. I close the door behind me and lock it. Grant's glare promised retribution but I'm not going to be interrupted until I figure out why she returned my ring.

"We really have nothing to say to each other," she says with her chin pointed in the air. Really? That attitude is not going to fly now that I have my wits about me.

"I have a helluva lot to say, Betty. I hope you do too. I need answers before I lose my temper." I fold my arms across my chest. "Let's start with what is making my blood pressure rise the fastest. Why don't you tell me the reason you are no longer wearing the ring I gave you?"

"I'm not marrying you so you can take care of us. I can do it myself. You can choose your level of involvement, but a marriage of obligation is off the table. We aren't Grant and Alison."

"Take care of us..." I raise my eyebrow at her. Our

conversation from the kitchen swirls in my mind. My brain recalls Betty's behavior in Molina's office and Molina's secret words to her. *Oh please. Please...* I need her to confirm she's pregnant. My heart can't take this rollercoaster.

"You hate sweets!" I lunge for the bag of chocolates on her desk. She reaches too, fighting me when my long arm reaches the bag first. I study the bag. A glittering red heart winks back at me. I can't help the smug smile tugging at my cheeks. "You are living on blood-laced chocolates. You are craving blood."

"You know why and I'm not sorry I just—"

"I'm not sorry either. I'm going to be a dad. We are having a baby! Does my mom know?"

"I had to tell her when she moved in, or Ally would have told her too." Betty tears her chocolates from my hands.

"Too? Princess, Alison never told me about a baby. Bela had kittens, four kittens, under my bed. In the kitchen, I was talking about kittens."

"You wanted to marry me without knowing about Little Batman?"

"I would get down on one knee right now if I was confident, you would stay conscious."

"Well, I never answered you before…"

I pull the ring out of my pocket. "Because I didn't ask. I told you to marry me."

She holds out her hand for me to slip the ring back in place. She places our joined hands to rest on her lower belly, taking my breath away. She smiles through glassy tears and slides into my embrace. I rain kisses onto her freckles until she giggles, and I savor the music.

"Shhhh." She smashes her hand over my mouth. We

listen to Grant's heavy footsteps and Alison's giggles approach. A resounding click alerts us to the bears retiring to their bedroom followed by the whirl of fans. "My sister puts on noise-canceling fans so Henrik and I can't hear them…um…retire."

"Perfect, they won't hear us." I take off my jacket to sling it over her desk chair. She stares with her mouth hanging open as I kick my boots under the chair and continue to remove my clothes. I can't help but do a slow turn under her gaze when I am naked. She blushes pink and bites her lip as she notices my arousal. I brush against her as I cross the room to her bed. Pulling open the lacy covers, I climb in and hold them ajar for her to join me.

"You are staying the day here?" She continues to worry her bottom lip with a small smile peeking through. Her eyes twinkle with mischief and I can't help but egg her on.

"When is the next time we are going to have a chance to christen your sister's house?" I ask the question with an eyebrow raised, and my voice a purr. The scent of her arousal fills the room.

"My bed, my rules. I won't be subjected to your games and wake everyone with my screams." She unbuttons her shirt. I become increasingly compliant as the creamy swells of her breasts are revealed. When she steps out of the matching pajama bottoms, I get a glimpse of blue boyshorts clinging to her hips and I'm putty in her hands.

"I'm yours, princess. Tell me your desires," I practically pant. She takes a boulder-sized pillow from the bed and tugs the flowered case off it, scrunching it into a tube shape.

"My desire? To have my way with you without your judgy face judging my novice moves."

"Be warned when I lose control, I bite. I cannot do that to you." She straddles me on the bed and reaches forward with the pillowcase. I latch onto her tempting nipple hanging at the end of my nose. I catch a glimpse of her expression of rapture before I am blindfolded.

"I'm not as averse to it now…"

"We could exchange—" She doesn't let me finish my sentence but feeds me her other nipple. I nurse the tip until her husky groan rings in my ears. The sound travels straight to my groin and I roll my hips beneath her. I repeat the movement with increasing tempo until her breathing catches in shallow pants.

"My pace," she commands, lifting from contact with me. The breathless quality to her voice bolsters my masculine pride. I'm on the edge but so is she.

"Your wish is my command, princess." She pushes at my shoulders and I lay flat at her urging. I have been tied up, strapped down, blindfolded, and suspended from the ceiling but I have never been at a woman's mercy like this. A makeshift blindfold and her tiny warm hands are molding me into her plaything. *I surrender*.

"May I touch you, Princess?" I ask to play her game.

"Mmmm hmmm," she half moans, half hums. Following her thighs, I score my claws along her sides. Her skin feels like silk as my palms trail behind them to cup her breasts. I waste no time kneading them as my princess needs a rougher touch. I tug and pull at her nipples until she starts to rock.

"May I taste you, Princess?"

She whimpers when I let go of her breasts to settle closer to the foot of the bed. The motion rocks her forward and she tunnels her fingers into my hair to gain purchase. I nuzzle her with my nose and draw lazy circles on her thighs in concert with the motion until she grabs my wrists.

"Rip them off."

"Your wish is my command, princess," I reply with heated breath blowing over her most sensitive bundle of nerves. She loses focus and releases my wrists. *Silly Princess.* My fangs pierce the fabric at the delicate junction between her thigh and core. A swing of my neck and they are reduced to a glorified belt. A moan in appreciation sings over me. I get to work lapping, teasing, nipping, and sucking as my princess writhes with wanton abandon. I wish I could see her face.

"Let it go, princess. Let me drink from you." Her muscles go rigid from head to toes, squeezing me delicately. She mutes her screams but a small mew escapes before the waves of her orgasm crash over us. I turn my head to sink my fangs into the delicate vessel within her thigh. I drink slowly, knowing with each pull of blood, her orgasm lengthens. When the drumming of her cervix weakens, I release her vein and lick over the wound to seal it.

"Would you drink from me too, princess?"

She melts from her stance, sliding along my body, and the blindfold travels with her. She lays in a boneless heap at my side with a beaming smile on her face.

"I don't have fangs." I kiss the little frown lines on her forehead with tiny pecks while arranging her to lie on her back. She turns her head to the side with her legs wide open. I puncture the vein at my elbow and press it to her lips, wrapping my arm around her head to cradle it. She experiments with little licks, flicks, and sips. She judges my face for approval, asking for guidance.

"It would please me if you sucked on it, princess," I say between puffs of air. When she latches, my eyes roll back in ecstasy. *Holy hell.* I'm not going to last. I fold her in half to wrap one of her legs over my feeding arm. I glide myself into her waiting core and wrap the other leg around my waist. I swivel my hips slowly until she rocks with impatience.

"May I move faster Princess?"

She nods but doesn't let go of my vein. I guess she has decided I taste as delicious as she does. I piston my hips and get lost in her. I nuzzle her hair aside and bite her neck like my stereotype. I draw hard on the vein to trigger her next orgasm. My release hits me with the force of a freight train. We lay panting for a few moments before I seal our wounds. Tucking her into my side, I pull the covers over us.

She falls asleep before I whisper, "I will love you forever" into the darkness.

Sometime during the day, I am awoken by the clinking of china. Through cracked eyelids, I watch a small figure place a tray of dishes on the desk. Alison gives me a lesson on what it means to be royalty when she picks up Betty's pajamas from the center of the floor and tosses them into the laundry basket in the corner. She then picks up my boots and silently backs out of the room. The most powerful woman in Strawberry is not a queen to be worshipped as Ryan expects, but a servant to her people. Her actions humble me beyond measure. My last thoughts are how much I wish to rule like Alison when I take the throne from Ryan. In a partnership with a Sluagh, he is no longer worthy of ruling our colony.

Chapter 36

Laying in the crook of Luc's arm while we stare at our phones should feel like the most natural position in the world. However, our perfect fit is tainted by the gaudy décor of my sister's house. Yesterday, I treated her like shit but I'm not ready to apologize. I drop my phone on the bedspread with a huff and it bounces amongst the lacy ruffles. My impatient nature bubbles to the surface and I can't resist opening my mouth. "Luc, when am I moving into your house?"

"I love how I didn't have to ask you." The gruff tone of his voice has my glare snapping to his face. I breathe a sigh of relief when his smile lifts his lips. "As soon as possible, I'm messaging everyone I know to find Ryan. I don't want him flashing into my house where my mom is alone. Nate says Ryan wasn't at work last night even though he signed the paperwork in my place for Kimberly to be hired as my new employee. He must have come in, moved the work from his desk, and left without anyone seeing him. Molina says if he took blood from the bank, he didn't sign it out. She is doing an inventory tonight to see if anything is missing."

"I was so sorry to witness your fall out with him. I know how you idolized him as a teen," I say while he retrieves a breakfast tray from the desk.

"Alison brought breakfast in during the day, despite the tiff you have going. You need to patch things up with her. Your sister is still alive. My mother is all I have left. I've lost my relationship with Ryan. My uncle may as well be dead. He resented my father and made my life a living hell. It couldn't have been easy to be king at age fifteen, but my dad was there to answer questions. It's not like Dad was dead for those first few years."

"I'm not ready to face her. I lost my temper and acted irrationally, par for the course with me. Why did Ryan take the throne so young?"

"My dad crowned Ryan so he could marry my mother before I was born. It is illegal for a human to be queen, so my dad abdicated. Ryan was petulant but ultimately grew addicted to the position's power and lifestyle."

"Are you giving up the throne for me? Is that why Ryan insisted you are just like your father?"

"Yes and no. I would choose you if I had to, so yes, I am my father's son. However, I'm healthier and plan to fight challengers when I crown you queen."

"Luc, please—"

"Non-negotiable," he says with a scary glare. "When the colony knows about the medical advances you are doing with Dr. V and how I'm bringing those advances to them, they will love you." He pauses to kiss the ring on my hand. "The ruby in this ring was the colony's gift to my father. Ryan had a larger ruby ring made and gave me this ruby when my father died. I had it made into an earring so I could hold him close to me. Josh was talented enough to make it into an engagement ring for you."

"Wait…What?"

"So, before you told me about Little Batman, I was building the courage to propose. I would have earlier, but the death of my sister had me bedridden with grief for days. When I am with you, I can open up without my social anxiety getting in the way. You clear my thoughts and settle my mind. Now I just have to find Ryan to abdicate the throne."

"And if no one can find him…"

"If he misses more work, Grant and I will go pay him a visit. Miles in the daytime QA department can't handle all the projects alone. Everything will come to a screeching halt which is bad news for the vampires. We need Bergan not only for the blood bank but for the front to research areas of need, like Molina's fertility project."

"Why isn't anyone coordinating research with Dr. V into IVIG, bone marrow transplants, and further stem cell treatments?"

"The simple answer is manpower, lack of expertise, and lack of direction." He puffs so hard his hair flutters over his forehead. I give in to the impulse and smooth it back over his head. He leans into my caress and sighs.

"As the king, you can change that…"

"One step at a time, my power-hungry wench," he says with a lop-sided grin. "We need to eat, check on my mother, move you into our house, find Ryan to sanction our marriage, have a wedding, bring Little Batman into the world, and then we can plot out our world domination."

I throw my head back and laugh at his ridiculous list. We are nuts. He freezes and watches me until I feel self-conscious.

"Sorry, I will never take your sound for granted again. Be careful with that laugh. You have the power to bring a king to his knees."

I fuse my lips to his in a tender duel for who loves

the other more. We part when the cooled coffee splashes from Luc's cup onto his lap.

"Eat," he says with a homemade pumpkin donut in his lifted hand. "Eat like a good princess and when we get home, I will let you take my vein again." He winks at me and I feel my face flame. As much as I hate to admit it, Luc was right about vampires and blood exchanges. I eat twice as much as he does and pack my small set of belongings. Everything I own fits into my parent's car, so the task takes minutes.

I pause to take in my temporary residence one last time. It was a refuge when I was dying inside and the location of my rebirth. I owe my recovery to my sister. *Ugh.* No more prevaricating. Time to make up with Ally. This room was a place of growth for me. To prove it, I need to act like a grown-up. "Luc, could I meet you at your place? I need to make up with Ally before we leave."

"No, but I can meet you at *our home* after you thank your sister for me. Oh, and get my boots back. What is it with the Weston sisters and shoes? Are you descendants of the fabled cobbler's elves?"

"You have no boots?"

"Not unless you have a pair of men's size-elevens lying in your closet," he says with a chuckle. "I'm going to flash to my car and drive straight home." He takes my meager luggage in his arms and kisses me softly before disappearing before my eyes. I'm left alone holding my car keys in one hand and the other grasping air where Luc's bicep once was. The room feels lonely as if he has taken all the warmth with him. My skin prickles with the need to get out of here. Placing my hand over Little Batman's growing baby bump, I go down to confront my ill-treatment of my biggest supporter.

I clomp down the stairs and pound my way into Ally's kitchen, following the clang of dishes in the sink. I hope she's preparing crow. "Ally, I need to apologize..."

My normally sunny sister turns to me with a stormy expression. She spins so fast her sundress twirls around her legs. "Sorry isn't enough," she snaps before turning back to the dishes. Oh...I never brought down the breakfast tray she brought us as we slept...in her home. I have been such a brat.

"You are right. I have a habit of taking you for granted," My words surprise her and draw her attention from the pot from which she was removing the Teflon with a soft sponge. "You stood by me and I never thanked you once. You took me in when I invited myself into your home. I lashed out at you for telling secrets that you never told. I've been a brat since I came here, and you bore the brunt of my tantrums."

"I'm not the doormat I used to be," she says, wiping her hands dry on a towel. "I still serve others, but I demand respect in return. Please do not mistake my gentle nature for weakness again. I am confident enough in my strength to be sweet."

"No, you aren't a doormat anymore, Madam Commander." I drop my gaze. Perhaps I should imitate one of Luc's obsequious bows or fully prostrate like Nate.

"Even though you are moving out, I still expect you to visit often. I also expect to have dinner at Rosie's with you before work on occasion. Oh, and I'm planning a joint baby shower for you and Aurora. No boys allowed." Her words start out stern but she's giggling by the end.

"Yes, Ma'am."

"Furthermore, Grant is already researching how to become ordained to perform the ceremony. Ryan will not come within miles of the wedding to crash it with his Sluagh friend. The Strawberry Shifters pack is behind your family. We will ensure Lucien succeeds Ryan as Vampire King with you at his side."

"Thank you, Ally." I rush into her arms. Tears flow from my cheeks as the dam on my emotions breaks loose. "I am honored you are my sister, and that we watch out for each other."

She pushes me off her shoulder to raise her pinky finger between us. "No more squabbling. It's us against the Vampire King, the Sluagh, and those who underestimate us. If we are going to invite a bunch of witches to Strawberry for your wedding, the pack will have to work overtime to keep them safe."

I wrap my pinky around hers and swear: "No more squabbling. Luc and I will need all the help we can get. Ryan is in league with a female Sluagh. Her name is Orchid and is after a witch's soul to get home. I think Luc wants to be face-to-face with him not to rule on our marriage but to take his royal ring."

"The pack will stand behind whatever decision Luc makes and fight the Sluagh for our territory, whether she's in alliance with Ryan or not. The feud between the shifters and the Sluagh goes back further than our alliance with the vampire colony, even longer than Ryan's lifespan. You just be careful and protect my winged nephew."

"With my life."

Chapter 37

Is there anything more thrilling than sneaking through the shadows of your own home? I'm practically giddy as I creep into the house where my pregnant bride awaits her father. I left the witchy Weston family to sort out Alison's elaborate flower arrangements, all six members scrambling to untangle a garland from inside a VW bug. I could have flashed but I wanted the satisfaction of crossing Grant's secret practice location where anyone in a three-mile radius can hear him repeating the most poignant parts of our pagan ceremony.

I'm holding in my laughter when I pass the kitchen where my mother and Rosie Paulino are placing chocolate bats, blood-laced of course, and roses, sans blood, on cupcakes. In lieu of a cake, my princess opted for a cupcake tree which I thought delightful as she should avoid knives with her temper these days. Just when I think I am in the clear, my mother calls my name.

"Lucien, aren't you supposed to be outside?"

"Nope, I would just be in the way of the flowers. Everyone has a job to do except me." I grab a bag of blood from my fridge. I rip off the port and drink while my mother's face drops in horror.

"Really Lucien, you shouldn't do that in your father's royal jacket. What if you drip on it?" Now it is my turn to be horrified when she wraps a length of paper towels around my shoulders like a barber's cape.

"Oh, what I wouldn't do for a camera," Rosie says before her fit of giggles. I can only flick her off in defense.

"Lucien, your manners. Not only has Rosie done the catering but her boys are patrolling your property to keep your guests safe. It is a lot of stress for a mother to send her sons into danger."

I say a garbled apology around my bag and Rosie waves it away. "I have them linked via headset and paired off. Tommy, Anthony, and Henrik are with Alison setting up. Knowing my youngest boys are being protected by the witches helps to balance the rest. By the way, Frank Junior found this by the alter." She hands me a small box wrapped in Christmas wrapping paper with a big red bow. The tag has my full name scrawled across it in the ancient lettering of the colony.

"Only Ryan would use that lettering," I mumble around the blood bag.

Rosie stops me by covering my hands with hers, "What if it is a bomb?"

"He would have blown us up while delivering it. Ryan doesn't have the patience for the long game." I reveal Ryan's royal ring on a cloud of cotton within the box. The silver letters "VP" beneath the ruby are unique to the ring he had made to signify the increase in the Von Popescu's wealth. I remove the ring from the box and hand it to Mother. I cannot form the words for what I'm feeling and apparently Ryan couldn't either.

"He's giving you the colony, Lucien." She beams at me with glee.

"What's the price? There is no note."

Rosie chooses to answer me when Mom can only

stare at the ring. "Why does there have to be a price? You are better suited to the job, better aligned with us..."

"He never saw me as ready." I lay my blood bag on the counter. Mom grabs it and throws the bag into the trash with a glare. "See I don't even throw my trash away. This changes a lot of things. Are you sure you aren't going to stay with us until the baby is born?"

"Lucien," she says as she removes my paper towel cape. "I have dedicated my life to this family, but I want a little space to live alone for a while. I need to go back and sell the house. It holds more sad memories than sweet at this point. I came to fulfill Terika's last wishes and make sure you are happily settled in America. You belong here and I belong there."

"When I crown you Queen Regent, Betty and I will come to you to visit. The people need to see their royal family, even if we shirk some of the royal customs. It will be nice to have you managing that side of the colony and help me link the two halves. I have many ideas to better their lives, just the transportation and healthcare improvements will take a lifetime."

"You always were a dreamer—" she pats my cheek "—but you sound just like your father. He would be proud of who you have grown to be."

"Love you too, Mom." I try to memorize her embrace as I missed out on a decade of her care being Ryan's stooge.

"I hope my boys have moments like these with me on their wedding day," Rosie sniffles. The two women embrace and blow their noses on paper towels while I quietly slip away, leaving my father's clinking jacket with them. While I did refuel, I have been sidelined from my original mission. I slink through my now clean front rooms to my creaky stairs. *Three…two…one…* I run up them while the grandfather clock loudly chimes ten o'clock. Hanging out in the kitchen, I almost missed my cue.

I pass the newly decorated guest room where my mother has stayed for the past few weeks. Using my credit card, she turned the empty room into a goth princess paradise. Black lacy curtains hang from the window as well as the four-poster bed. A gray bedspread decorated with black roses embroidered on it matches the pile of decorative pillows. Even the dresser, vanity table, and bookcase are a dusky shade of charcoal. Of all the decorating schemes, she claimed this fit her best because "her fondest memories are from living a goth girl's dream." She had exchanged knowing smiles with Betty…*Betty*.

I inhale deeply to confirm my bride is locked in our son's nursery. Despite the new wards Henrik put on the house to keep Ryan out, I flash through the door. Betty is standing at the full-sized mirror from my bedroom, which I carried upstairs just for today. Anything for my princess, like I ever cared if the antique oak frame clashed with the batman theme.

The room is a vision of my sweetest dream. A cradle is on the left and a small bed is on the right topped with comic book-themed soft furnishings. An empty toy box and a changing table sit idle, with carved bats and runes to protect my growing family. While I put our relationship back together, Alison and my mother bought Betty's entire baby registry and set up this sacred space. I can't wait to fill it with memories raising our son…or daughter…but I have been told by not one, but a half dozen witches, I should be proud of my growing *son*.

I stand there staring until Betty's glare reaches me from the mirror's reflection. She looks like a fairytale in my mother's dress. Mom's wedding photos hang in galleries in the Old Country, her beauty more legendary than the scandal of the day, but Betty outshines her in my eyes. Even with rage flashing in her eyes, I'm dumbstruck this gorgeous creature is going to stand at my side for the rest of my days. I am humbled and speechless as she rails at me. My fingers find the door lock and check it to ensure our privacy.

"Luc, it is bad luck for you to see me in this dress before the ceremony. Didn't that info reach the Old Country? You will doom our future," she snaps at the mirror.

"I couldn't stay away. Not when my nose found your sweet happiness through the door."

"Down the stairs," I say with the next step.

"Across the first floor…" I stand directly behind her so my breath drifts over the soft junction between her neck and shoulder.

"Into my bedroom." I wrap my arms around her to grind my pelvis into her backside.

"Luc, everyone we know is somewhere on your property. What are you thinking? Sneaking in here?"

"I *was* thinking we never follow the rules and soon we will be making them. *Now* I'm thinking about how to access you in this dress when it annoyingly laces up the back and front."

"You wouldn't dare." The eyes say no but the small hand cupping my groin says otherwise. It hardens me to a steel post as I kneel at her feet.

Whoosh! I catch her completely off-guard when I reach under her dress to dump her on the bed by her thighs. The whalebone in the skirt retains its shape as it flips over my bride's torso. The result is a mountain of red satin with delicious legs protruding from it. Her thigh-high stockings are irresistible as is the tiny blue thong—that has to go. The top of the stockings draws my mouth like a magnet and Betty is writhing in minutes…or perhaps she is fighting her way through the layers of fabric to control the situation.

"Let me undo the garters so you don't—" Her rushed whisper is cut off by the rip of her panties being destroyed. "Damn it, Luc, that was my something blue. At this rate, we are going to be forever doomed."

"I'm crowning you the Queen of the Damned, so get ready for it." I feast like a starving man. She sings a symphony of delight with no more coherent words. Knowing the danger of our position to her father's proximity, I bring her up faster than I would normally dare. Her legs kick and fight my shoulders to close against the onslaught of pleasure before the blossom of her orgasm. I make quick work of my pants and plunge inside her.

A guttural moan escapes the mound of fabric as I stand before her. I tug the closest whalebone, crinkling the opaque layers of fabric. I uncover the sultry image of her face lost in rapture and obscured by the lace. The combination of her dazed expression and husky sounds sends me over the edge of my control. I piston to my own climax, thankful that the soft headboard silently hits the wall. Collapsing on the bed beside her, she twists to my side and paints my face with her lipstick.

"You know I don't have a backup pair in this room and cannot get to our room without passing every member of my family. Are you going to flash somewhere to get me another pair of blue panties or am I walking down the aisle without them?"

"What do you think?"

Chapter 38

"It's not that he's an idiot. It's that I am totally badass," I mutter to myself as an icy draft blows up my wedding dress. An outdoor wedding in February, at night with no panties, is the hallmark of a badass bride. The breeze threatens to freeze solid the residual moisture from my lover to my thighs. The secret sensations electrify the atmosphere and remind me that I'm getting what I always wanted...a bad boy to call my own.

"Alison says he will take good care of you," my father says while reaching for my elbow. We crunch through the snow together guided by heat lamps I wish were a little lower.

"He loves me, Daddy."

"That's a good start, I guess, but are you sure? He's got that disease..."

"It's worth it to be with someone who complements me. I don't have to take care of him. We take care of each other."

"Then he must be the right one." He pats my hand in support.

When we turn the corner, I gasp with delight. Fairy lights and garlands of night-blooming jasmine connect the house, a floral arch, a Maypole, and the few trees at the far side of Luc's property. The result is an aroma of magical floral notes. The entire town of Strawberry sits in circles of chairs constructed of mini-Bonsai trees except for Henrik who sits at Luc's keyboard which is also covered in flowers. Henrik sings Luc's song to me and his voice rings into the night.

"Wait, Daddy." I yank my father's arm to allow Nate and Gran to cross my path. Nate is nearly carrying her. Gran's glittery purple dress hangs loosely on her gaunt frame. Her twinkling eyes seem to have dulled over the past month and her mouth is set into a determined frown. The pair shuffle into the back circle where James holds onto Aurora protectively. Who put my best friend in the back? I pull my dad to their side where I confront my friends before the entire town.

"Back row?" I hiss between clenched teeth. Only the noisy shuffling of the guests standing at my entrance muffles the unfolding scene.

"Fewer steps for my date. She's hit the punch already," Nate says with a wink. Gran gasps at Nate's outrageous lie and slaps him with her cane. James and Aurora nod over his shoulder.

"Stop telling people that," Gran scolds him with an extra whack with her cane.

"Oh…well…perfect then," I sputter. Of course, Nate would invite Gran to sit with them. The rest of the Paulino's have been busy behind the scenes.

"Thank you for coming," my father whispers to bring me back to the present.

At the center of the circle, Grant and Luc stand under the arch. Luc looks like an emo fairytale in his red jacket covered in metals and military honor stripes. Around them is a smaller ring of chairs holding our closest family members. Ally turns to beam at me and waves the ornamental broom. She must have used her magic to weave vines, roses, lavender twigs, and rosemary branches into such a stunning piece. Henrik's tune changes to a slower softer song which is my cue to enter the circle and let my dad hand me over to Luc. I try to lock eyes with Luc but something over my head has caught his attention. *Really Luc?*

****

If he takes a swipe at my bride, I will torture him for the rest of my days. I will torture the Sluagh as well. The pair are sitting under the garland anchor trees like they are included in the ceremony but on the outside of our circle of family. The Sluagh is cuffed to Ryan but curled into a ball at his side. She looks cold, pitiful, and almost depressed about being here. Ryan sits on the ground looking like he just rolled out of bed and drinking wine directly out of a giant bottle.

We lock gazes and my fangs itch to descend. My eyes are glowing which I hope alerts the werewolves protecting the witches. My wings rustle with the urge to fly over and rip his face off. The years we had after my father died root me where I stand. He was a second father to me. Ryan slowly raises his wine bottle in salute. Whatever is going on with him and the Sluagh, he has no intention of ruining my wedding. I breathe a sigh of relief and salute him in return. *Blessed be, Old Friend. I hope you find peace with what you have done.*

In the Old Country, vampire weddings were lavish parties celebrating two mates who found each other. Only the royals had true ceremonies and those were more coronations than weddings. My parents broke the rules by having a huge wedding in a human church in Moldova with all the Protestant traditions of my mother's family. Following my father's footsteps, I trusted Alison and Grant to give Betty all of her family's pagan traditions.

"Please put her first," Mr. Weston says, pulling me out of the staring contest with Ryan.

"Her heart beats in place of my own." He squints as if testing my honesty before opening Betty's veil and removing her hand from his elbow. I cross my arms, so she awkwardly takes my far elbow. The gesture allows her alone a view up my sleeve. My prank is rewarded with her deep flush. Beneath my black leather gauntlet, her blue thong is tied around my arm. Her father squeezes her hand over it, pressing the shape into her palm. We both bite our lips to contain our giggles, while Rosie snaps a picture. In the photo album, I hope we look in love, not about to explode with forbidden secrets.

"Spirits of the waters, blessed be this ritual. I call to you. And so above," Gran calls from her side of the outer circle to the sky. Lightning flashes and thunder booms overhead. She's clapping her hands and laughing as she crumples into Nate's arms. When it was suggested she miss the ceremony to rest, she threw a fit. No one dared to take the water witch honor from her.

"Mother Earth, Spirit of the soil, blessed be this ritual. I call to you. And so below," Alison calls to the sky. The ground quakes and seedlings erupt around her feet.

"Father Sky, Spirit of the air we breathe, blessed be this ritual. I call to you. And so within," Henrik calls from behind the piano bench. A strong wind gushes behind him ruffling the garland and showering us with flower petals.

"Spirit of the fires within our earth, blessed be this ritual. I call to you. And so without," Betty's Aunt Sarah calls while holding a candle. Being an Earth-bound witch just like Alison, she cannot make her own fire. However, a staff of twisted trees reaches from the Earth to take the candle from her hand. The image is enough to make the hairs on the back of my neck stand on end.

Grant takes a bell from his jacket pocket and rings it. The outer circles take the strand of sleighbells from the backs of their chairs and ring them in chorus to Grant's music. The ringing calls the spirit guides to make a protective circle around the circle of family, protecting us on the Earthly and spiritual plane. Further cleansing and protection are performed by Alison and my mother. The women receive smudge sticks from Grant and walk in opposite directions around the inside of the circle. When the women meet back at Grant's sides, the audience puts their bells back on the chairs.

"It is an honor to introduce the world to a new family. One the world has never seen before," Grant thunders without a microphone. His cadence rolls over the barren landscape. I bet Ryan can hear every word. Hell, I bet Louisville can hear every word. "This new family is the resultant of the union of the Westons and the Von Popescu families, but one unique to both clans. The new family comprised of Lucien Von Popescu, Prince of Darkness joined here today to Betty Weston with Little Batman in attendance, though not yet old enough for his own piece of cake." Betty's face flames bright red at the mention of our child not-yet-in-wedlock. She looks like she could tear Grizzly Grant to pieces with her bluntly-manicured nails. The image is adorable considering everyone has snooped through my home and seen the nursery.

"I would like to bless this new family with the gift of air," Grant says before signaling Henrik to play a soft melody on a flute. "Air carries the gifts of intellect, patience, and rational decision making."

"Better give Luc a double shot of that, Henrik," calls one of Betty's brothers before he is shushed by Alison. Much to Alison's horror, Henrik plays the melody again and her brothers burst into giggles.

"I would like to bless this new family with earth." Alison approaches us with a small jar. As she pours dirt into our palms, she says: "Earth carries the security, physicality, and stability to your joyous home." She hugs Betty as tears fill her eyes. Where Alison's tears hit the mound of dirt in Betty's palm a tiny plant grows and a violet blooms.

"I would like to bless this new family with water." My mother takes Alison's place with her small jar filled partially with a clear liquid. "Water to gift to you: adaptability, flexibility, and imagination as you navigate life's challenges." She sprinkles the water over us and hugs Betty.

"I will bless this new family with fire," says Mrs. Weston, approaching us with a small candle in a jar. "Fire to light the passion, ambition, and dedication that resides in you both." She takes a flower out of Betty's blue and black bouquet and drops it into the jar. It incinerates on contact with a pop of sparks.

"Blessed be these elements as they live in harmony in your home," Grant says, pulling the binding cord and rings from his pocket. The twinkling of his bell accompanies their emergence.

"That extra ringing means they will have lots of children," Mrs. Weston says while clapping her hands.

"I could have told you that one." Betty's ire is fired at one of her brothers for that remark. The pair earn glares from Alison and their mother too.

"The next comment from the peanut gallery gets both of you pounded into a pulp," yells my blushing bride. She's about as sweet and Lilly-fair as the red dress she's wearing, and I wouldn't have it any other way.

Grant hands me both rings and I hand Ryan's ring to Betty. Her eyes expand to saucers, filled with hundreds of questions. I nod my head toward Ryan's perch, and she looks right at him. He raises his giant bottle at her, and she nods demurely in return.

"Within this circle, you are witnessed by your closest confidants as you choose to enter an everlasting union. This cord symbolizes the bonds that tie your souls together not only in this life but when you regain your place within the earth's soil. You recognize the stardust in one another. It calls to the stardust within yourself. The dust originated in the same fusion of elements within the same star only to be reunited within this circle of friends." Grant pauses and looks to us expectantly.

My mind whirls as I remember my lines. Good thing they are in unison with Betty so I can read her lips. "I understand the union I enter tonight. I promise not to stretch the threads which tie my soul to yours. I promise to do everything in my power to honor those bonds as I honor you."

Satisfied with our garbled mutters, Grant binds our wrists with the cord symbolizing the ties of marriage. Great, it is time for the difficult part. The rings. I stupidly pushed for us to write our own vows instead of the pagan traditional ones. Writing verse to celebrate Betty comes as naturally as breathing. Too bad public speaking makes my brain spin like a top. I thought I could read the vows I wrote but with the ring in one hand and the other tied to Betty's, that's impossible. Clearing my throat, I hold

Betty's custom ring to slide on her finger and…blank out.

"I… I…" My mouth has forgotten how to form words. My breathing accelerates. The world begins tilting back and forth like a ship in a storm. I can't ruin this. I can't function. *Oh my God…*

"Shhhhh," Betty places her hand over my mouth. "Talk to me, just me. Take all the time you need. I will wait and so they will wait." I don't deserve her. My body relaxes as our hearts beat together. When she is satisfied, she lowers her hand and smiles at me.

****

He looks so terrified I fear he will pass out on the spot. I want to drag him over the broom and into his house where I can hide him from all this. Sudden feelings of guilt wash over me like a tidal wave as I recall the planning of this shenanigan. Luc puts my desires above everything else…including his own comfort.

"Betty," he sighs and pushes the ring onto my finger, "I don't deserve you…"

With the ring snugly on my finger, he wipes my tears with his thumb. I tilt my head upward to receive a small peck that blooms into a deeper kiss. My brothers snicker and Grant clears his throat, but I have never followed the rules. Now, I follow Luc.

Epilogue

"Did you bring me here to torture me, Ryan, as a reminder I will never have a wedding of my own?"

"Shut up, Orchid," I reply. "I want to see it and I don't want you to burn down my house. I need the closure of this thirty-five-year period of my life. That is all. No ulterior motives."

I couldn't stay away. I had to witness the end of my Golden Age as Betty slips my ring onto Lucien's finger. There will be an official coronation in Moldova, but this is the snowball to start the avalanche. Most will see it as my downfall, a madman in ruins, however, I see it as my last act in control. While Lucien's birthright puts him next in line, I wanted the final say as to who and when I was succeeded.

"I can't believe he sang his vows to her," Orchid says with a feminine sigh. "Can all vampires sing like him?" She folds her hands under her chin and gazes at the happy groom with a wistful countenance.

Jealousy, uninvited, flares in my chest. "A true king would never sink to his knees in public even before his intended queen." I can't carry a tune in a bucket, but Orchid doesn't know that. I hate true love. I hate Fate for picking Orchid as mine. I hate the face she's making at Lucien. What I hate most is how much I wish she looked at me that way.

"He's a romantic prince—"

"—with a stutter." My comment earns a glare from the Fae Princess.

"Tiny flaws make him relatable and even more endearing," she says with another sigh.

"Shut up, Orchid." I punctuate the sentiment with a swig from my wine bottle. I've made a bucket list now I know the timeline for the rest of my life. Drinking the contents of my wine cellar is on it but quickly rose to the top of the list when the flash test worked with the spoiled brat at my side. The realization that I was enamored with the bubble brain had me running for my more expensive bottles.

Orchid shivers as Betty says her vows to Lucien. Betty talks about having a safe harbor in his arms and feeling secure enough to let down her guard. Orchid never has her guard up. That's why she's constantly abused. She trusts everyone and is surprised when they take advantage of her—myself included. I have done my best to resist her charms but even I couldn't keep my hands off her. A mild regret.

Since my teens, I have dreamt of my queen. She would be a debonaire vampire with a blueblood pedigree and expensive vocabulary. She would glide in high heels without teetering and never have a hair out of place. Together we would look down our noses at our subjects. She would be my perfect, barren vampiress because I already have an heir. No reason for a mistress or the messiness of parenting. As four decades flew by, the dream faded into the lonely reality. I had resigned myself to being alone.

At one point, I thought Alison might be the queen of my dreams. My attention focuses on her as she lays the broom at the happy couple's feet. Ugh, another royal kneeling in the dirt. Her thin white dress shifts up her thighs as she stretches at their feet. *Yeah, it would have been no hardship to hit that.* "The red-haired witch is the polar bear," I say with a wave of my bottle at Alison. "Stay away from her. She looks like a nice lady, but she is the Fae-eater."

Orchid leans forward to get a better look. "No way. She's smaller than I am. How did she beat Maple and Oak in combat?"

Stupid Fae customs, giving men tree names and females flower names as if they are one with nature. Orchid cried for days after getting a grass stain on her perfectly white dress. "Alison was pretty motivated from what I understand,"—pausing to pull a swing from my bottle— "Maple was molesting her while your precious Oak watched, taunting her with their intended murder of her son. The son, by the way, is the number one witch to avoid. He's the one at the piano and you saw the wind power he brought. That kid closed the portal on you."

I could have softened the story. However, Bubble-brain needs to realize the Fae General wasn't the perfect boyfriend she thought he was. How else can I demonstrate he was her downfall without sounding like a jealous lover?

"That must be an exaggeration or an outright lie to justify the witch's need to eat him. I bet she lusted after his flesh until she couldn't withstand his allure," Orchid says between choking sobs.

My eyes roll before I can sanction them. *Give me a break.* Alison doesn't have lustful thoughts. She's the tightest schoolmarm I have ever encountered. I doubt she even has those thoughts of her husband let alone a decaying phantom who kidnaps her. Not that I have an iota of sympathy for Grant. Getting to tutor her body in bedroom arts would be an opportunity of a lifetime. I look to Orchid with regret. She's spoiled in more ways than one.

"What are they doing now?" Only the fiftieth time she asked that question during the ceremony after I told her, I had never been to a witchy pagan wedding.

"They are jumping over a broom. Do you need binoculars?"

"A broom? Why would cleaning supplies be part of a wedding? Is it a symbol of the bride's pure reputation?"

I laugh so hard wine shoots out my nose, spraying the snow with plum droplets. "The bride's purity is nonexistent. Prince Romantic, your words not mine, has already knocked her up," I say before wiping my nose with the back of my hand.

Orchid looks at me with disgust, but the wine has taken away my ability to care. I have become accustomed to the numb feeling I get from a full-to-empty bottle. Not only does the pain in my joints, the wheezing of my chest, and the aches in my wings subside with wine but also the internal ache over my loss of the throne is numb. I gave my life to the colony. I brought them from poverty to thriving with my investments. What do I have to show for it? My wine cellar and Orchid.

"Can we go now?" Her voice is small, and tears stain her face. She is rocking slightly as she hugs her knees for comfort or maybe just warmth. I want to watch the party all night long with my dark mood. The expression on her face squashes my pity party. The need to end her suffering trumps any other thought in my head.

"Yeah." I throw my now empty bottle in Lucien's

yard. As I stand, she struggles to get up resulting in a yank of the tether between us. At her yelp, I reach down to cradle her in my arms. I may not be Prince Romantic, but I can sweep the emaciated fairy off her feet. As my muscles atrophy, this will no longer be the case. I race my disease to get immortality in the Fae Realm with my body intact. While I'm at it, I might as well shoot for the stars. If I can manipulate Orchid's attention in my direction, I may luck into being King of the Fae.

A word about the author…

Marilyn Barr currently resides in the wilds of Kentucky with her husband, son, and rescue cats. She has a diverse background containing experiences as a child prodigy turned medical school reject, published microbiologist, special education/inclusion science teacher, homeschool mother of a savant, certified spiritual/energy healer, and advocate for the autistic community. This puts her in the position to bring tales containing heroes who are regular people with different ability levels and body types, in a light where they are powerful, lovable, and appreciated.

When engaging with the real world, she is collecting characters, empty coffee cups, and unused homeschool curricula. She is a sucker (haha) for cheesy horror movies, Italian food, punk music, black cats, bad puns, and all things witchy.

She would love to hear from readers via her website:

www.marilynbarr.com

Or Instagram @marilyn_barr_author

Thank you for purchasing
this publication of The Wild Rose Press, Inc.

For questions or more information
contact us at
info@thewildrosepress.com.

The Wild Rose Press, Inc.
www.thewildrosepress.com

Milton Keynes UK
Ingram Content Group UK Ltd.
UKHW030414170224
437973UK00012B/1131